DANTDM (REAL NAME DAN MIDDLETON) IS ONE OF THE WORLD'S TOP YOUTUBERS. DAN STARTED MAKING VIDEOS WHILE HE WAS A STUDENT AT THE UNIVERSITY OF NORTHAMPTON. SOON AFTER, IN 2012, HIS CURRENT MINECRAFT-FOCUSED CHANNEL WAS BORN—*THE DIAMOND MINECART // DANTDM*. HE NOW HAS FANS ALL AROUND THE GLOBE AND MAKES VIDEOS THAT ARE WATCHED BY MILLIONS OF PEOPLE EVERY DAY.

DAN LIVES IN THE UK WITH HIS WIFE, JEMMA, (ALSO KNOWN AS *XXJEMMAXX*) AND THEIR TWO PUGS, ELLIE AND DARCIE. THIS IS HIS FIRST BOOK.

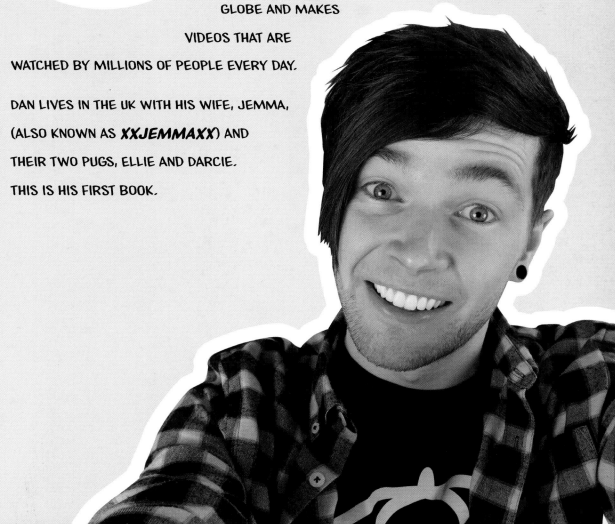

THIS BOOK IS FOR MY WIFE, JEMMA.
MY PUGS. EVERY SINGLE MEMBER OF TEAMTDM.
AND EVERY MEMBER OF MY FAMILY THAT
SUPPORTS ME; YOU KNOW WHO YOU ARE.

TRAYAURUS AND THE ENCHANTED CRYSTAL

Dan•TDM

ILLUSTRATED BY
DOREEN MULRYAN AND **MIKE LOVE**

HARPER
An Imprint of HarperCollinsPublishers

DANTDM: TRAYAURUS AND THE ENCHANTED CRYSTAL

FOR INFORMATION ADDRESS HARPERCOLLINS CHILDREN'S BOOKS, A DIVISION OF HARPERCOLLINS PUBLISHERS, 195 BROADWAY, NEW YORK, NY 10007.
WWW.HARPERCOLLINSCHILDRENS.COM

ISBN 978-0-06-257432-9 (TRADE BDG.)

16 17 18 19 20 PC/RRDW 10 9 8 7 6 5 4

❖

FIRST AMERICAN EDITION
ORIGINALLY PUBLISHED IN GREAT BRITAIN IN 2016 BY TRAPEZE,
AN IMPRINT OF THE ORION PUBLISHING GROUP LTD.

TRAYAURUS AND THE ENCHANTED CRYSTAL

DanTDM

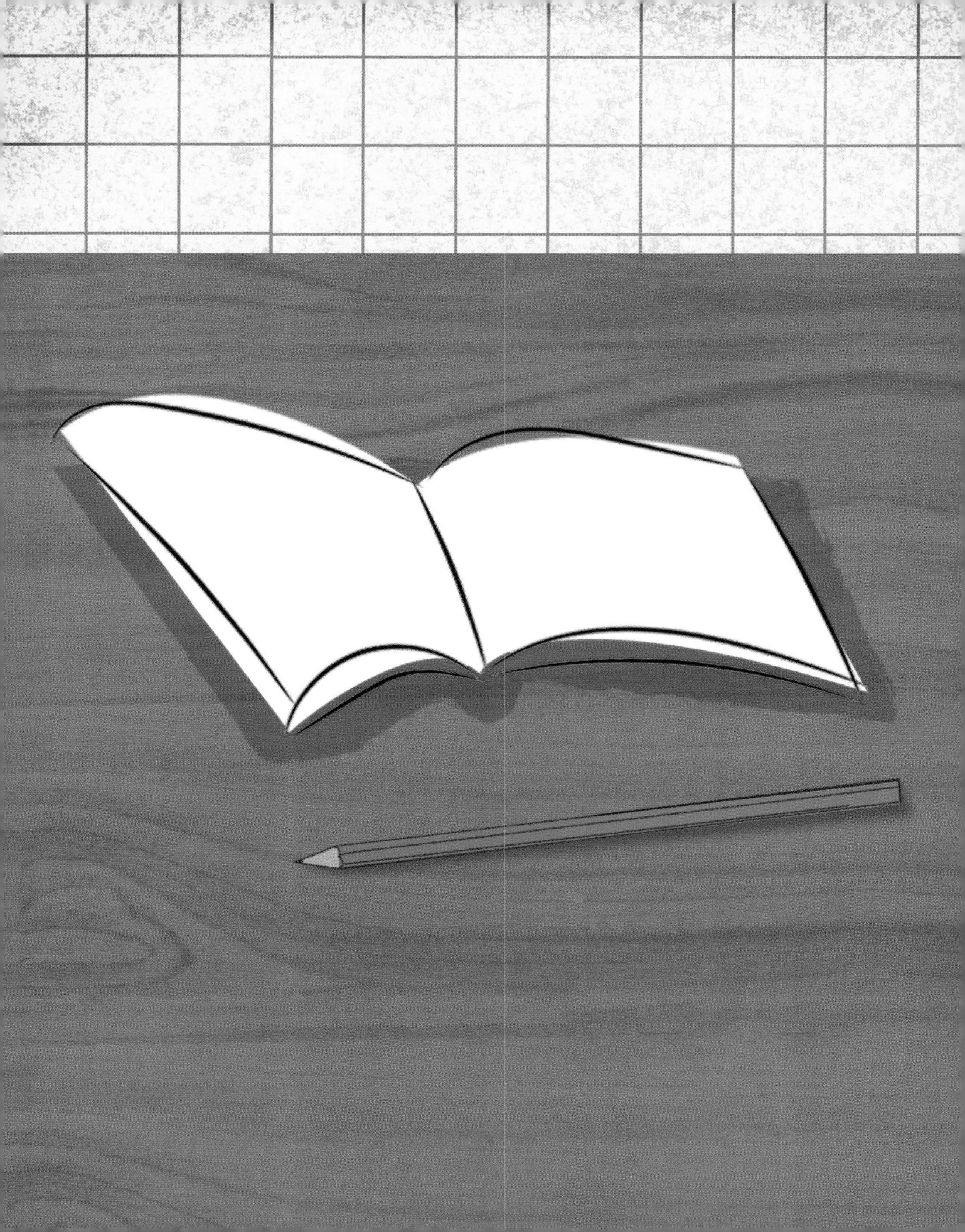

HEY THERE, EVERYONE—DAN HERE AND WELCOME TO MY BOOK! THANK YOU SO MUCH FOR CHOOSING TO BUY MY FIRST EVER GRAPHIC NOVEL. IT'S BEEN A VERY SPECIAL PROJECT, AND I'M SO GLAD YOU'VE DECIDED TO TAKE THIS JOURNEY WITH ME.

YOU MIGHT KNOW ME FROM MY VIDEOS, ESPECIALLY MESSING AROUND WITH MY FAVORITE MINECRAFT CHARACTERS LIKE TRAYAURUS, GRIM, CRAIG, AND MANY OTHERS. I LOVE CREATING STORIES AND ADVENTURES FOR THEM ONLINE SO MUCH THAT I WANTED TO TAKE THEIR STORY FURTHER IN A MEGA-QUEST—AND THAT'S RIGHT HERE IN THE FOLLOWING PAGES. WITH NO LIMITS TO THE KIND OF ESCAPADES WE COULD GET UP TO IN THIS BOOK, WE DELVE HEADFIRST INTO AN EPIC ADVENTURE, A STRUGGLE FOR POWER, AND WE MAKE BOTH FRIENDS AND ENEMIES ALONG THE WAY.

I DECIDED TO WRITE THIS BOOK FOR THE SAME REASONS I STARTED DOING YOUTUBE VIDEOS— BECAUSE I LOVE BEING CREATIVE, PLAYING GAMES, INVENTING STORIES AND HAVING FUN IN THE PROCESS. WHEN I FIRST BEGAN MAKING VIDEOS, HARDLY ANYONE VIEWED THEM, BUT NOW I HAVE ONE OF THE MOST-WATCHED CHANNELS IN THE WORLD—AND IT'S ALL DOWN TO YOU GUYS! YOU HAVE ALL BEEN A HUGE SUPPORT; WATCHING, LIKING, AND INTERACTING WITH MY VIDEOS EVERY SINGLE DAY, MAKING ALL OF THE HARD WORK WORTHWHILE. I HOPE THIS PROVES THAT IF YOU KEEP DOING SOMETHING WITH PASSION, WORK HARD, AND NEVER GIVE UP, YOU'LL EVENTUALLY HAVE OPPORTUNITIES TO DO BRILLIANT THINGS.

THIS GRAPHIC NOVEL IS ONE OF THOSE THINGS. THE IDEA CAME ABOUT BECAUSE I WANTED TO CREATE SOMETHING NEW FOR ALL OF US TO ENJOY, AND THIS HAS DEFINITELY BEEN ONE OF THE MOST EXCITING THINGS I'VE WORKED ON. FROM PLOTTING THE STORY, EVOLVING MY CHARACTERS, ADJUSTING THE COLORS, PLANNING THE BACKGROUNDS, AND LAYING IT ALL OUT, THIS BOOK HAS SURE BEEN A WHIRLWIND COMPARED TO MAKING VIDEOS! I HAVE LOVED BEING ABLE TO TELL A STORY VISUALLY, AND HAVING THE CHANCE TO WORK WITH AMAZING ARTISTS HAS BEEN A BLAST. I AM A HUGE GRAPHIC NOVEL FAN, AND I HOPE THAT BY READING THIS, YOU WILL BE TOO (IF YOU'RE NOT ALREADY).

SO HERE GOES. THIS IS MY WORLD OF IMAGINATION ON A PAGE—YOU CAN NOW SIT DOWN WITH A STORY STRAIGHT OUTTA MY BRAINBOX! HOPEFULLY YOU WILL ENJOY IT AND IT WILL INSPIRE YOU TO KEEP BEING CREATIVE, FOLLOWING YOUR DREAMS, AND MAKING STUFF—JUST LIKE DAN AND TRAYAURUS IN THEIR LAB.

OK, INTRODUCTION OVER. LET'S DO THIS!

DanTDM

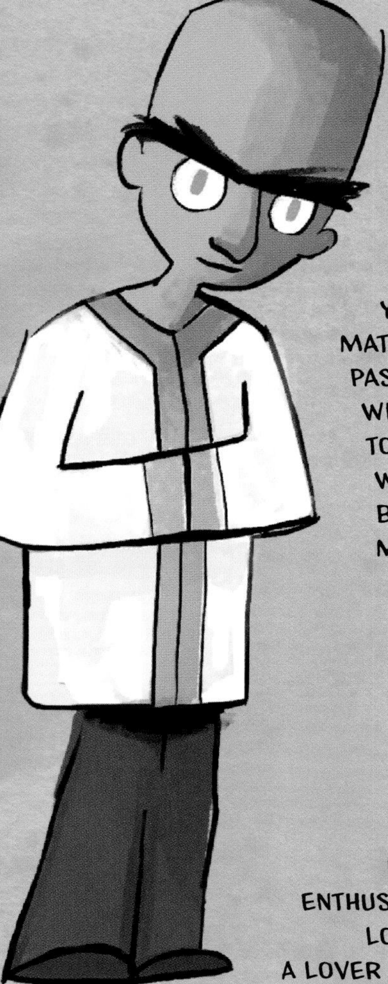

TRAYAURUS

DR. TRAYAURUS (OR JUST TRAYAURUS FOR SHORT) IS A BUDDING SCIENTIST WITH HIS VERY OWN LAB. FROM A YOUNG AGE, TRAYAURUS STARTED MIXING LIQUIDS, COMBINING MATERIALS, AND STUDYING ANYTHING HE COULD TO FULFILL HIS PASSION FOR SCIENCE. UNFORTUNATELY FOR HIM, HE WAS BORN WITH EXTREME CLUMSINESS, A CONDITION THAT CAUSES HIM TO MAKE LITTLE MISTAKES IN HIS AMBITIOUS EXPERIMENTS WITH DISASTROUS RESULTS. HOWEVER, WITH HELP FROM HIS BEST FRIEND, DAN, THINGS ALWAYS WORK OUT IN THE END, NO MATTER HOW BIG THE MESS.

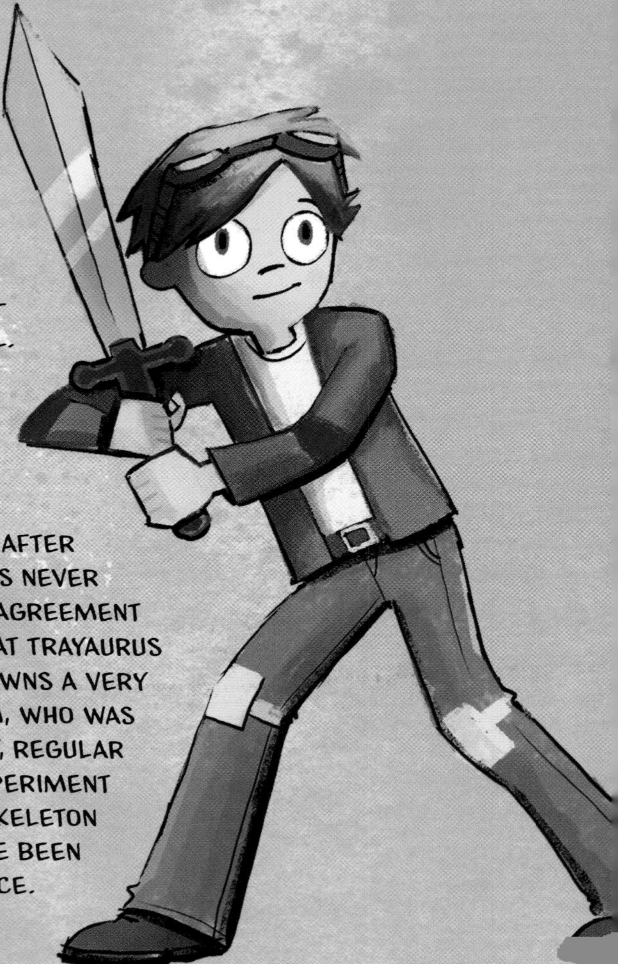

DAN

DAN IS A HAPPY, ENTHUSIASTIC, AND FUN-LOVING INDIVIDUAL. A LOVER OF ADVENTURE AND PURSUER OF ALL THINGS EXTRAORDINARY. DAN AIDS TRAYAURUS WITH HIS EXPERIMENTS DAY IN, DAY OUT, INTENT ON EXPLORING ALL THINGS WEIRD. DAN MET TRAYAURUS AFTER MOVING NEXT DOOR TO HIS LAB AND HAS NEVER LOOKED BACK, DESPITE A SLIGHT DISAGREEMENT ABOUT A GIANT PET DRAGON THAT TRAYAURUS ONCE OWNED. DAN ALSO OWNS A VERY SPECIAL DOG CALLED GRIM, WHO WAS ONCE A PERFECTLY HEALTHY, REGULAR DOG, BUT ONE UNFORTUNATE EXPERIMENT LATER, GRIM IS NOW A LIVING SKELETON VERSION OF HIMSELF. THEY HAVE BEEN INSEPARABLE EVER SINCE.

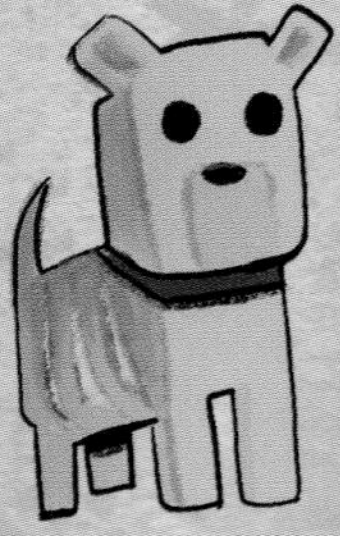

DENTON

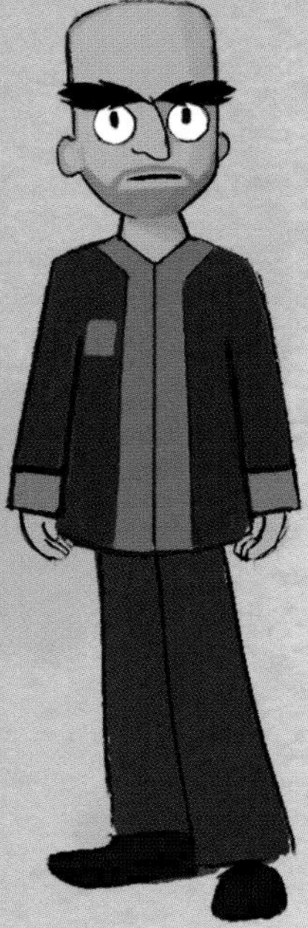

NO ONE IS SURE WHERE DENTON CAME FROM OR WHY HE IS SO UPSET WITH EVERYONE HE MEETS. HE RUNS HIS OWN LAB, WHERE HE CONDUCTS EVIL EXPERIMENTS TO AID HIS ULTIMATE PLAN OF WORLD DOMINATION. AT HIS COMMAND IS A GROUP OF ELVES, ALL OF WHOM WERE EMPLOYED BY HIM AFTER HE BUILT OVER THEIR SETTLEMENT WITH HIS GIANT LABORATORY. WITH THEIR LEADER, FIN, AS DENTON'S RIGHT-HAND MAN, THE ELVES NOW AID DENTON IN HIS EVIL PLANS. DAN, TRAYAURUS, AND DENTON HAVE CROSSED PATHS IN THE PAST, WITH DENTON BEING BEATEN EACH TIME, LEAVING HIM WITH A STRONG DISLIKE TOWARD DAN AND TRAYAURUS AND SEEKING REVENGE!

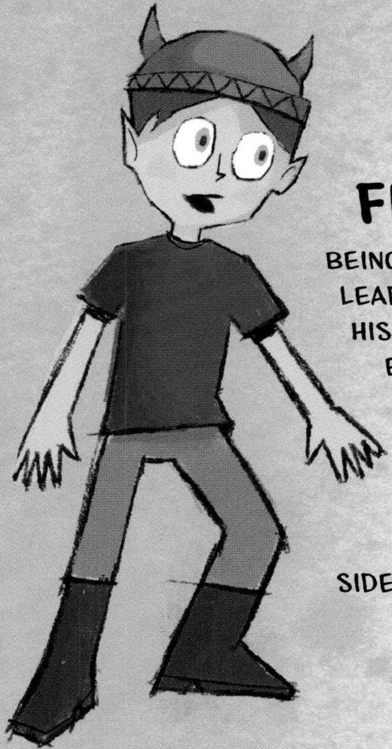

FIN

BEING THE LARGEST IN SIZE, FIN WAS THE NATURAL LEADER OF THE ELF COMMUNITY. BUT WHEN DENTON BUILT HIS LAB OVER THEIR SETTLEMENT, IT THREATENED THEIR VERY EXISTENCE. NATURALLY PERSUASIVE, FIN USED HIS CHARMS TO ENCOURAGE DENTON TO TAKE HIM AND THE ELVES ON AS LAB ASSISTANTS SO THEY WOULDN'T BE LEFT HOMELESS. DENTON RECOGNIZED FIN'S QUICK THINKING AND EFFICIENCY AND EMPLOYED HIM AS HIS SECOND-IN-COMMAND. EVER SINCE, FIN HAS STOOD LOYALLY BY DENTON'S SIDE, LEADING MANY OF HIS EXPERIMENTS.

PIGS

THE PIGS WERE YOUR NORMAL, EVERYDAY PIGS UNTIL ONE OF THE YOUNGER FEMALES WAS BESTOWED WITH THE POWER OF SPEECH. IT TURNS OUT THAT SHE IS VERY GRUMPY MOST OF THE TIME, THOUGH SHE HARBORS A SECRET SOFT SPOT FOR DAN AND TRAYAURUS. BUT DON'T YOU GO TELLING THEM THAT!

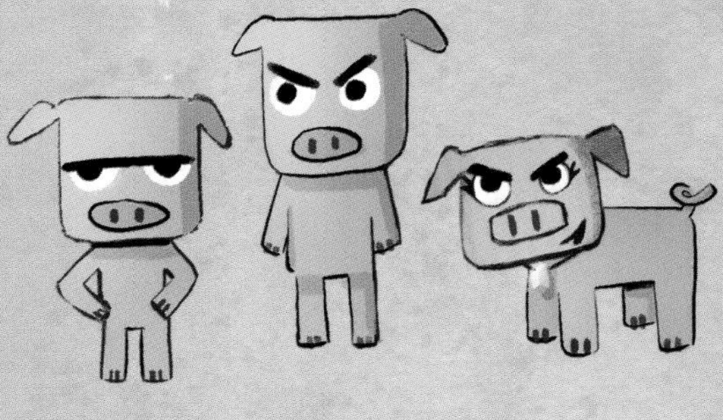

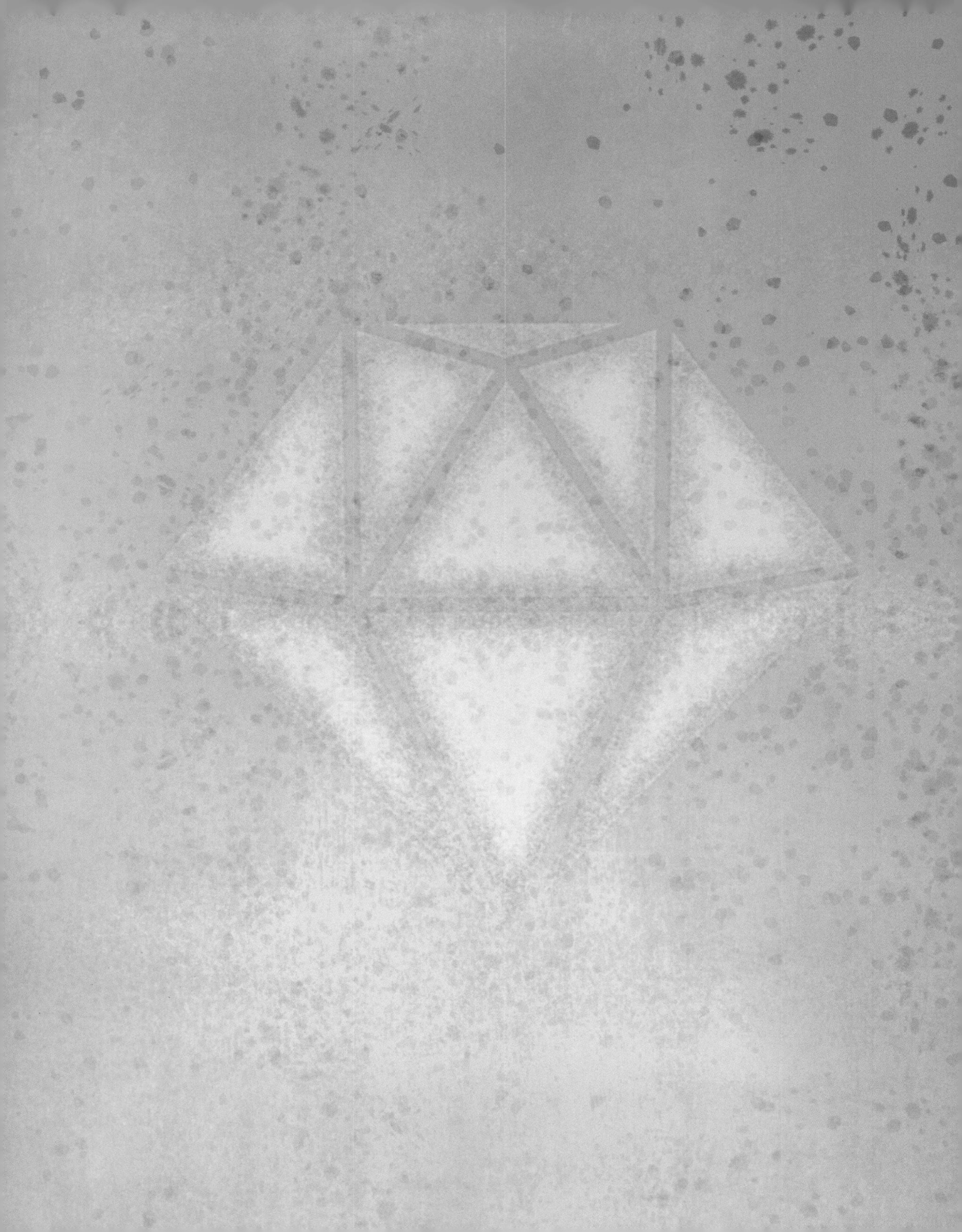

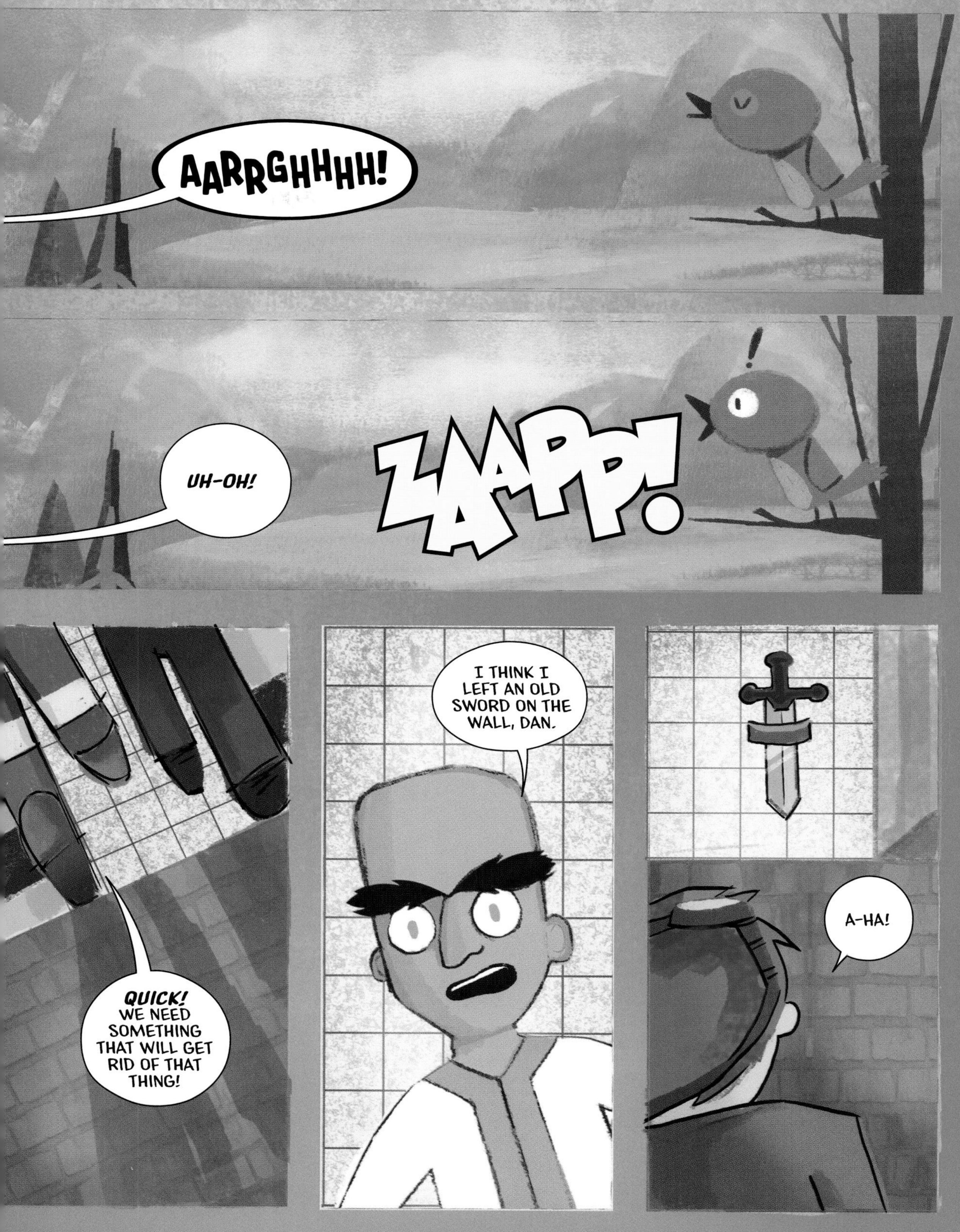

AARRGHHHH!
UH-OH!
ZAAPP!
QUICK! WE NEED SOMETHING THAT WILL GET RID OF THAT THING!
I THINK I LEFT AN OLD SWORD ON THE WALL, DAN.
A-HA!

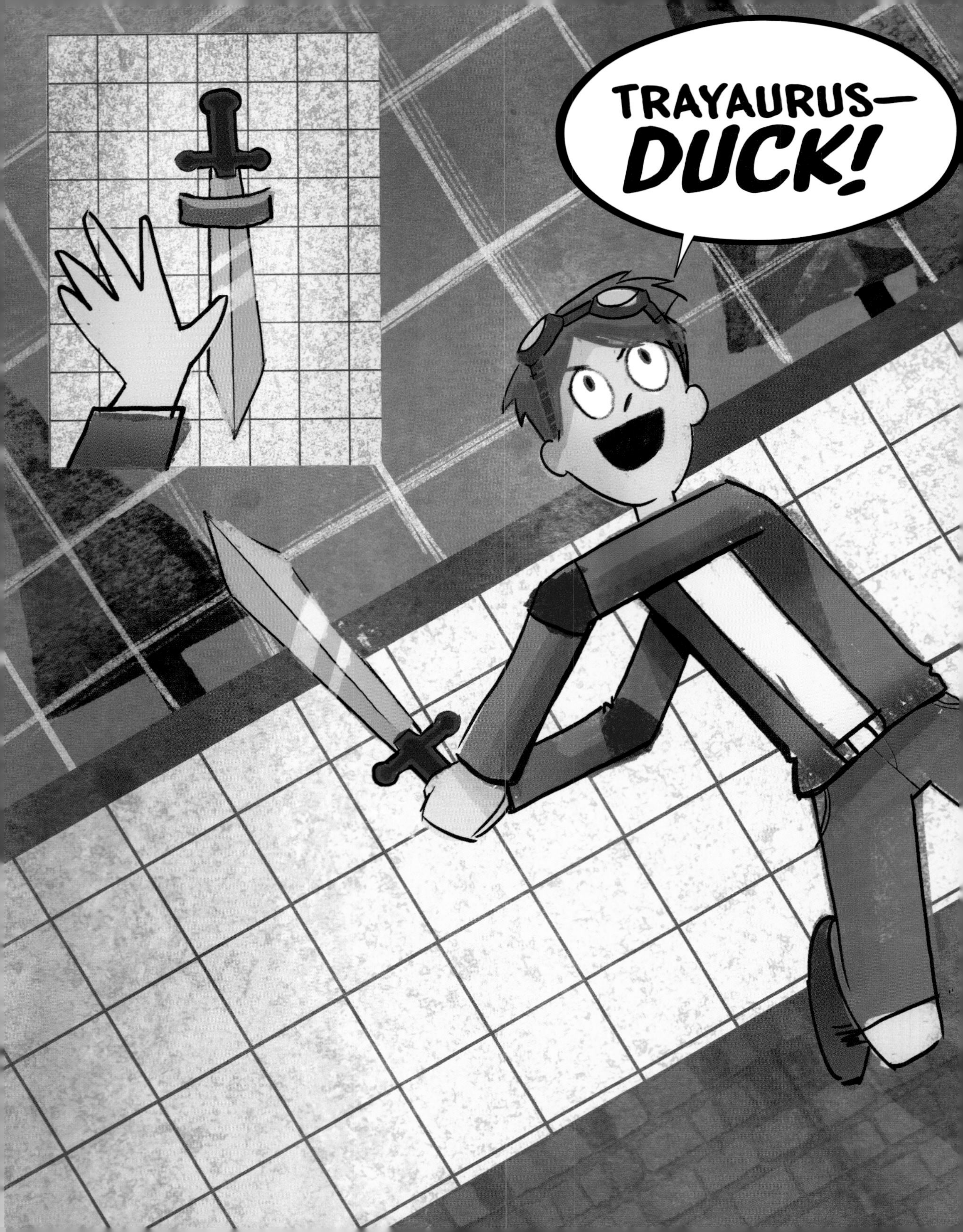
TRAYAURUS—
DUCK!

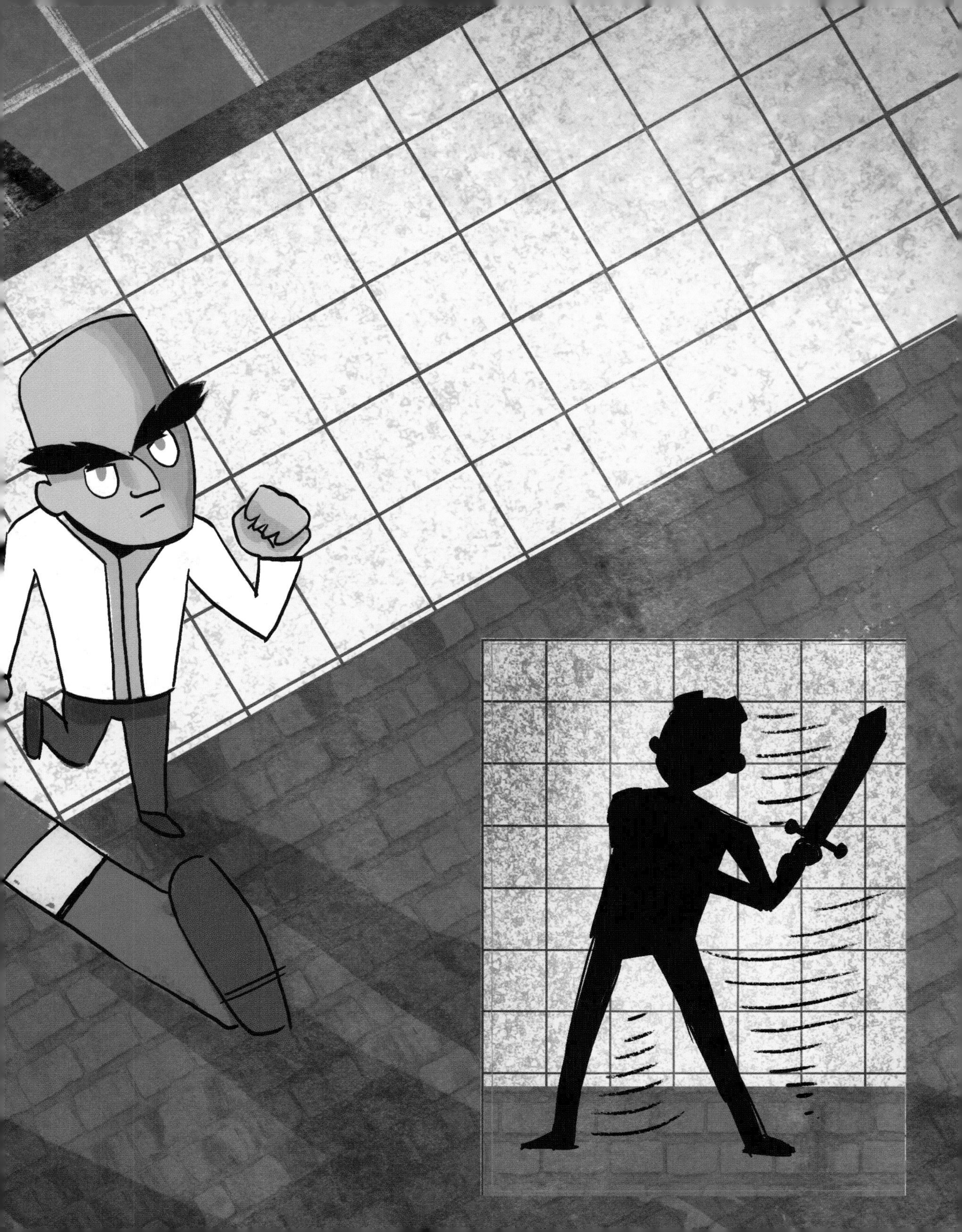

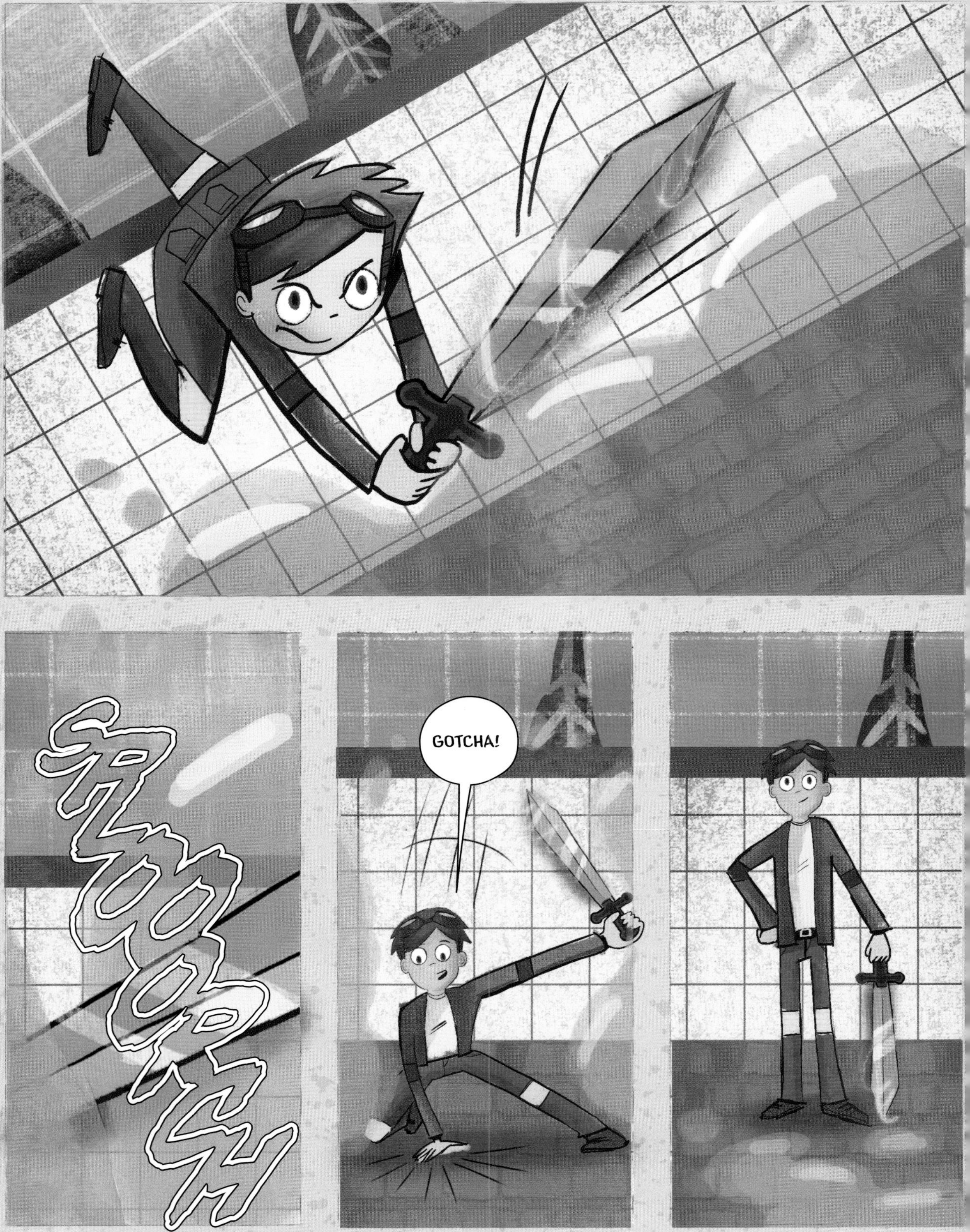
GOTCHA!

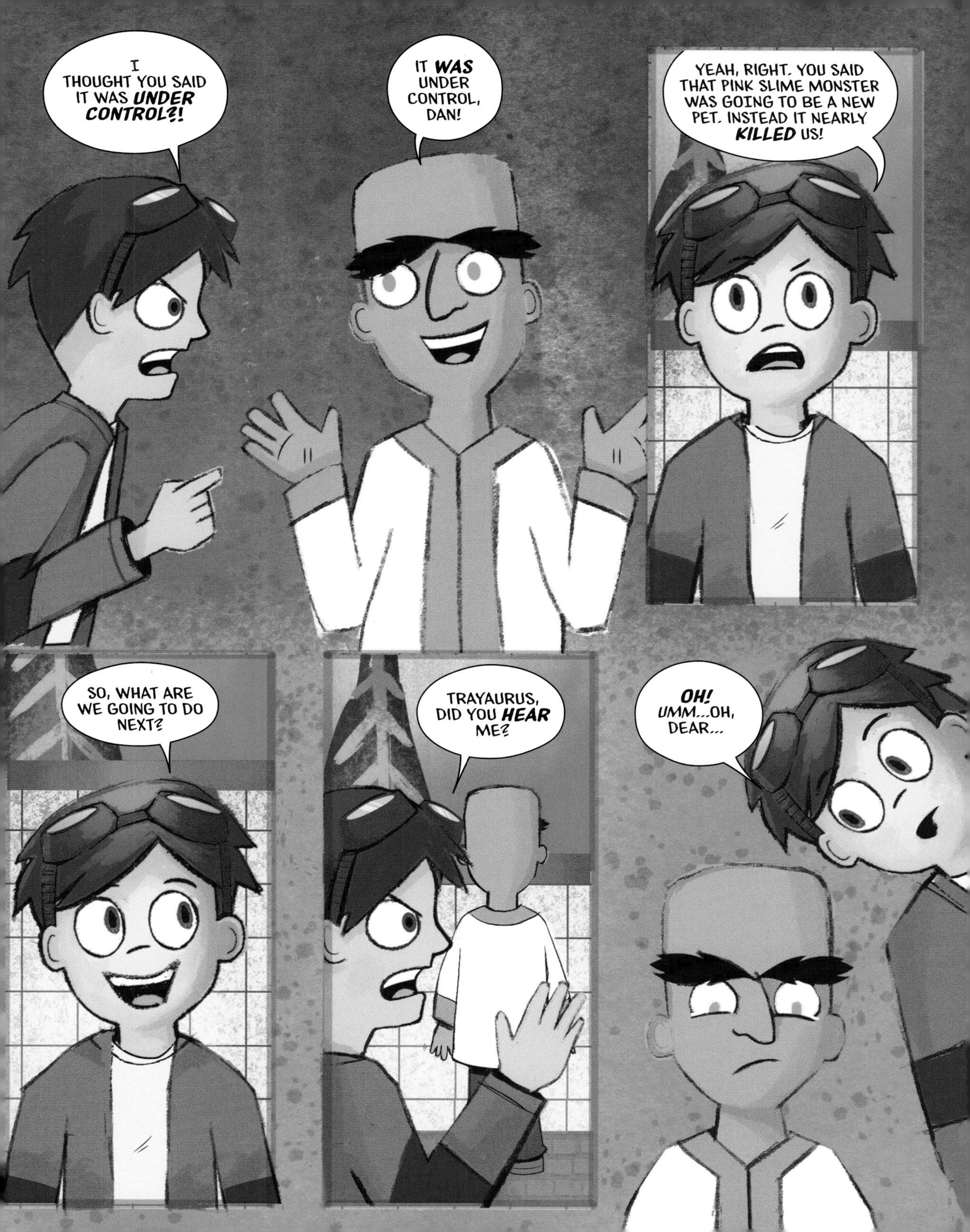
I THOUGHT YOU SAID IT WAS UNDER CONTROL?!
IT WAS UNDER CONTROL, DAN!
YEAH, RIGHT. YOU SAID THAT PINK SLIME MONSTER WAS GOING TO BE A NEW PET. INSTEAD IT NEARLY KILLED US!
SO, WHAT ARE WE GOING TO DO NEXT?
TRAYAURUS, DID YOU HEAR ME?
OH! UMM...OH, DEAR...

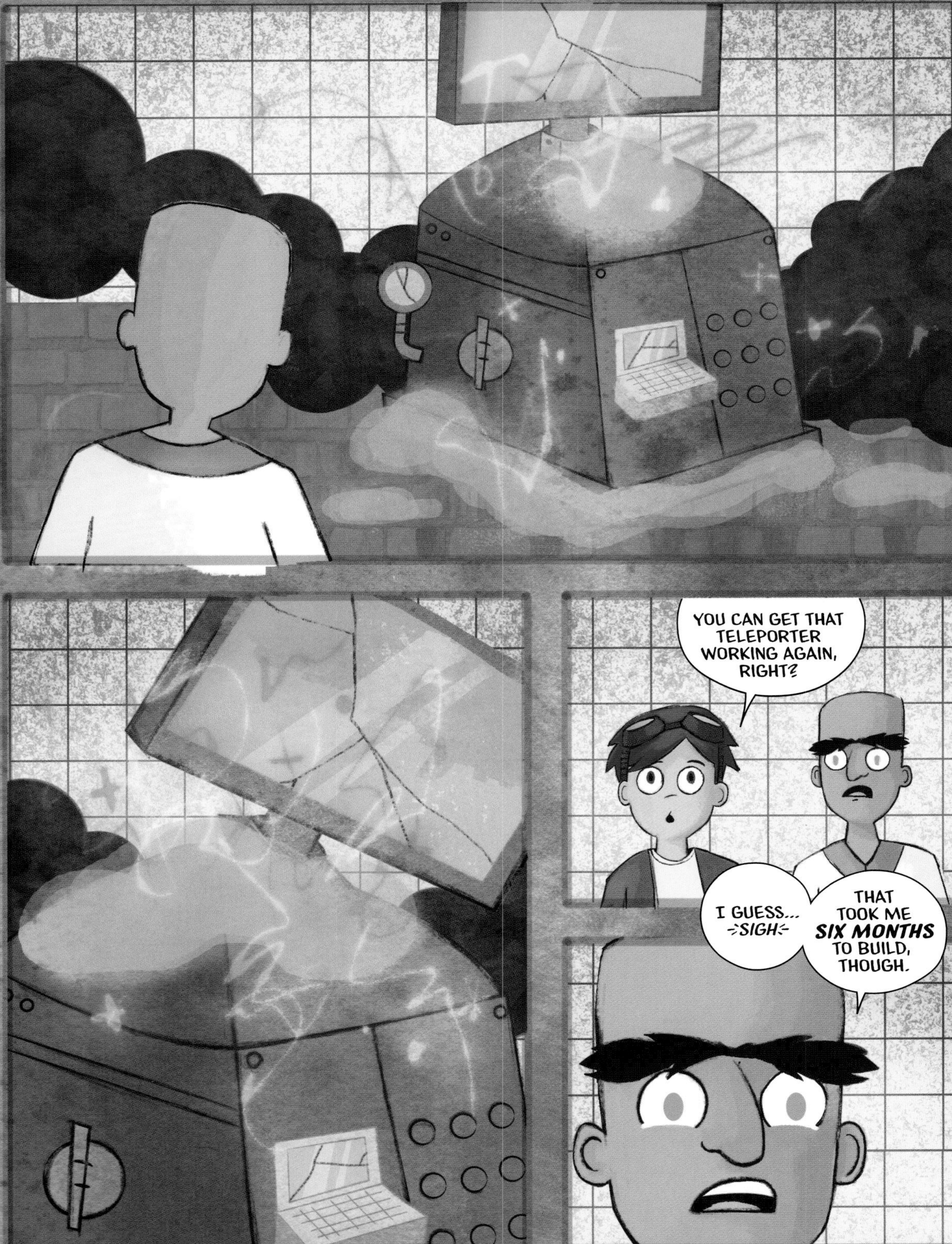
YOU CAN GET THAT TELEPORTER WORKING AGAIN, RIGHT?
I GUESS... ~SIGH~
THAT TOOK ME SIX MONTHS TO BUILD, THOUGH.

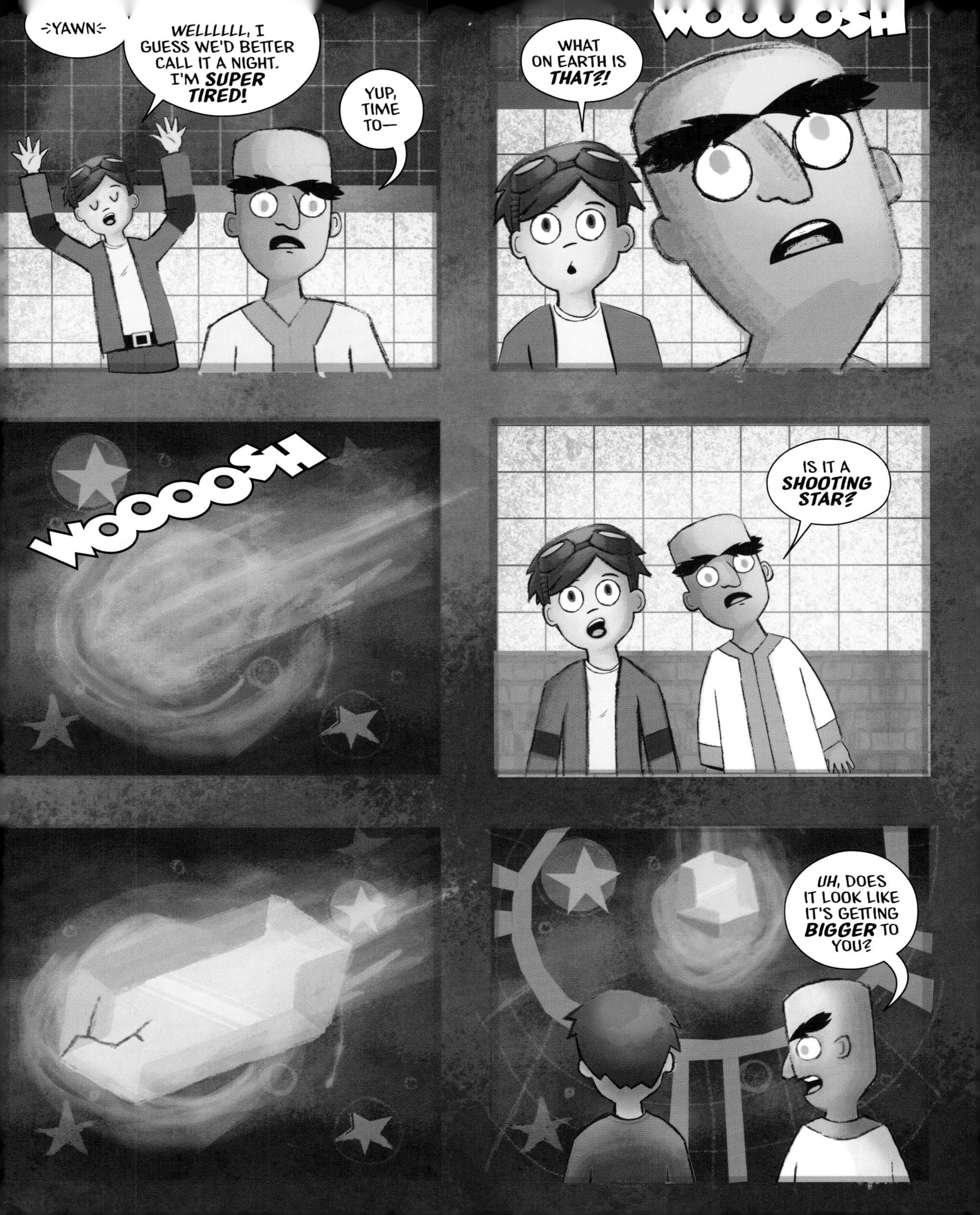
-YAWN-
WELLLLLLL, I GUESS WE'D BETTER CALL IT A NIGHT. I'M SUPER TIRED!
YUP, TIME TO—
WOOOOOSH
WHAT ON EARTH IS THAT?!
WOOOOSH
IS IT A SHOOTING STAR?
UH, DOES IT LOOK LIKE IT'S GETTING BIGGER TO YOU?

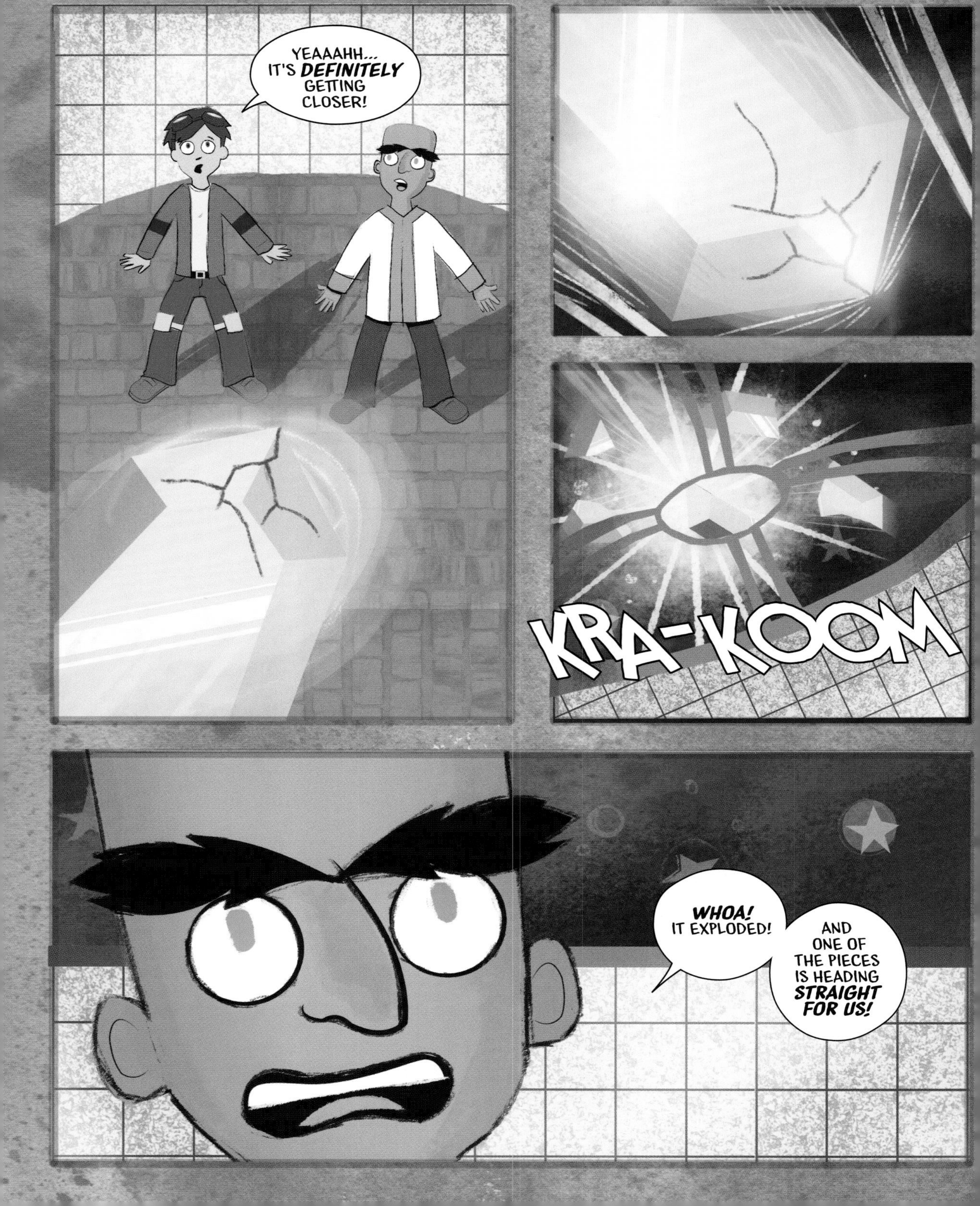
YEAAAHH... IT'S ***DEFINITELY*** GETTING CLOSER!
KRA-KOOM
WHOA! IT EXPLODED!
AND ONE OF THE PIECES IS HEADING ***STRAIGHT FOR US!***

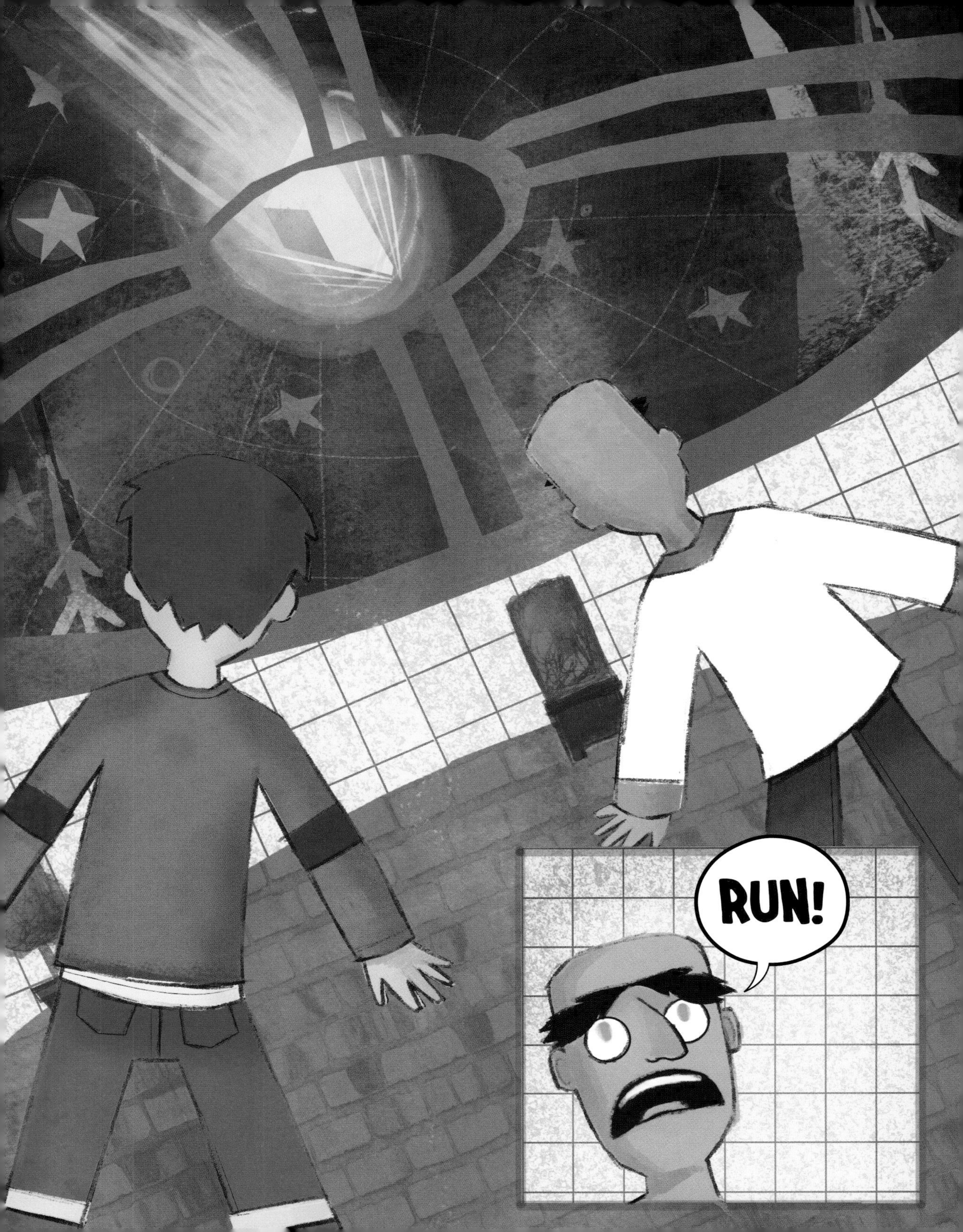
RUN!

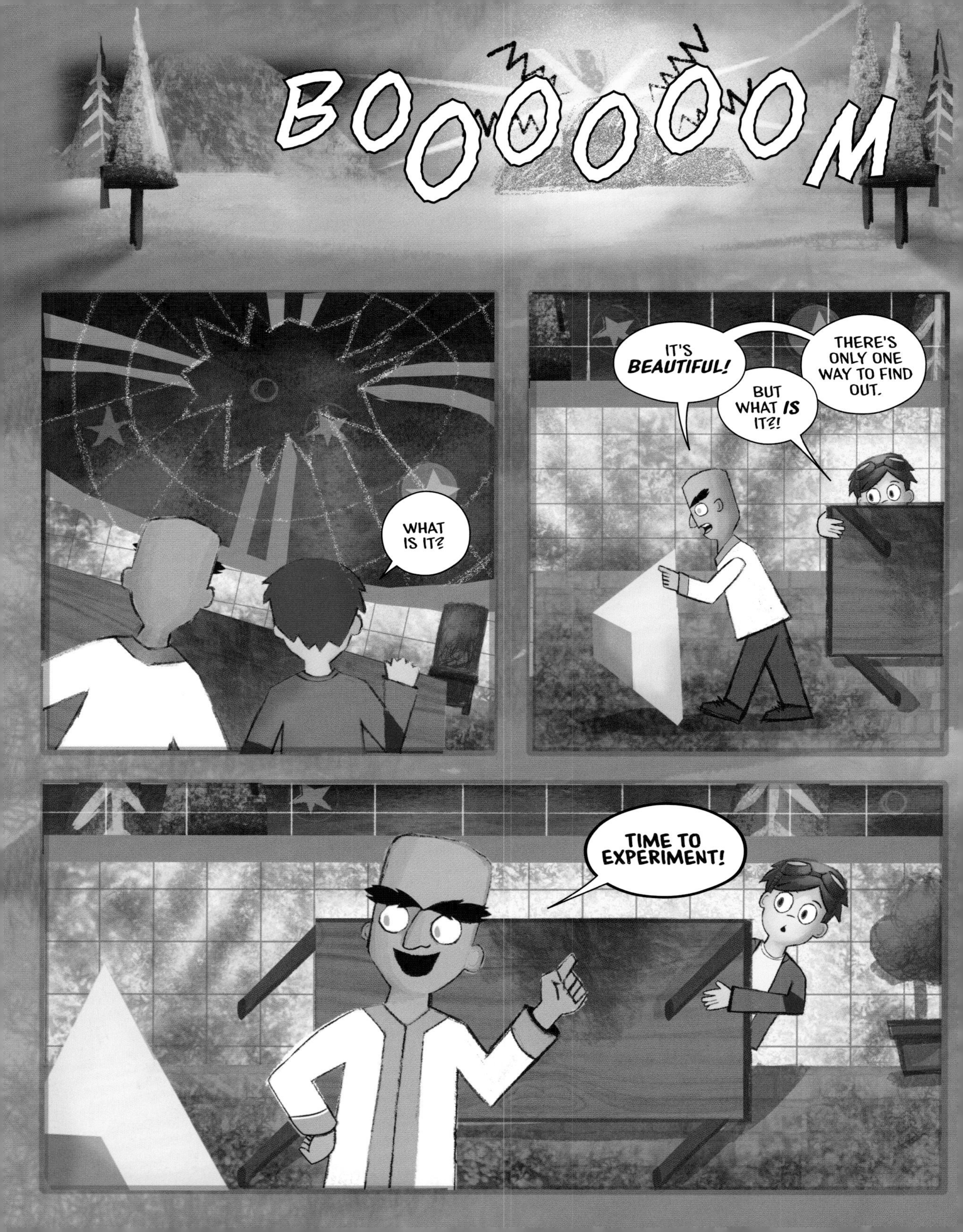
BOOOOOOM
WHAT IS IT?
IT'S BEAUTIFUL!
BUT WHAT IS IT?!
THERE'S ONLY ONE WAY TO FIND OUT.
TIME TO EXPERIMENT!

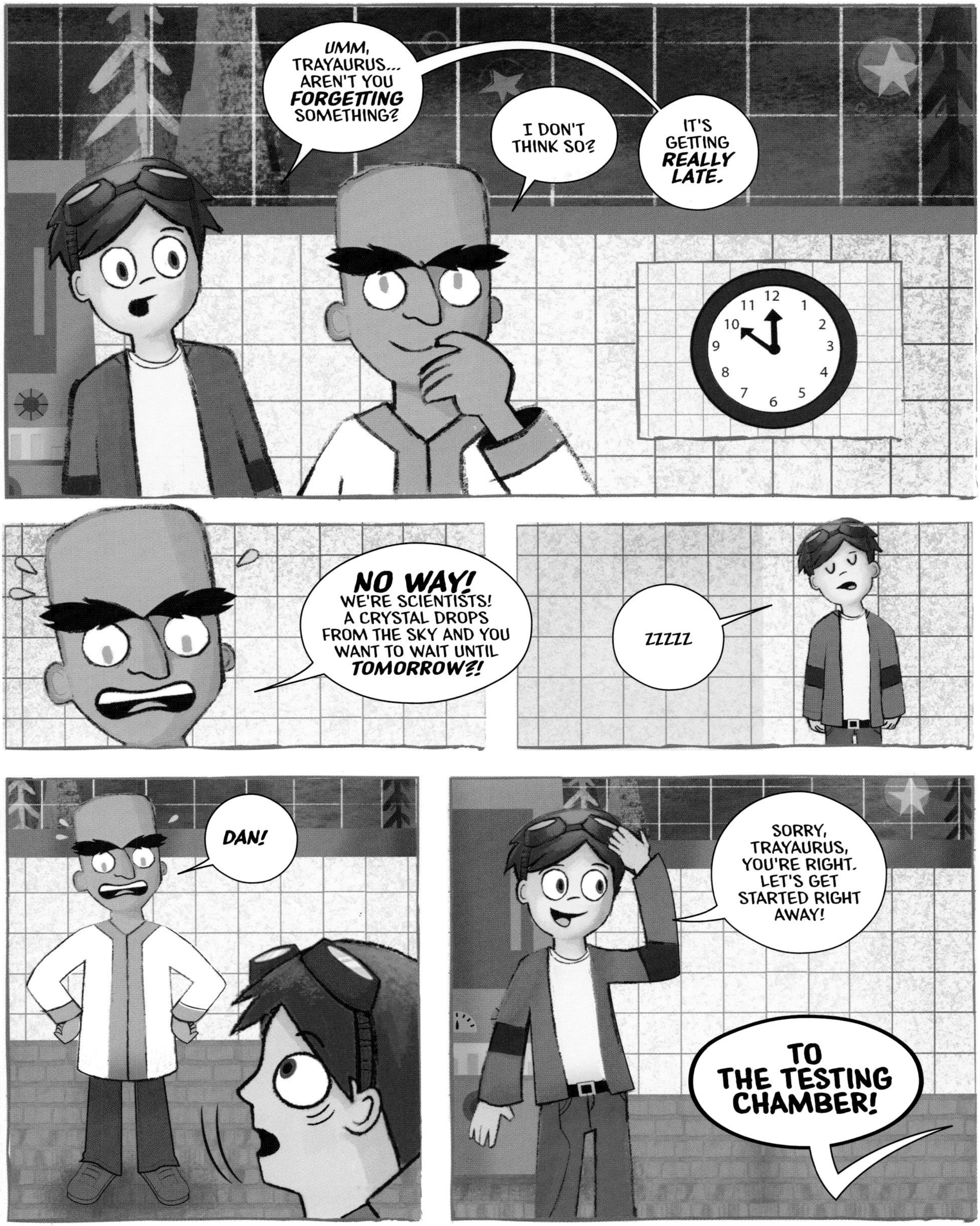
UMM, TRAYAURUS... AREN'T YOU FORGETTING SOMETHING?
I DON'T THINK SO?
IT'S GETTING REALLY LATE.
NO WAY! WE'RE SCIENTISTS! A CRYSTAL DROPS FROM THE SKY AND YOU WANT TO WAIT UNTIL TOMORROW?!
ZZZZZ
DAN!
SORRY, TRAYAURUS, YOU'RE RIGHT. LET'S GET STARTED RIGHT AWAY!
TO THE TESTING CHAMBER!

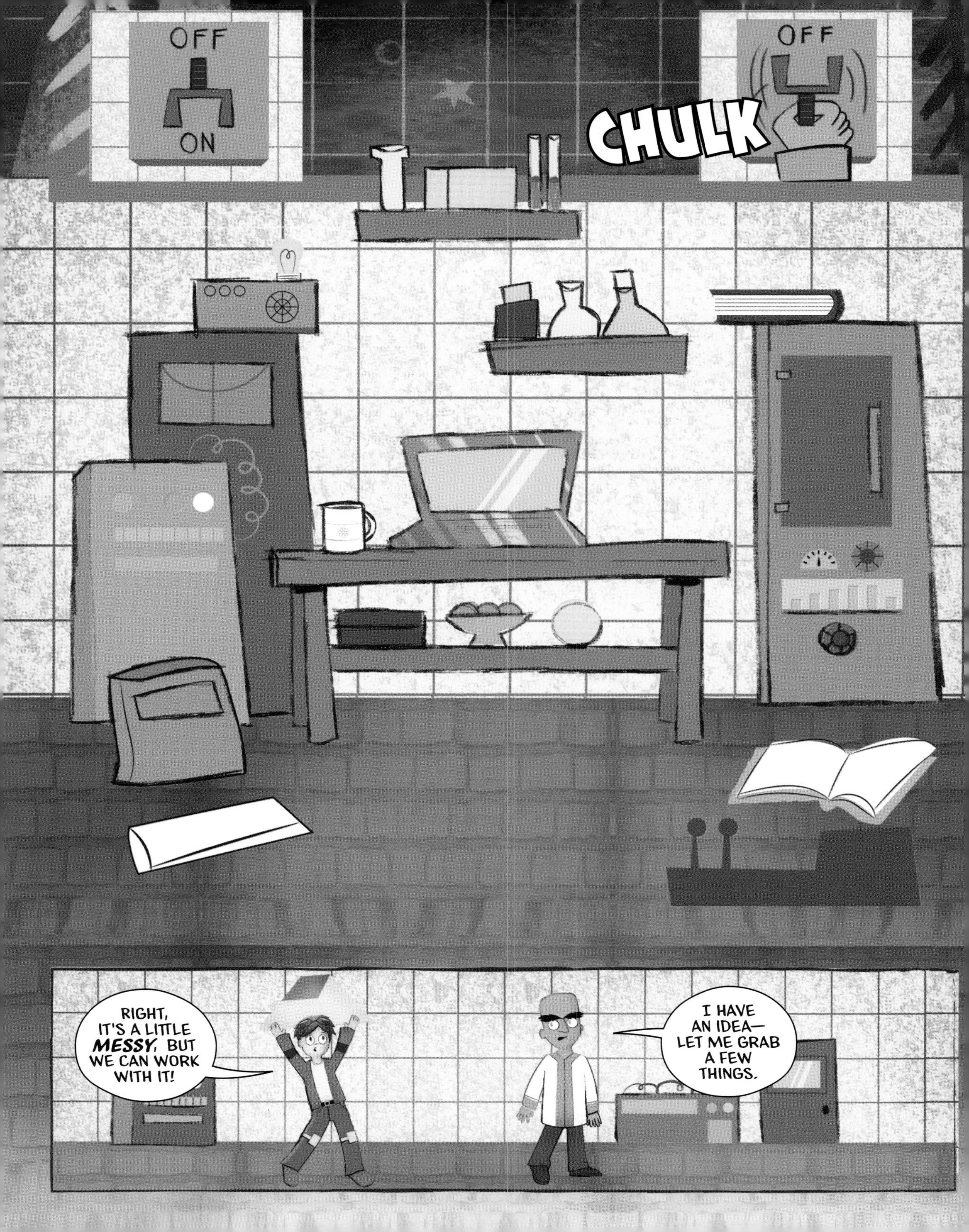
OFF
ON
OFF
CHULK
RIGHT, IT'S A LITTLE MESSY, BUT WE CAN WORK WITH IT!
I HAVE AN IDEA— LET ME GRAB A FEW THINGS.

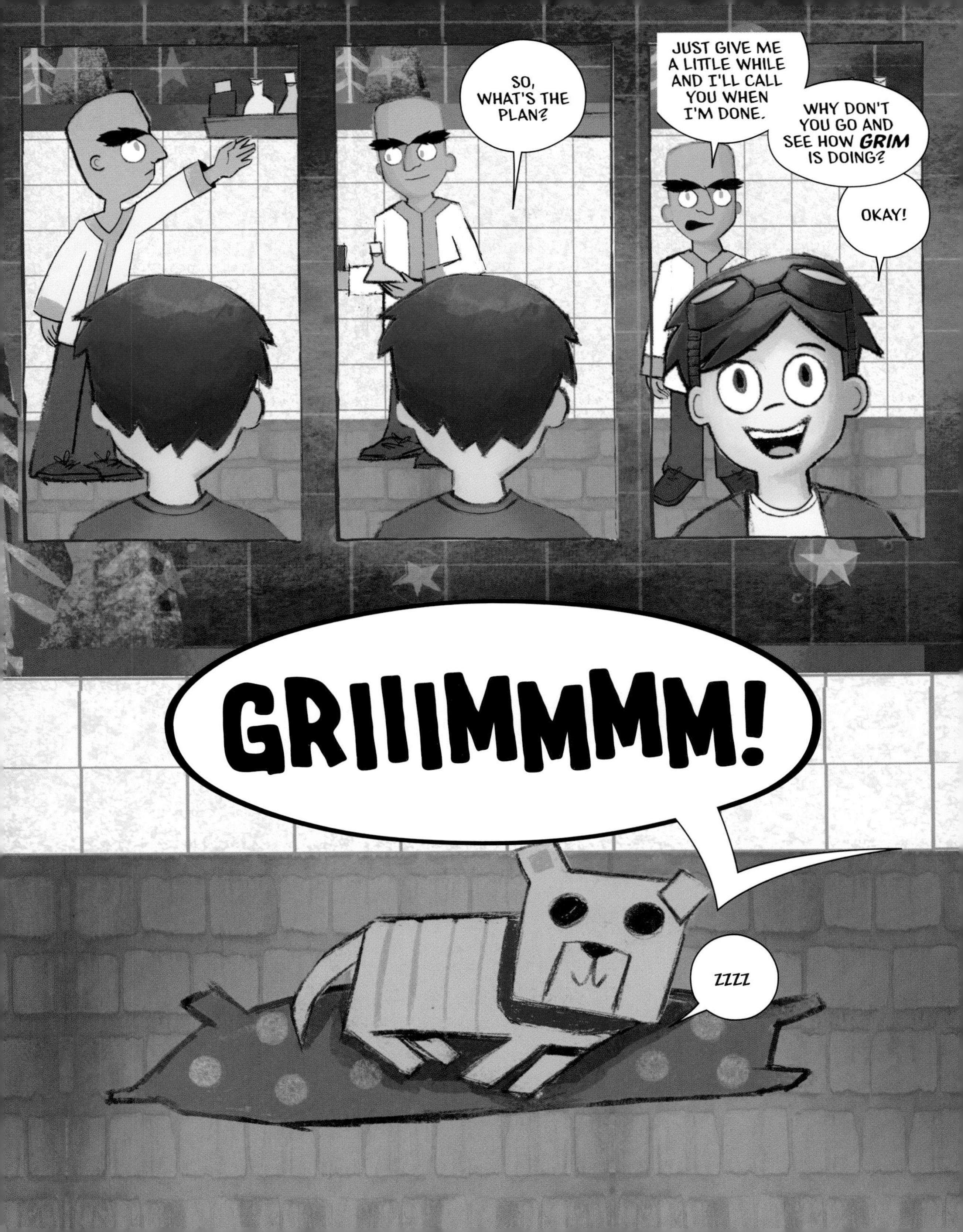
SO, WHAT'S THE PLAN?
JUST GIVE ME A LITTLE WHILE AND I'LL CALL YOU WHEN I'M DONE.
WHY DON'T YOU GO AND SEE HOW GRIM IS DOING?
OKAY!
GRIIIMMMM!
ZZZZ

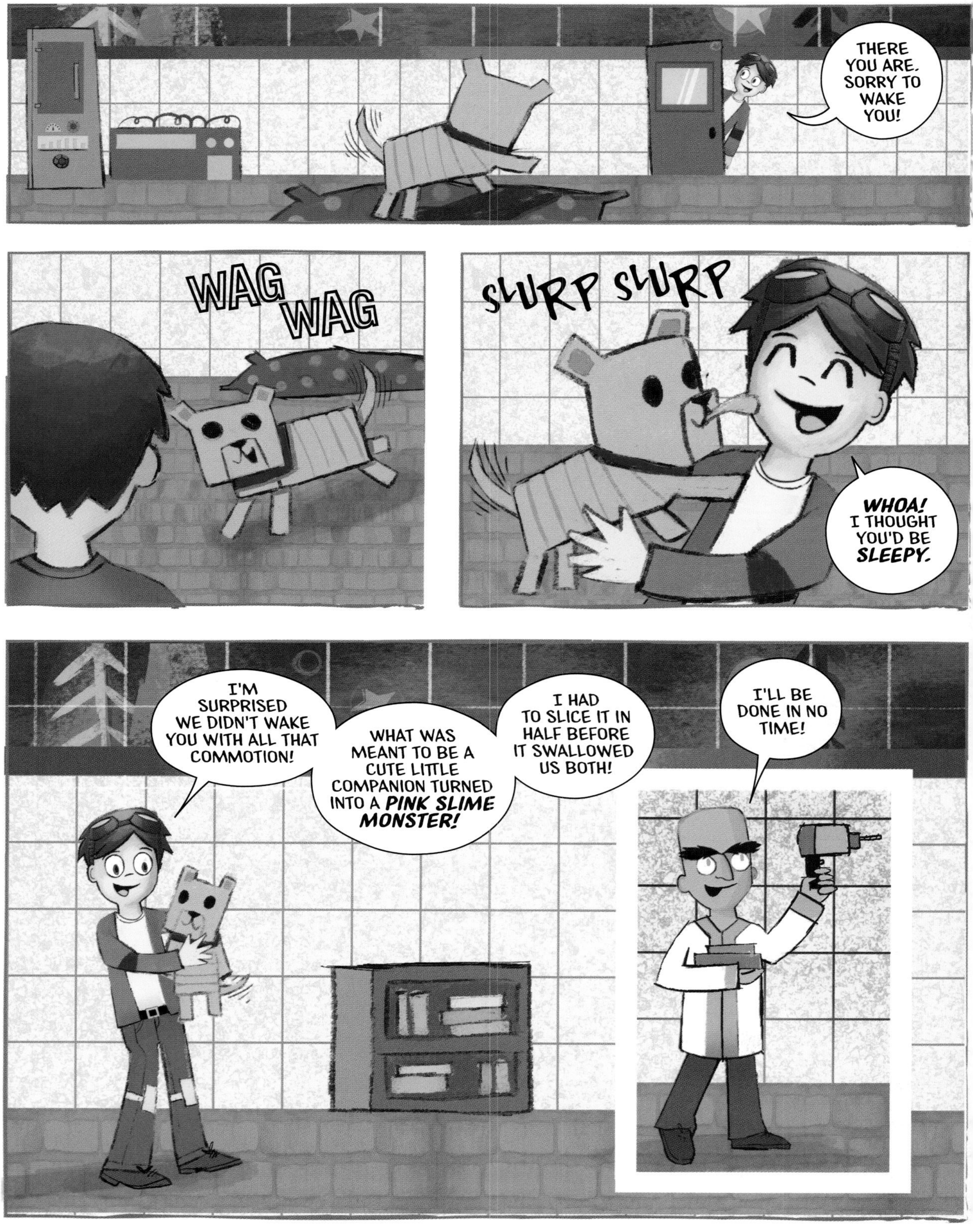
THERE YOU ARE. SORRY TO WAKE YOU!
WAG WAG
SLURP SLURP
WHOA! I THOUGHT YOU'D BE SLEEPY.
I'M SURPRISED WE DIDN'T WAKE YOU WITH ALL THAT COMMOTION!
WHAT WAS MEANT TO BE A CUTE LITTLE COMPANION TURNED INTO A PINK SLIME MONSTER!
I HAD TO SLICE IT IN HALF BEFORE IT SWALLOWED US BOTH!
I'LL BE DONE IN NO TIME!

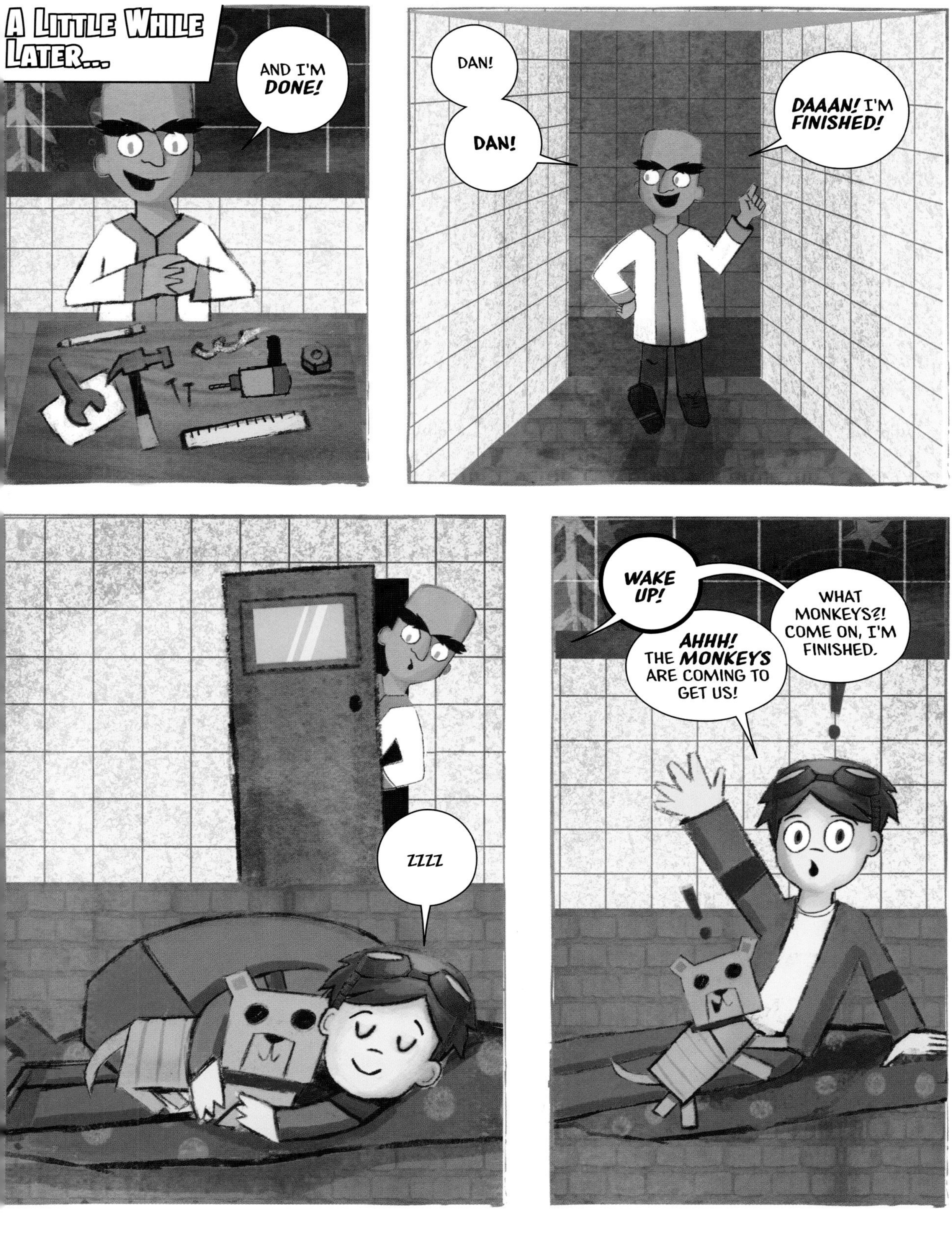
A LITTLE WHILE LATER...
AND I'M DONE!
DAN!
DAN!
DAAAN! I'M FINISHED!
ZZZZ
WAKE UP!
AHHH! THE MONKEYS ARE COMING TO GET US!
WHAT MONKEYS?! COME ON, I'M FINISHED.

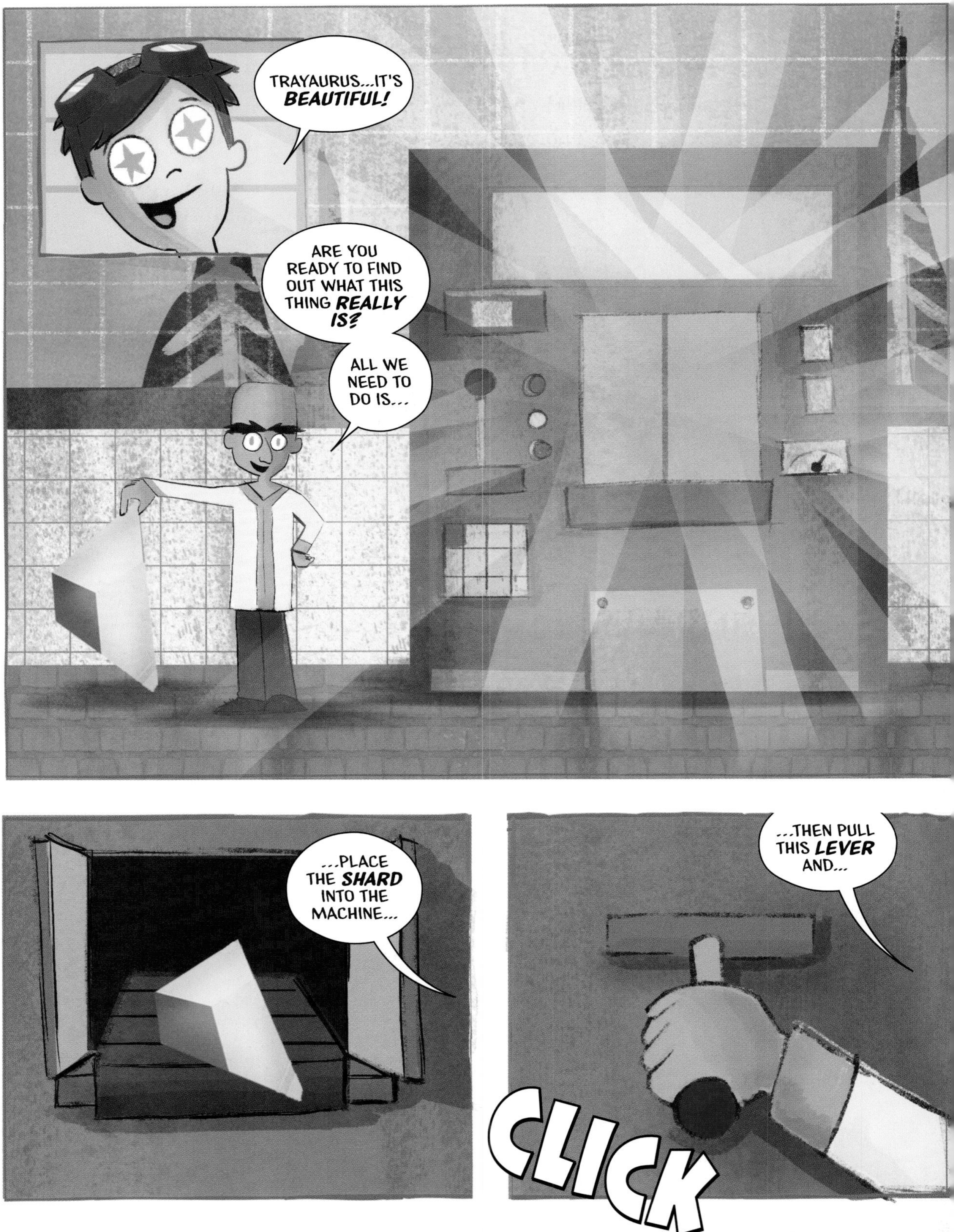
TRAYAURUS...IT'S BEAUTIFUL!
ARE YOU READY TO FIND OUT WHAT THIS THING REALLY IS?
ALL WE NEED TO DO IS...
...PLACE THE SHARD INTO THE MACHINE...
...THEN PULL THIS LEVER AND...
CLICK

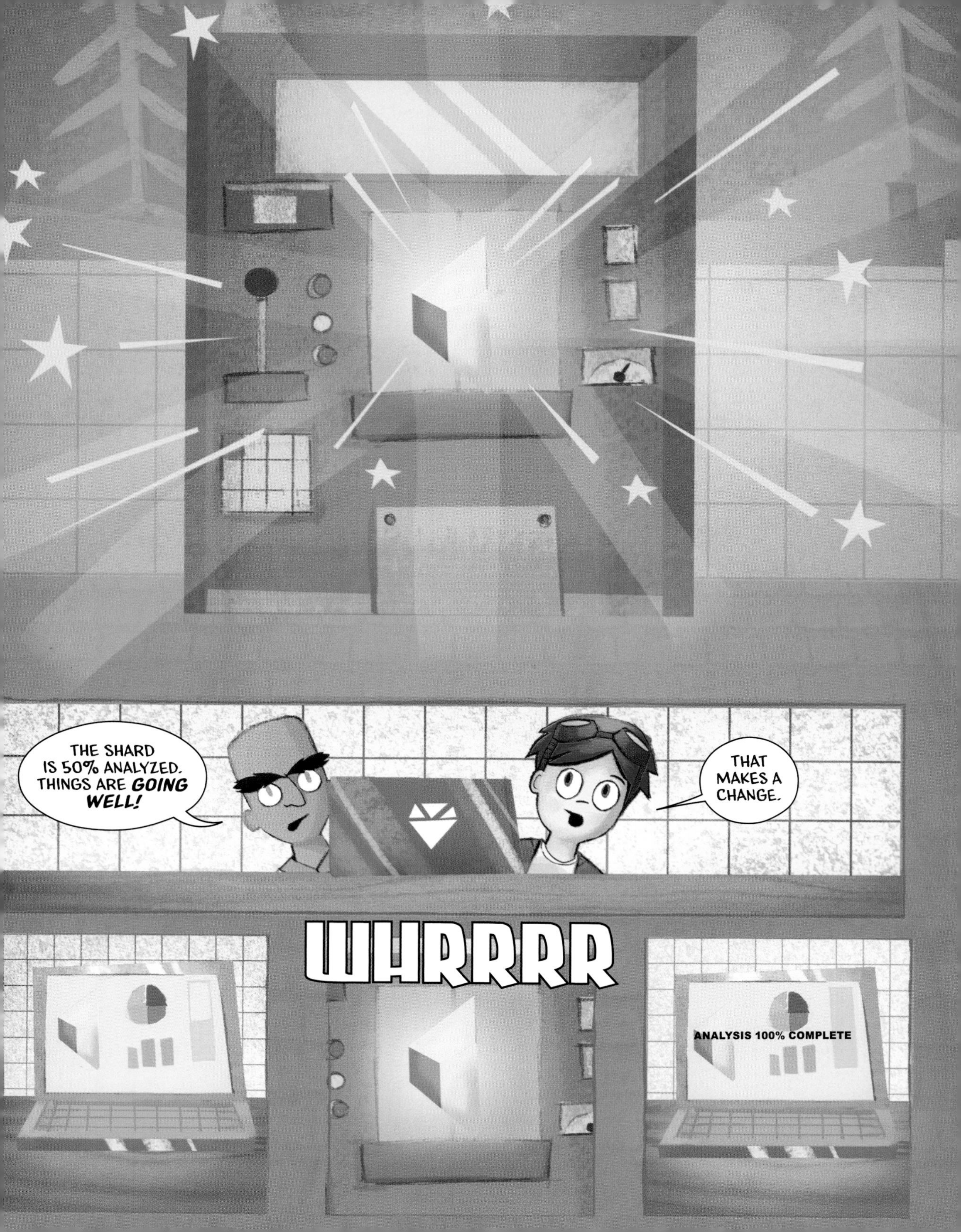
THE SHARD IS 50% ANALYZED. THINGS ARE GOING WELL!
THAT MAKES A CHANGE.
WHRRRR
ANALYSIS 100% COMPLETE

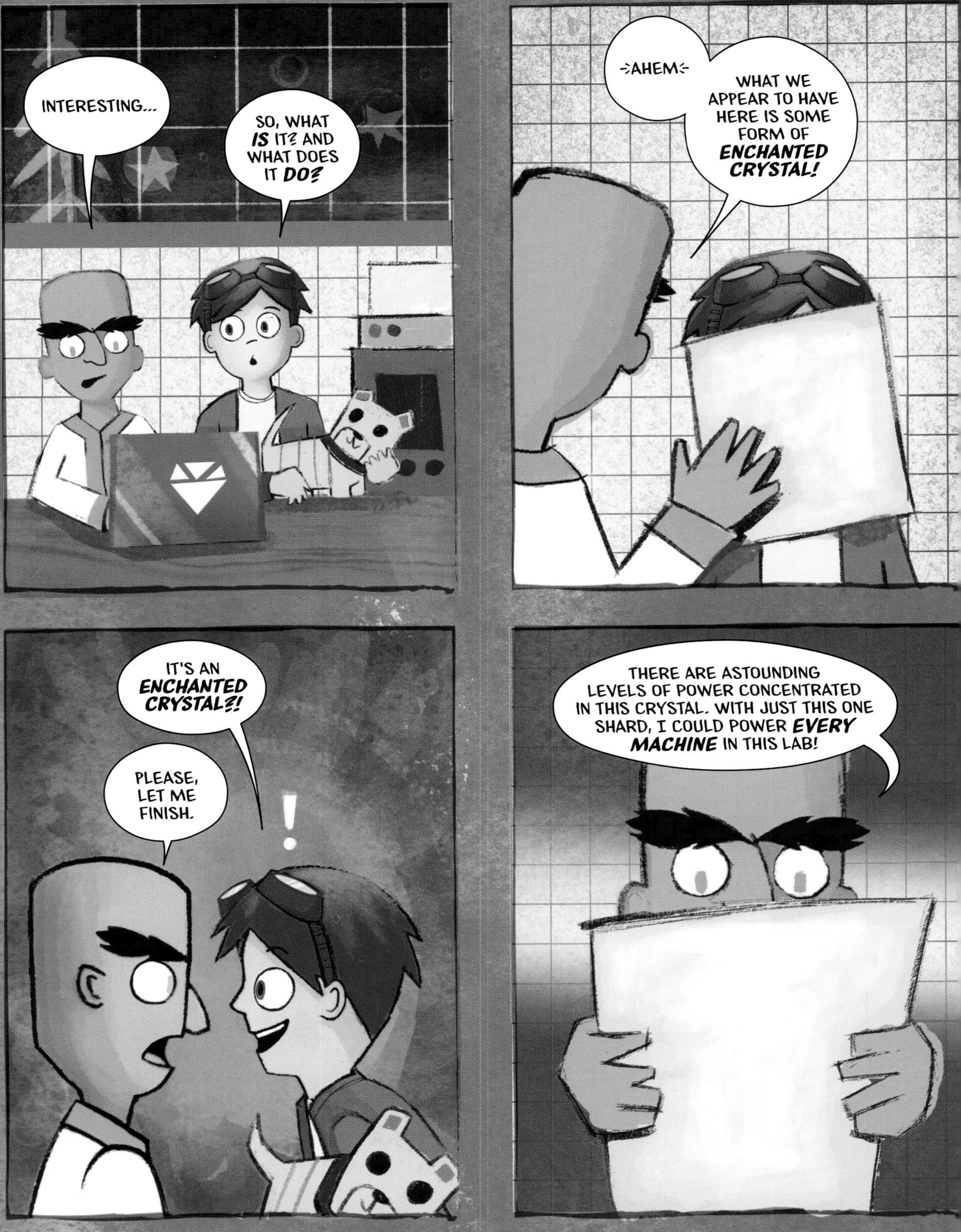
INTERESTING...
SO, WHAT IS IT? AND WHAT DOES IT DO?
AHEM
WHAT WE APPEAR TO HAVE HERE IS SOME FORM OF ENCHANTED CRYSTAL!
IT'S AN ENCHANTED CRYSTAL?!
PLEASE, LET ME FINISH.
!
THERE ARE ASTOUNDING LEVELS OF POWER CONCENTRATED IN THIS CRYSTAL. WITH JUST THIS ONE SHARD, I COULD POWER EVERY MACHINE IN THIS LAB!

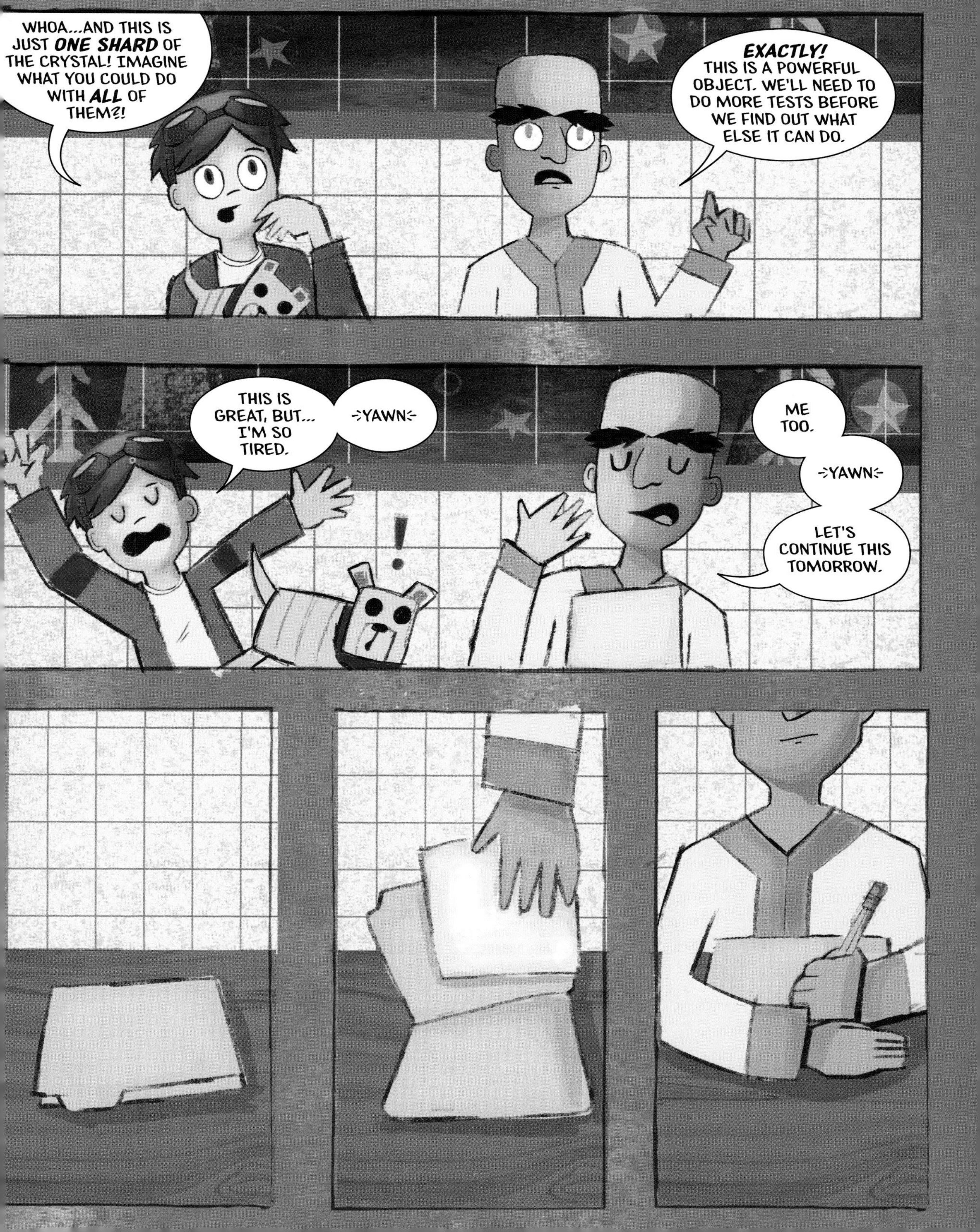
WHOA...AND THIS IS JUST ONE SHARD OF THE CRYSTAL! IMAGINE WHAT YOU COULD DO WITH ALL OF THEM?!
EXACTLY! THIS IS A POWERFUL OBJECT. WE'LL NEED TO DO MORE TESTS BEFORE WE FIND OUT WHAT ELSE IT CAN DO.
THIS IS GREAT, BUT... I'M SO TIRED.
YAWN
ME TOO.
YAWN
LET'S CONTINUE THIS TOMORROW.

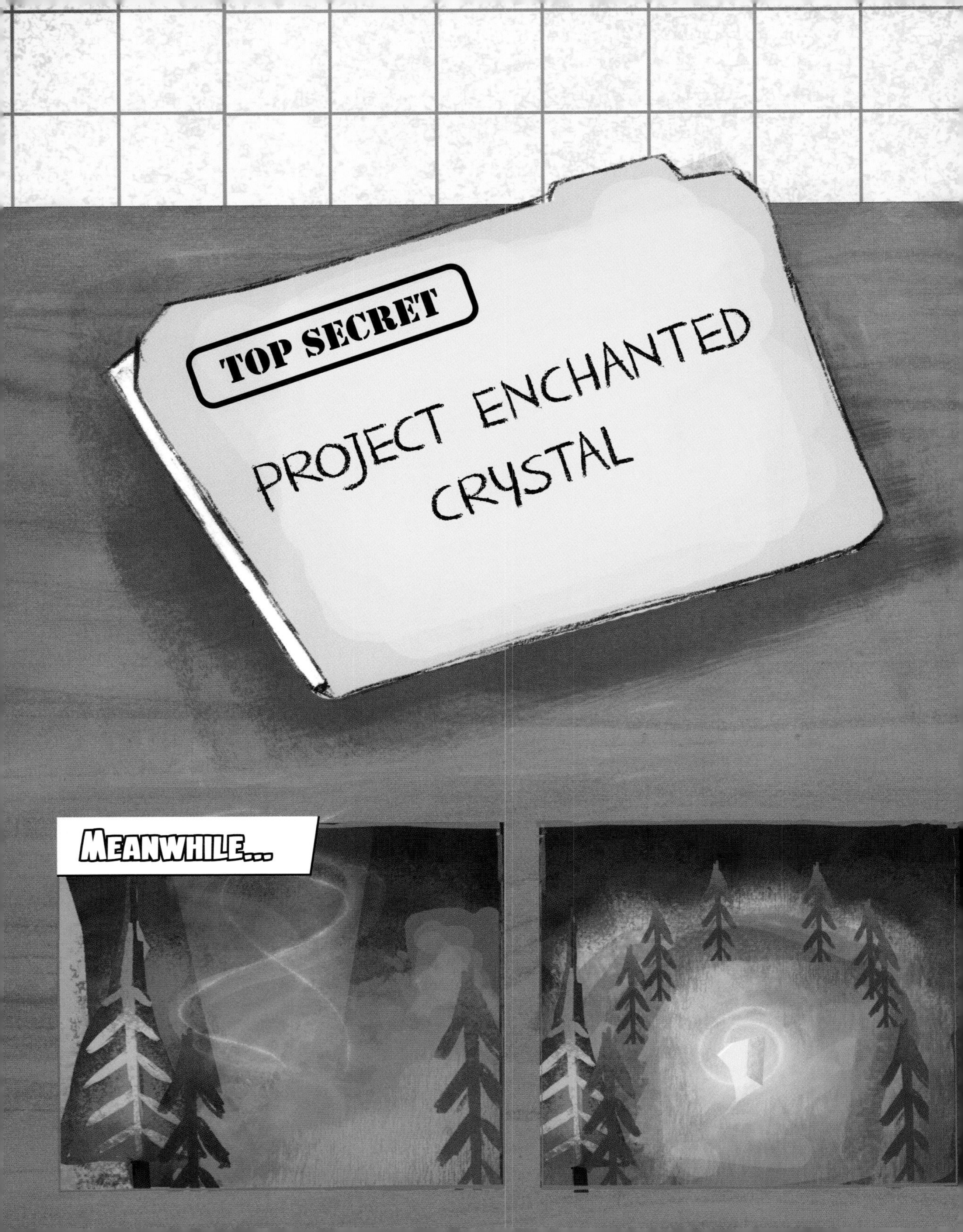
TOP SECRET
PROJECT ENCHANTED CRYSTAL
MEANWHILE...

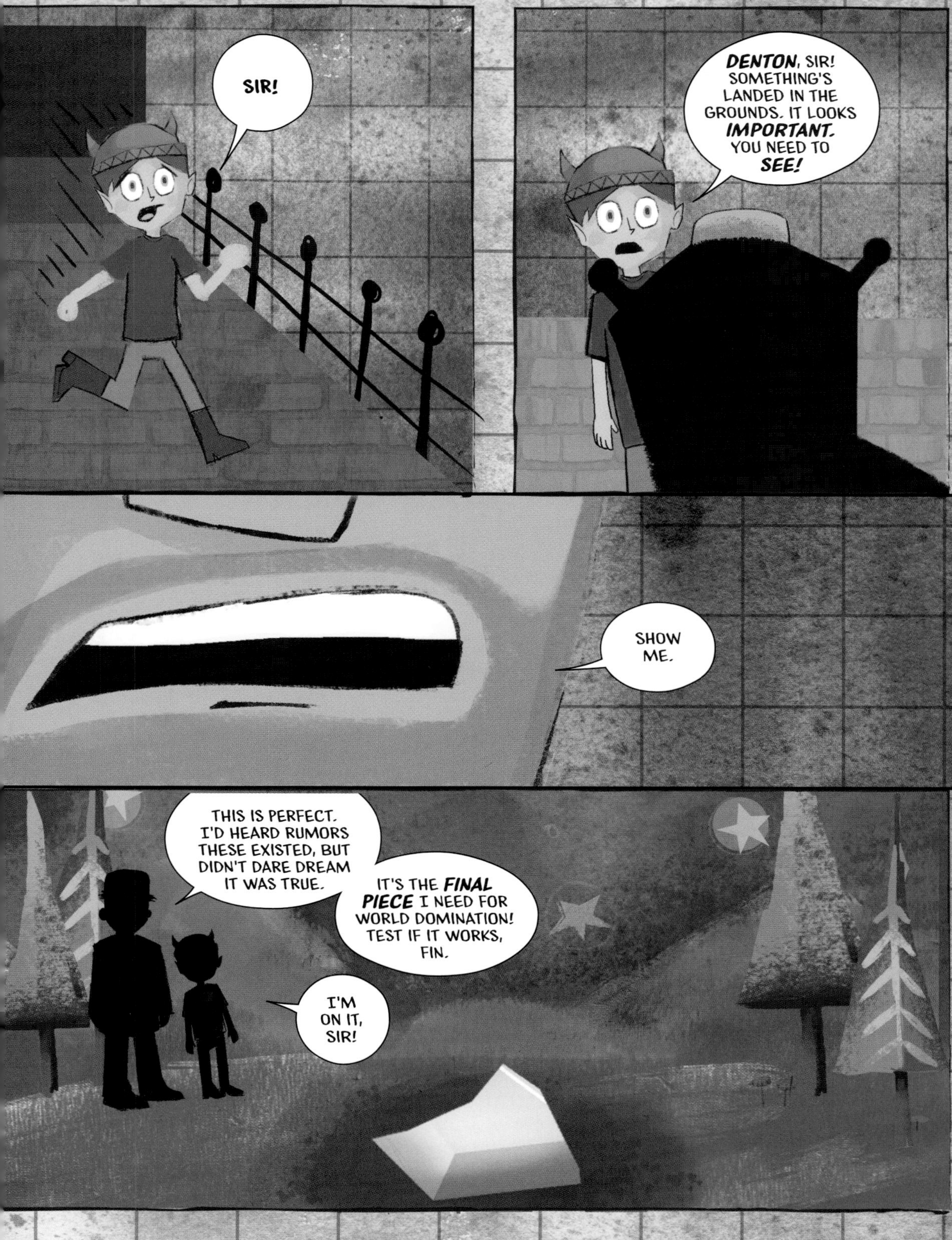
SIR!
DENTON, SIR! SOMETHING'S LANDED IN THE GROUNDS. IT LOOKS **IMPORTANT.** YOU NEED TO **SEE!**
SHOW ME.
THIS IS PERFECT. I'D HEARD RUMORS THESE EXISTED, BUT DIDN'T DARE DREAM IT WAS TRUE.
IT'S THE **FINAL PIECE** I NEED FOR WORLD DOMINATION! TEST IF IT WORKS, FIN.
I'M ON IT, SIR!

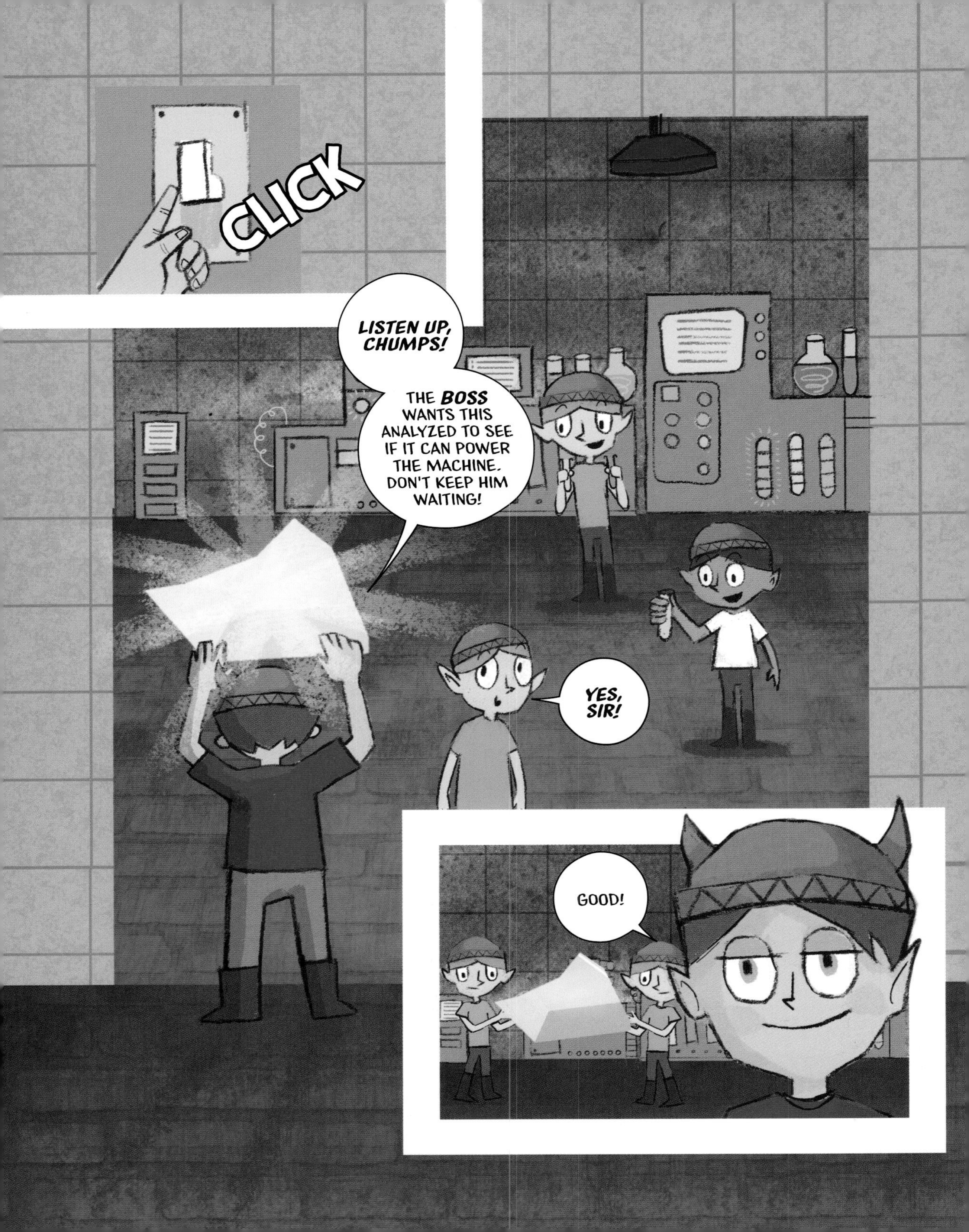
CLICK
LISTEN UP, CHUMPS!
THE BOSS WANTS THIS ANALYZED TO SEE IF IT CAN POWER THE MACHINE. DON'T KEEP HIM WAITING!
YES, SIR!
GOOD!

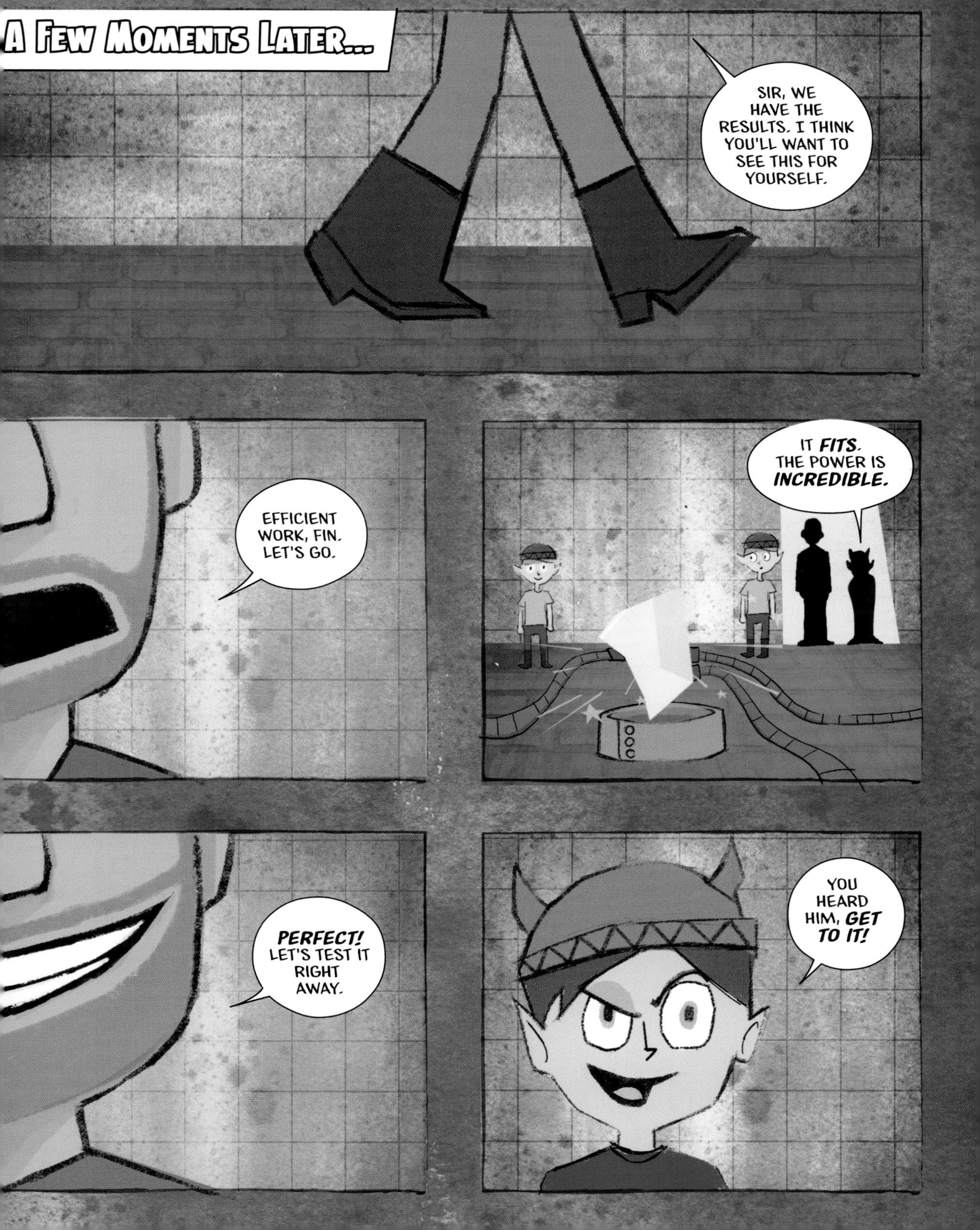
A FEW MOMENTS LATER...
SIR, WE HAVE THE RESULTS. I THINK YOU'LL WANT TO SEE THIS FOR YOURSELF.
EFFICIENT WORK, FIN. LET'S GO.
IT FITS. THE POWER IS INCREDIBLE.
PERFECT! LET'S TEST IT RIGHT AWAY.
YOU HEARD HIM, GET TO IT!

CLICK
WUMMMMMMM
WUMMMMMMMM
IT'S FULLY POWERED, SIR!
ALL YOU NEED TO DO IS STEP IN. ARE YOU READY?

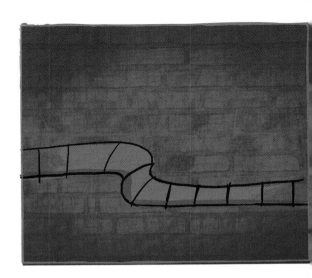

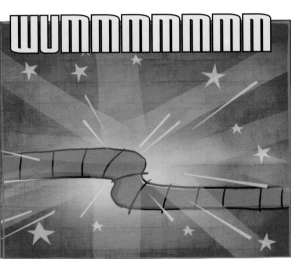

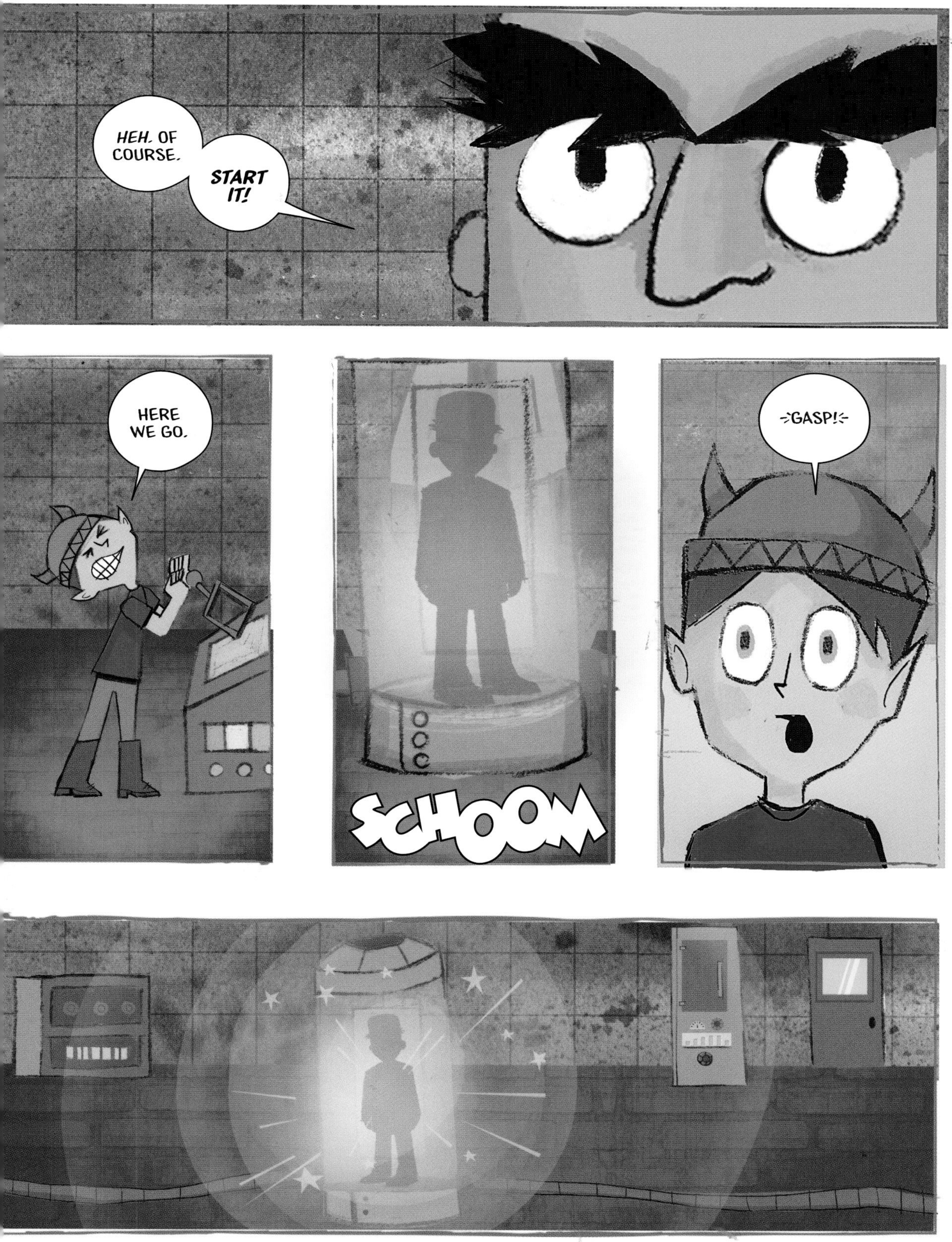
HEH. OF COURSE.
START IT!
HERE WE GO.
SCHOOM
-GASP!-

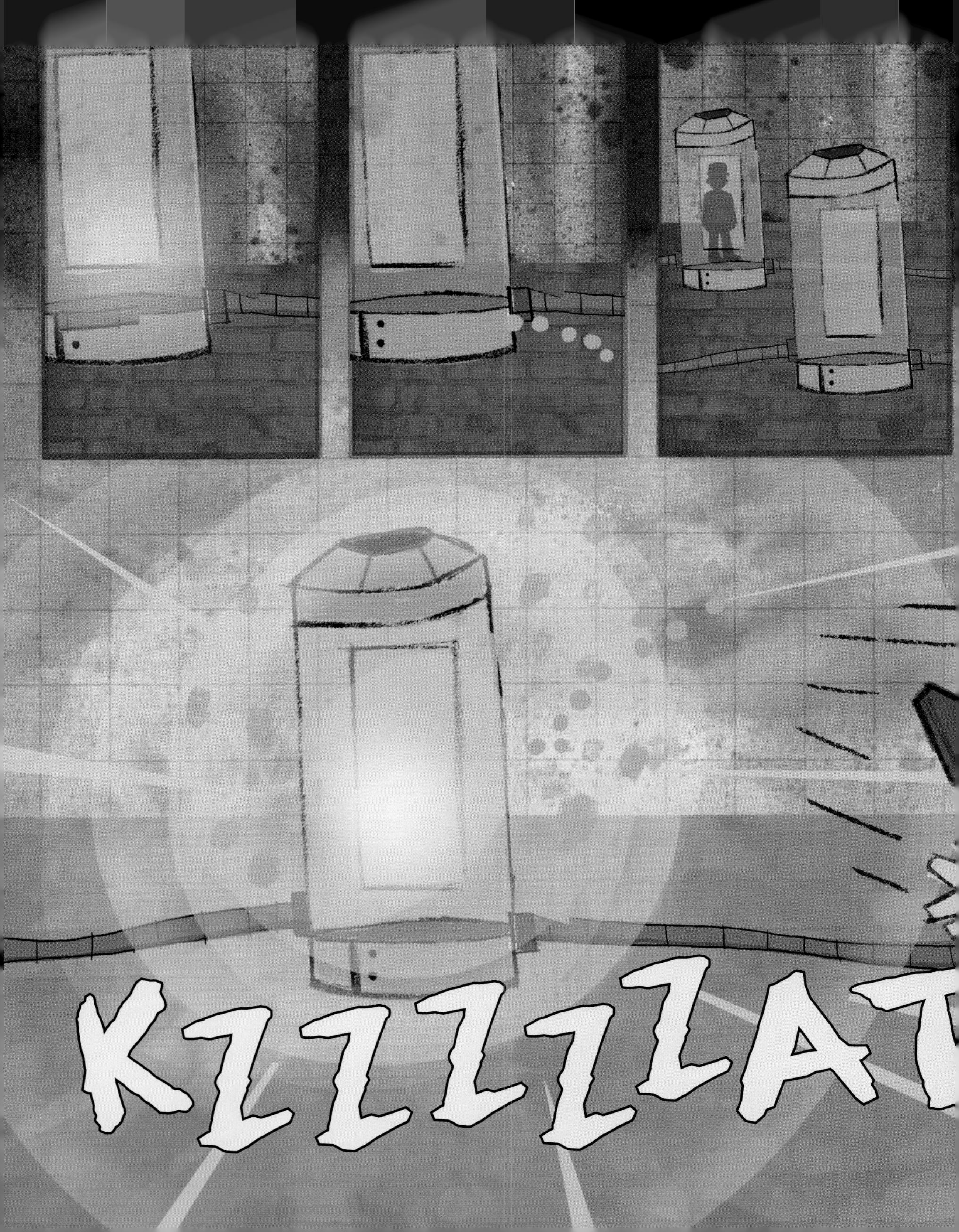
KZZZZZA

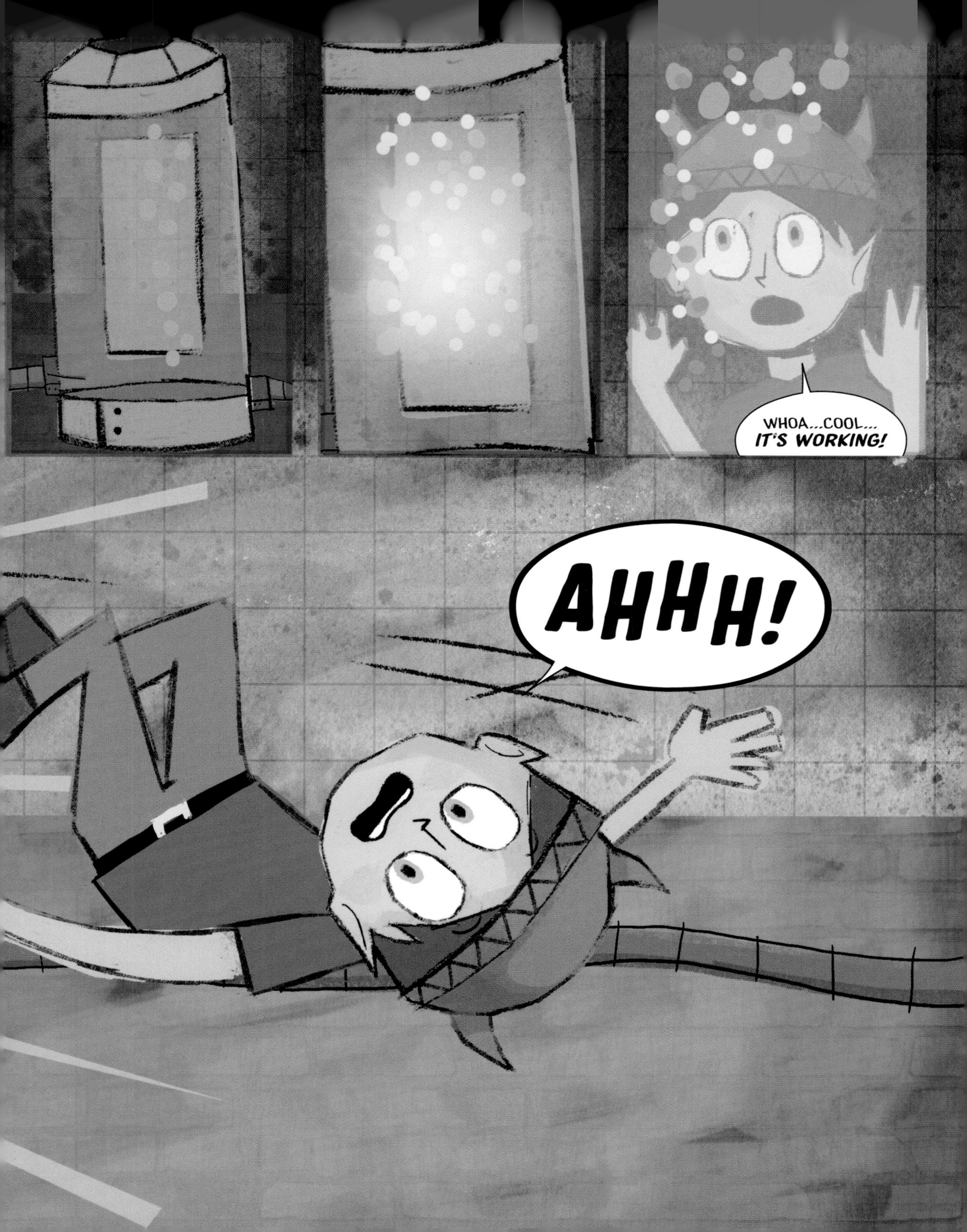
WHOA...COOL... IT'S WORKING!
AHHH!

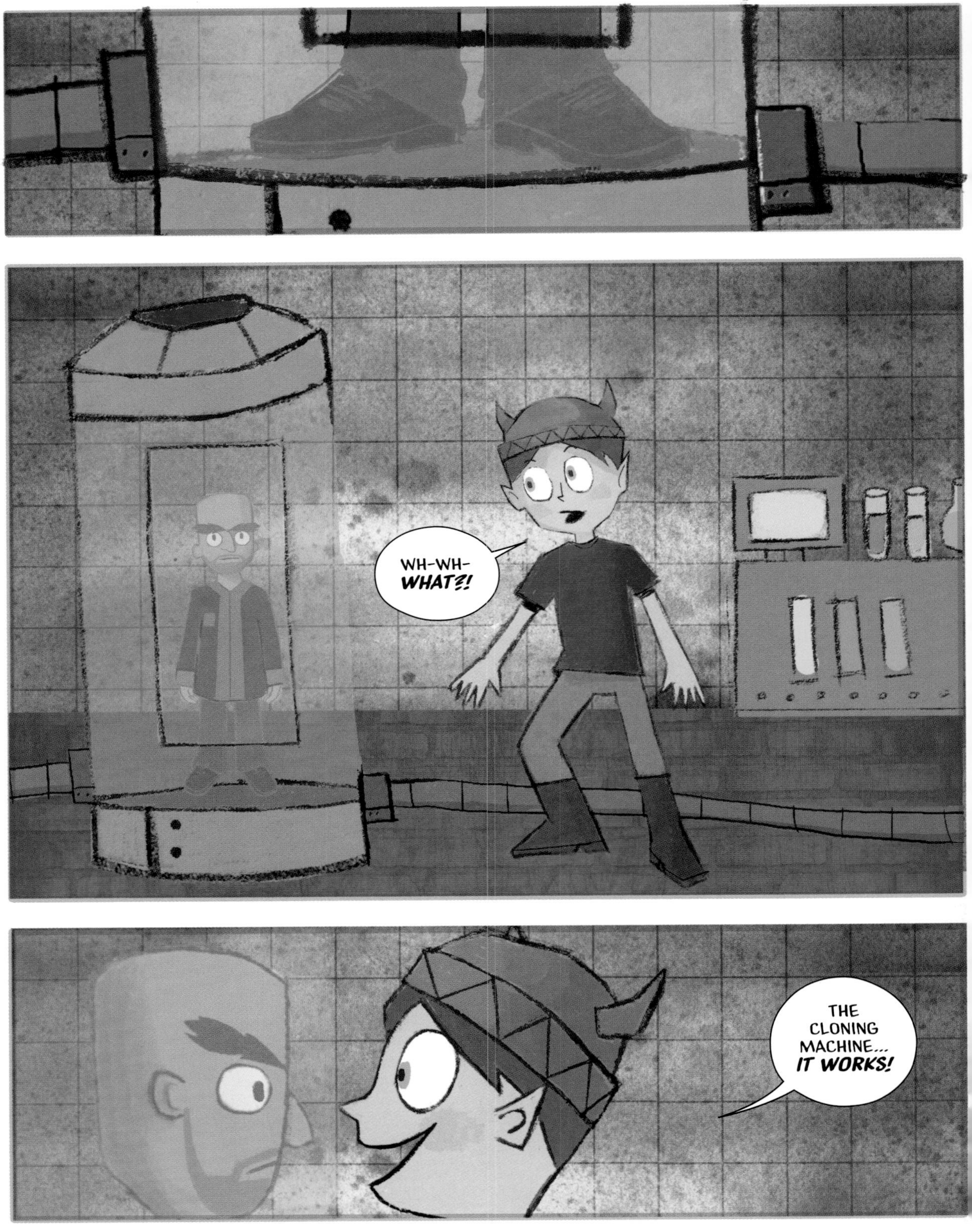
WH-WH-WHAT?!
THE CLONING MACHINE... IT WORKS!

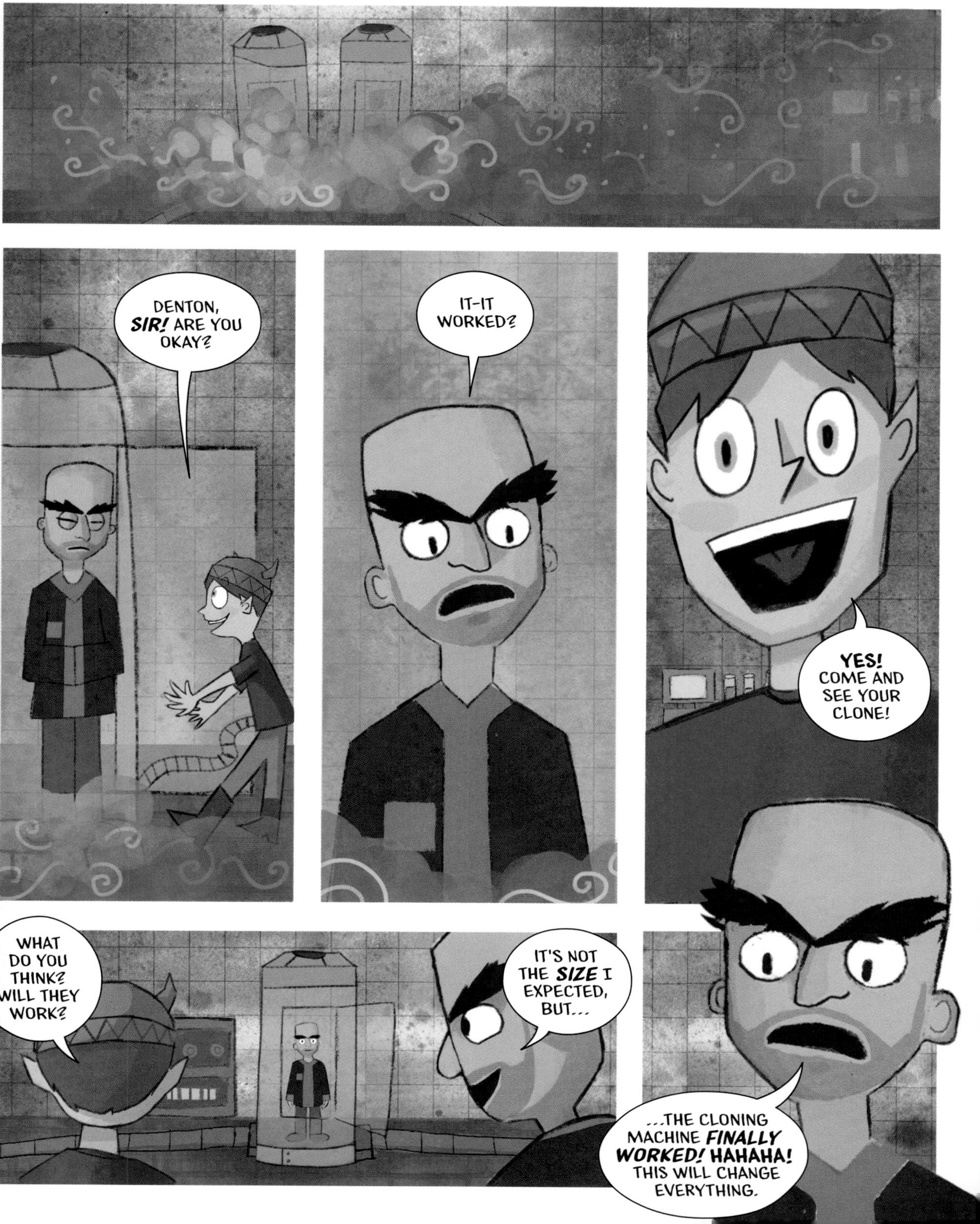

DENTON, SIR! ARE YOU OKAY?
IT-IT WORKED?
YES! COME AND SEE YOUR CLONE!
WHAT DO YOU THINK? WILL THEY WORK?
IT'S NOT THE SIZE I EXPECTED, BUT...
...THE CLONING MACHINE FINALLY WORKED! HAHAHA! THIS WILL CHANGE EVERYTHING.

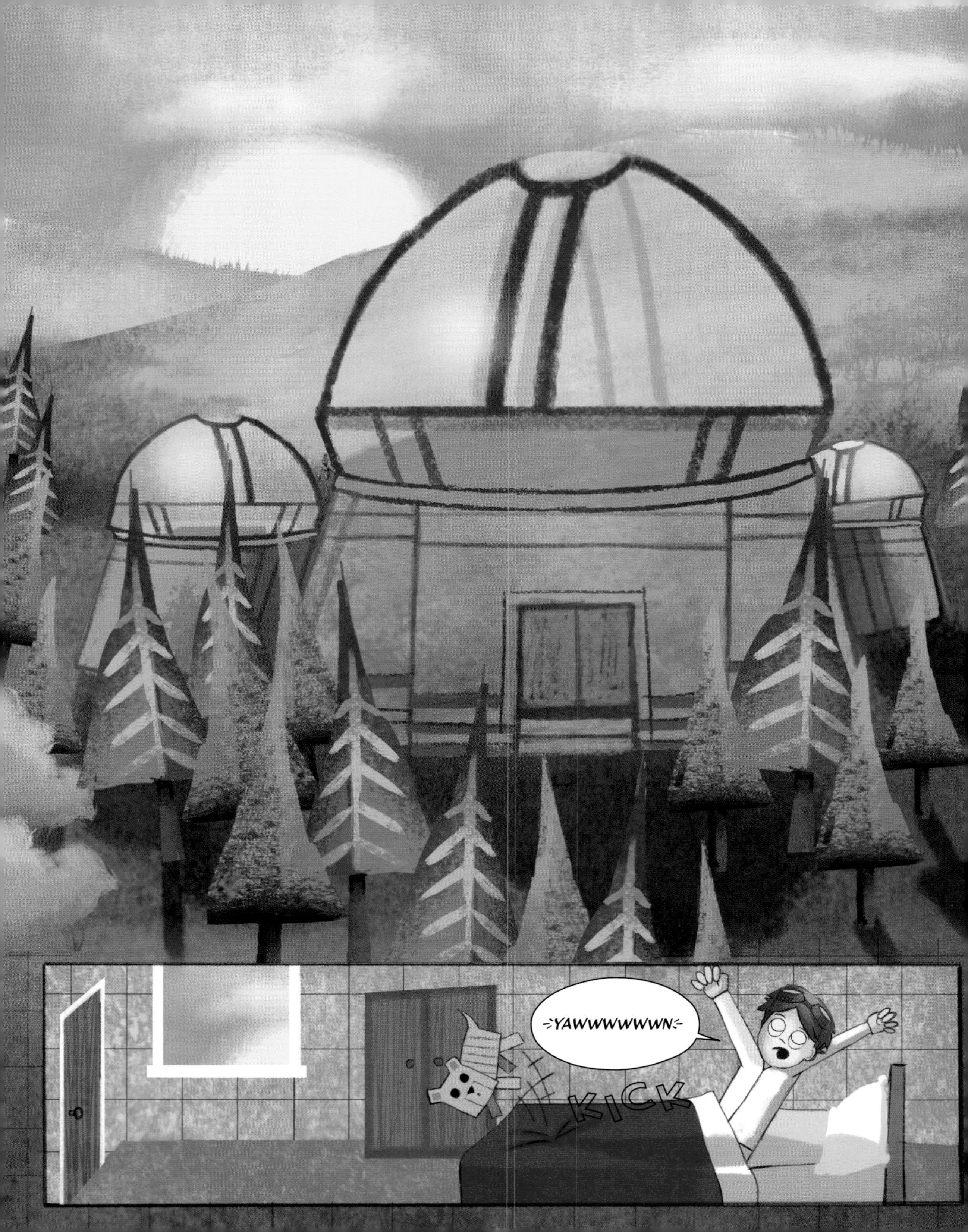
YAWWWWWWN
KICK

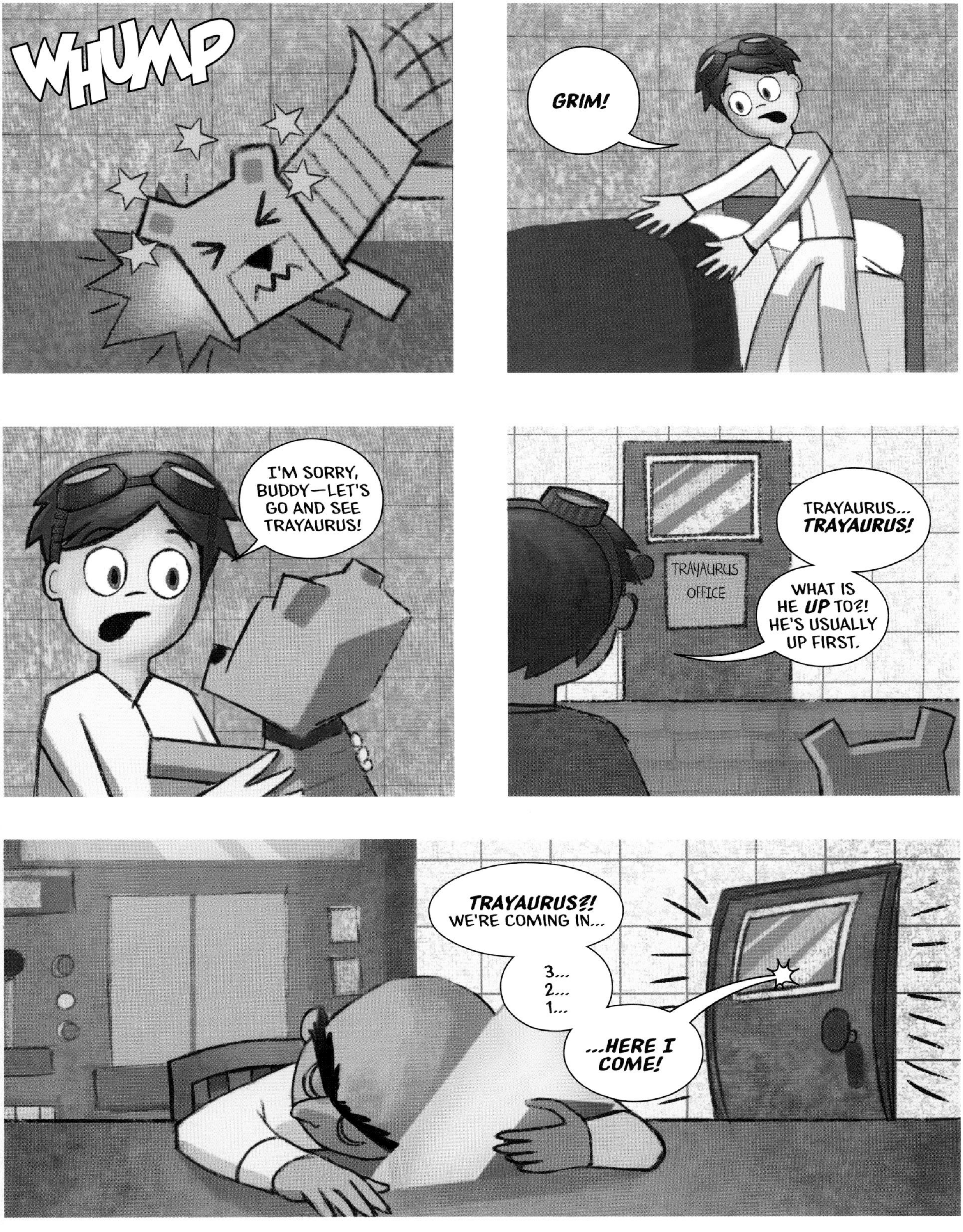
WHUMP
GRIM!
I'M SORRY, BUDDY—LET'S GO AND SEE TRAYAURUS!
TRAYAURUS... TRAYAURUS!
TRAYAURUS' OFFICE
WHAT IS HE UP TO?! HE'S USUALLY UP FIRST.
TRAYAURUS?! WE'RE COMING IN...
3... 2... 1...
...HERE I COME!

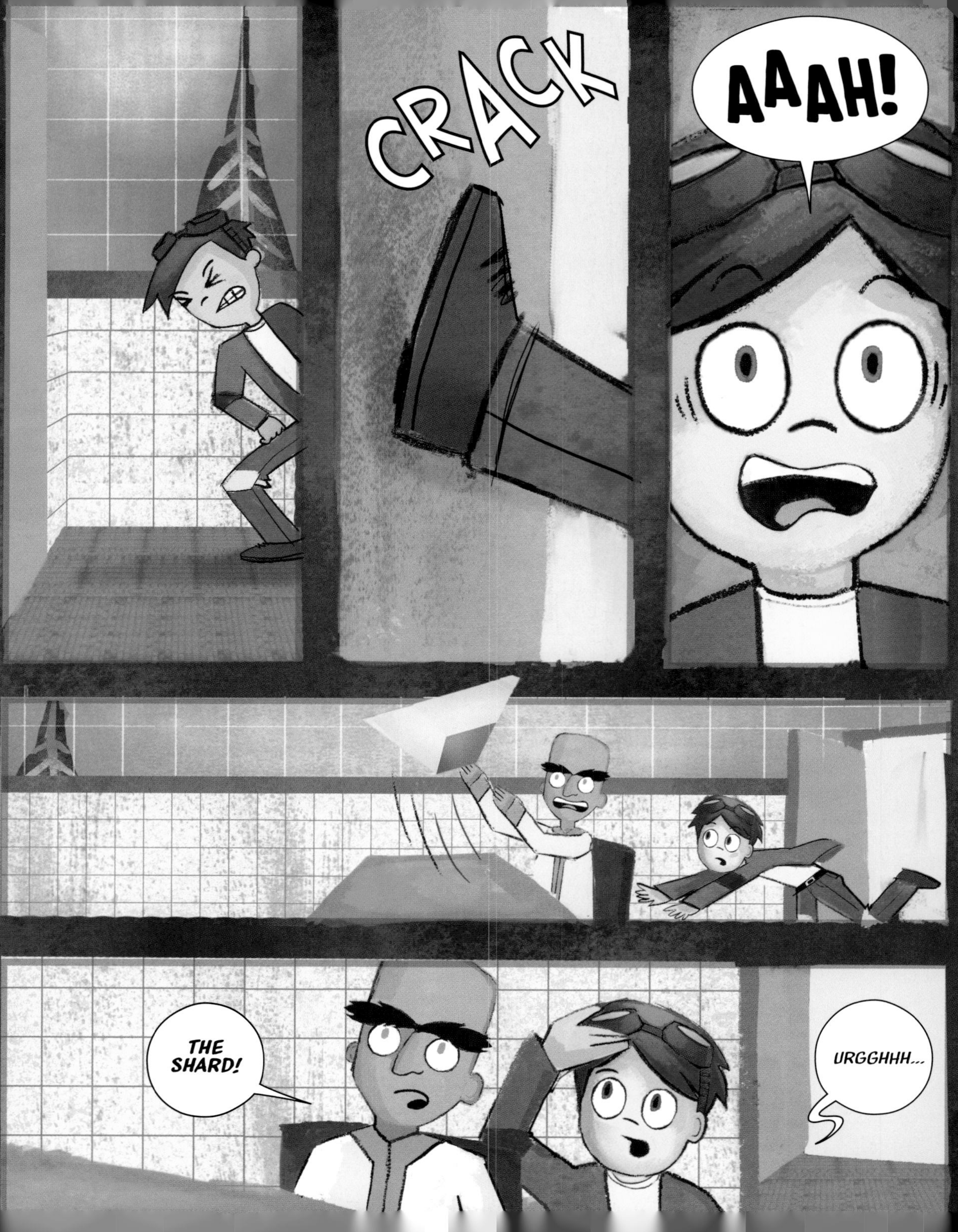
CRACK
AAAH!
THE SHARD!
URGGHHH...

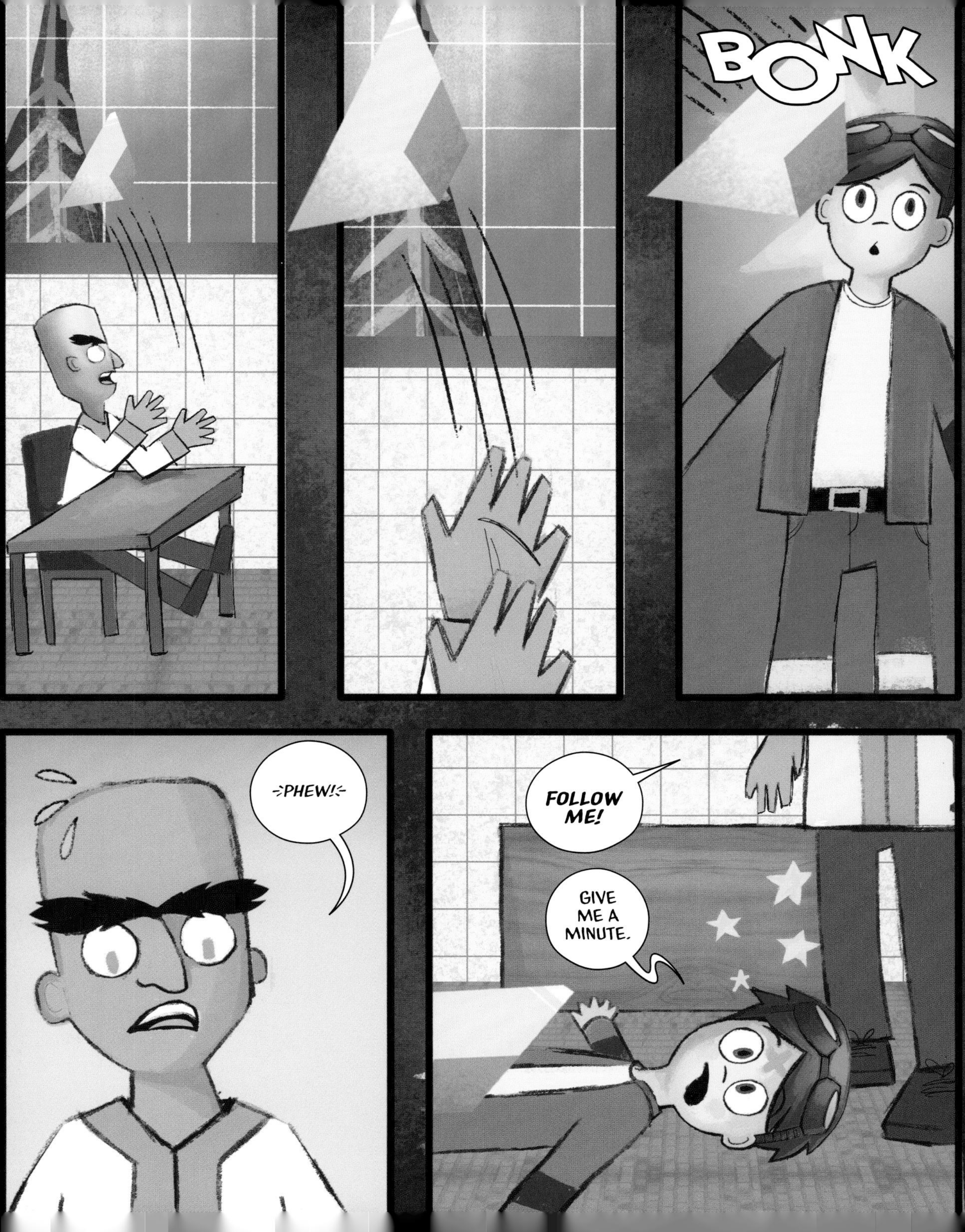
BONK
~PHEW!~
FOLLOW ME!
GIVE ME A MINUTE.

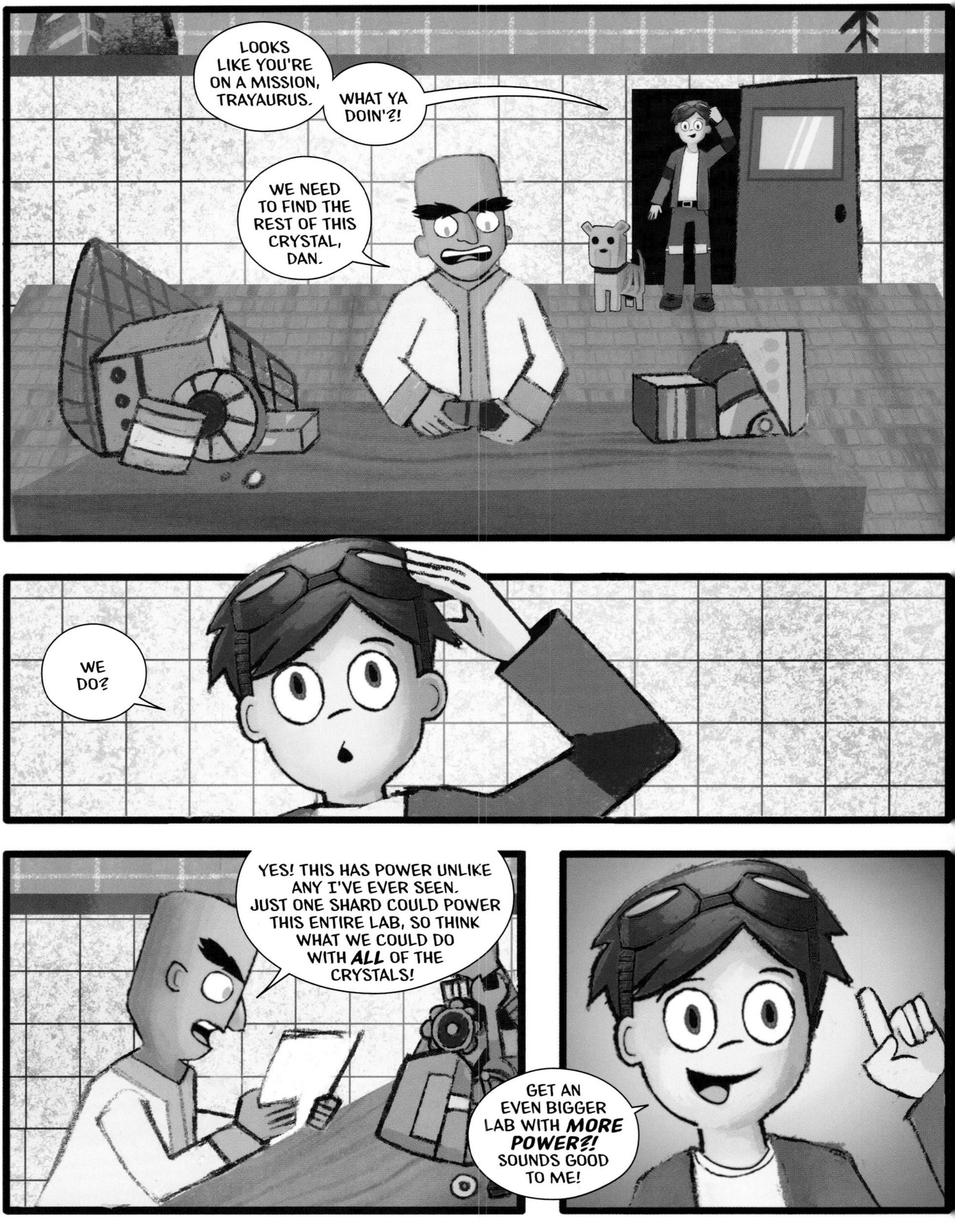
LOOKS LIKE YOU'RE ON A MISSION, TRAYAURUS.
WHAT YA DOIN'?!
WE NEED TO FIND THE REST OF THIS CRYSTAL, DAN.
WE DO?
YES! THIS HAS POWER UNLIKE ANY I'VE EVER SEEN. JUST ONE SHARD COULD POWER THIS ENTIRE LAB, SO THINK WHAT WE COULD DO WITH ALL OF THE CRYSTALS!
GET AN EVEN BIGGER LAB WITH MORE POWER?! SOUNDS GOOD TO ME!

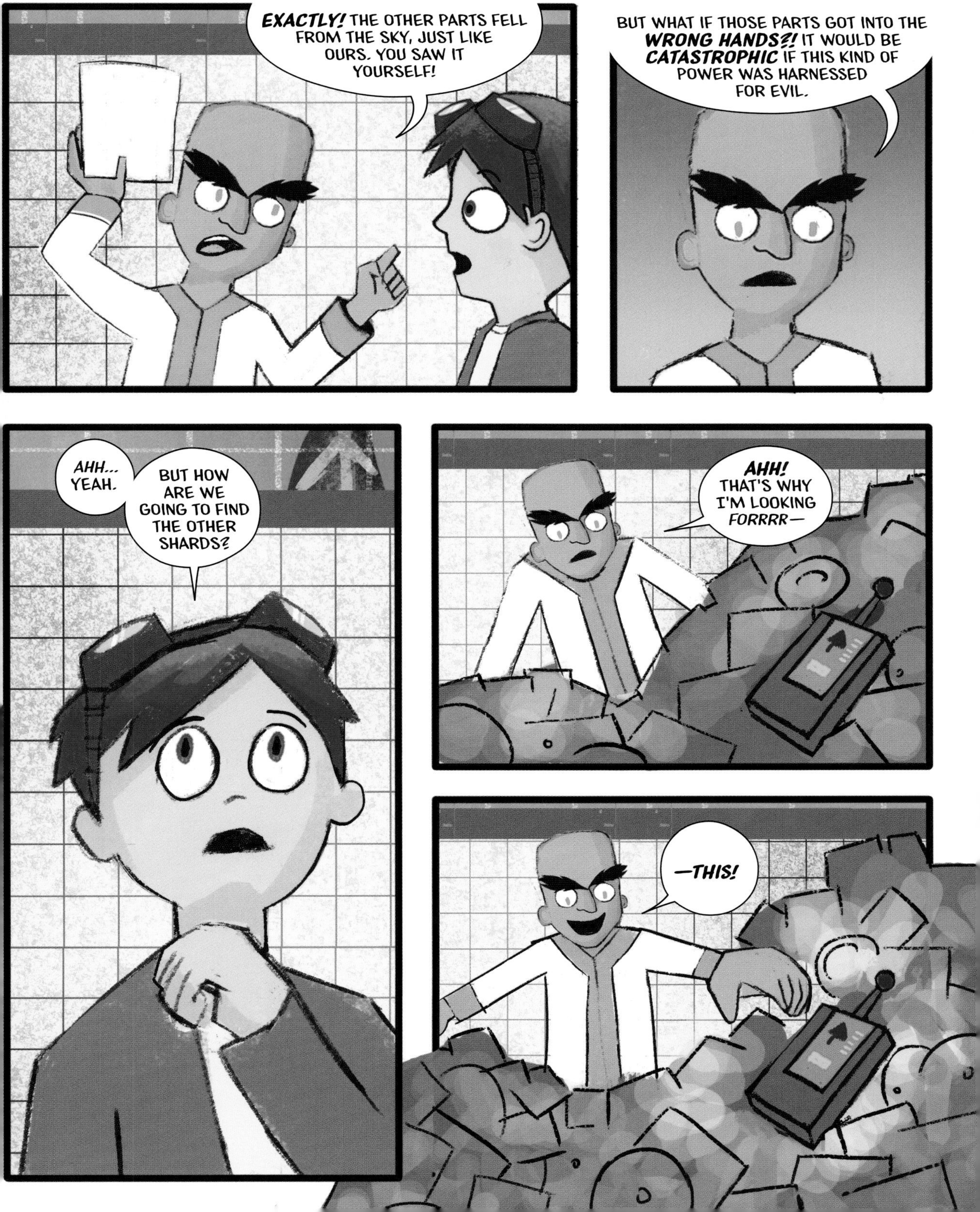
EXACTLY! THE OTHER PARTS FELL FROM THE SKY, JUST LIKE OURS. YOU SAW IT YOURSELF!
BUT WHAT IF THOSE PARTS GOT INTO THE WRONG HANDS?! IT WOULD BE CATASTROPHIC IF THIS KIND OF POWER WAS HARNESSED FOR EVIL.
AHH... YEAH.
BUT HOW ARE WE GOING TO FIND THE OTHER SHARDS?
AHH! THAT'S WHY I'M LOOKING FORRRR—
—THIS!

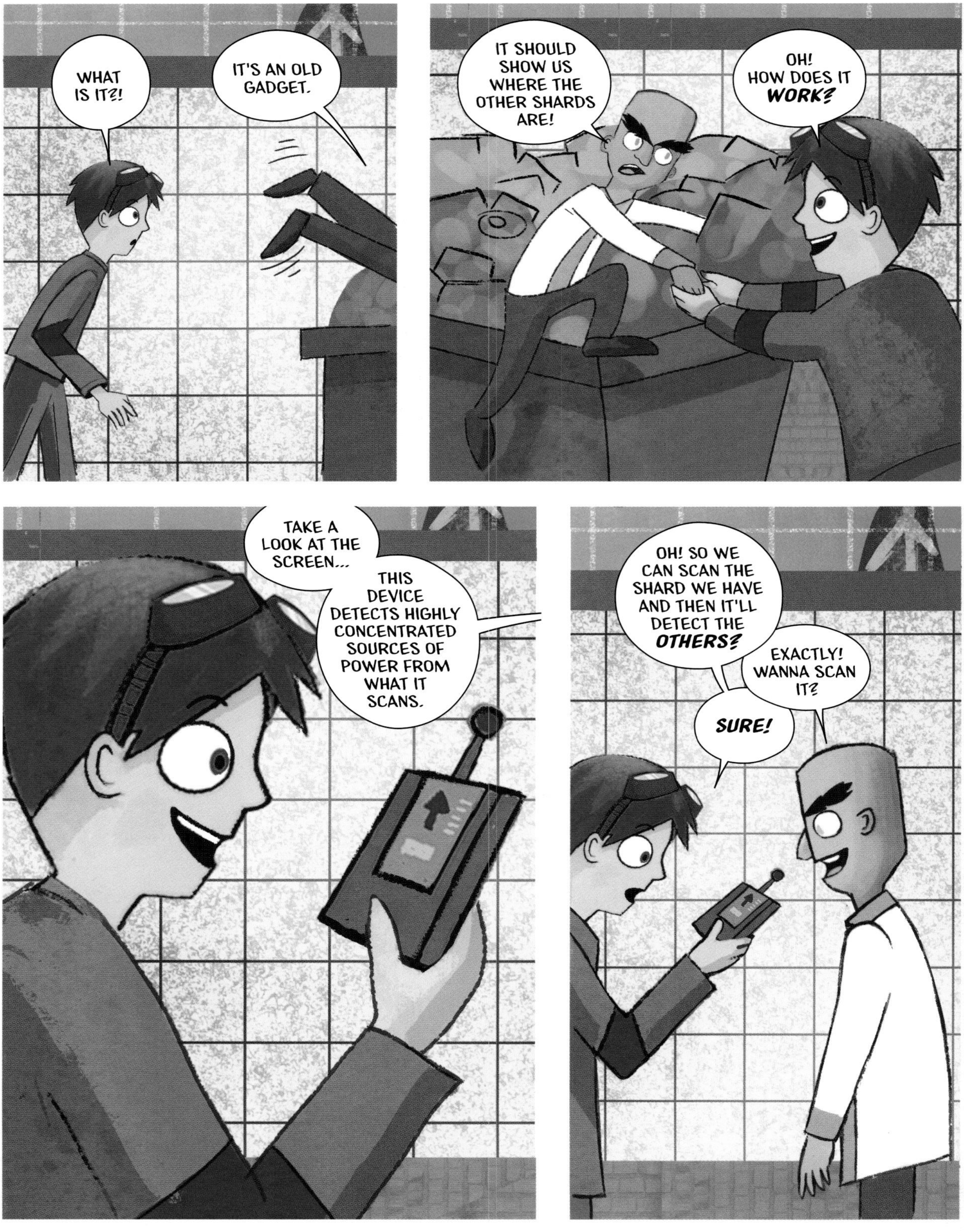
WHAT IS IT?!
IT'S AN OLD GADGET.
IT SHOULD SHOW US WHERE THE OTHER SHARDS ARE!
OH! HOW DOES IT *WORK?*
TAKE A LOOK AT THE SCREEN...
THIS DEVICE DETECTS HIGHLY CONCENTRATED SOURCES OF POWER FROM WHAT IT SCANS.
OH! SO WE CAN SCAN THE SHARD WE HAVE AND THEN IT'LL DETECT THE *OTHERS?*
EXACTLY! WANNA SCAN IT?
SURE!

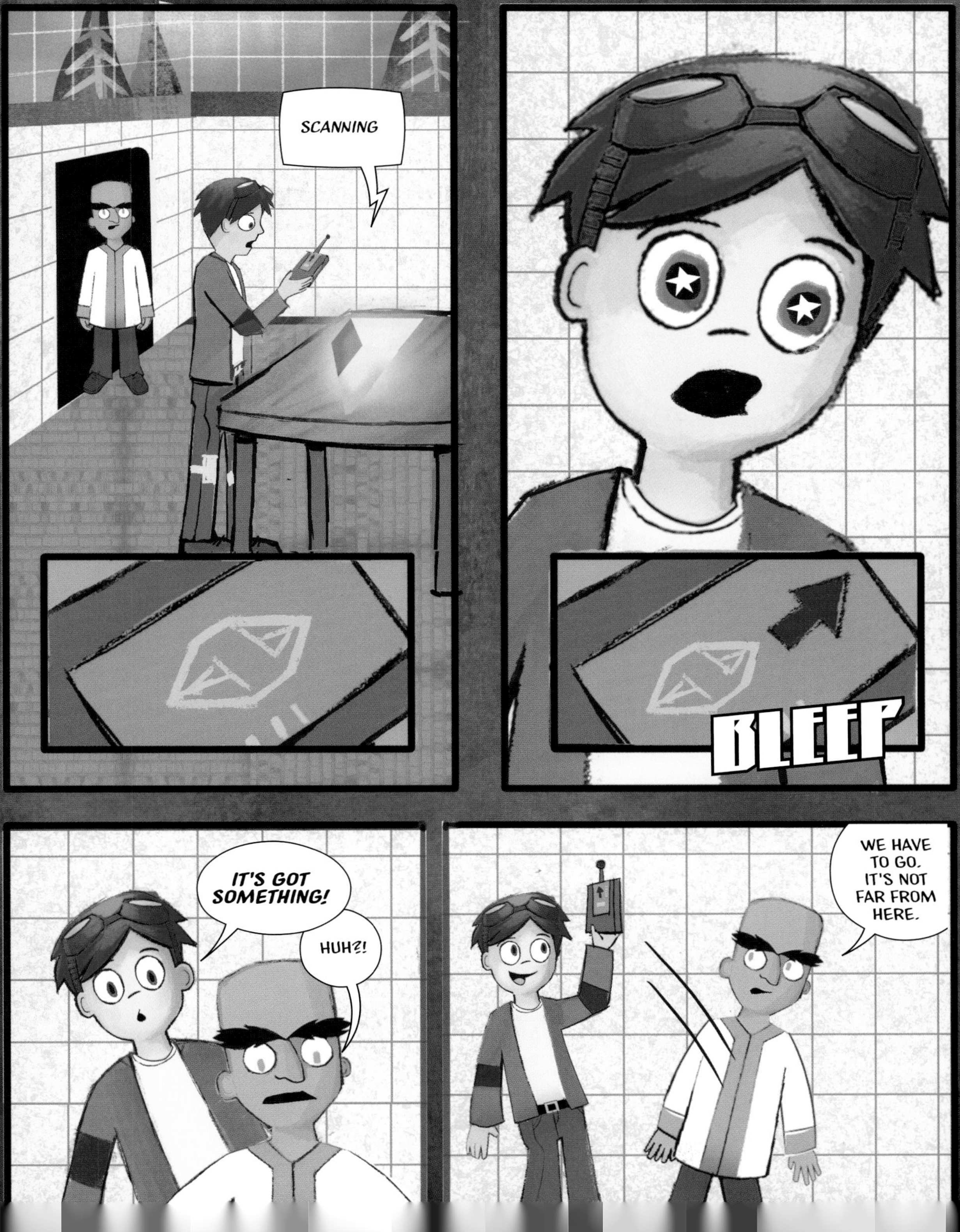
SCANNING
BLEEP
IT'S GOT SOMETHING!
HUH?!
WE HAVE TO GO. IT'S NOT FAR FROM HERE.

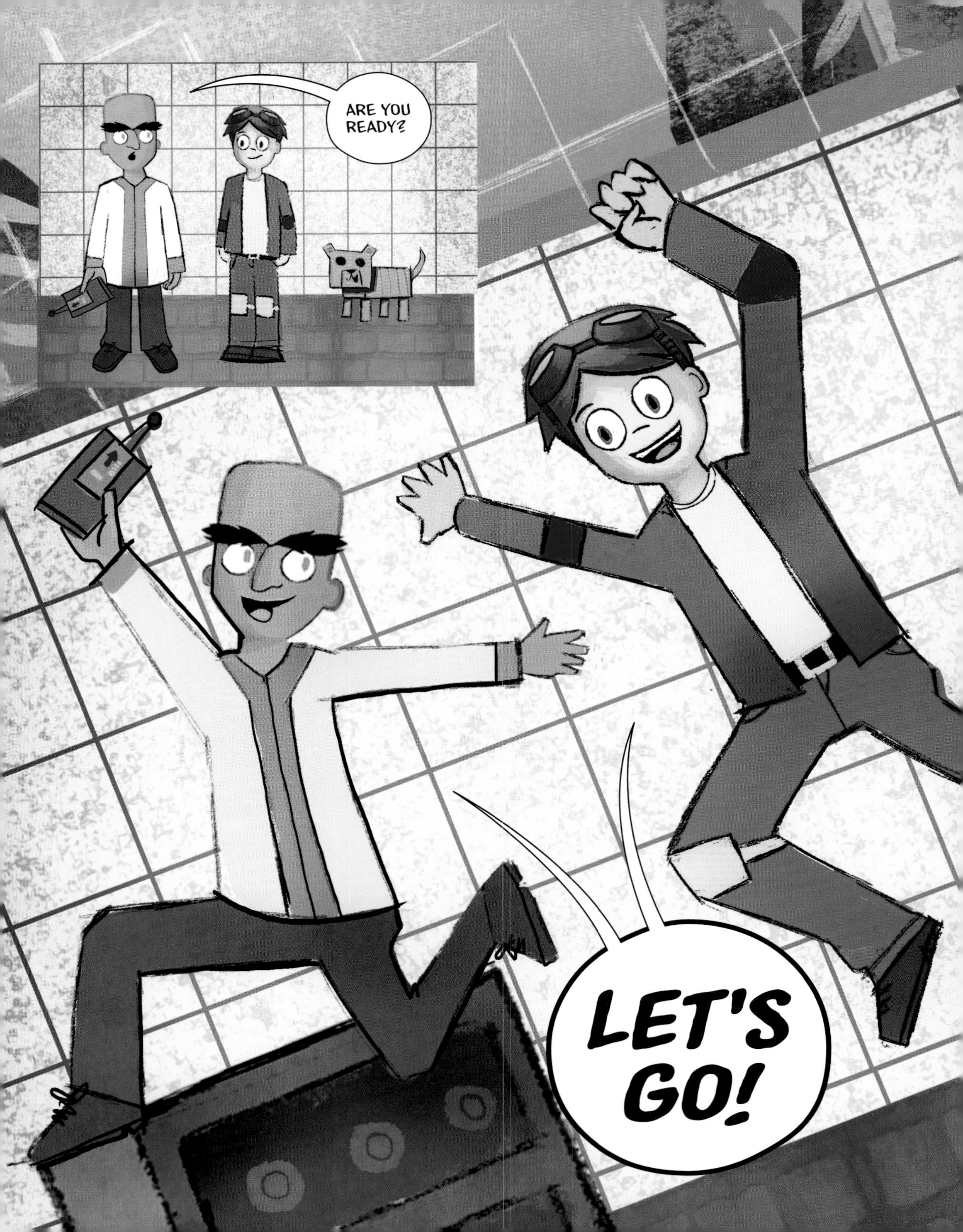
ARE YOU READY?
LET'S GO!

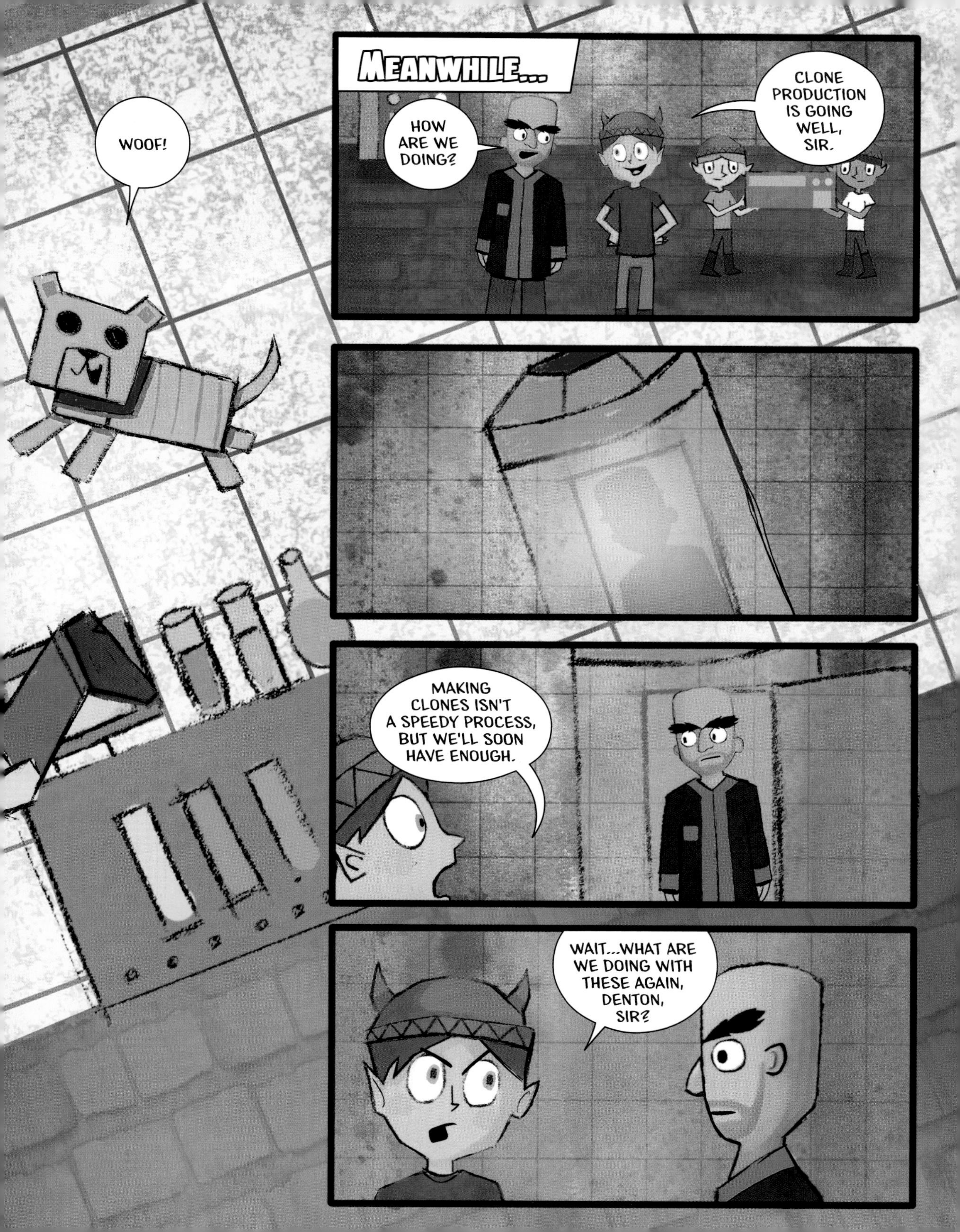
WOOF!
MEANWHILE...
HOW ARE WE DOING?
CLONE PRODUCTION IS GOING WELL, SIR.
MAKING CLONES ISN'T A SPEEDY PROCESS, BUT WE'LL SOON HAVE ENOUGH.
WAIT...WHAT ARE WE DOING WITH THESE AGAIN, DENTON, SIR?

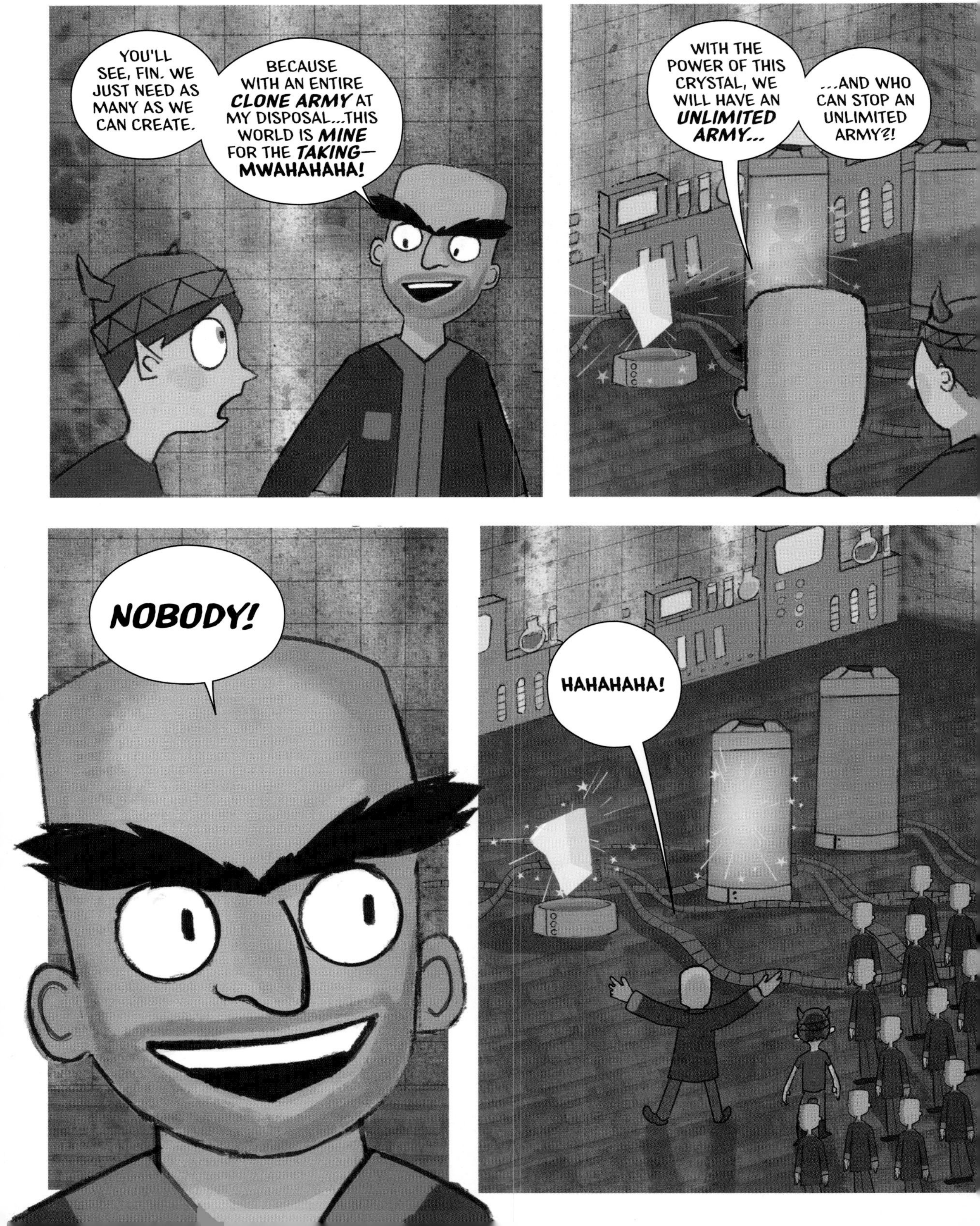
YOU'LL SEE, FIN. WE JUST NEED AS MANY AS WE CAN CREATE.
BECAUSE WITH AN ENTIRE CLONE ARMY AT MY DISPOSAL...THIS WORLD IS MINE FOR THE TAKING— MWAHAHAHA!
WITH THE POWER OF THIS CRYSTAL, WE WILL HAVE AN UNLIMITED ARMY...
...AND WHO CAN STOP AN UNLIMITED ARMY?!
NOBODY!
HAHAHAHA!

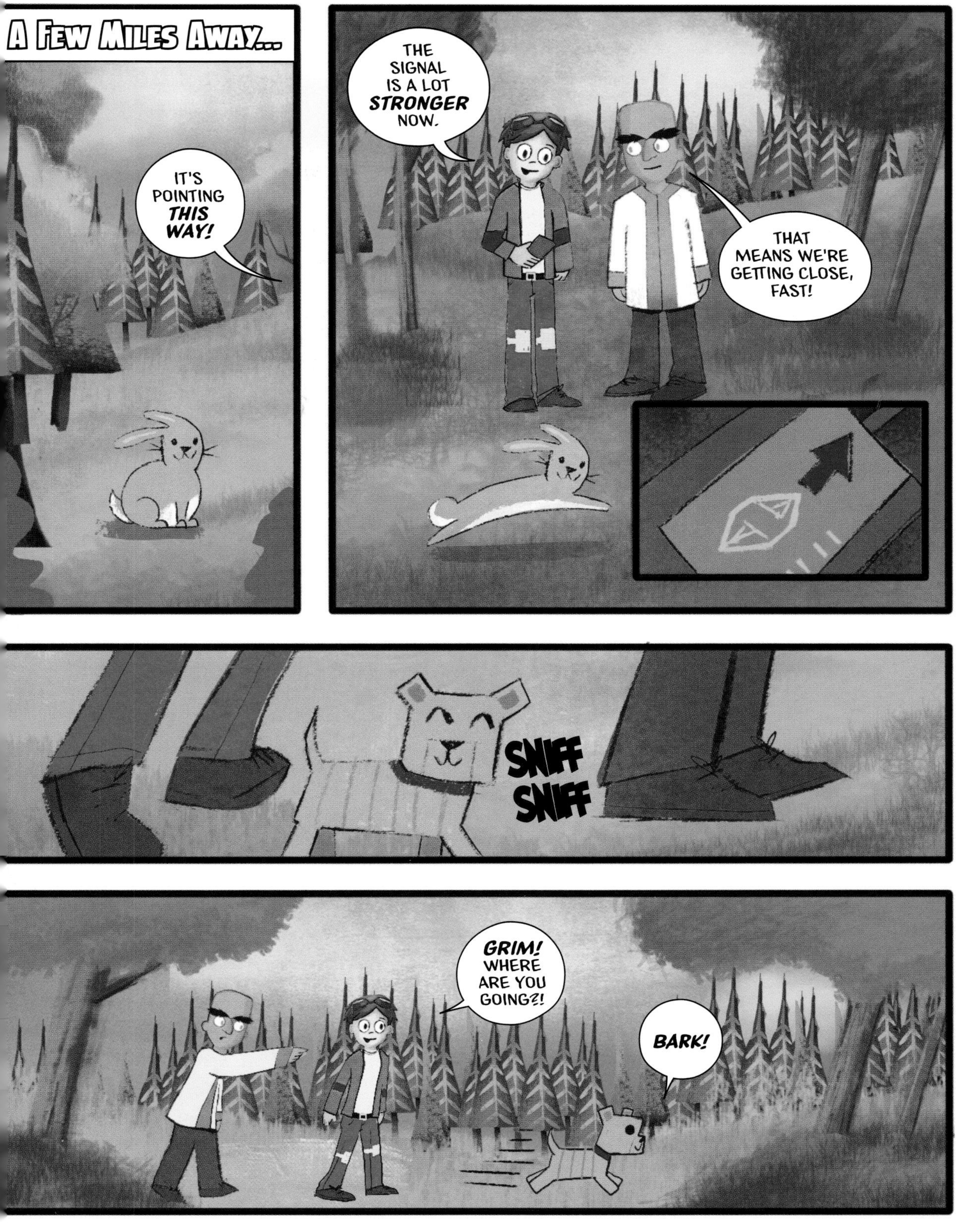
A FEW MILES AWAY...
IT'S POINTING THIS WAY!
THE SIGNAL IS A LOT STRONGER NOW.
THAT MEANS WE'RE GETTING CLOSE, FAST!
SNIFF SNIFF
GRIM! WHERE ARE YOU GOING?!
BARK!

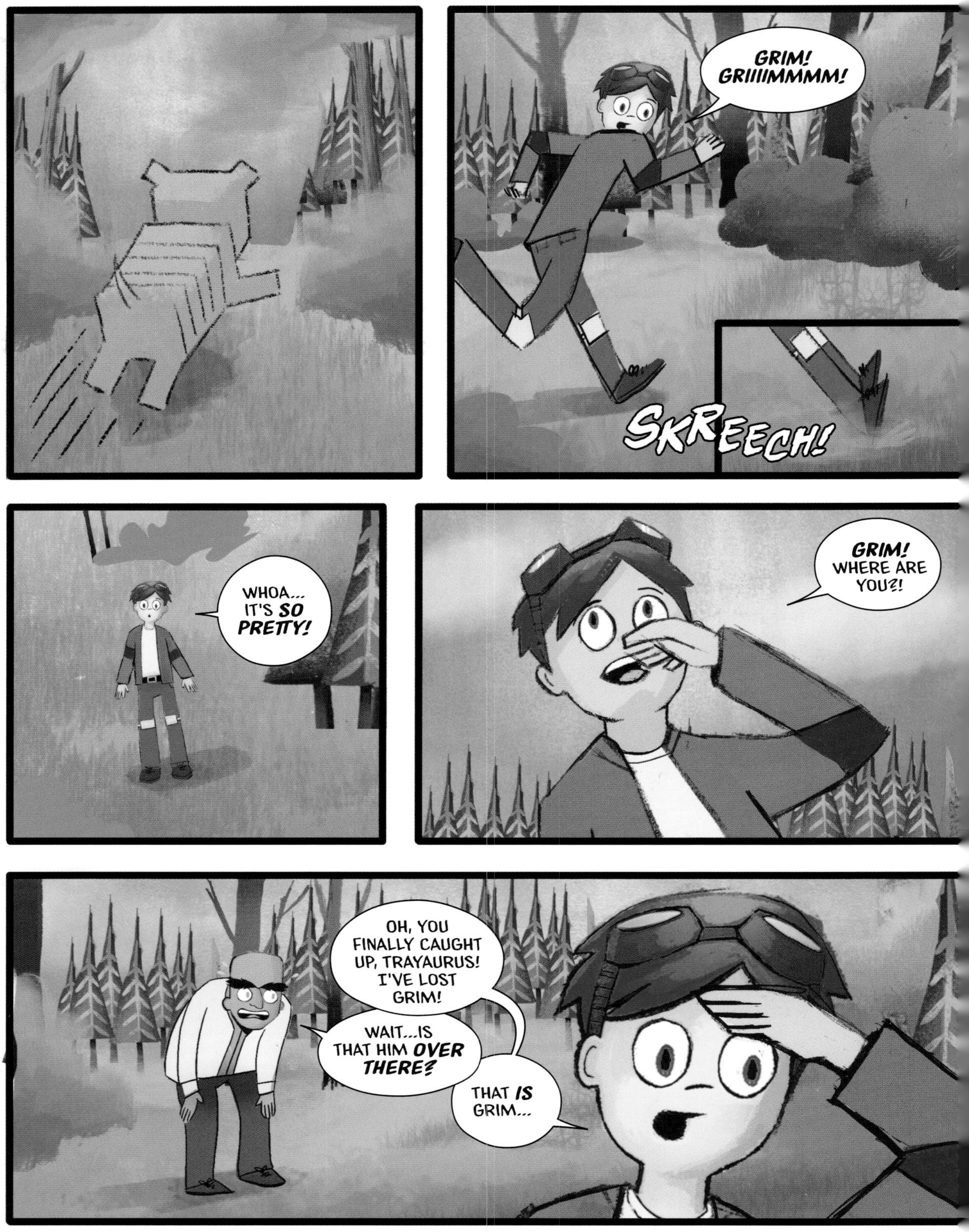
GRIM! GRIIIIMMMM!
SKREECH!
WHOA... IT'S SO PRETTY!
GRIM! WHERE ARE YOU?!
OH, YOU FINALLY CAUGHT UP, TRAYAURUS! I'VE LOST GRIM!
WAIT...IS THAT HIM OVER THERE?
THAT IS GRIM...

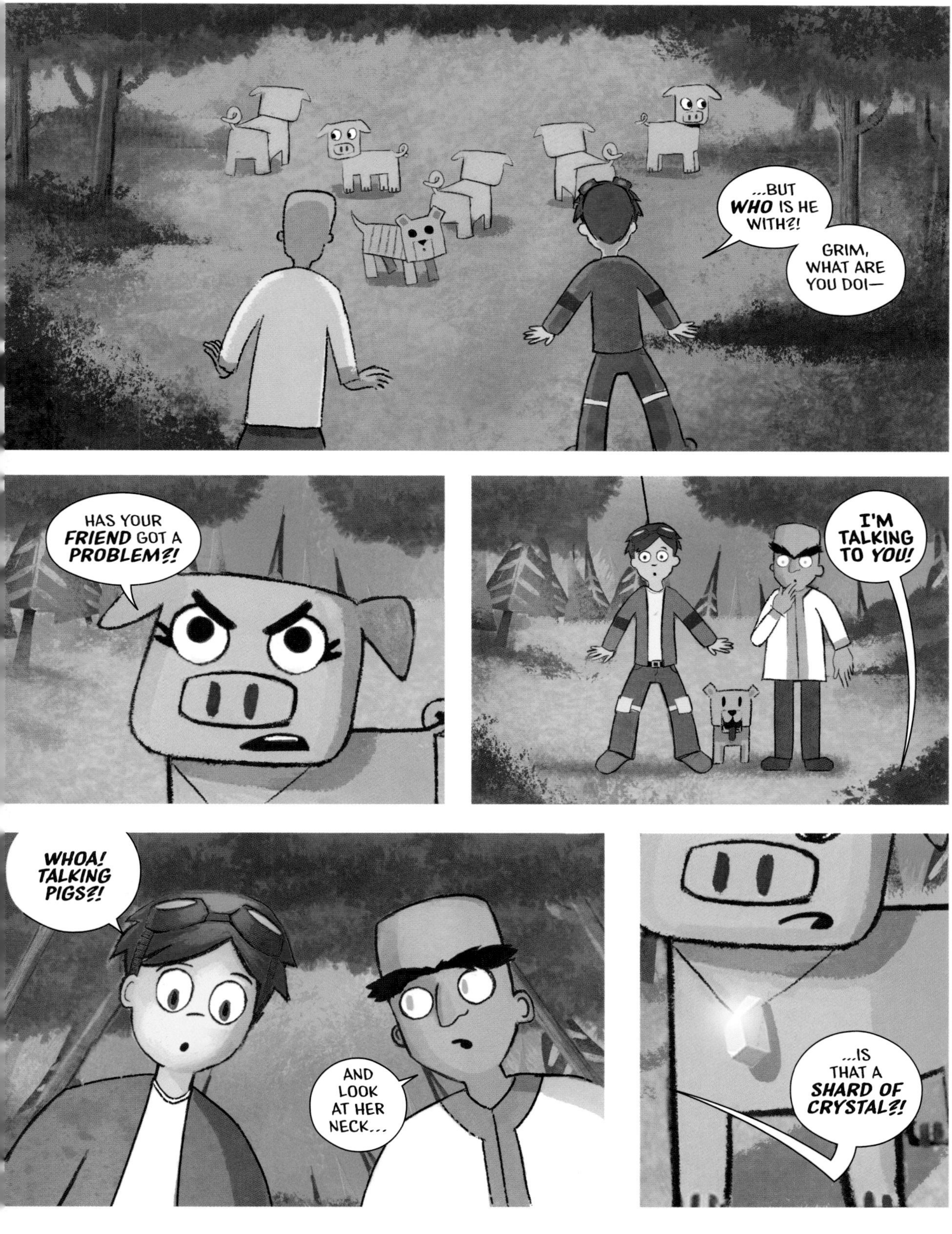
...BUT WHO IS HE WITH?!
GRIM, WHAT ARE YOU DOI—
HAS YOUR FRIEND GOT A PROBLEM?!
I'M TALKING TO YOU!
WHOA! TALKING PIGS?!
AND LOOK AT HER NECK...
...IS THAT A SHARD OF CRYSTAL?!

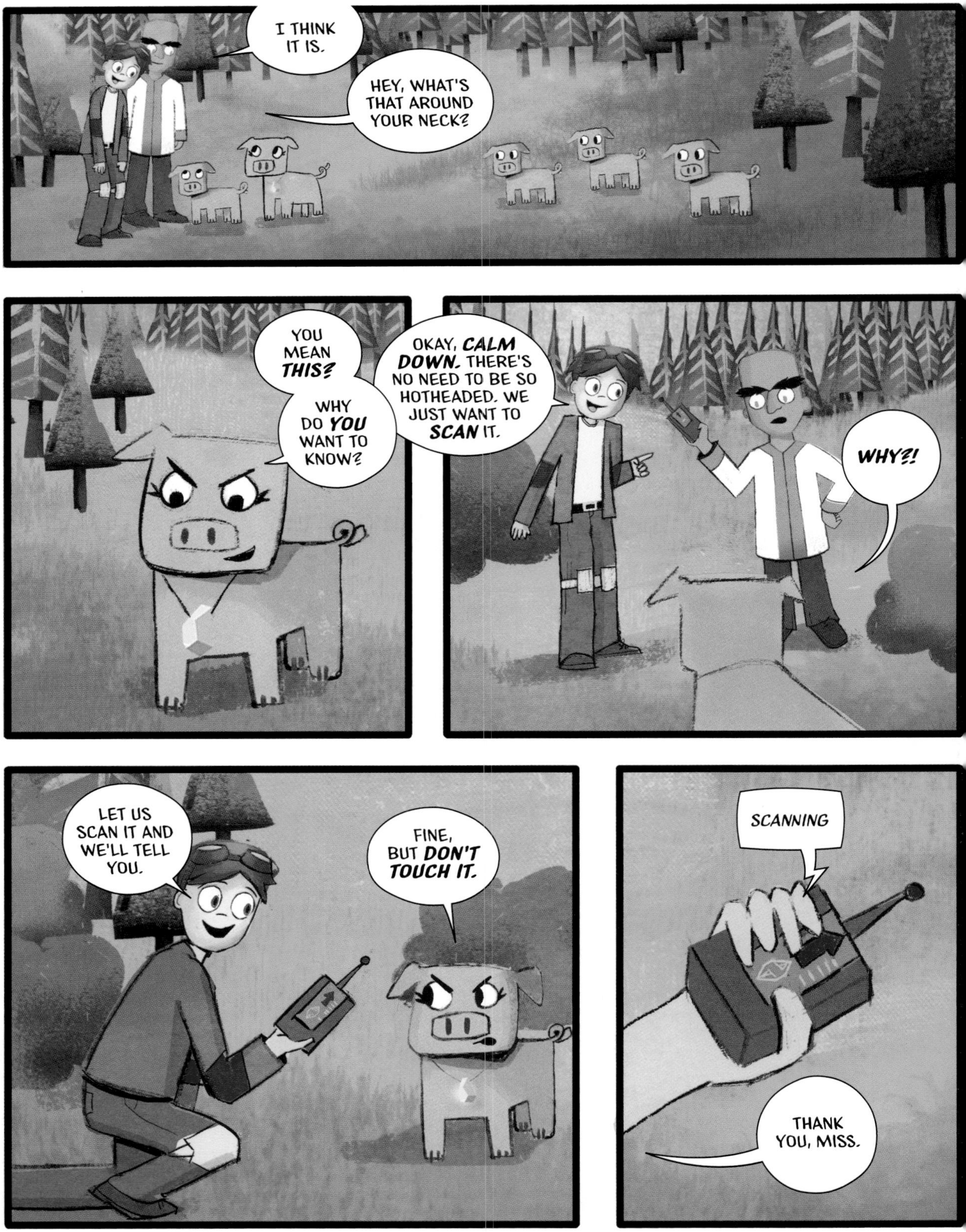
I THINK IT IS.
HEY, WHAT'S THAT AROUND YOUR NECK?
YOU MEAN THIS?
WHY DO YOU WANT TO KNOW?
OKAY, CALM DOWN. THERE'S NO NEED TO BE SO HOTHEADED. WE JUST WANT TO SCAN IT.
WHY?!
LET US SCAN IT AND WE'LL TELL YOU.
FINE, BUT DON'T TOUCH IT.
SCANNING
THANK YOU, MISS.

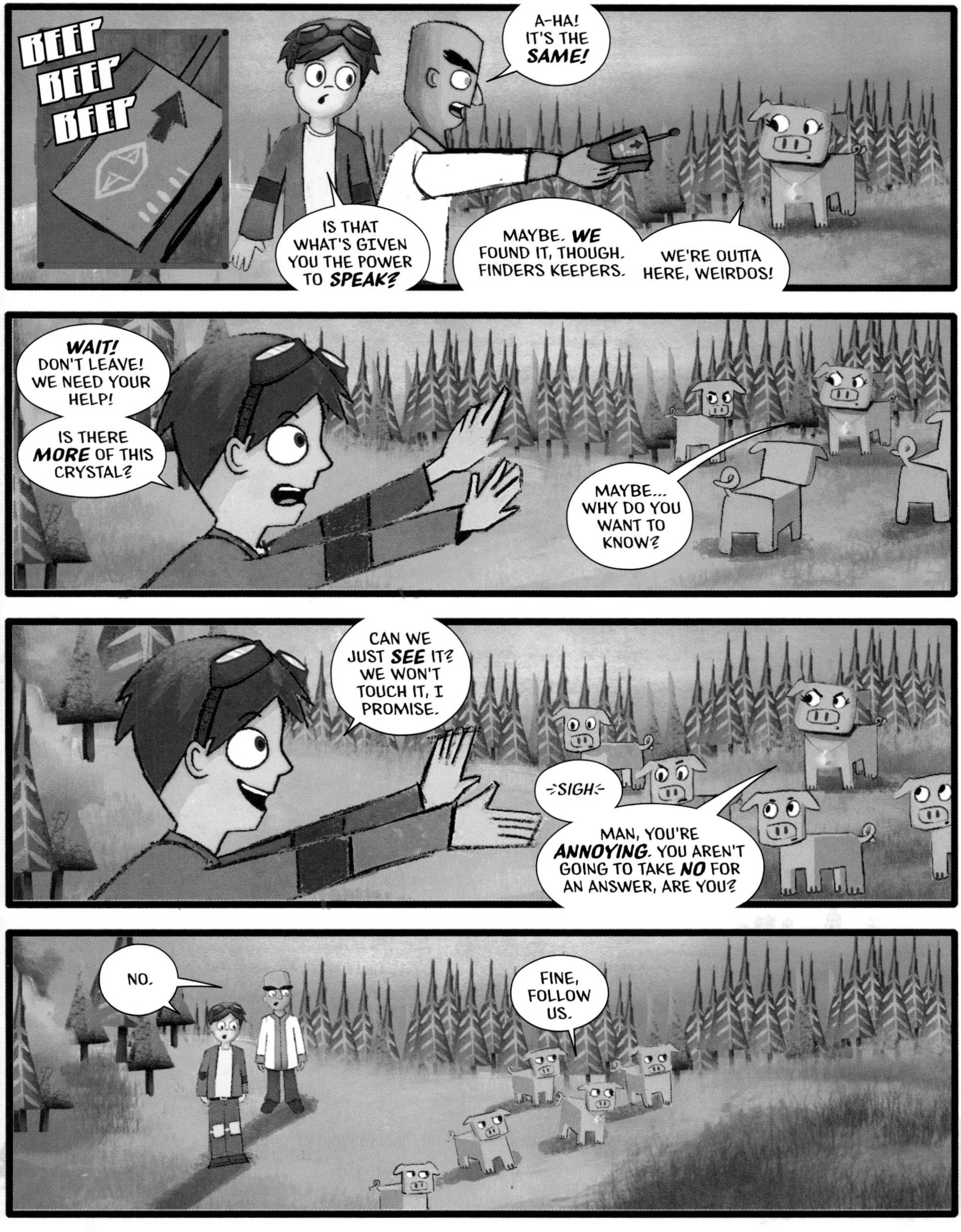
BEEP BEEP BEEP
A-HA! IT'S THE SAME!
IS THAT WHAT'S GIVEN YOU THE POWER TO SPEAK?
MAYBE. WE FOUND IT, THOUGH. FINDERS KEEPERS.
WE'RE OUTTA HERE, WEIRDOS!
WAIT! DON'T LEAVE! WE NEED YOUR HELP!
IS THERE MORE OF THIS CRYSTAL?
MAYBE... WHY DO YOU WANT TO KNOW?
CAN WE JUST SEE IT? WE WON'T TOUCH IT, I PROMISE.
SIGH
MAN, YOU'RE ANNOYING. YOU AREN'T GOING TO TAKE NO FOR AN ANSWER, ARE YOU?
NO.
FINE, FOLLOW US.

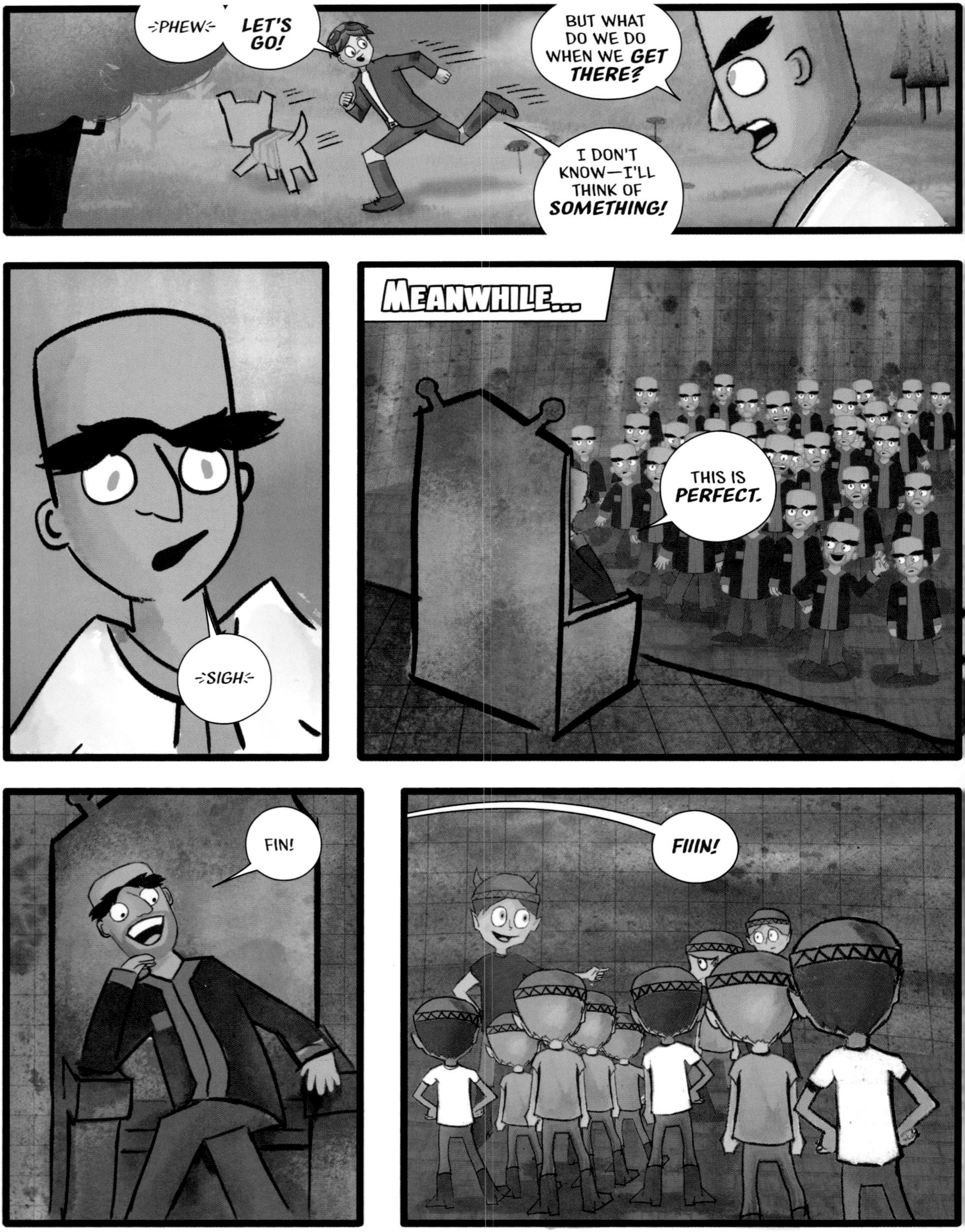

PHEW
LET'S GO!
BUT WHAT DO WE DO WHEN WE GET THERE?
I DON'T KNOW—I'LL THINK OF SOMETHING!
SIGH
MEANWHILE...
THIS IS PERFECT.
FIN!
FIIIN!

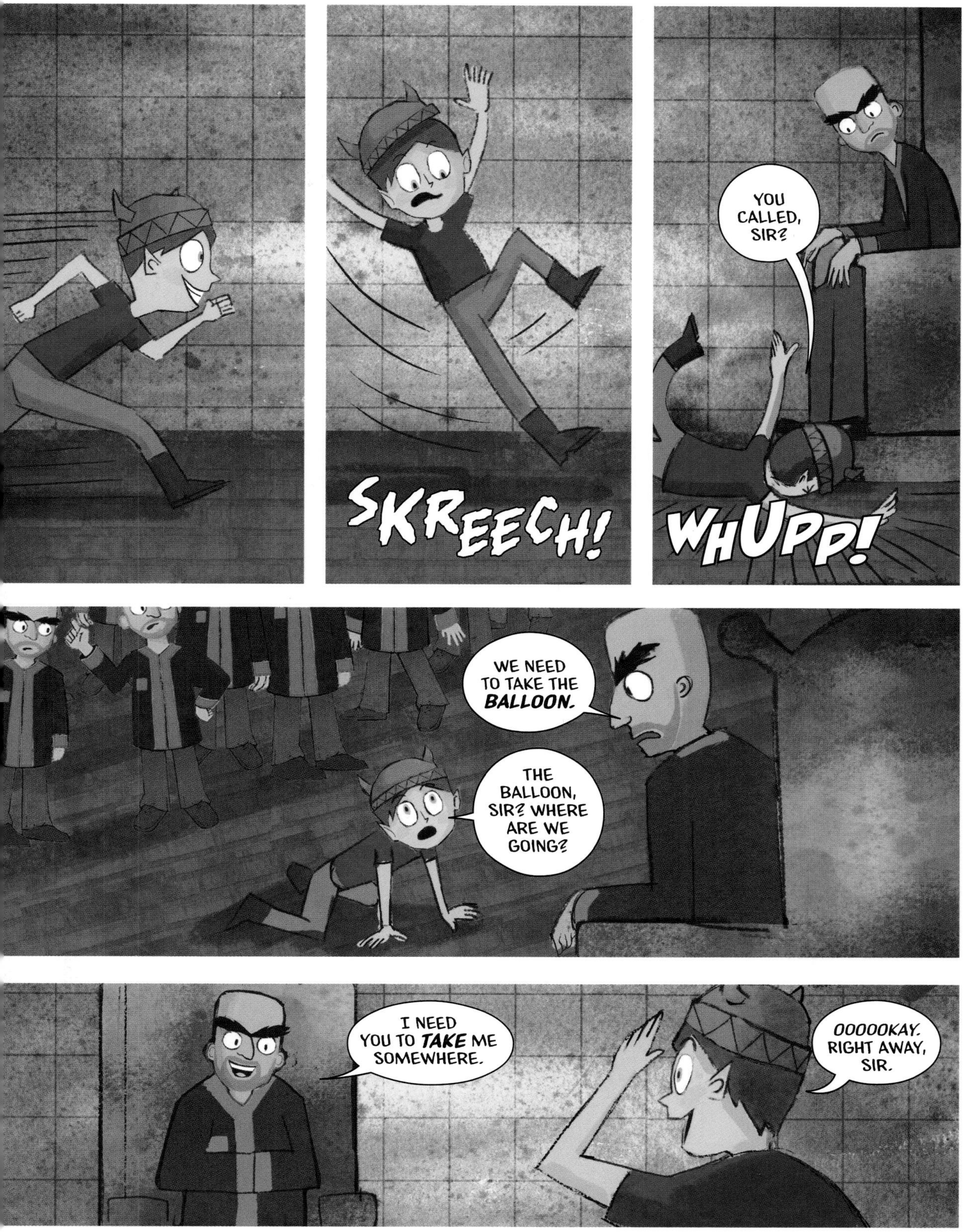
SKREECH!
YOU CALLED, SIR?
WHUPP!
WE NEED TO TAKE THE *BALLOON.*
THE BALLOON, SIR? WHERE ARE WE GOING?
I NEED YOU TO *TAKE* ME SOMEWHERE.
OOOOOKAY. RIGHT AWAY, SIR.

UH-OH...

...WHAT'S THE **CODE** AGAIN?

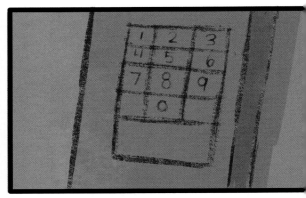

I THINK IT'S...

...3... 6...3... 6...

BEEP

INCORRECT

...UH-OH! I HAVE TWO MORE ATTEMPTS.

0... 6...2... 4...

BEEP

INCORRECT

ARGH, IF I GET IT WRONG AGAIN, IT'LL **LOCK ME OUT!**

I THINK I'VE GOT IT THIS TIME.

0... 9...0... 4...

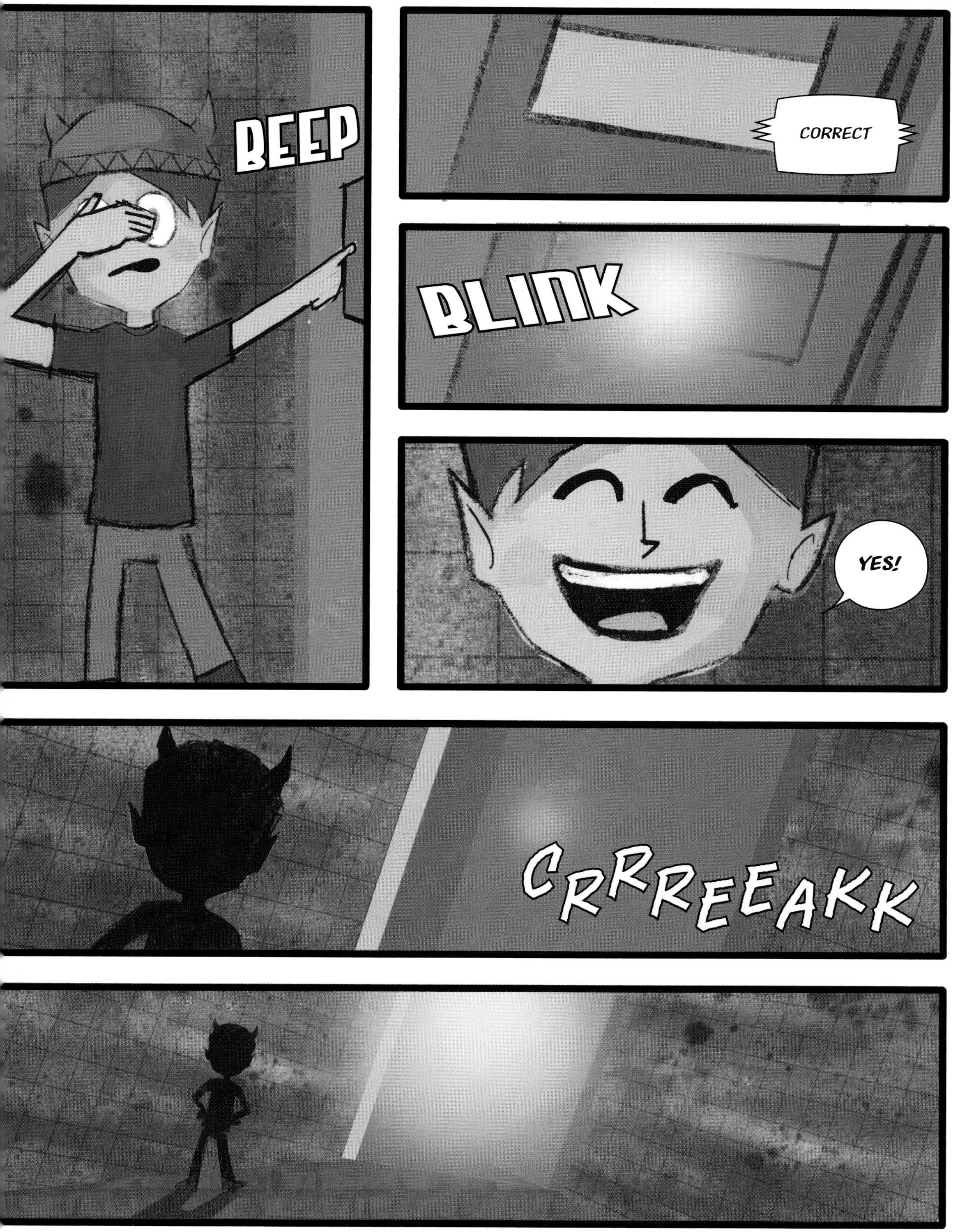
BEEP
CORRECT
BLINK
YES!
CRRREEAKK

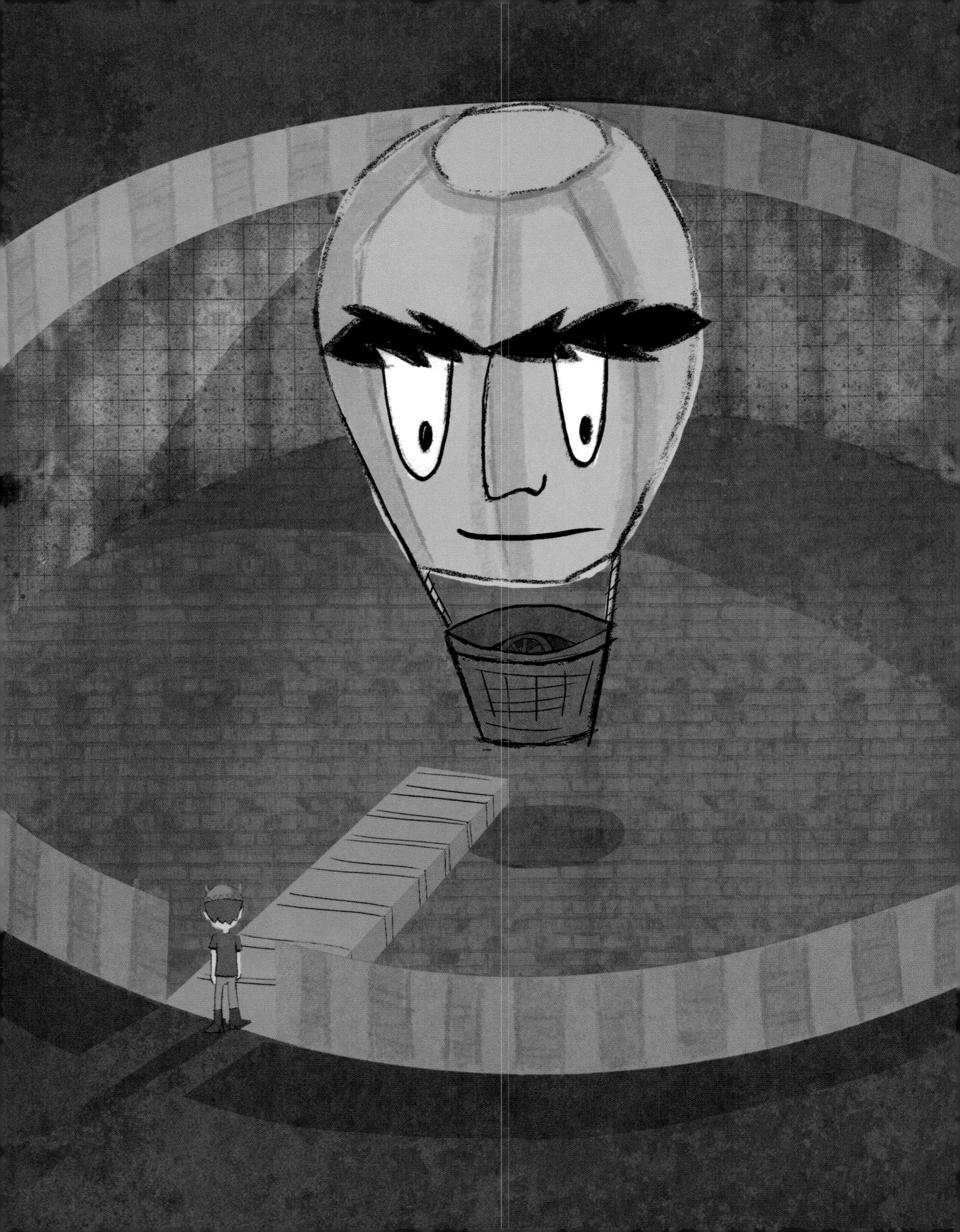

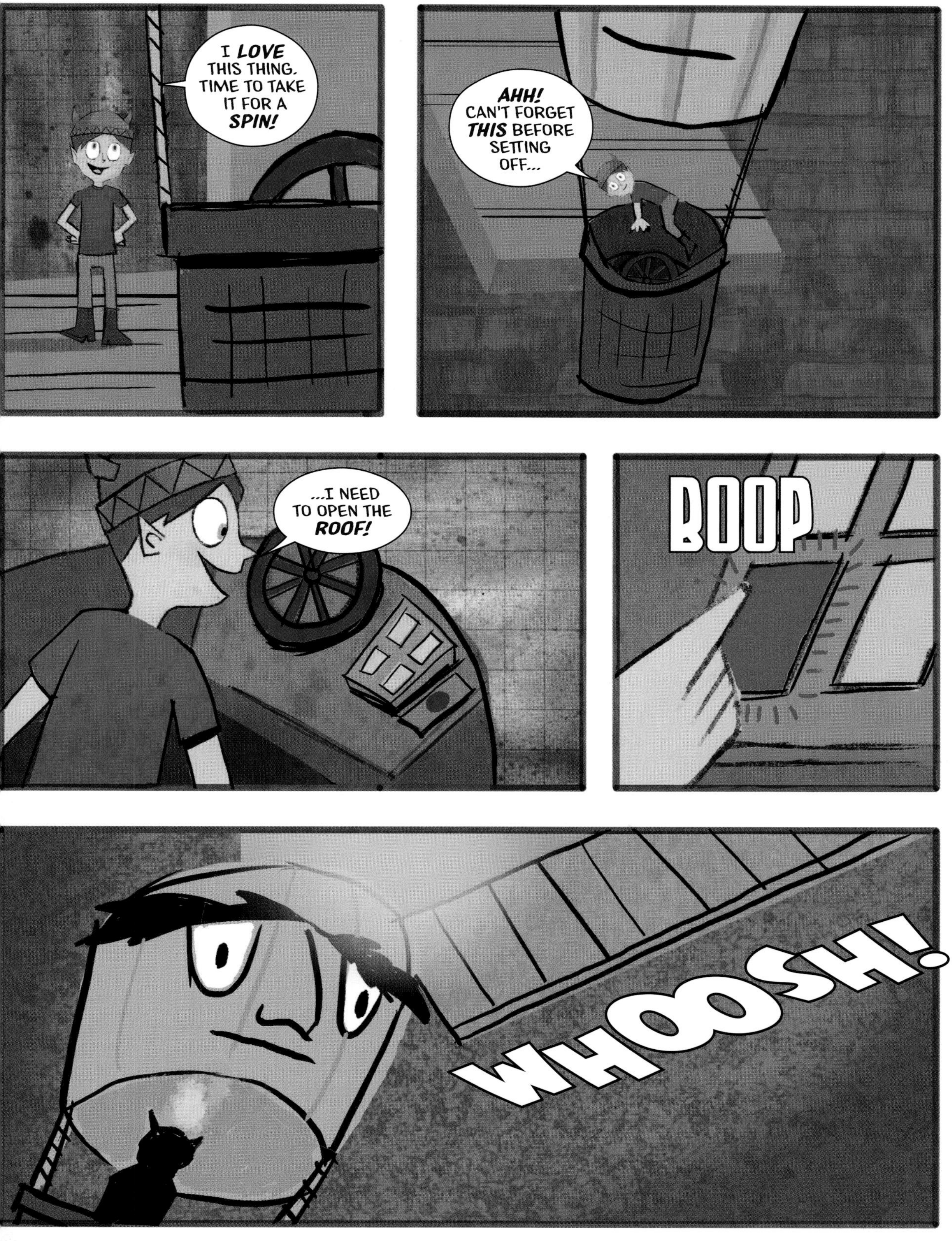
I LOVE THIS THING. TIME TO TAKE IT FOR A SPIN!
AHH! CAN'T FORGET THIS BEFORE SETTING OFF...
...I NEED TO OPEN THE ROOF!
BOOP
WHOOSH!

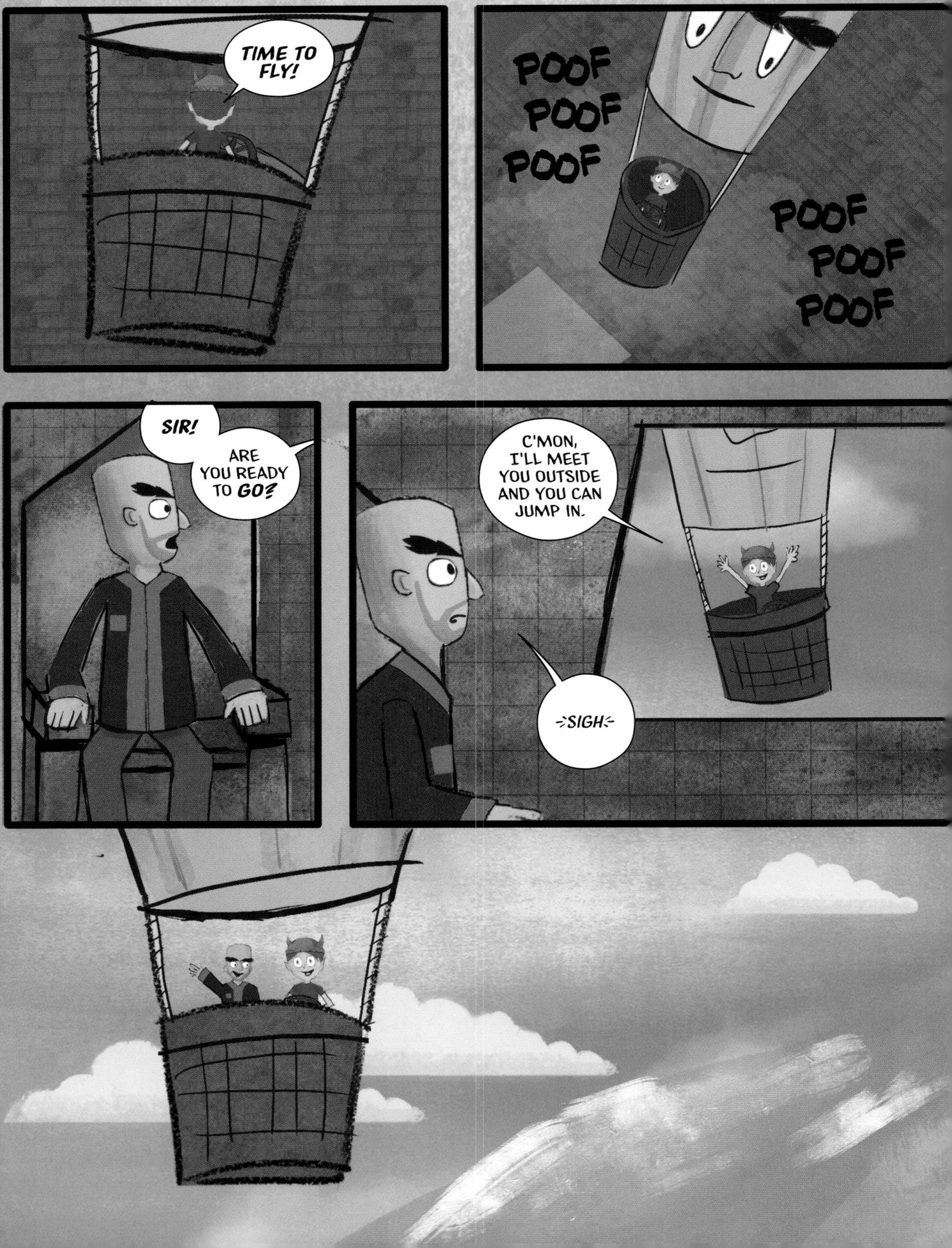
TIME TO FLY!
POOF POOF POOF
POOF POOF POOF
SIR!
ARE YOU READY TO GO?
C'MON, I'LL MEET YOU OUTSIDE AND YOU CAN JUMP IN.
SIGH

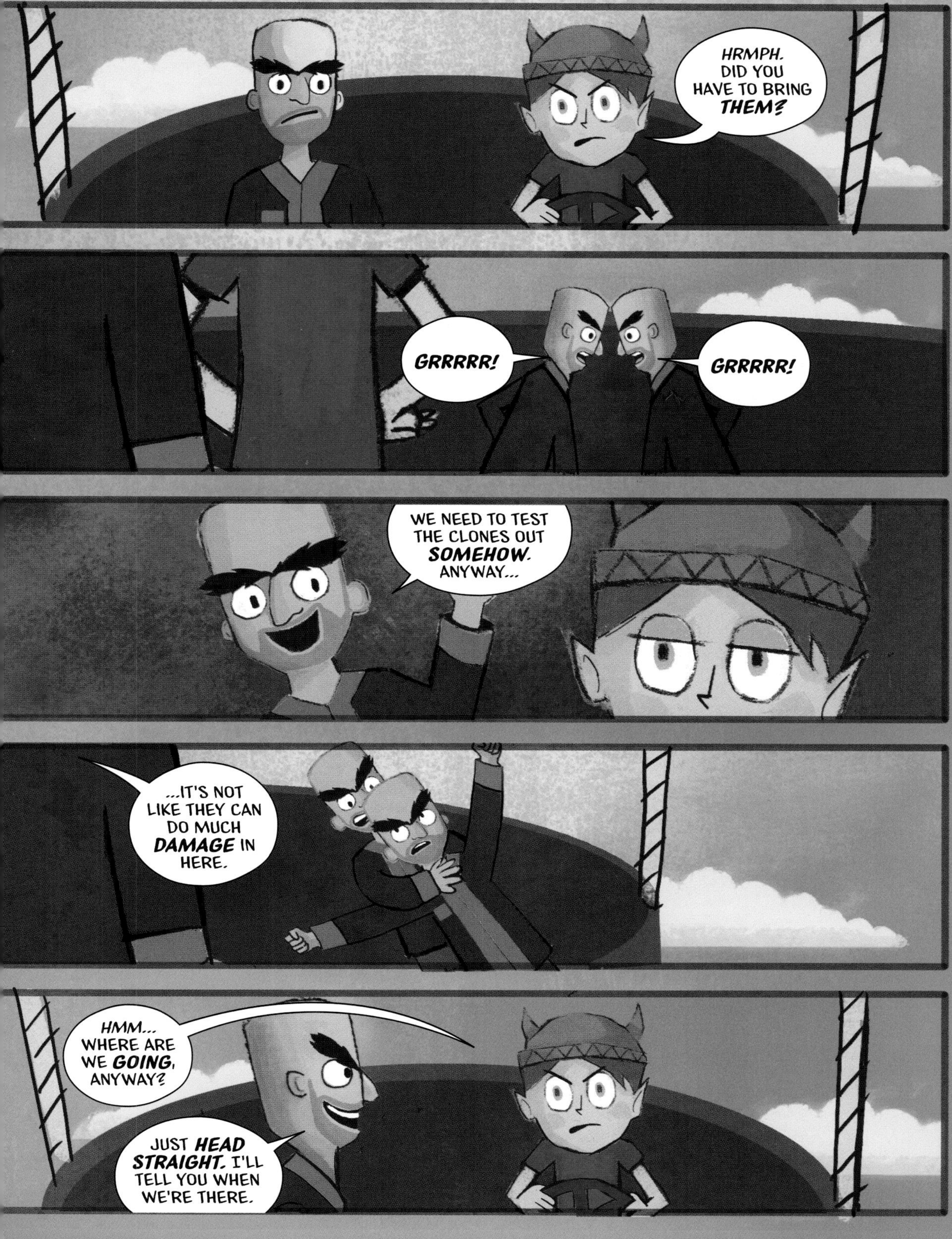
HRMPH. DID YOU HAVE TO BRING THEM?
GRRRRR!
GRRRRR!
WE NEED TO TEST THE CLONES OUT SOMEHOW. ANYWAY...
...IT'S NOT LIKE THEY CAN DO MUCH DAMAGE IN HERE.
HMM... WHERE ARE WE GOING, ANYWAY?
JUST HEAD STRAIGHT. I'LL TELL YOU WHEN WE'RE THERE.

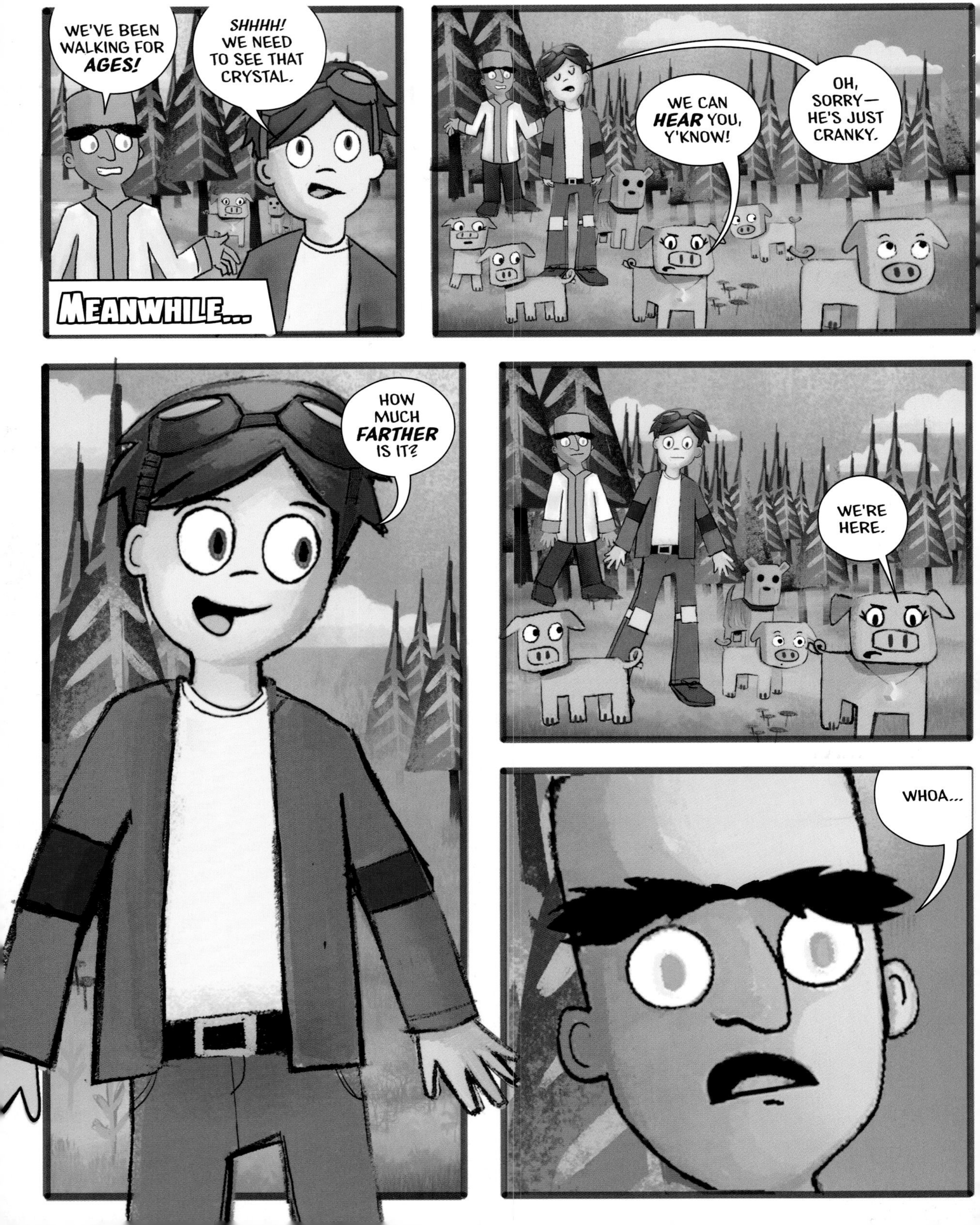
WE'VE BEEN WALKING FOR AGES!
SHHHH! WE NEED TO SEE THAT CRYSTAL.
MEANWHILE...
OH, SORRY— HE'S JUST CRANKY.
WE CAN HEAR YOU, Y'KNOW!
HOW MUCH FARTHER IS IT?
WE'RE HERE.
WHOA...

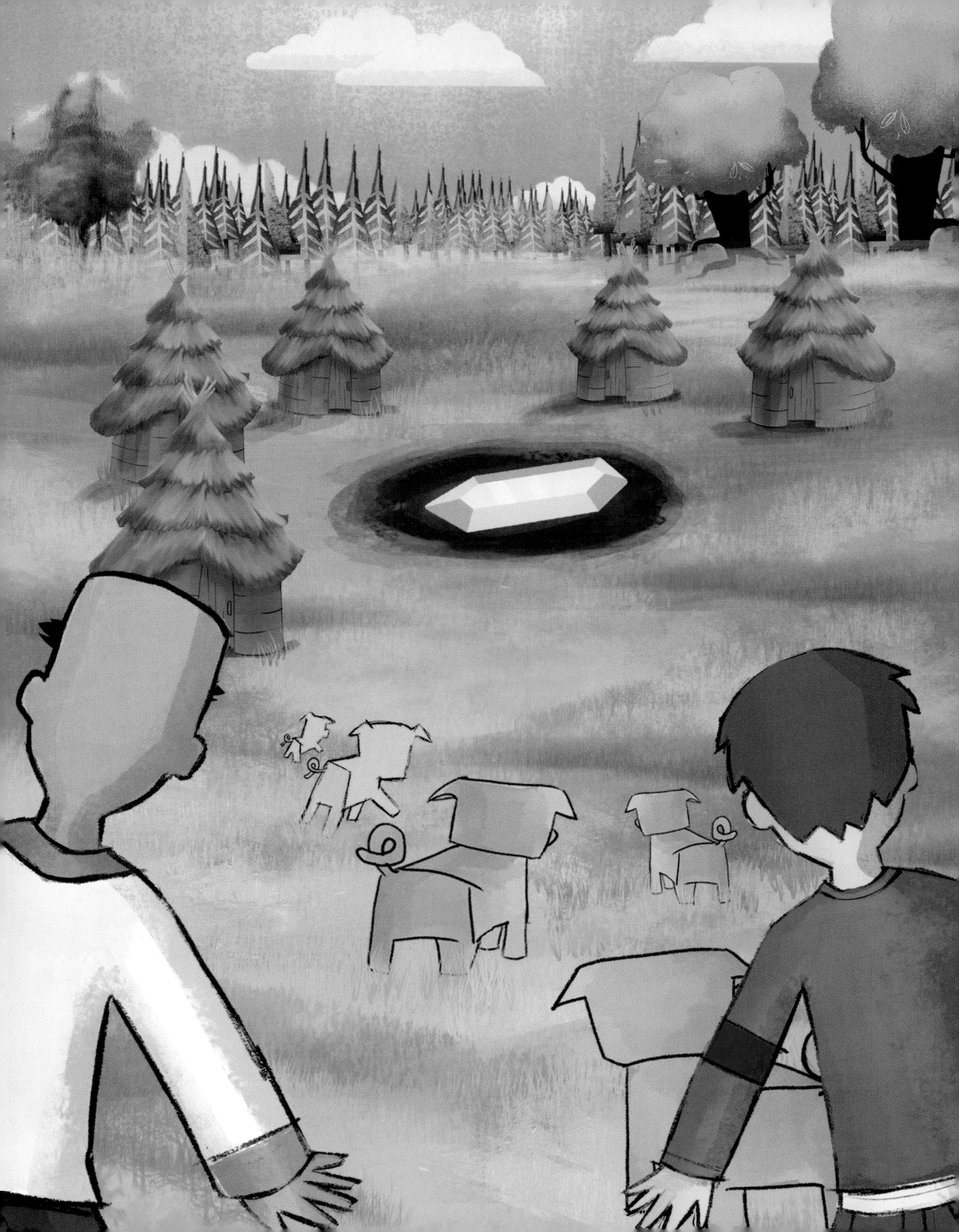

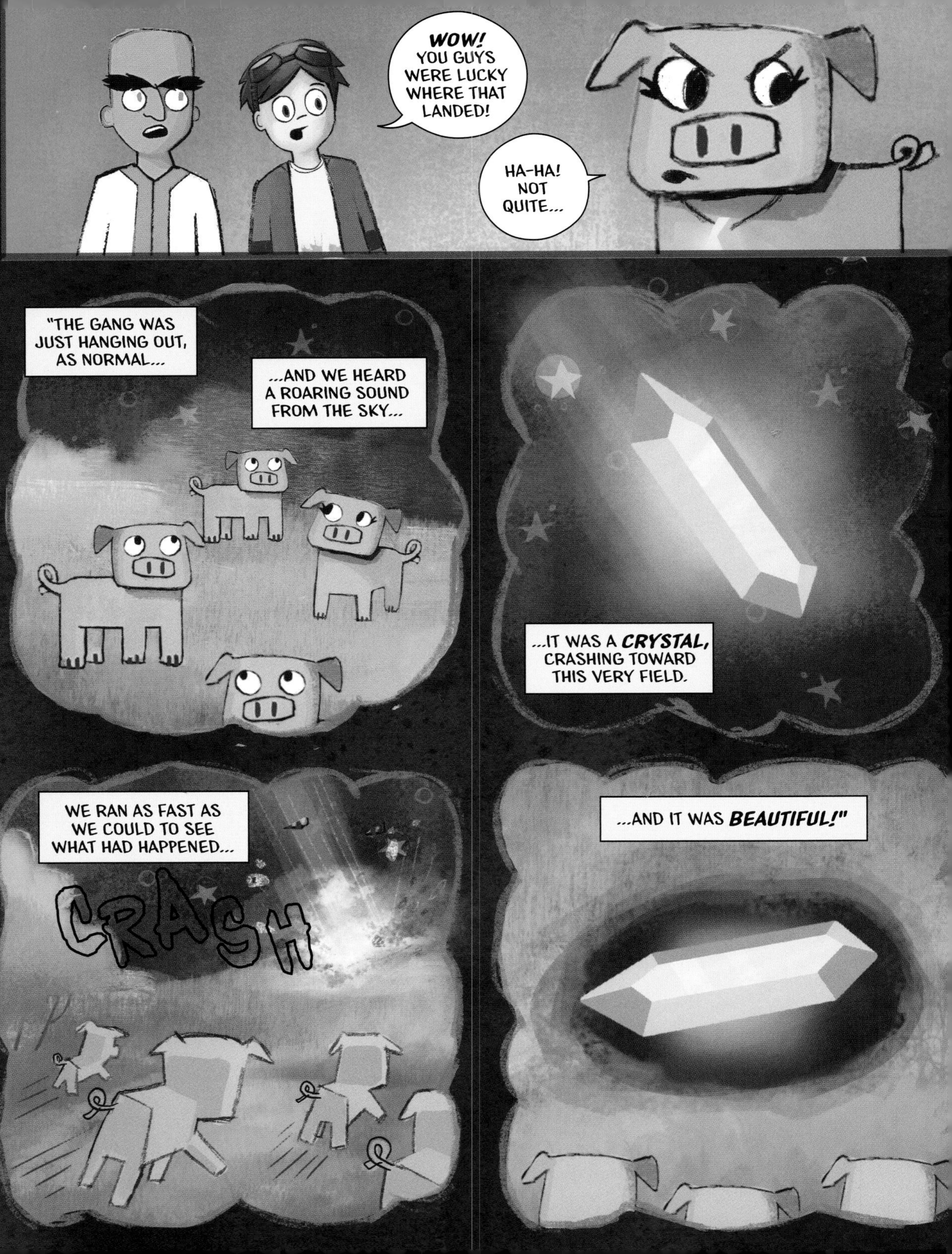

WOW! YOU GUYS WERE LUCKY WHERE THAT LANDED!
HA-HA! NOT QUITE...
"THE GANG WAS JUST HANGING OUT, AS NORMAL...
...AND WE HEARD A ROARING SOUND FROM THE SKY...
...IT WAS A CRYSTAL, CRASHING TOWARD THIS VERY FIELD.
WE RAN AS FAST AS WE COULD TO SEE WHAT HAD HAPPENED...
CRASH
...AND IT WAS BEAUTIFUL!"

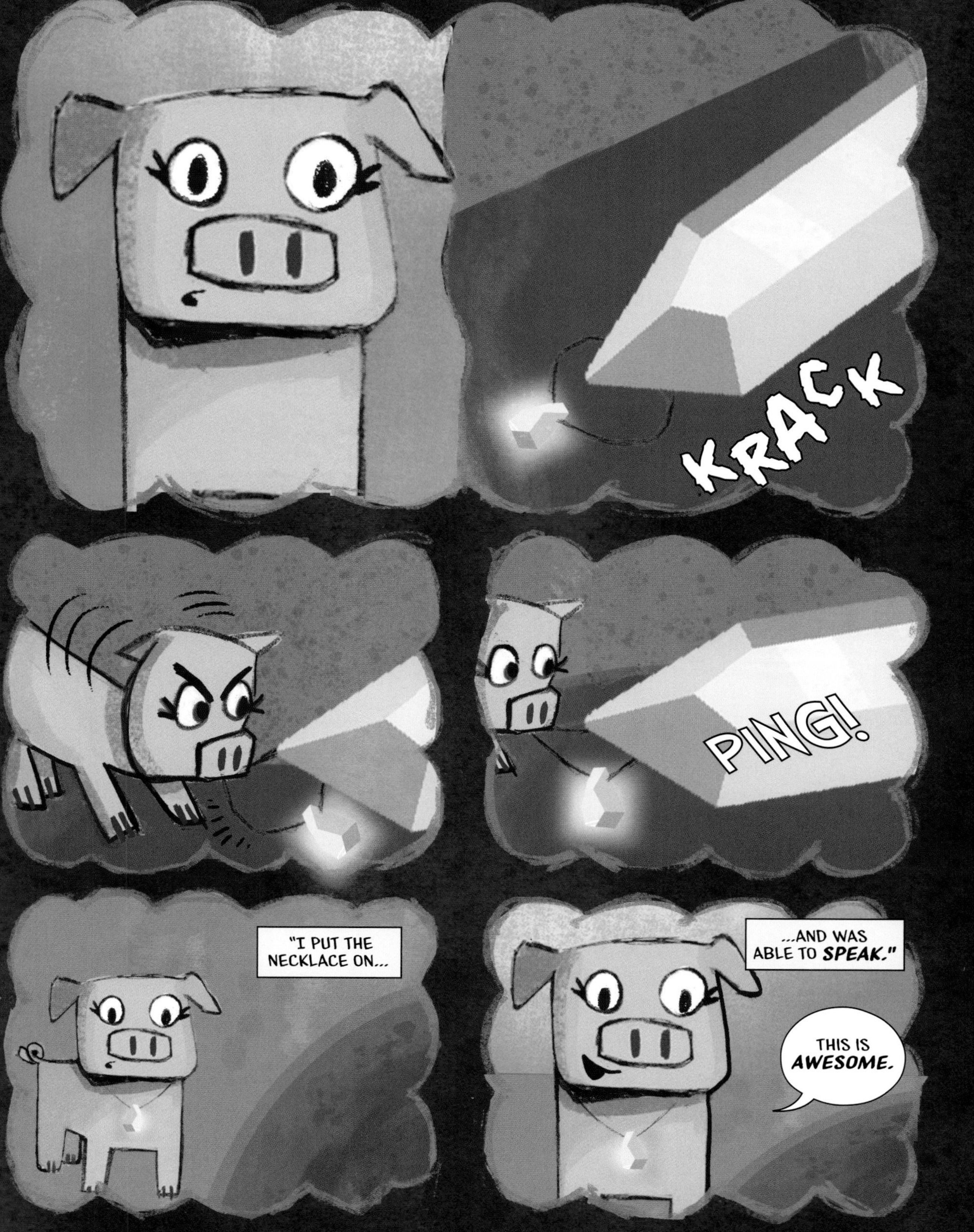
KRACK
PING!
"I PUT THE NECKLACE ON...
...AND WAS ABLE TO SPEAK."
THIS IS AWESOME.

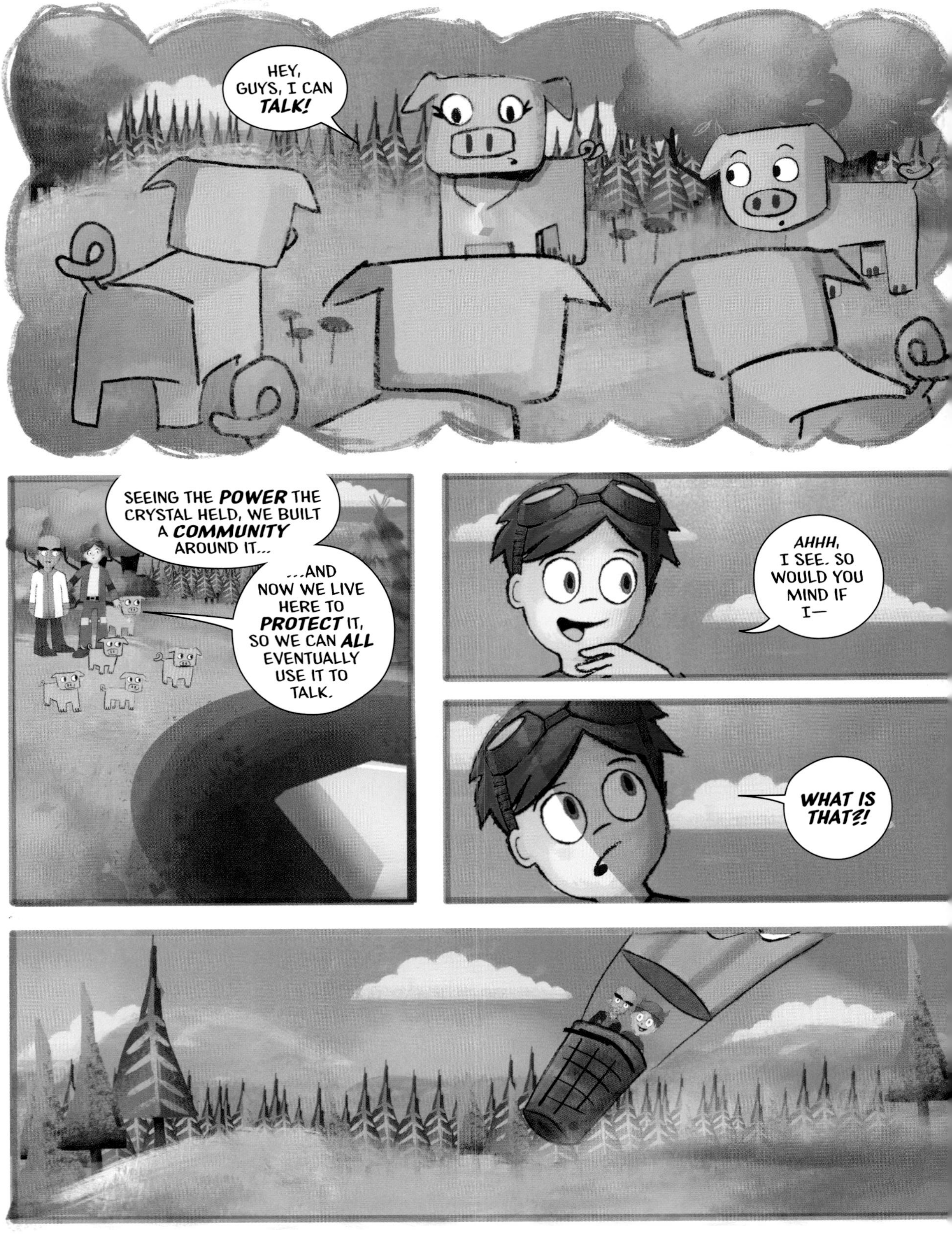
HEY, GUYS, I CAN *TALK!*
SEEING THE *POWER* THE CRYSTAL HELD, WE BUILT A *COMMUNITY* AROUND IT...
...AND NOW WE LIVE HERE TO *PROTECT* IT, SO WE CAN *ALL* EVENTUALLY USE IT TO TALK.
AHHH, I SEE. SO WOULD YOU MIND IF I—
WHAT IS THAT?!

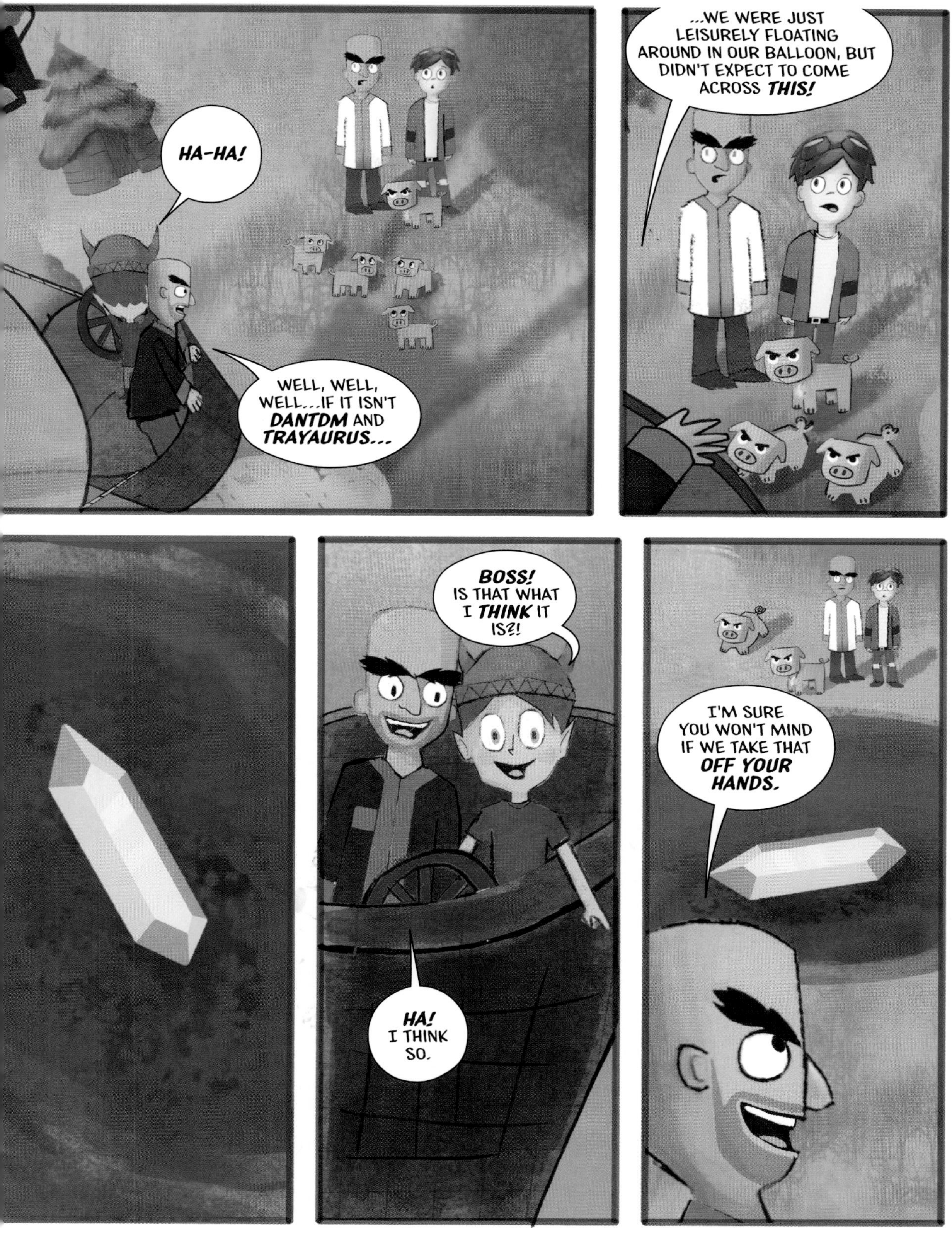
HA-HA!
WELL, WELL, WELL...IF IT ISN'T DANTDM AND TRAYAURUS...
...WE WERE JUST LEISURELY FLOATING AROUND IN OUR BALLOON, BUT DIDN'T EXPECT TO COME ACROSS THIS!
BOSS! IS THAT WHAT I THINK IT IS?!
HA! I THINK SO.
I'M SURE YOU WON'T MIND IF WE TAKE THAT OFF YOUR HANDS.

POOF!

IS THAT *DENTON?!*

DENTON! THIS DOESN'T BELONG TO YOU!

OH, *REALLY?*

FIN, YOU KNOW WHAT TO DO.

YES, SIR!

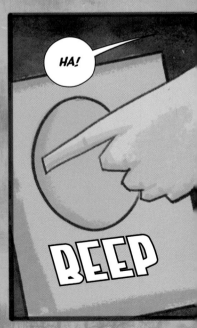

HA!

BEEP

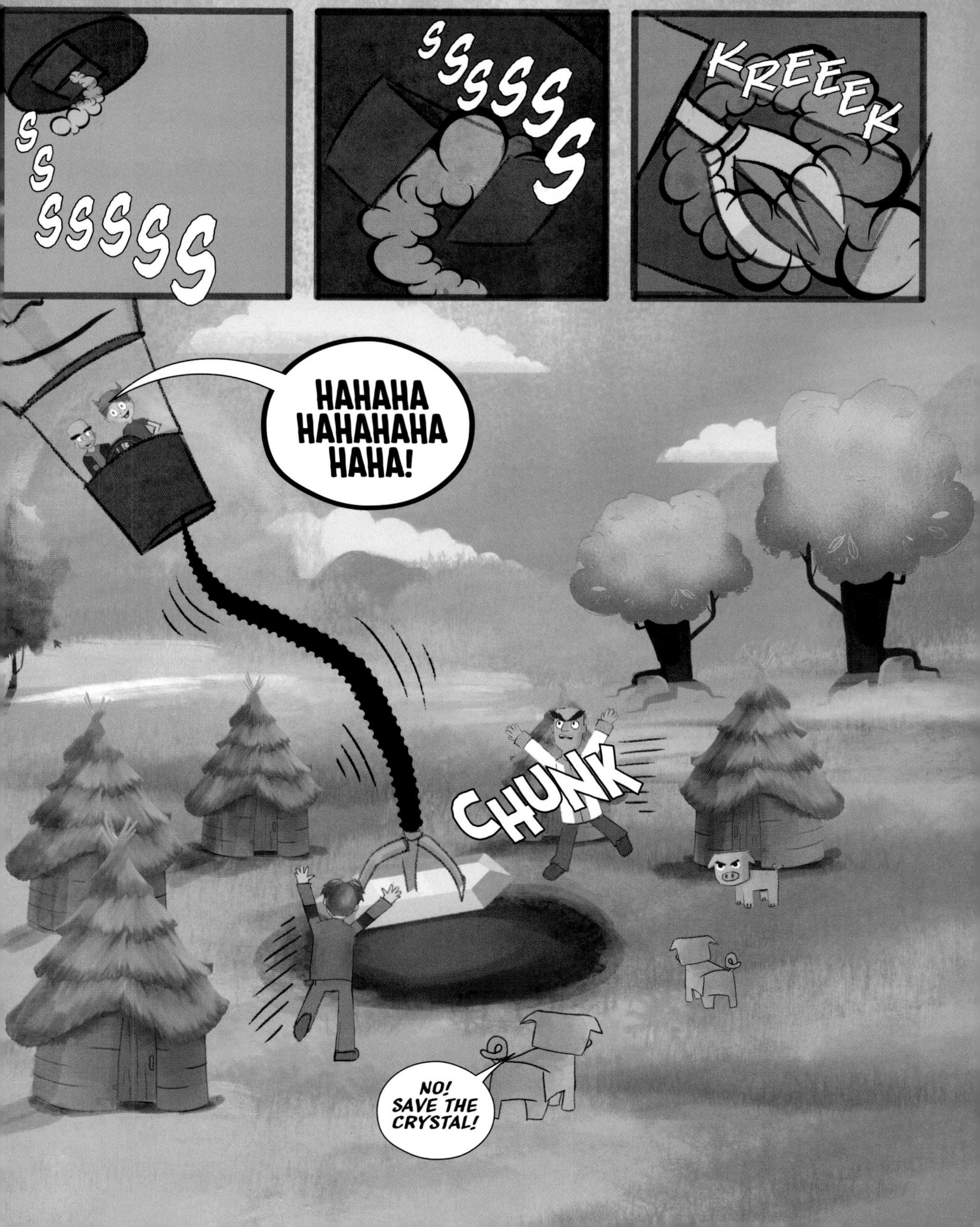
SSSSSSSS
SSSSSSS
KREEEK
HAHAHA HAHAHAHA HAHA!
CHUNK
NO! SAVE THE CRYSTAL!

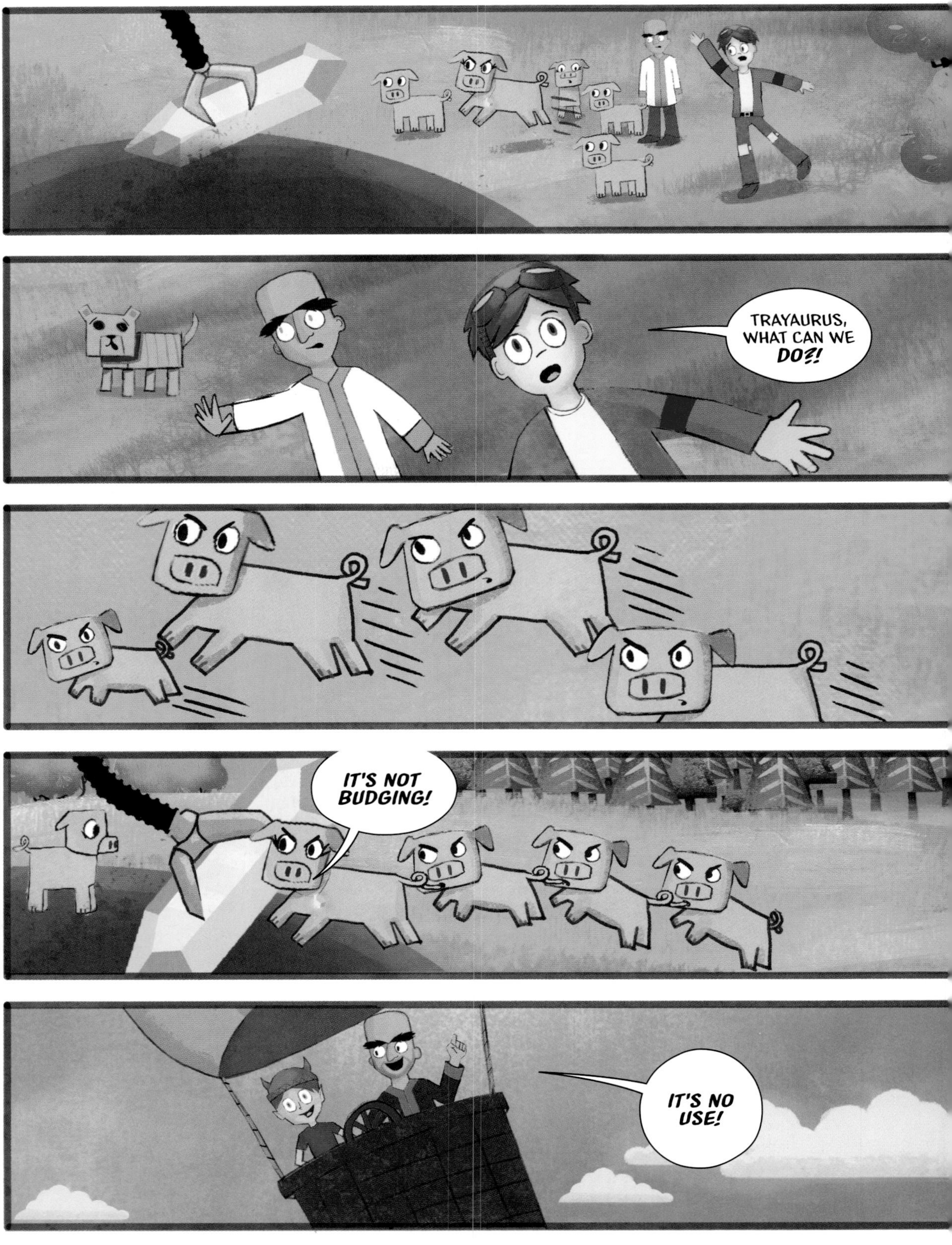
TRAYAURUS, WHAT CAN WE DO?!
IT'S NOT BUDGING!
IT'S NO USE!

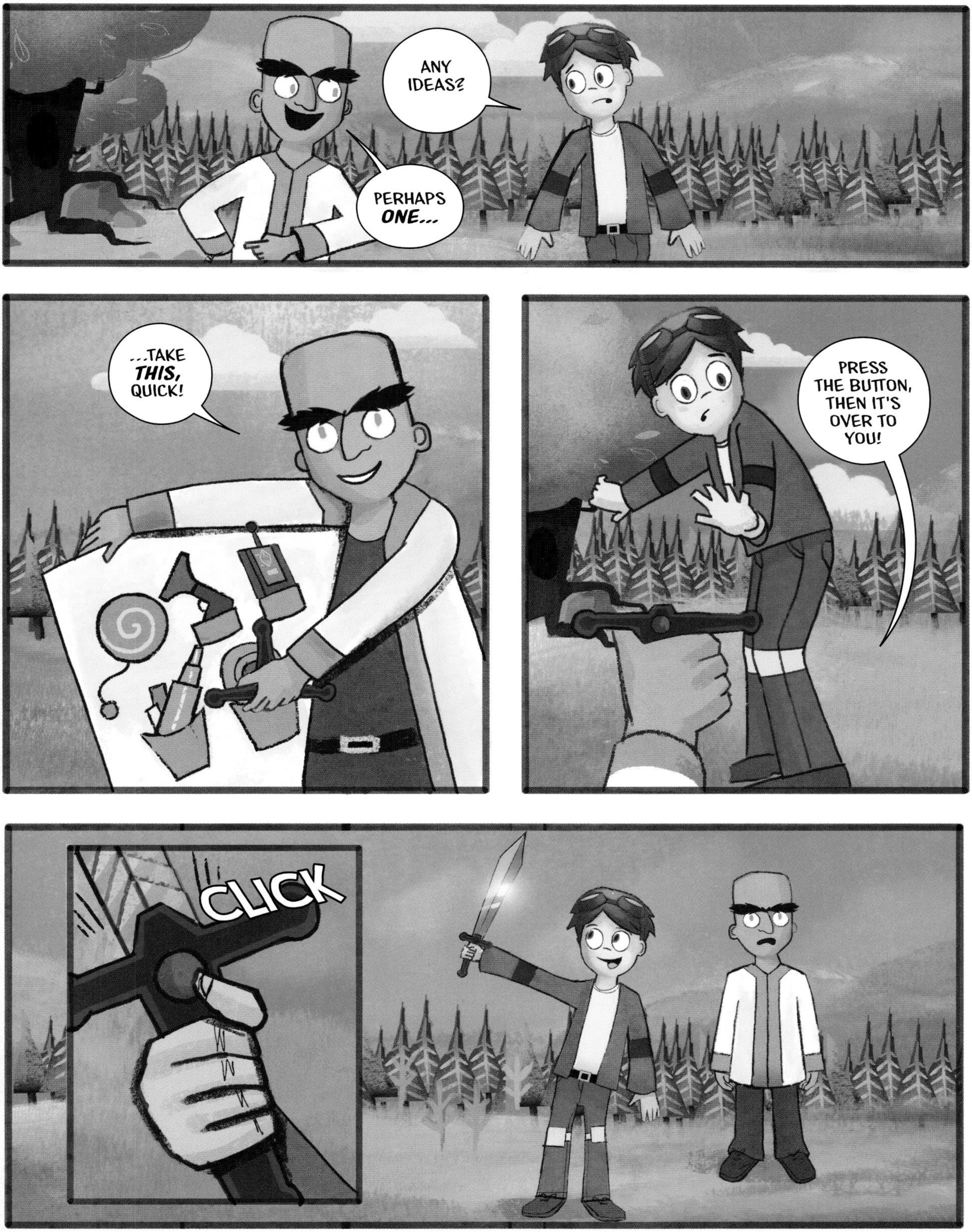
ANY IDEAS?
PERHAPS *ONE...*
...TAKE *THIS,* QUICK!
PRESS THE BUTTON, THEN IT'S OVER TO YOU!
CLICK

ZZZ

IIING!

CLANG!

TAKE THAT!

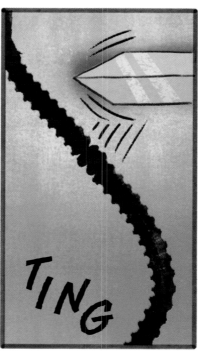

TING

IT JUST BOUNCED RIGHT OFF!

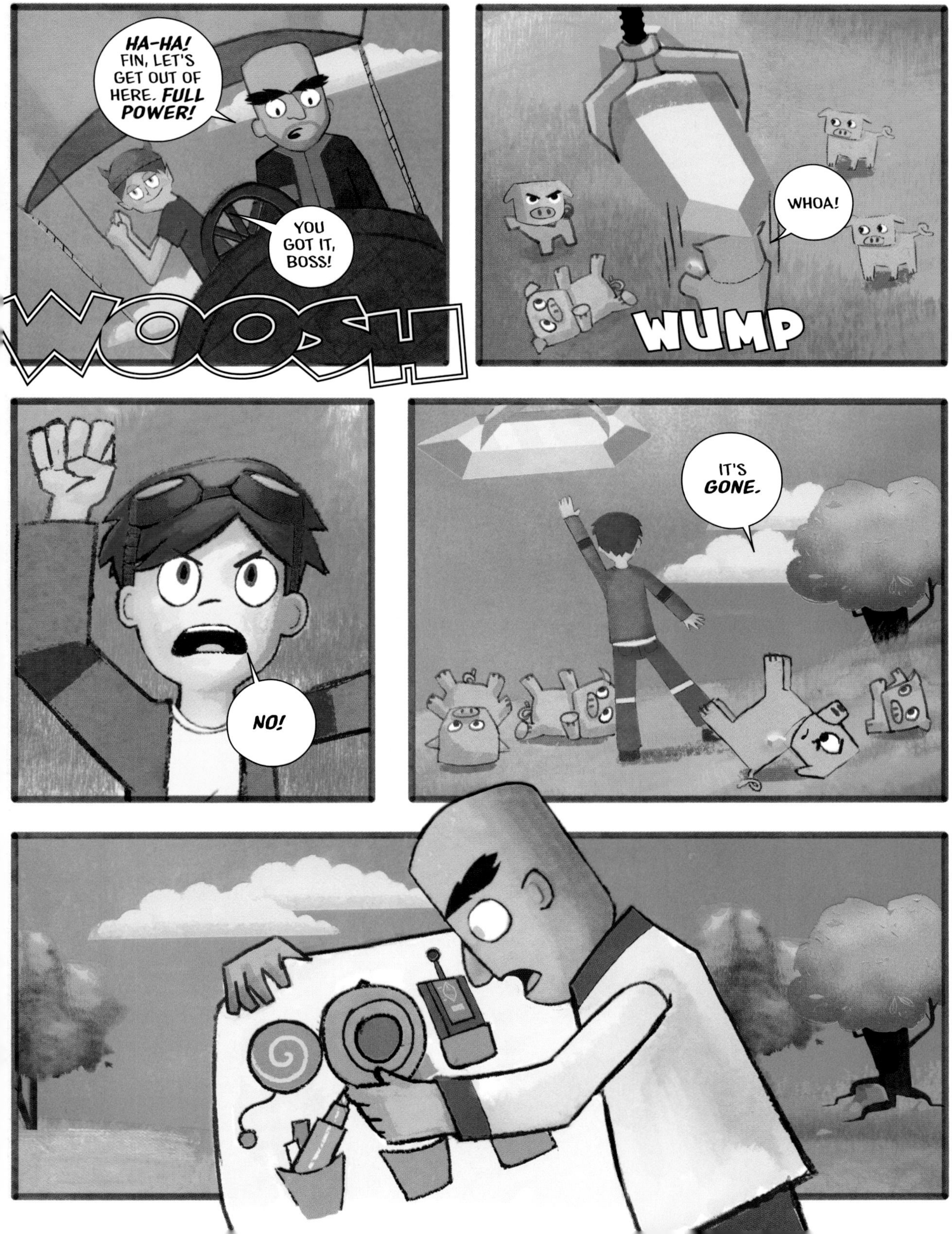
HA-HA! FIN, LET'S GET OUT OF HERE. FULL POWER!
YOU GOT IT, BOSS!
WOOSH
WHOA!
WUMP
NO!
IT'S GONE.

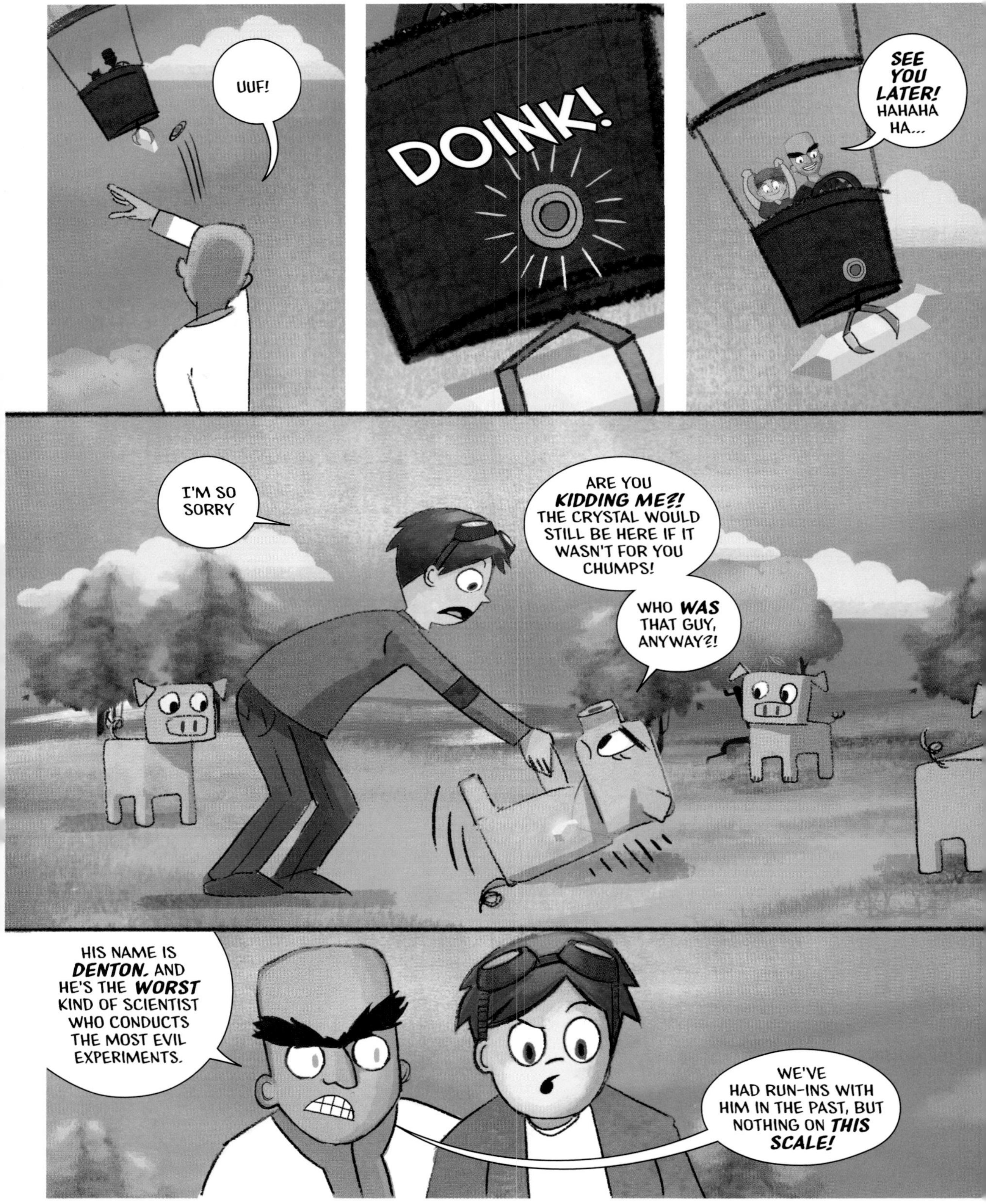
UUF!
DOINK!
SEE YOU LATER! HAHAHA HA...
I'M SO SORRY
ARE YOU KIDDING ME?! THE CRYSTAL WOULD STILL BE HERE IF IT WASN'T FOR YOU CHUMPS!
WHO WAS THAT GUY, ANYWAY?!
HIS NAME IS DENTON. AND HE'S THE WORST KIND OF SCIENTIST WHO CONDUCTS THE MOST EVIL EXPERIMENTS.
WE'VE HAD RUN-INS WITH HIM IN THE PAST, BUT NOTHING ON THIS SCALE!

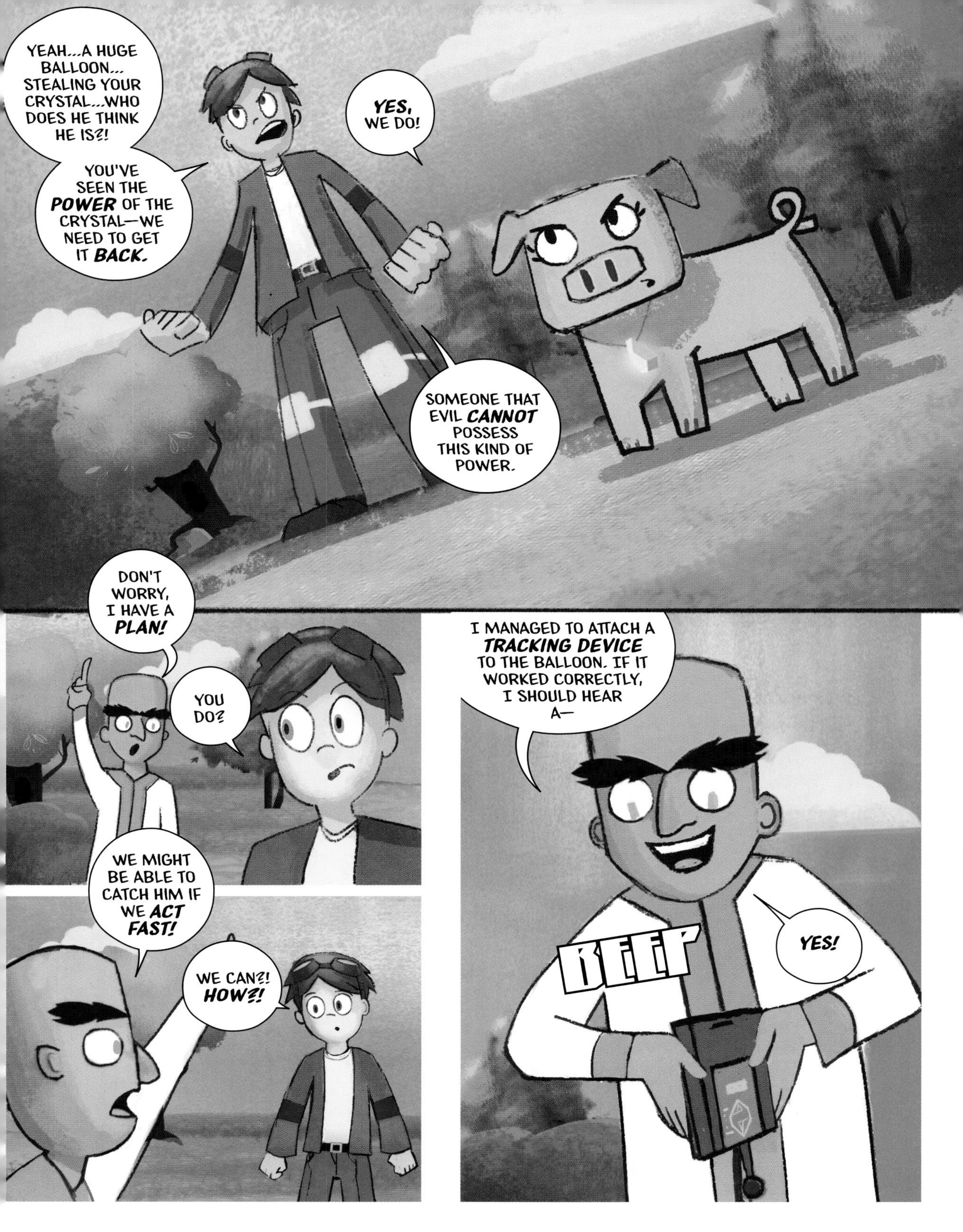
YEAH...A HUGE BALLOON... STEALING YOUR CRYSTAL...WHO DOES HE THINK HE IS?!
YOU'VE SEEN THE **POWER** OF THE CRYSTAL—WE NEED TO GET IT **BACK.**
YES, WE DO!
SOMEONE THAT EVIL **CANNOT** POSSESS THIS KIND OF POWER.
DON'T WORRY, I HAVE A **PLAN!**
YOU DO?
WE MIGHT BE ABLE TO CATCH HIM IF WE **ACT FAST!**
WE CAN?! **HOW?!**
I MANAGED TO ATTACH A **TRACKING DEVICE** TO THE BALLOON. IF IT WORKED CORRECTLY, I SHOULD HEAR A—
BEEP
YES!

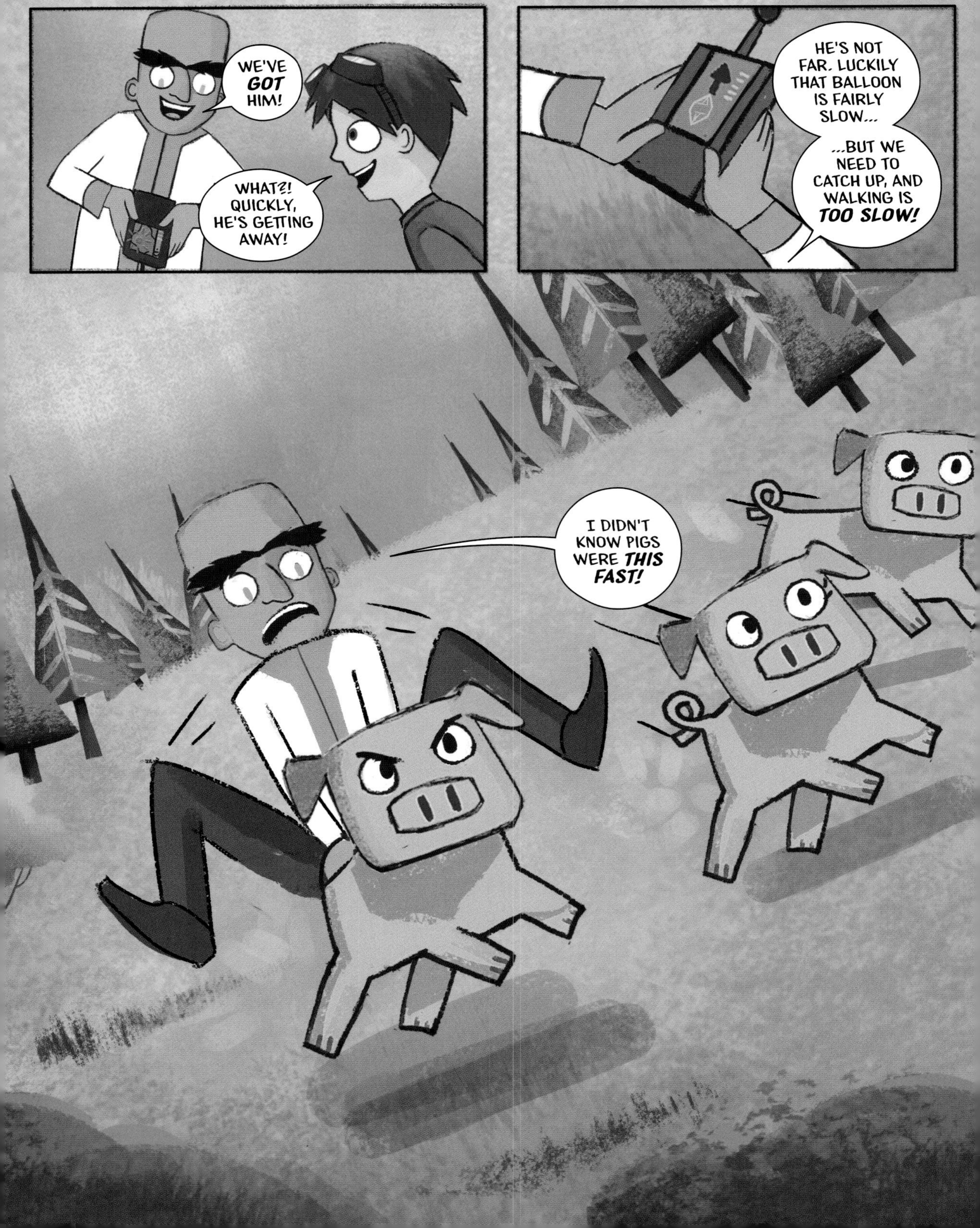
WE'VE GOT HIM!
WHAT?! QUICKLY, HE'S GETTING AWAY!
HE'S NOT FAR. LUCKILY THAT BALLOON IS FAIRLY SLOW...
...BUT WE NEED TO CATCH UP, AND WALKING IS TOO SLOW!
I DIDN'T KNOW PIGS WERE THIS FAST!

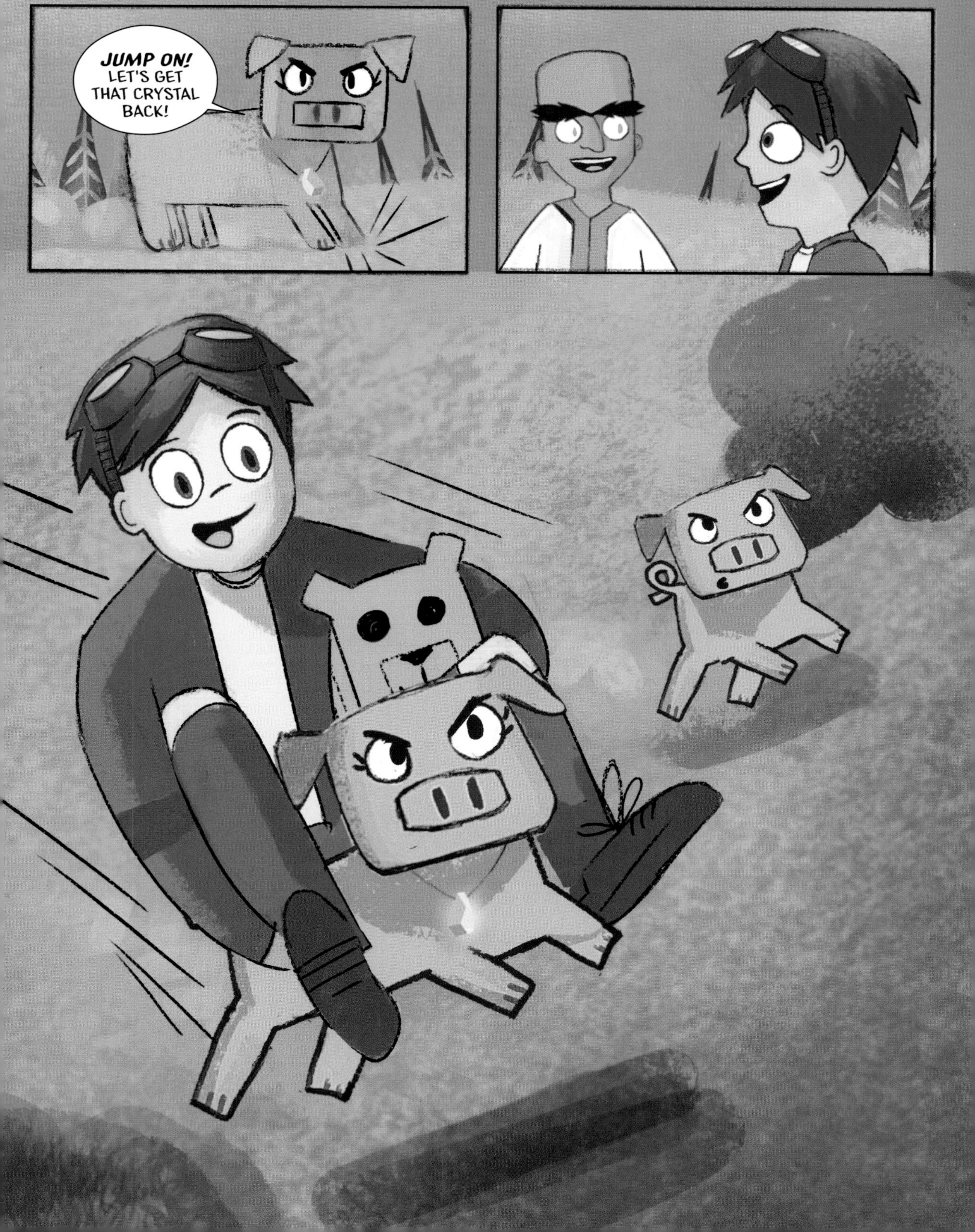
JUMP ON! LET'S GET THAT CRYSTAL BACK!

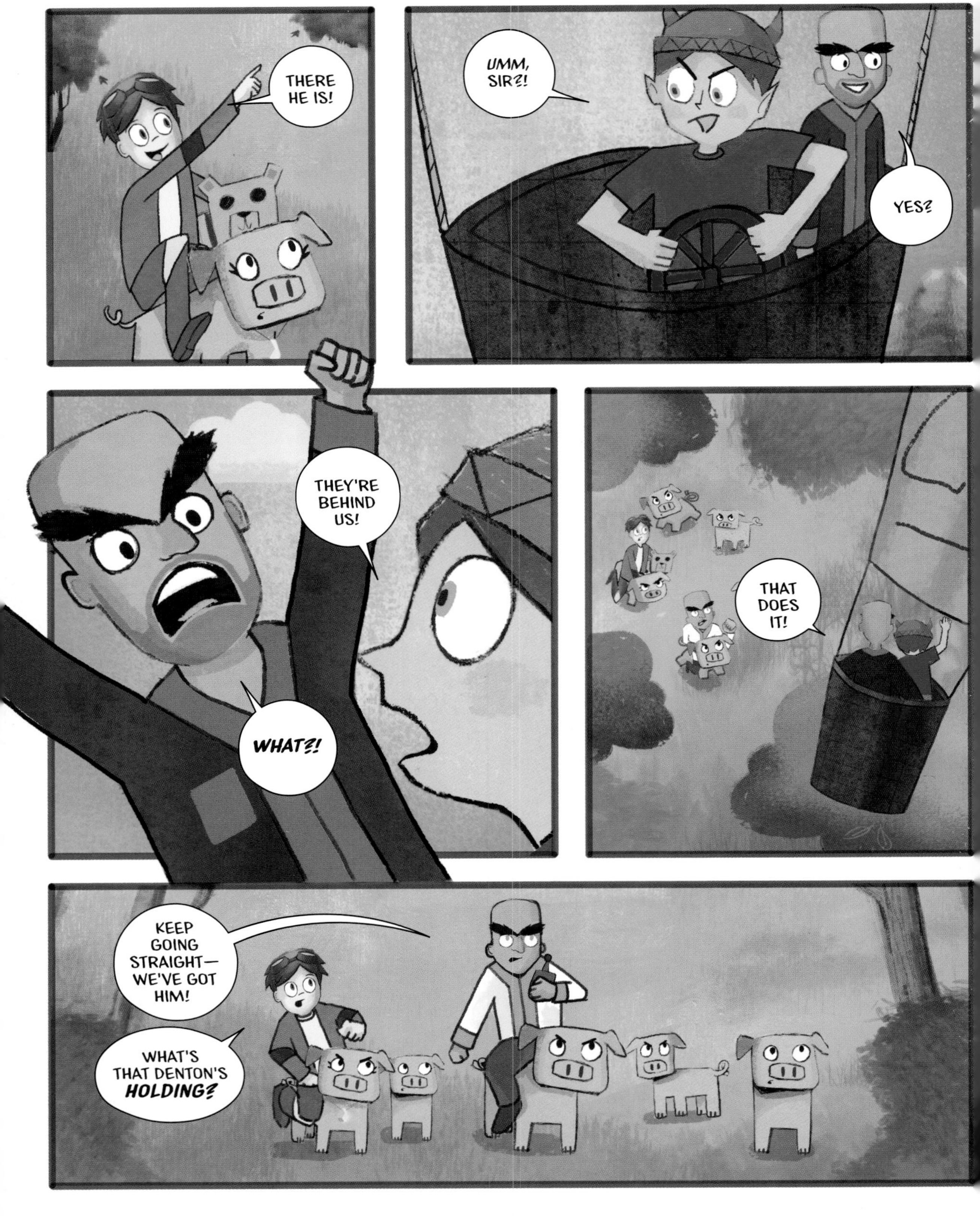
THERE HE IS!
UMM, SIR?!
YES?
THEY'RE BEHIND US!
WHAT?!
THAT DOES IT!
KEEP GOING STRAIGHT— WE'VE GOT HIM!
WHAT'S THAT DENTON'S ***HOLDING?***

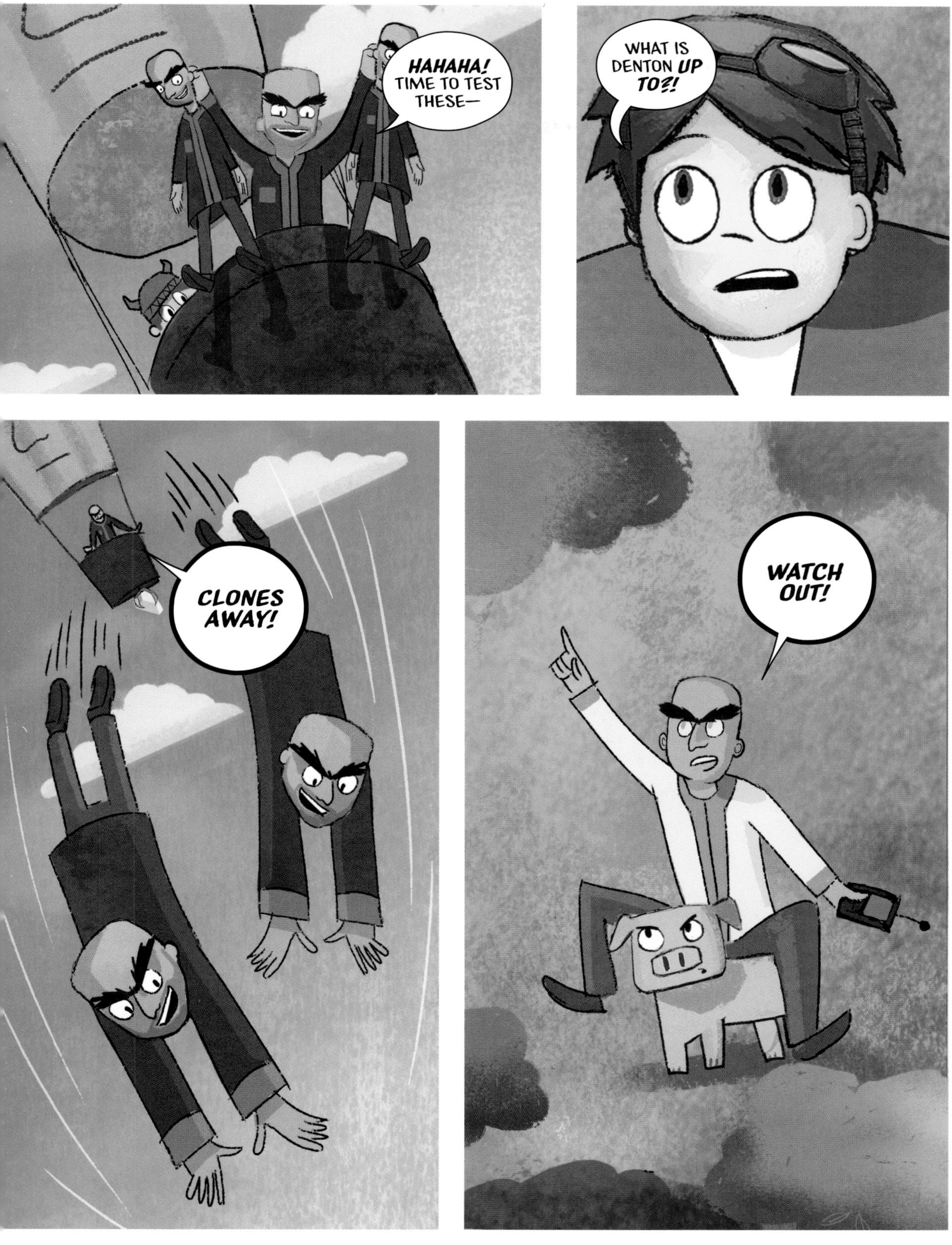
HAHAHA! TIME TO TEST THESE—
WHAT IS DENTON UP TO?!
CLONES AWAY!
WATCH OUT!

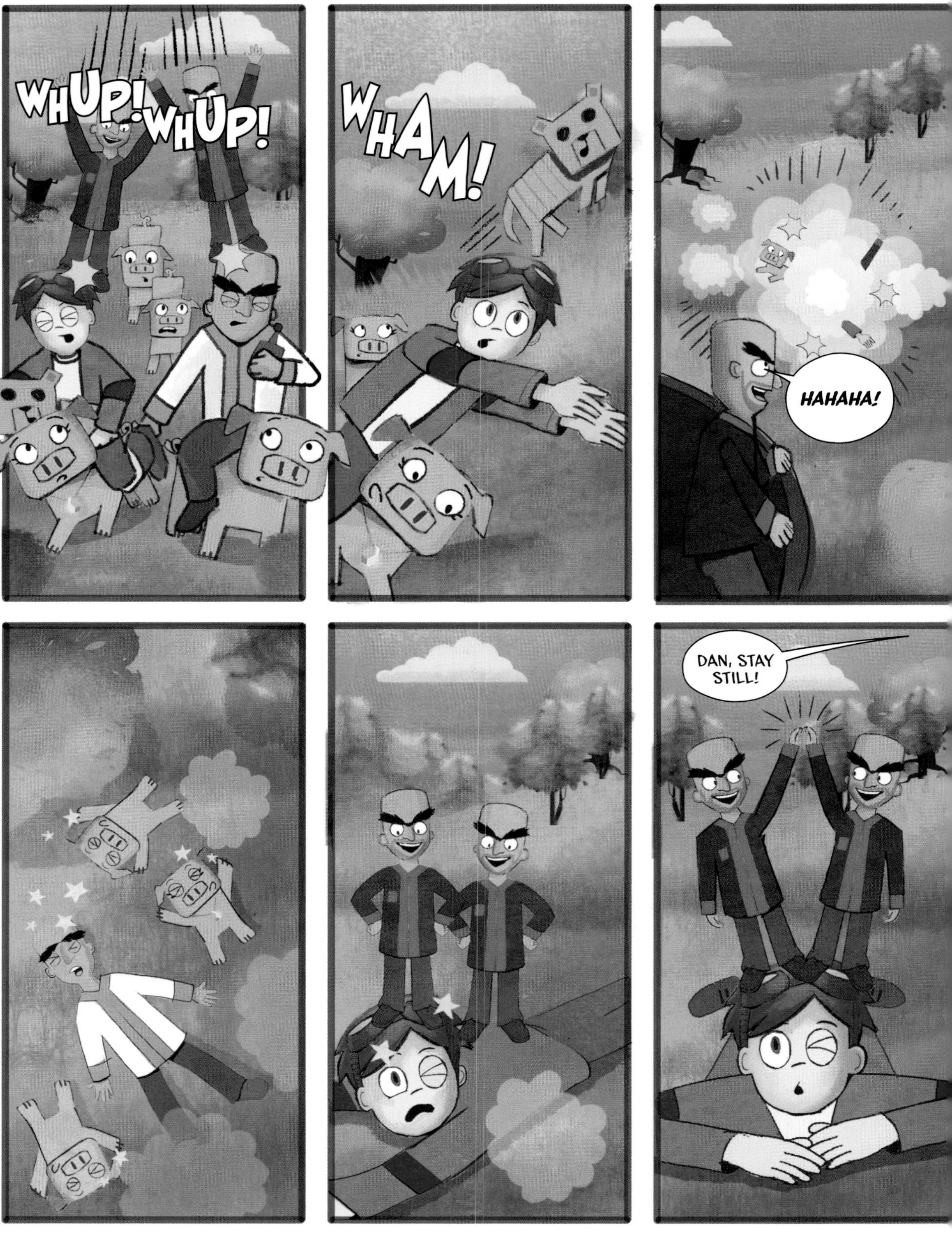
WHUP! WHUP!
WHAM!
HAHAHA!
DAN, STAY STILL!

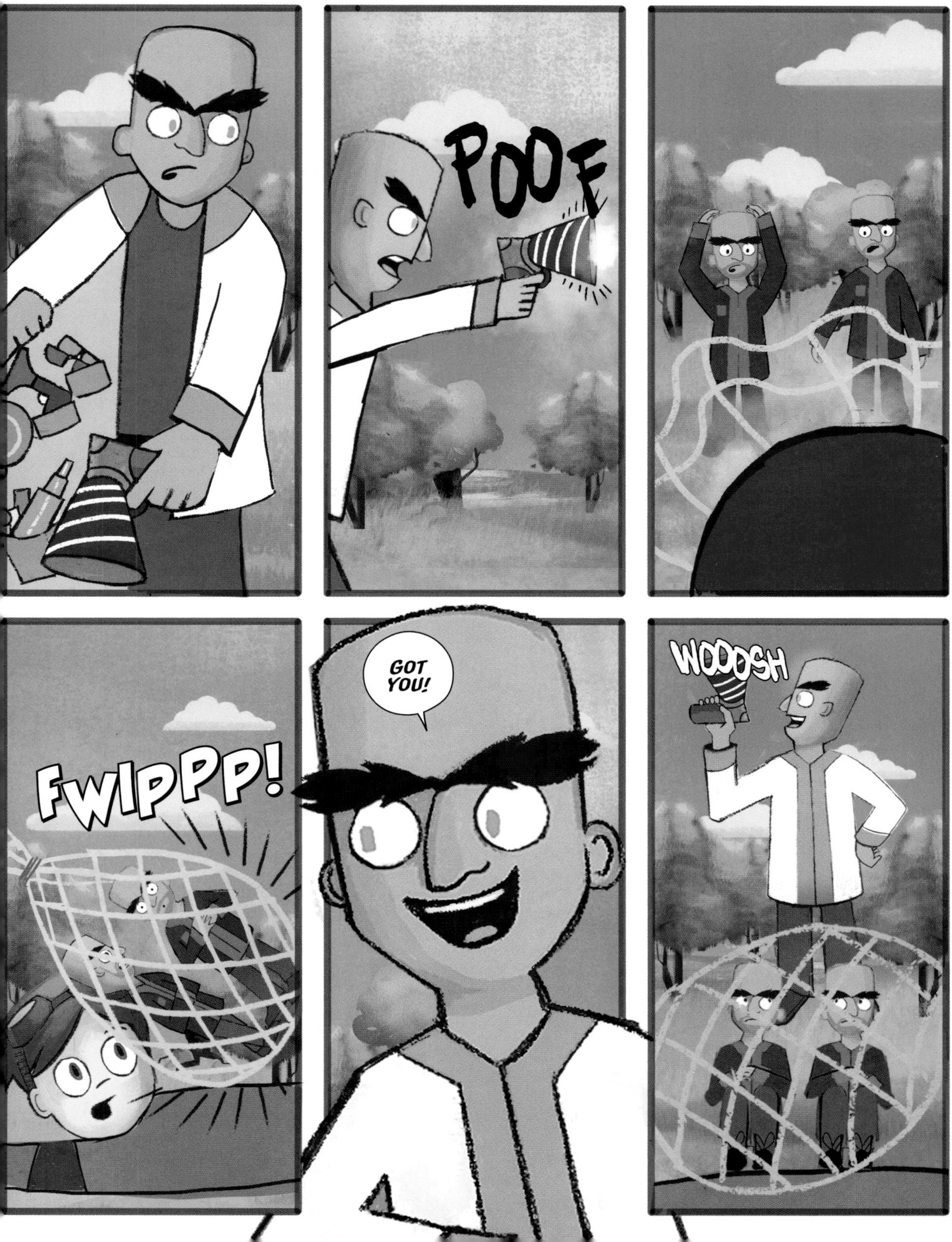
POOF
FWIPPP!
GOT YOU!
WOOOSH

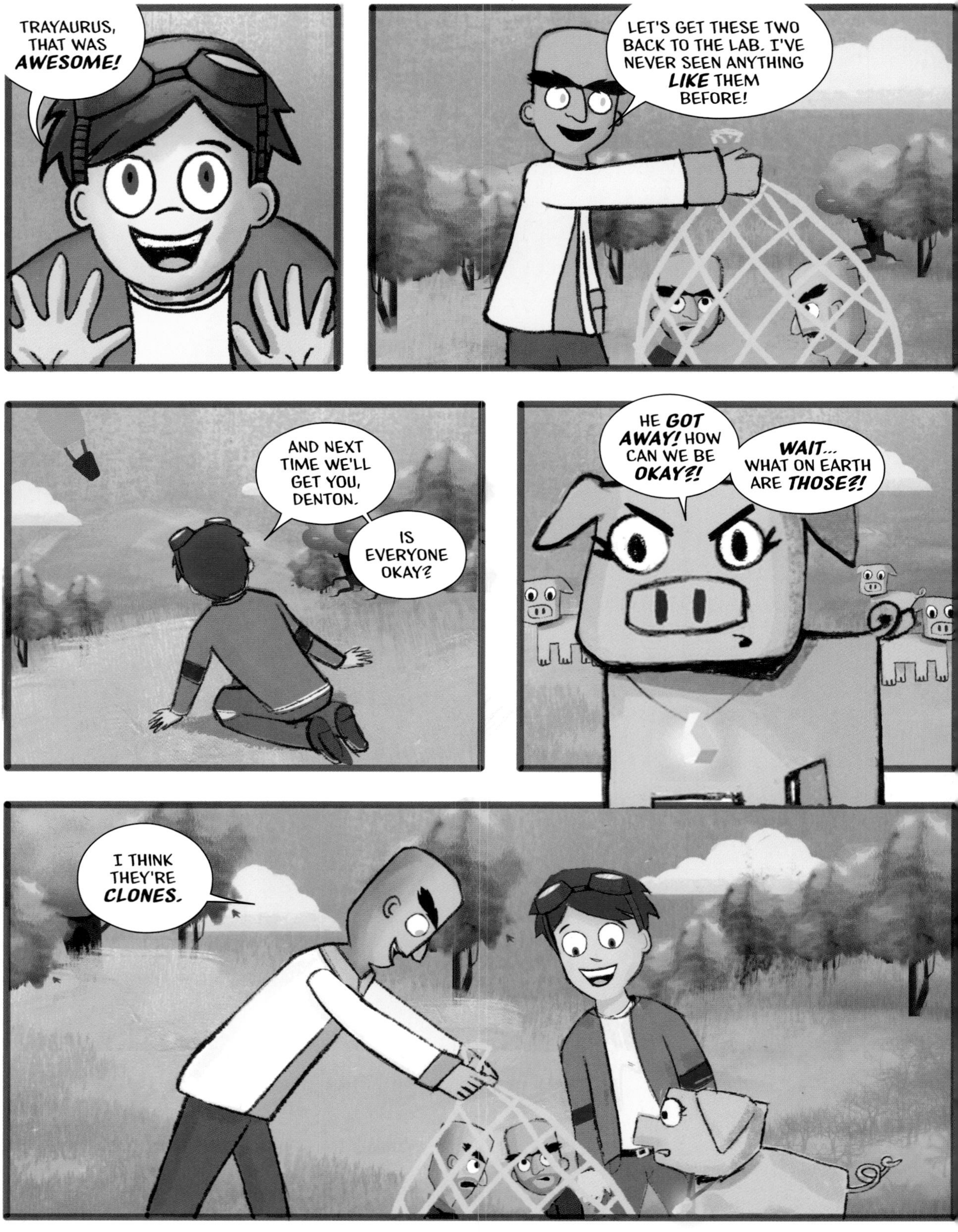
TRAYAURUS, THAT WAS AWESOME!
LET'S GET THESE TWO BACK TO THE LAB. I'VE NEVER SEEN ANYTHING LIKE THEM BEFORE!
AND NEXT TIME WE'LL GET YOU, DENTON.
IS EVERYONE OKAY?
HE GOT AWAY! HOW CAN WE BE OKAY?!
WAIT... WHAT ON EARTH ARE THOSE?!
I THINK THEY'RE CLONES.

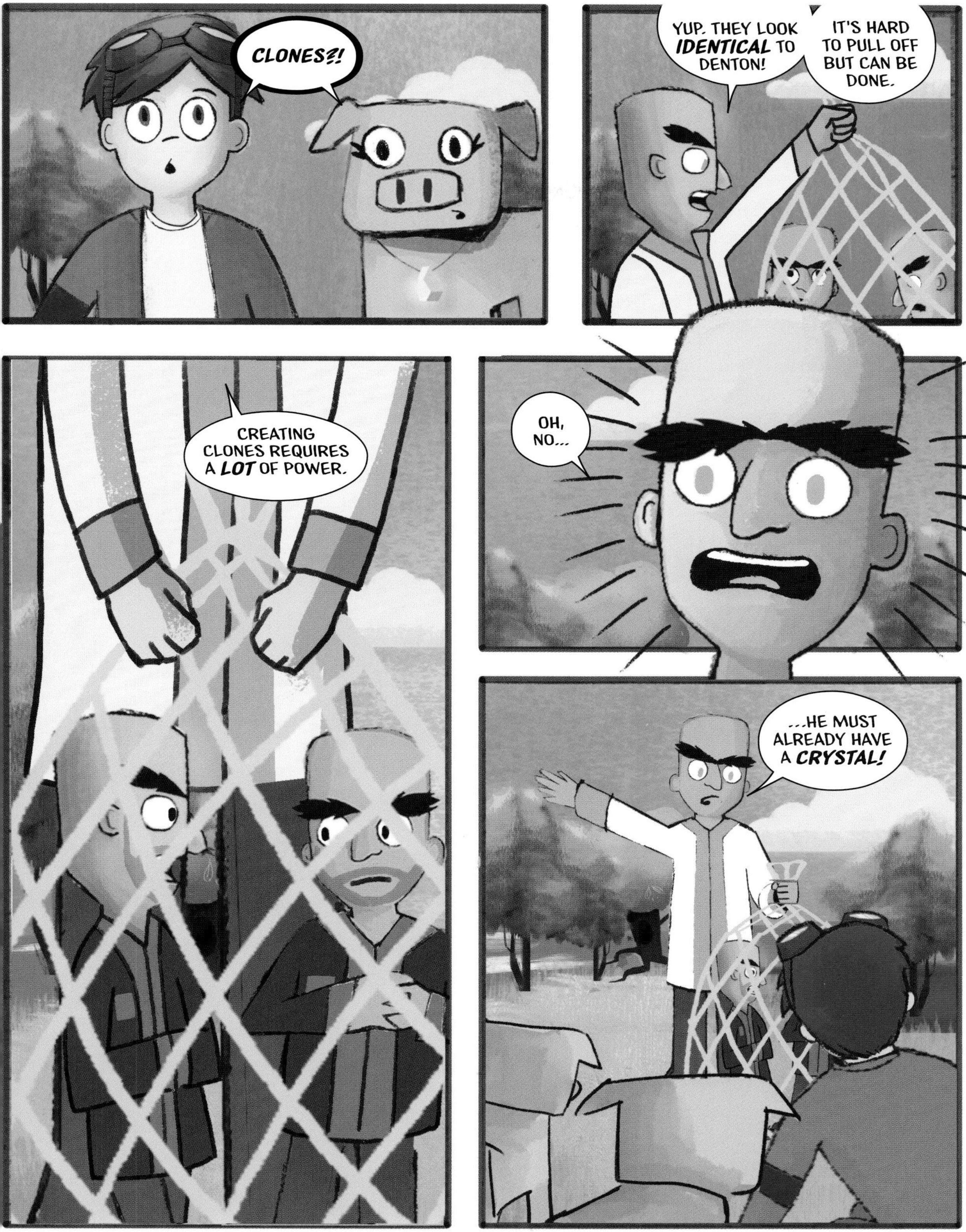

CLONES?!
YUP. THEY LOOK IDENTICAL TO DENTON!
IT'S HARD TO PULL OFF BUT CAN BE DONE.
CREATING CLONES REQUIRES A LOT OF POWER.
OH, NO...
...HE MUST ALREADY HAVE A CRYSTAL!

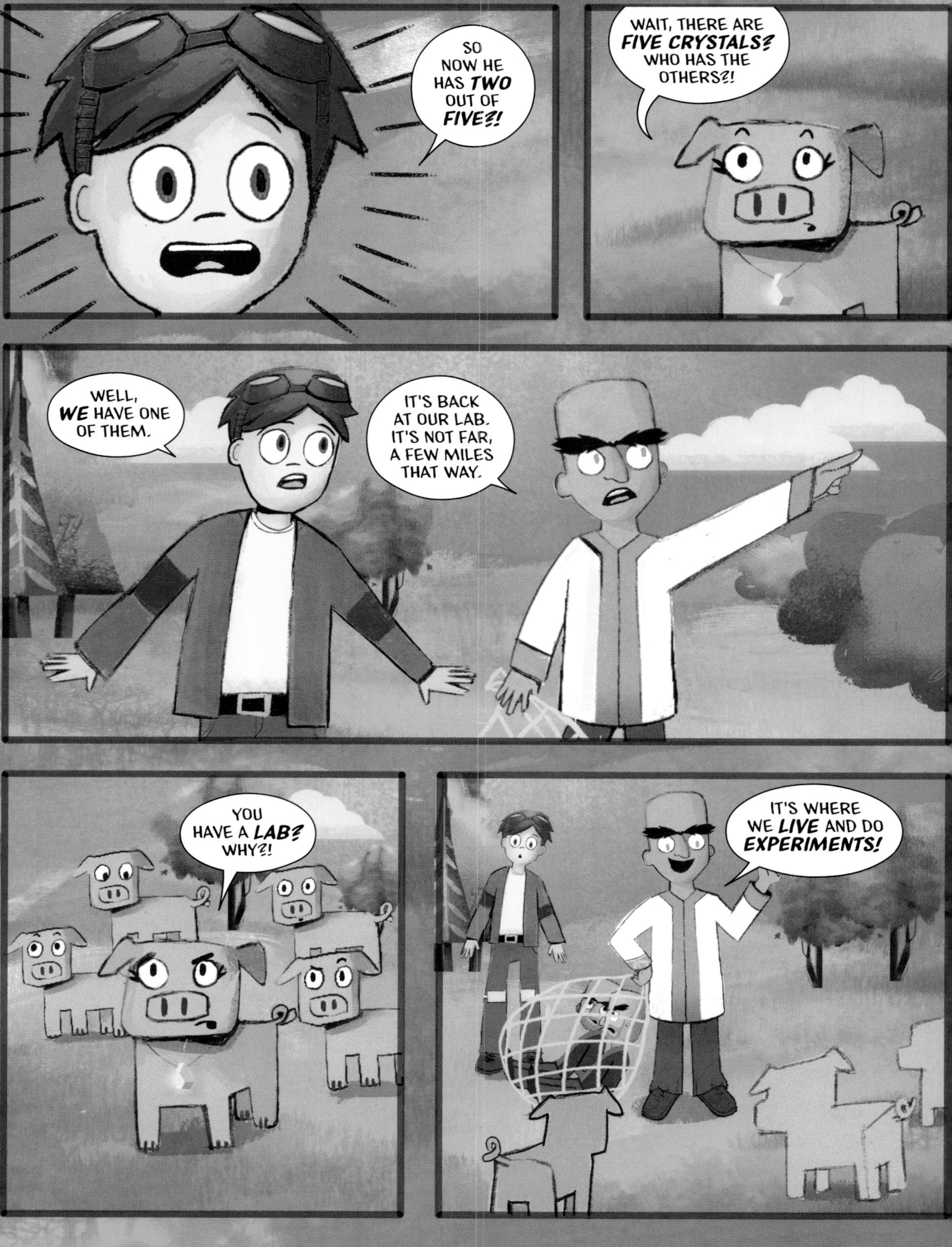
SO NOW HE HAS TWO OUT OF FIVE?!
WAIT, THERE ARE FIVE CRYSTALS? WHO HAS THE OTHERS?!
WELL, WE HAVE ONE OF THEM.
IT'S BACK AT OUR LAB. IT'S NOT FAR, A FEW MILES THAT WAY.
YOU HAVE A LAB? WHY?!
IT'S WHERE WE LIVE AND DO EXPERIMENTS!

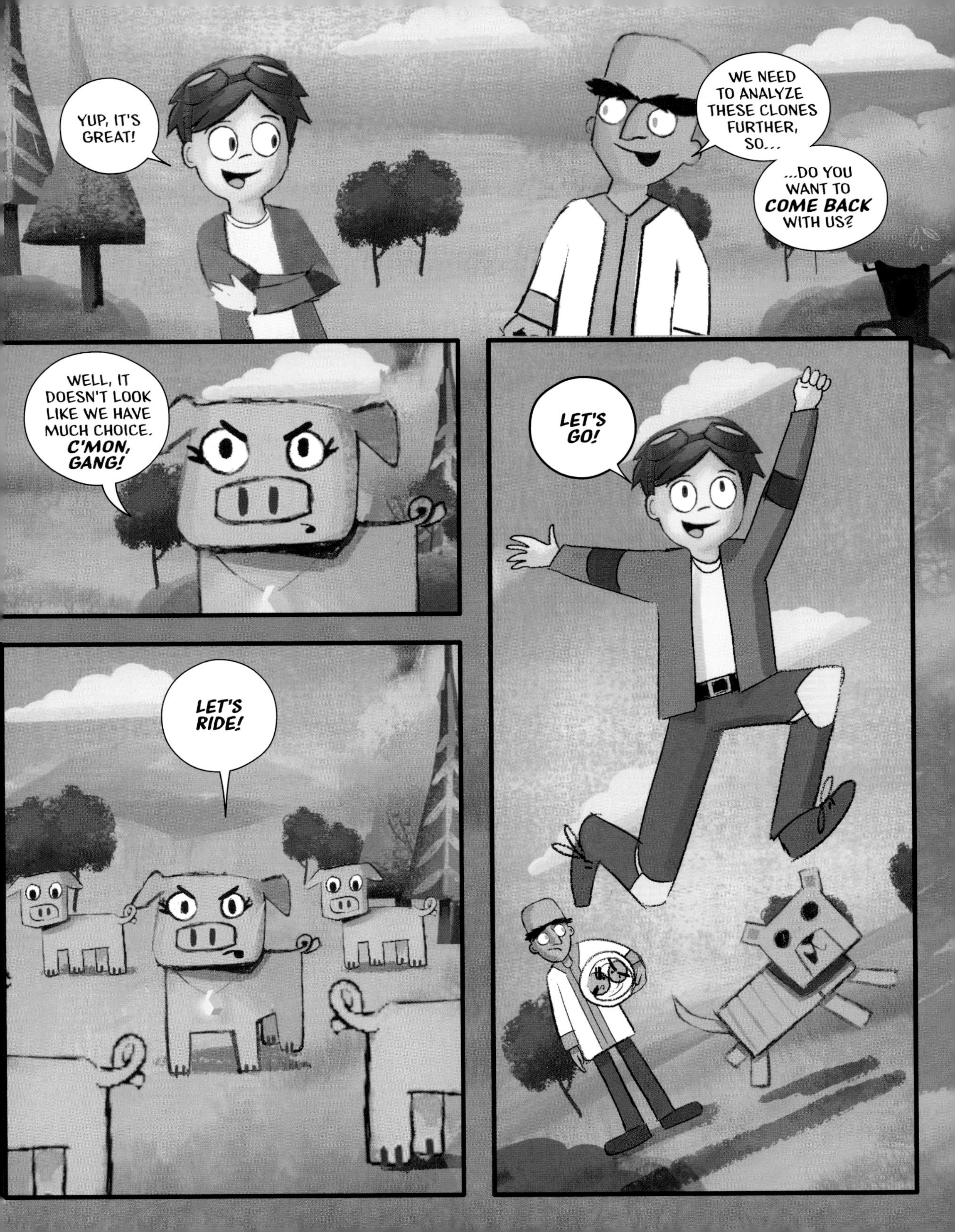
YUP, IT'S GREAT!
WE NEED TO ANALYZE THESE CLONES FURTHER, SO...
...DO YOU WANT TO **COME BACK** WITH US?
WELL, IT DOESN'T LOOK LIKE WE HAVE MUCH CHOICE. **C'MON, GANG!**
LET'S GO!
LET'S RIDE!

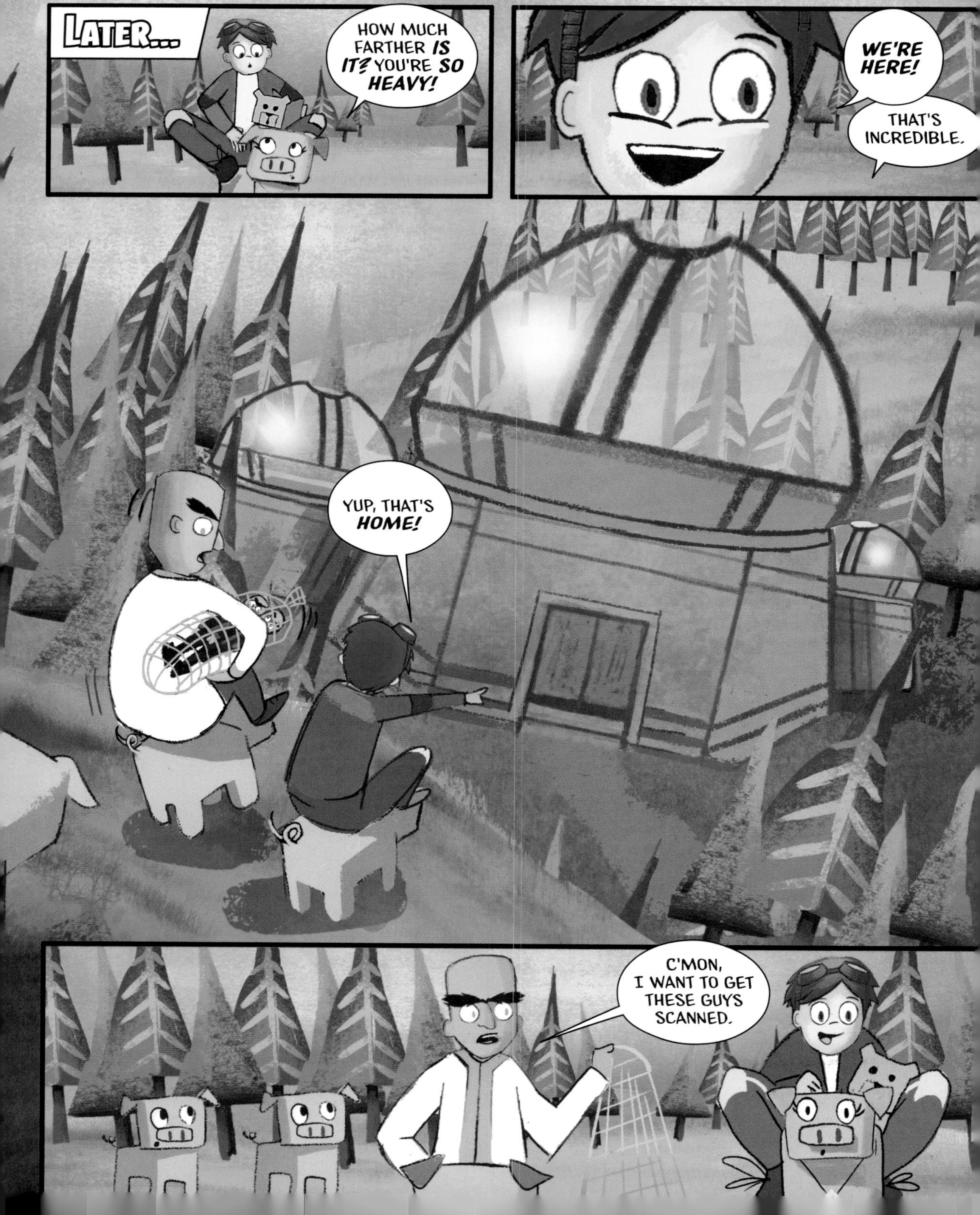
LATER...
HOW MUCH FARTHER IS IT? YOU'RE SO HEAVY!
WE'RE HERE!
THAT'S INCREDIBLE.
YUP, THAT'S HOME!
C'MON, I WANT TO GET THESE GUYS SCANNED.

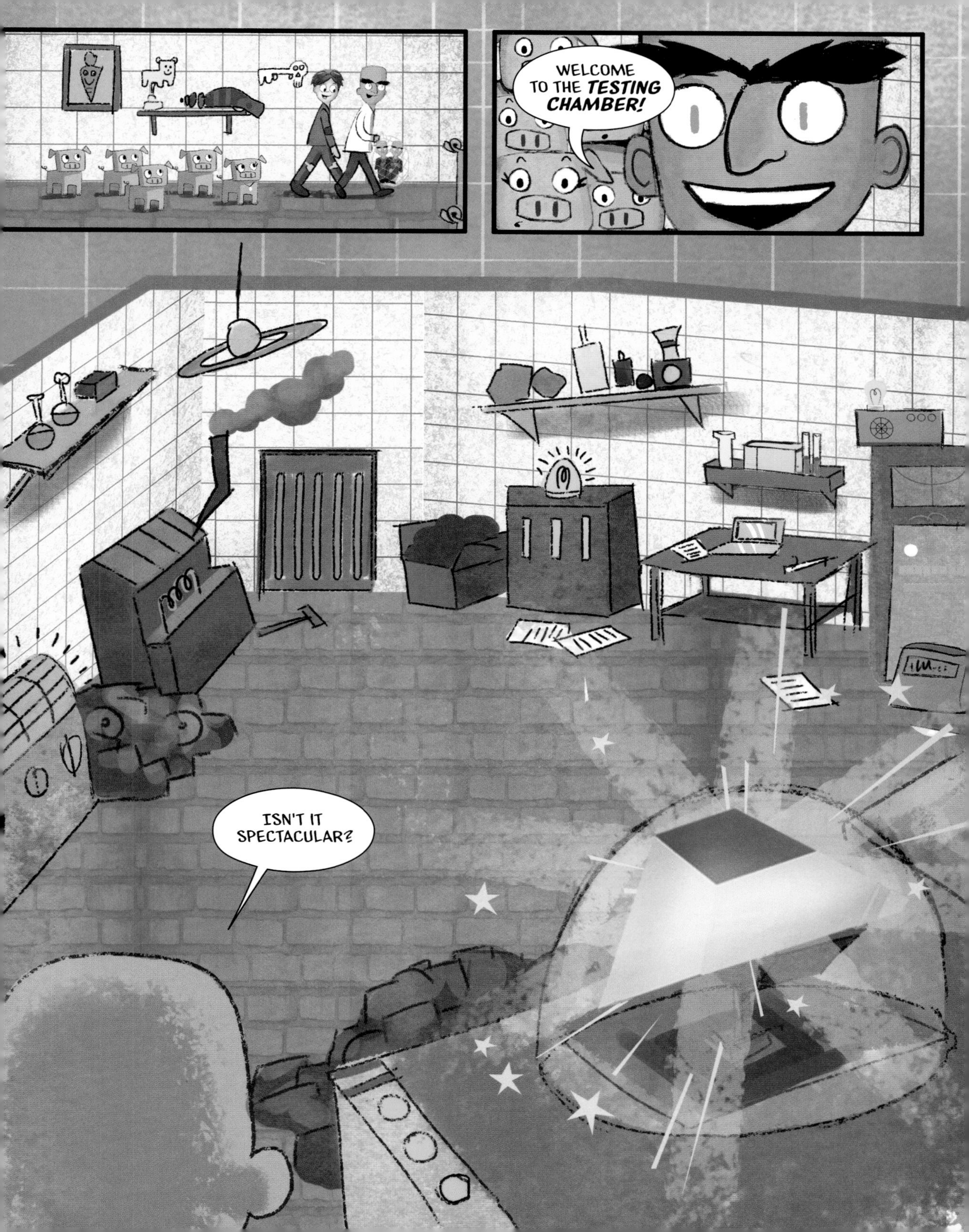
WELCOME TO THE TESTING CHAMBER!
ISN'T IT SPECTACULAR?

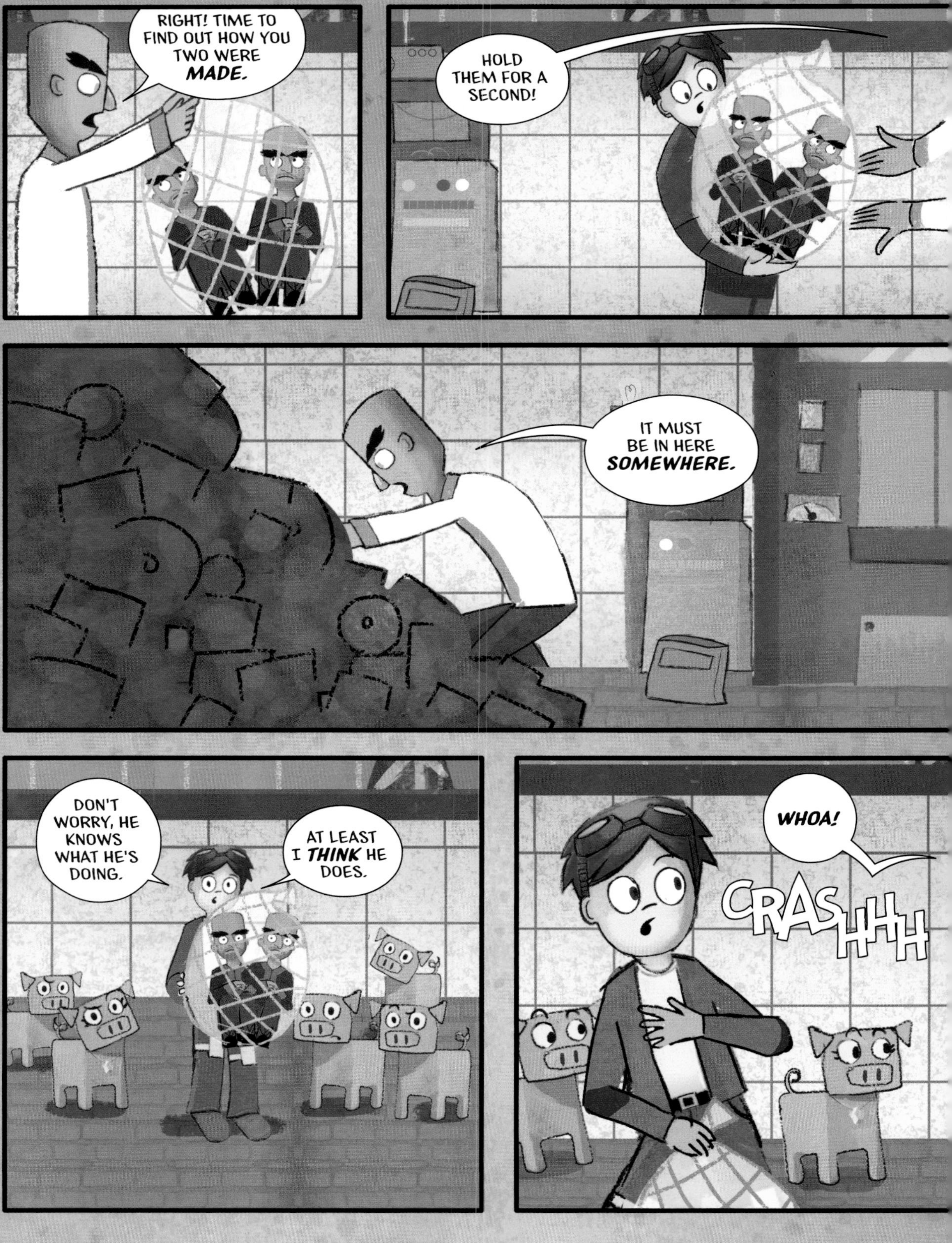
RIGHT! TIME TO FIND OUT HOW YOU TWO WERE *MADE.*
HOLD THEM FOR A SECOND!
IT MUST BE IN HERE *SOMEWHERE.*
DON'T WORRY, HE KNOWS WHAT HE'S DOING.
AT LEAST I *THINK* HE DOES.
WHOA!
CRASHHH

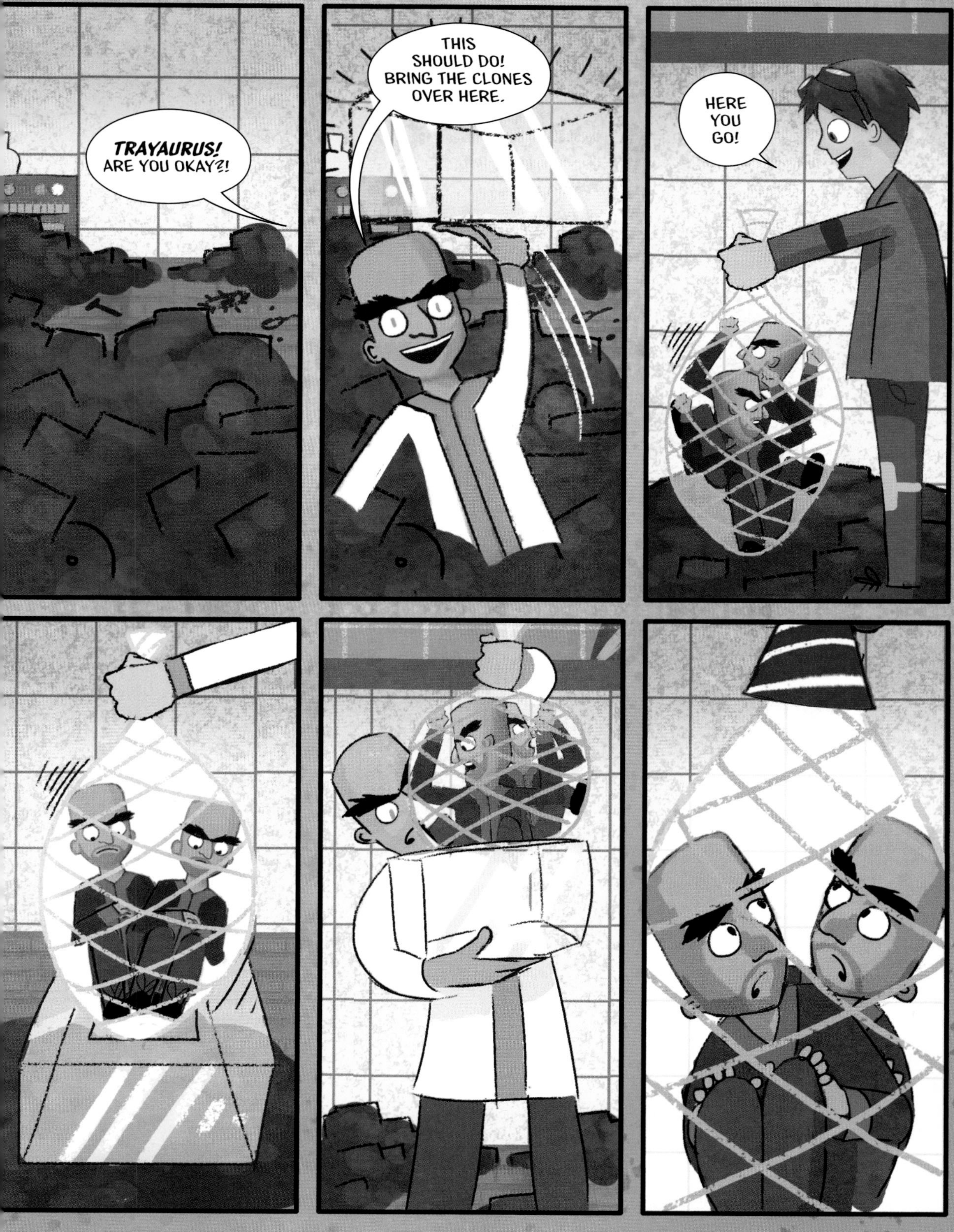
TRAYAURUS! ARE YOU OKAY?!
THIS SHOULD DO! BRING THE CLONES OVER HERE.
HERE YOU GO!

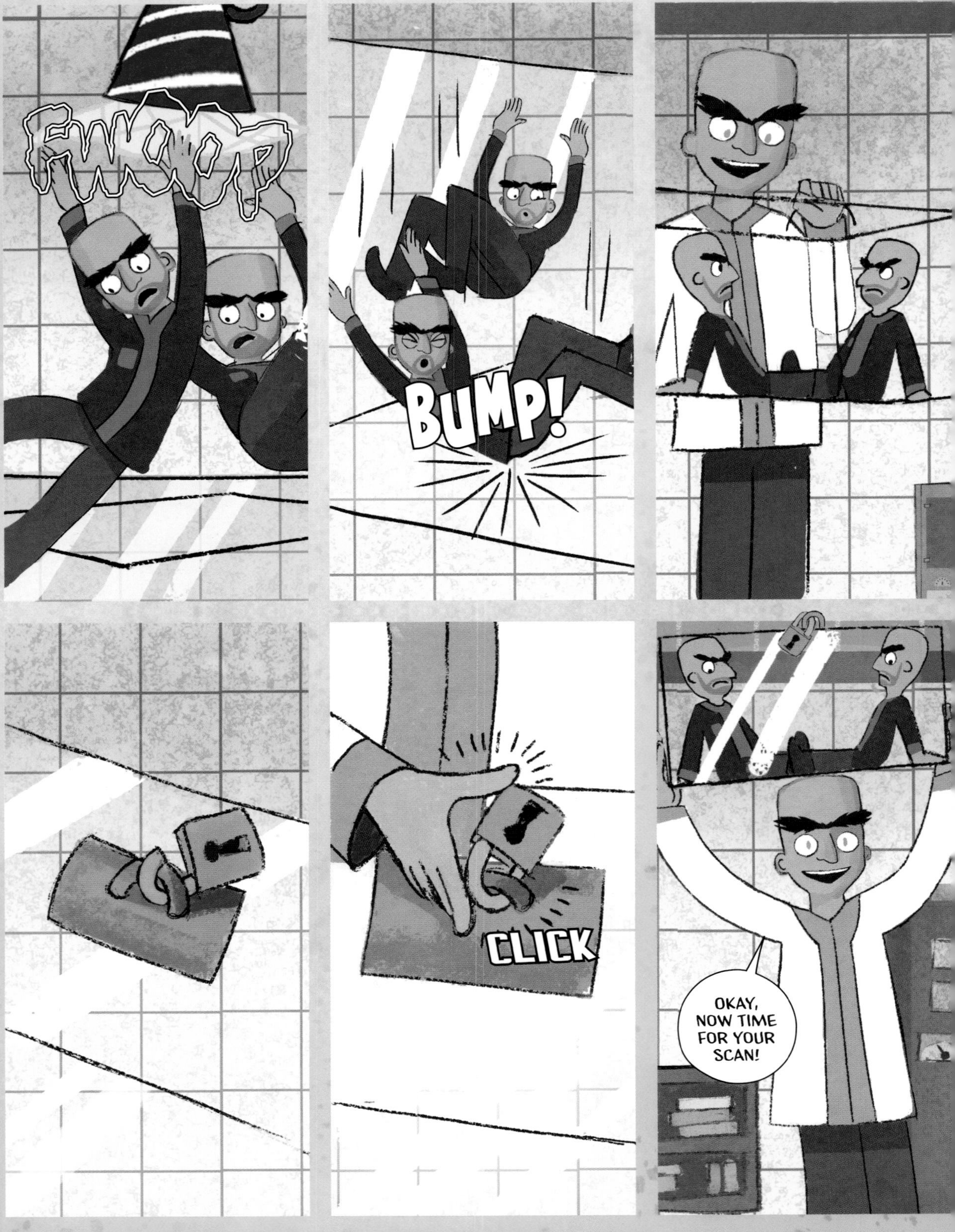
FWOOP
BUMP!
CLICK
OKAY, NOW TIME FOR YOUR SCAN!

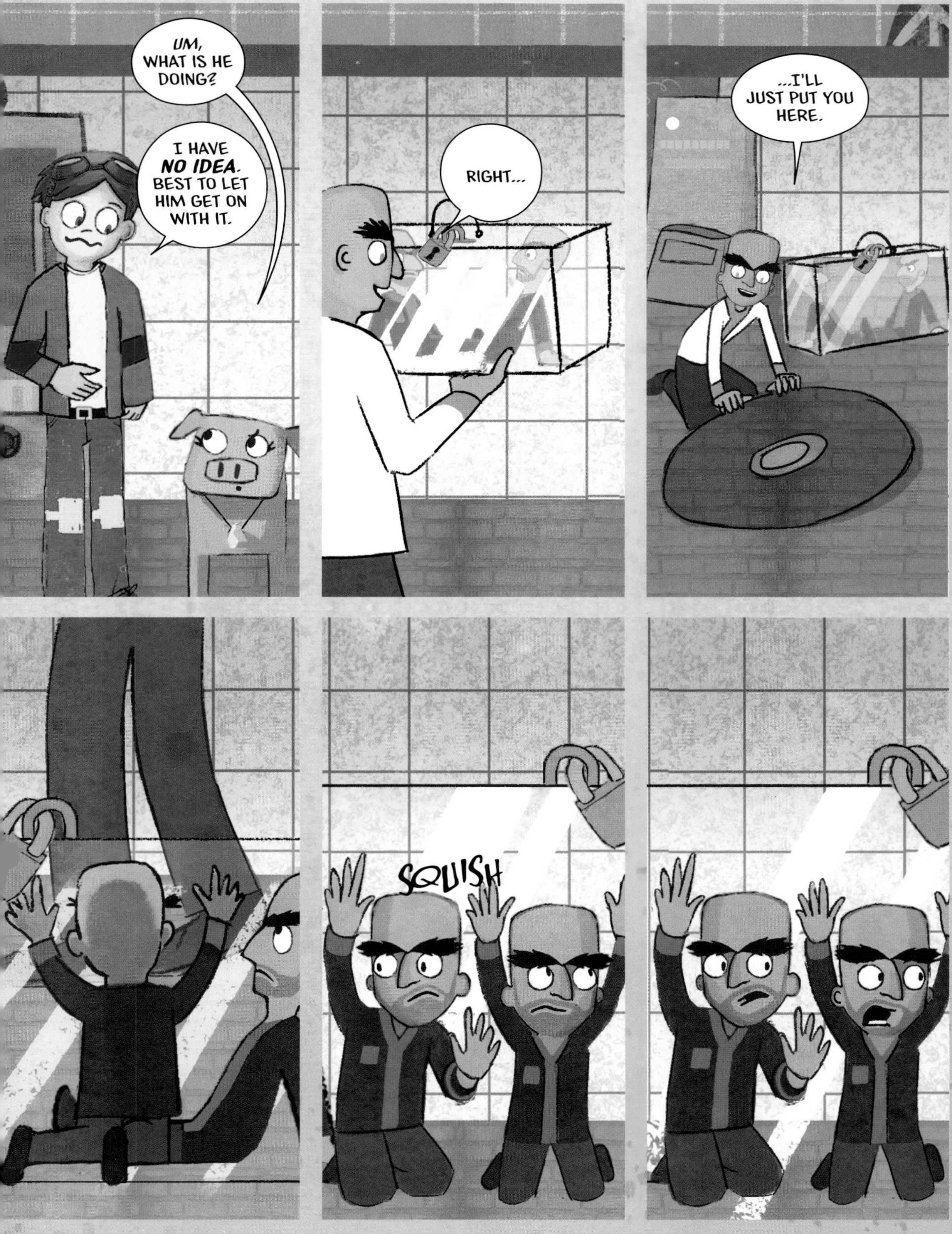
UM, WHAT IS HE DOING?
I HAVE **NO IDEA**. BEST TO LET HIM GET ON WITH IT.
RIGHT...
...I'LL JUST PUT YOU HERE.
SQUISH

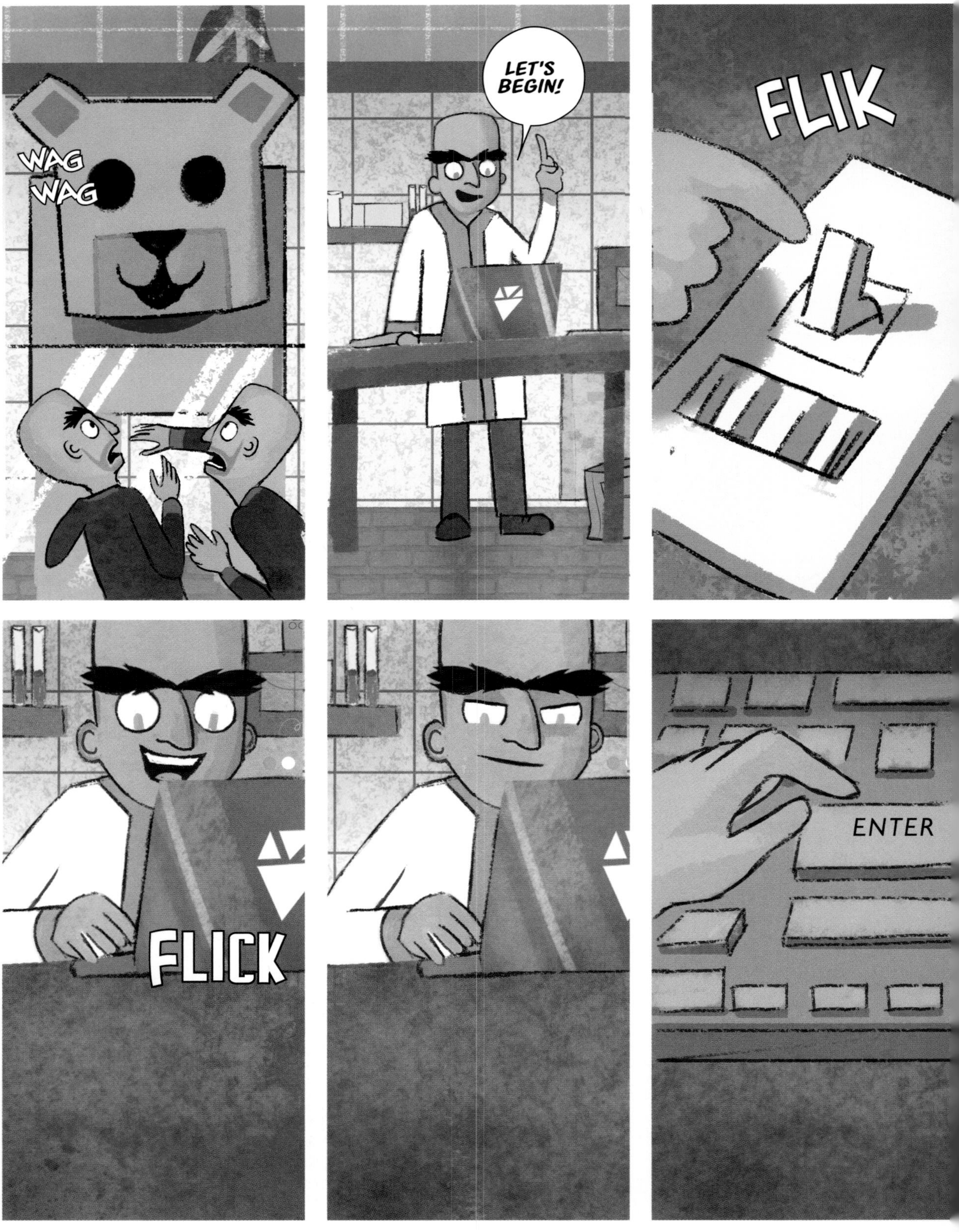
WAG
WAG
LET'S BEGIN!
FLIK
FLICK
ENTER

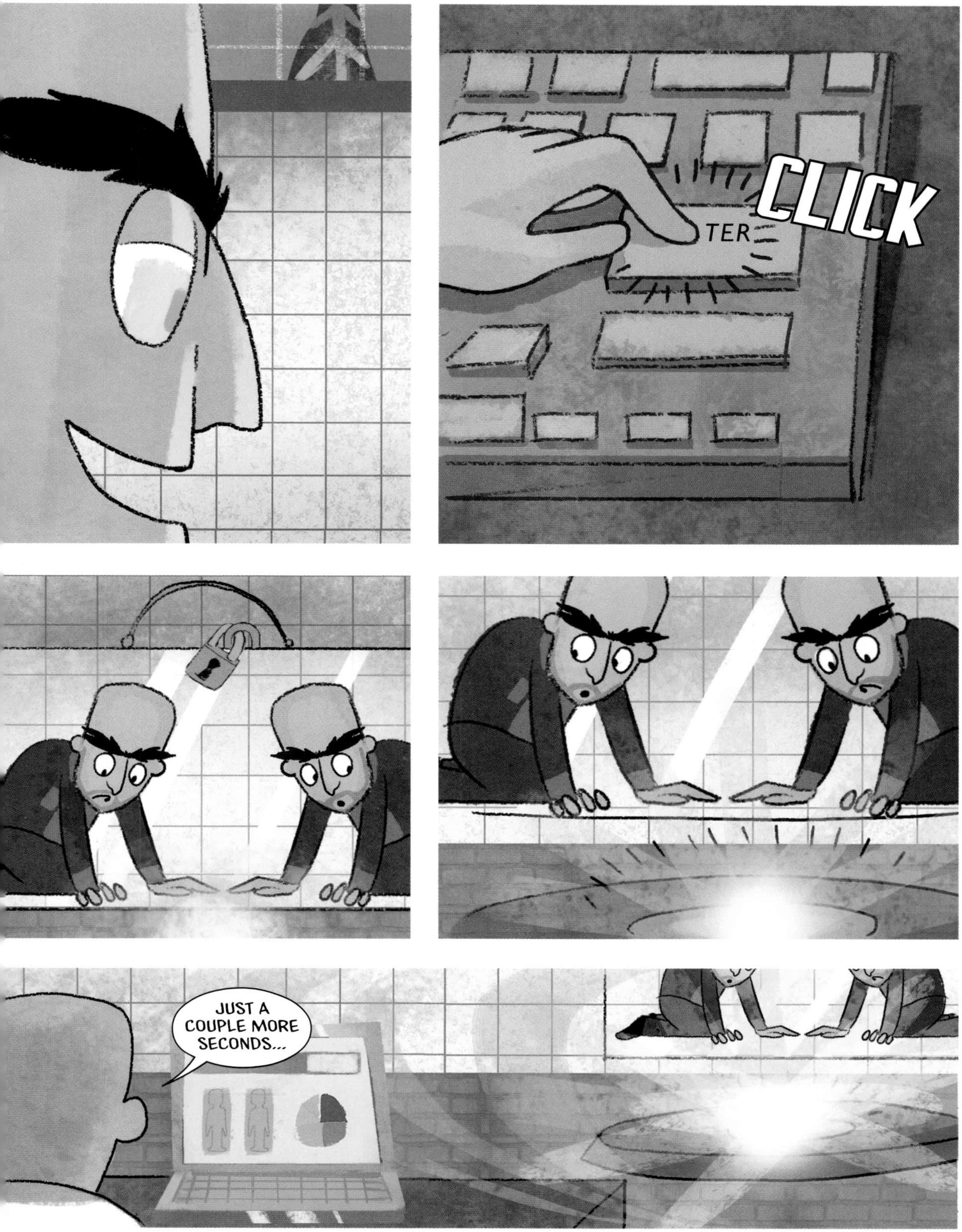
TER
CLICK
JUST A COUPLE MORE SECONDS...

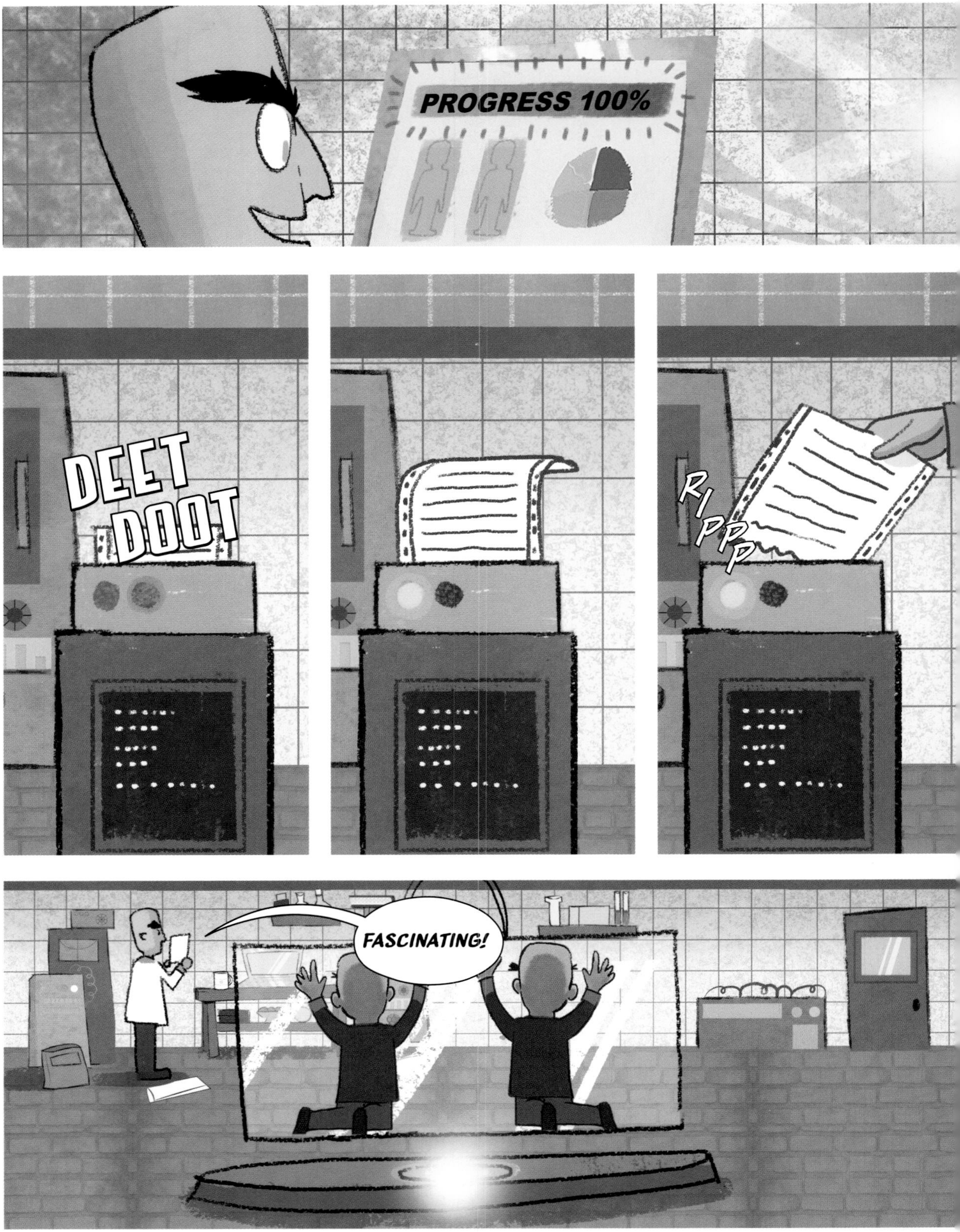
PROGRESS 100%
DEET DOOT
RIPPP
FASCINATING!

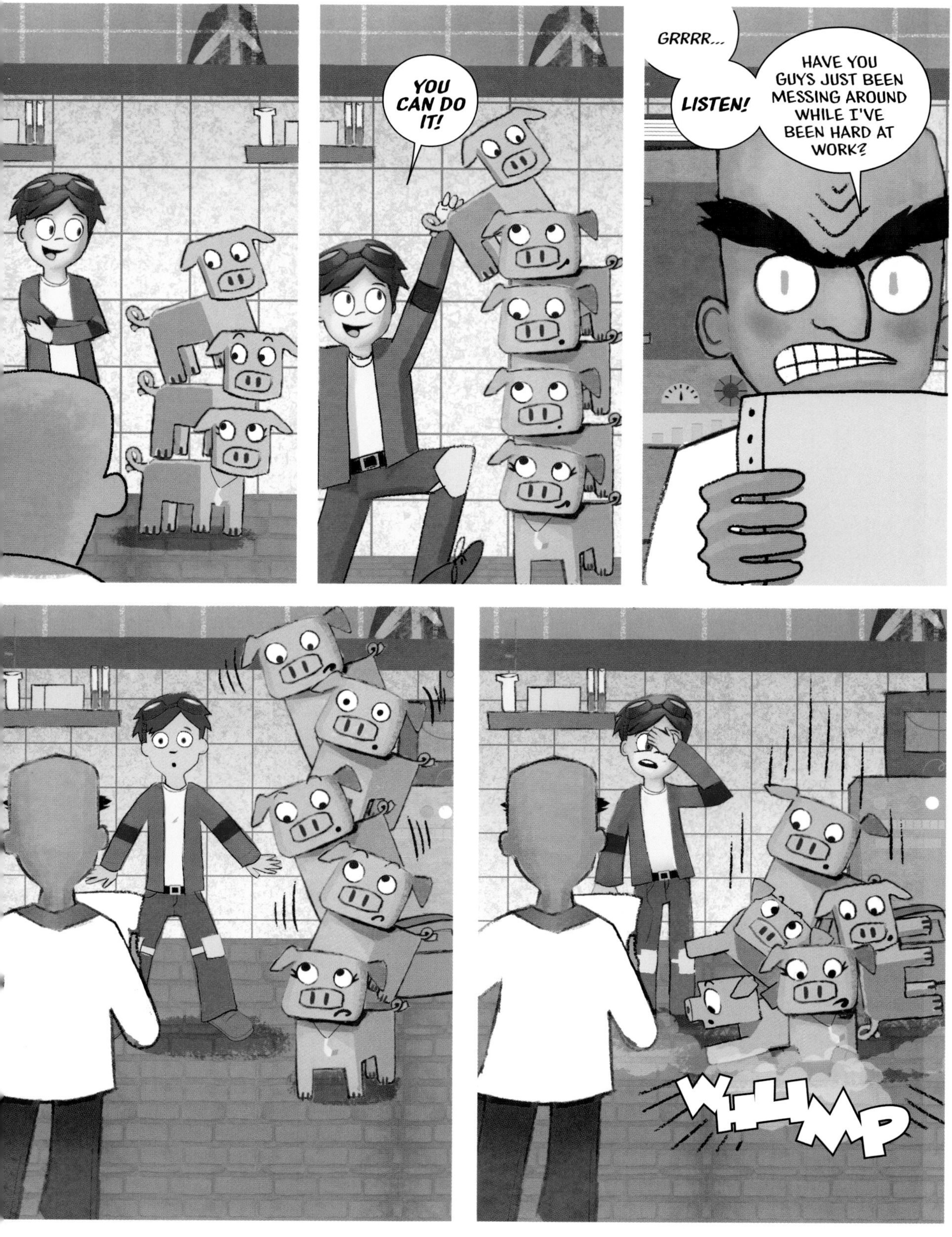
YOU CAN DO IT!
GRRRR...
LISTEN!
HAVE YOU GUYS JUST BEEN MESSING AROUND WHILE I'VE BEEN HARD AT WORK?
WHUMP

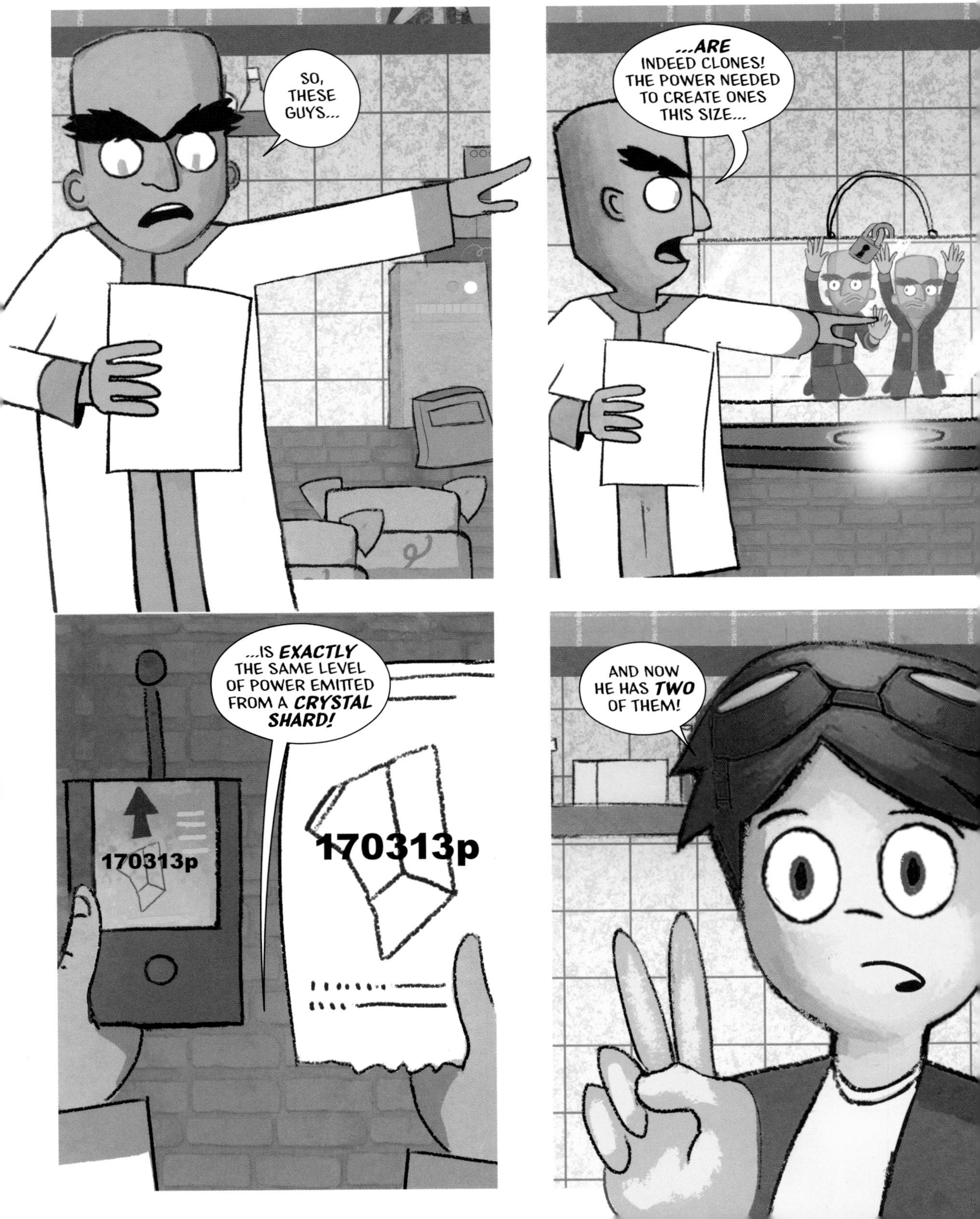
SO, THESE GUYS...
...ARE INDEED CLONES! THE POWER NEEDED TO CREATE ONES THIS SIZE...
...IS EXACTLY THE SAME LEVEL OF POWER EMITTED FROM A CRYSTAL SHARD!
AND NOW HE HAS TWO OF THEM!

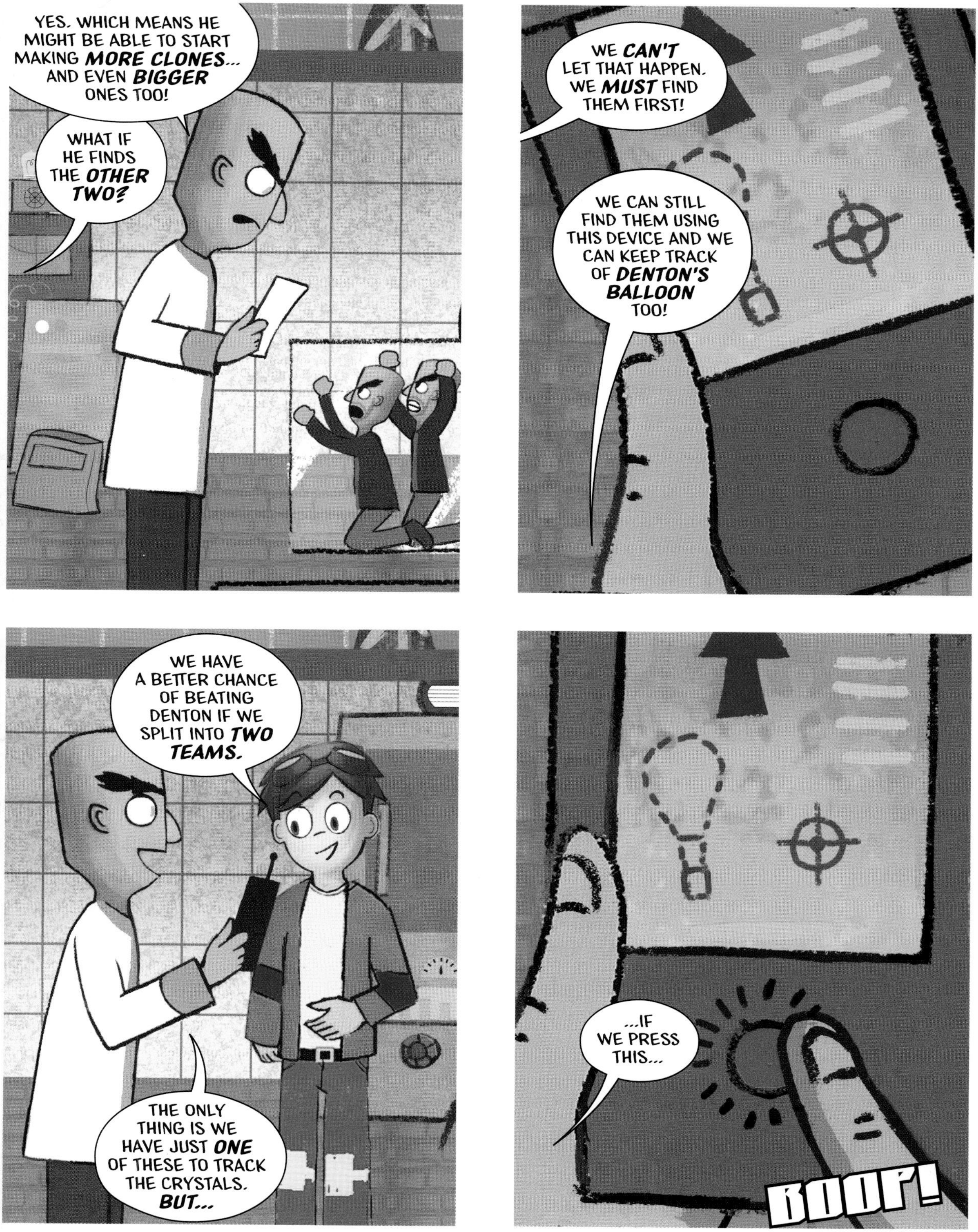
YES. WHICH MEANS HE MIGHT BE ABLE TO START MAKING MORE CLONES... AND EVEN BIGGER ONES TOO!
WHAT IF HE FINDS THE OTHER TWO?
WE CAN'T LET THAT HAPPEN. WE MUST FIND THEM FIRST!
WE CAN STILL FIND THEM USING THIS DEVICE AND WE CAN KEEP TRACK OF DENTON'S BALLOON TOO!
WE HAVE A BETTER CHANCE OF BEATING DENTON IF WE SPLIT INTO TWO TEAMS.
THE ONLY THING IS WE HAVE JUST ONE OF THESE TO TRACK THE CRYSTALS. BUT...
...IF WE PRESS THIS...
BOOP!

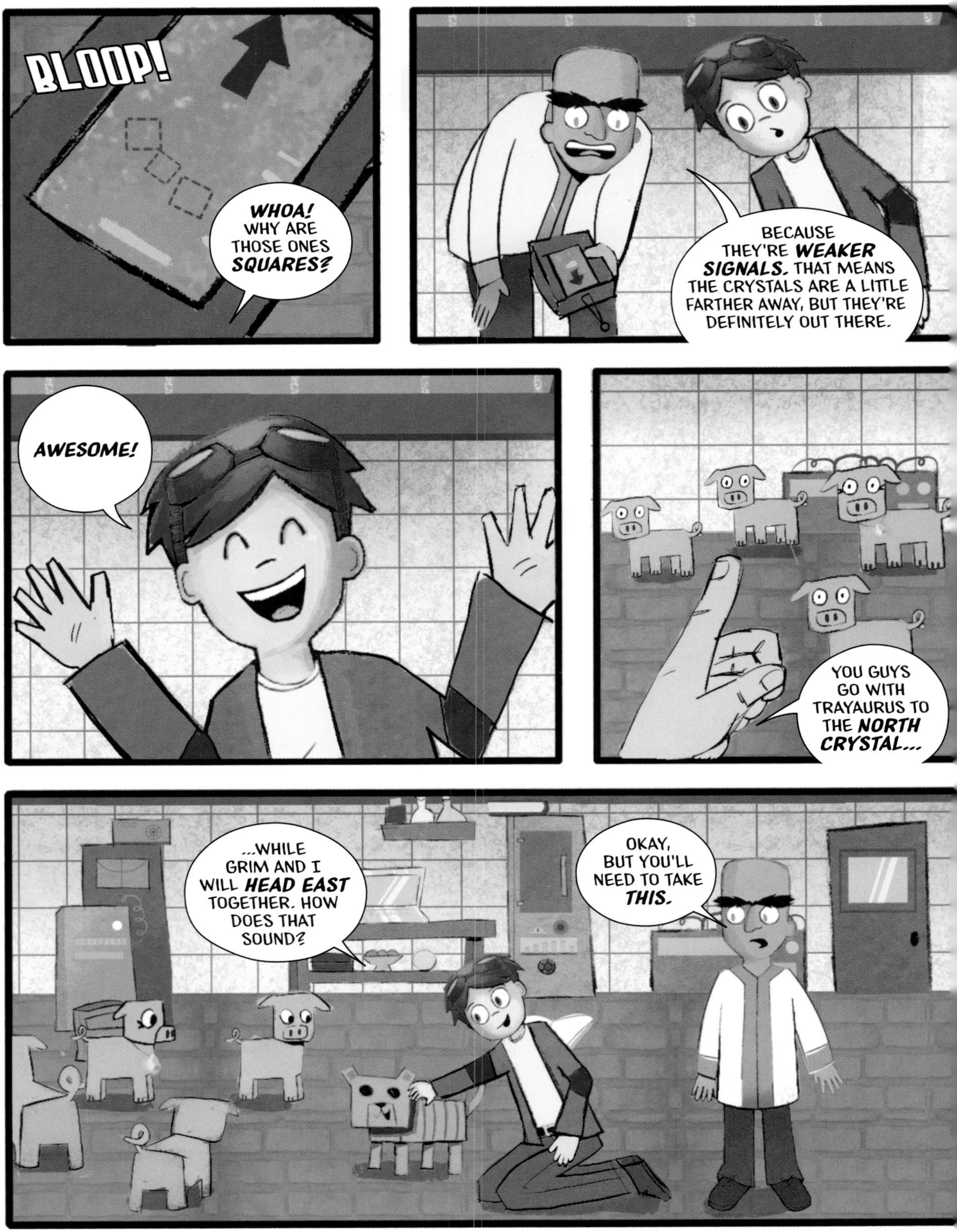
BLOOP!
WHOA! WHY ARE THOSE ONES SQUARES?
BECAUSE THEY'RE WEAKER SIGNALS. THAT MEANS THE CRYSTALS ARE A LITTLE FARTHER AWAY, BUT THEY'RE DEFINITELY OUT THERE.
AWESOME!
YOU GUYS GO WITH TRAYAURUS TO THE NORTH CRYSTAL...
...WHILE GRIM AND I WILL HEAD EAST TOGETHER. HOW DOES THAT SOUND?
OKAY, BUT YOU'LL NEED TO TAKE THIS.

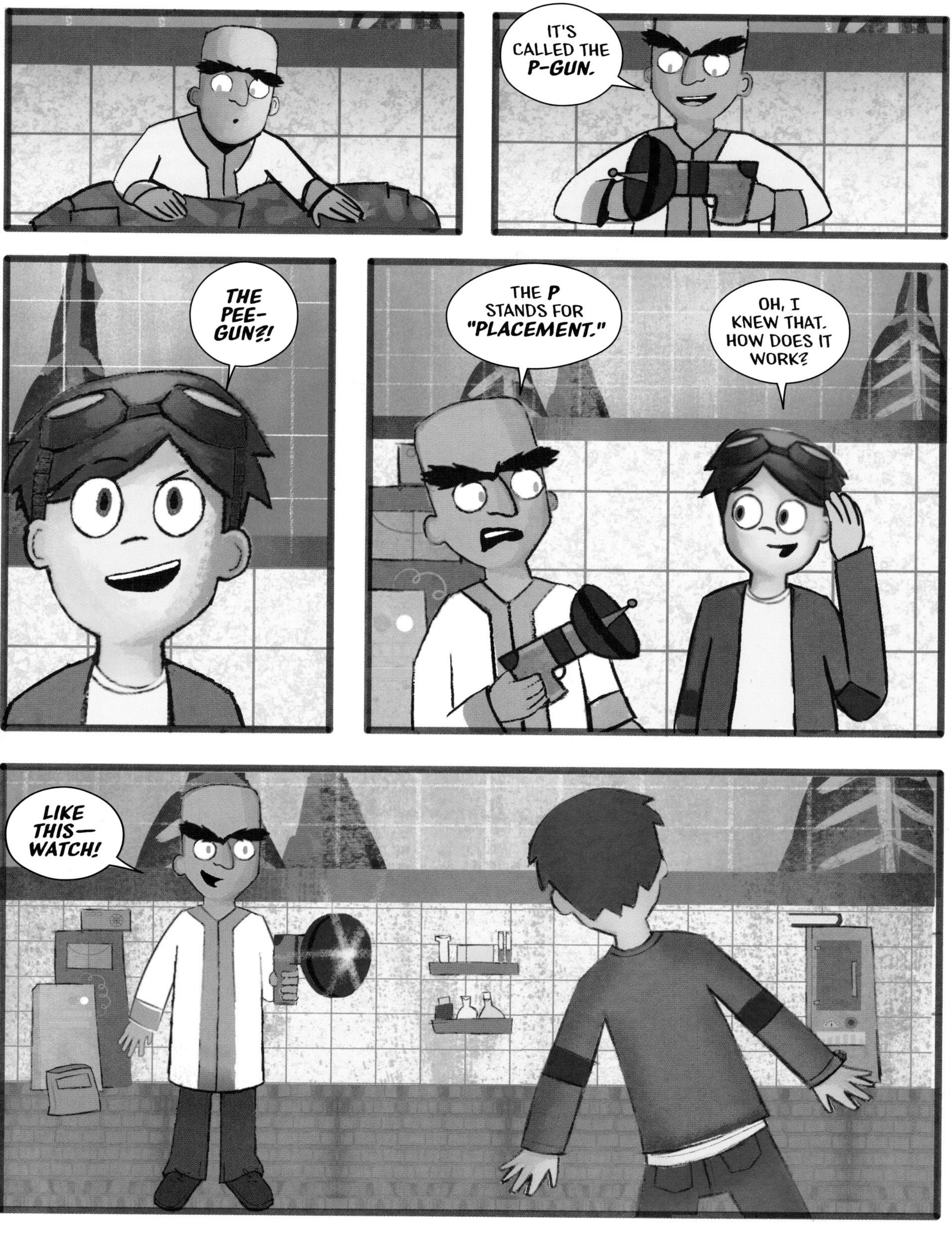
IT'S CALLED THE P-GUN.
THE PEE-GUN?!
THE P STANDS FOR "PLACEMENT."
OH, I KNEW THAT. HOW DOES IT WORK?
LIKE THIS— WATCH!

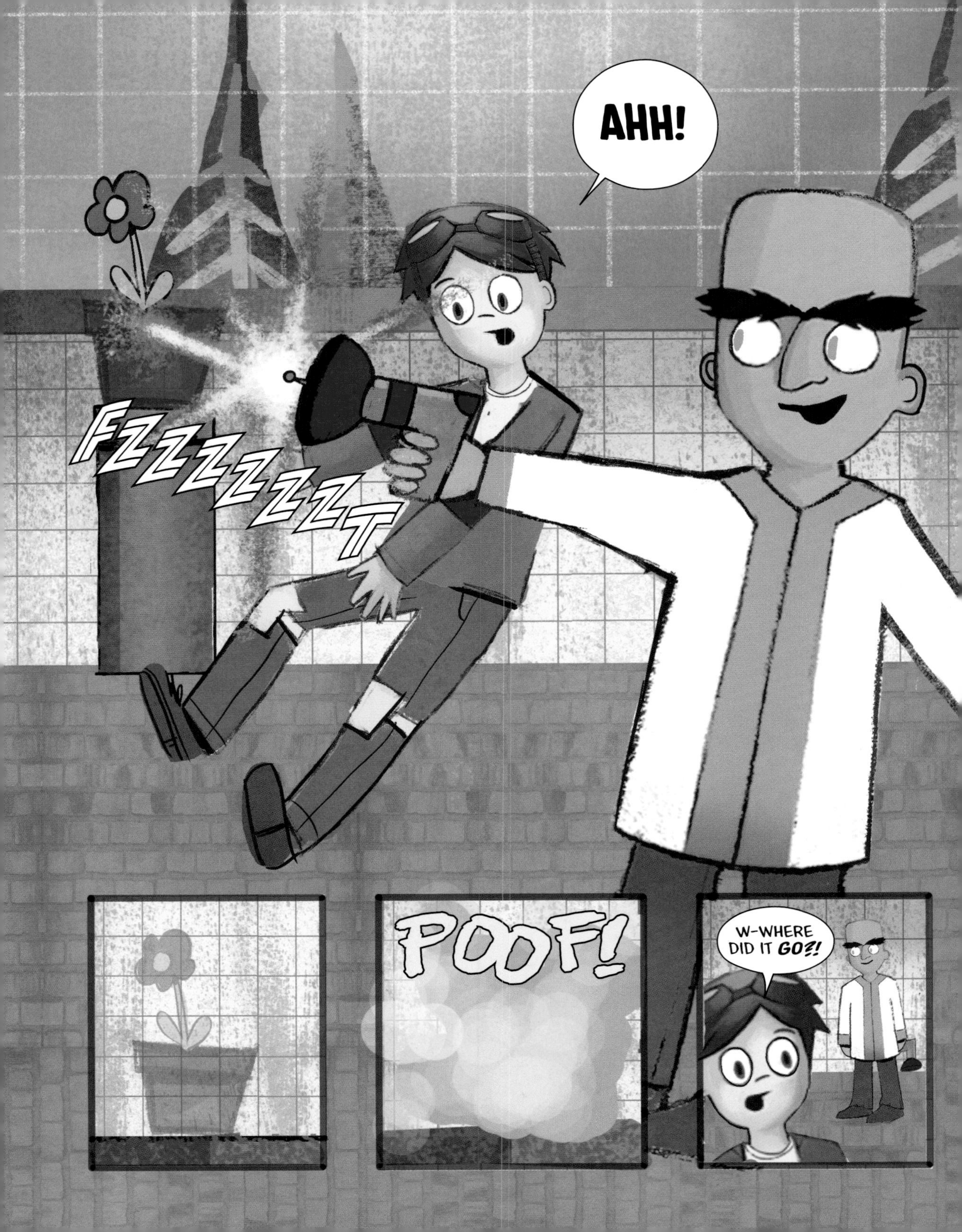
AHH!
FZZZZZZZZT
POOF!
W-WHERE DID IT GO?!

JUST LOOK OVER THERE.
WHOOSH!
CRASH!
IT'S **COOL**, RIGHT?!

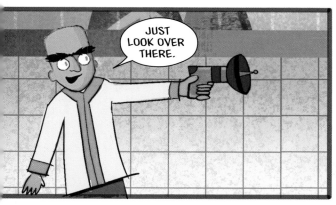

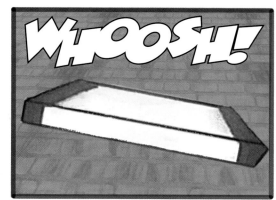

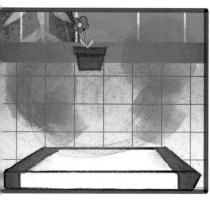

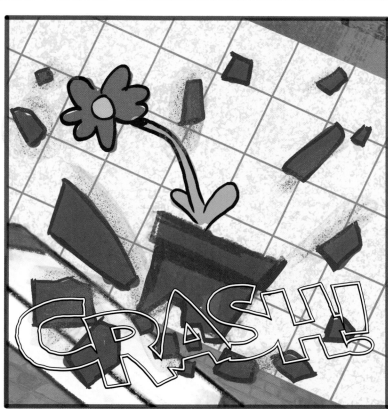

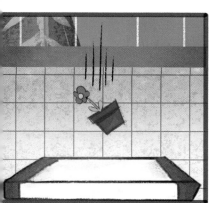

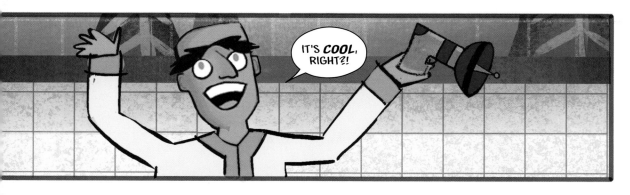

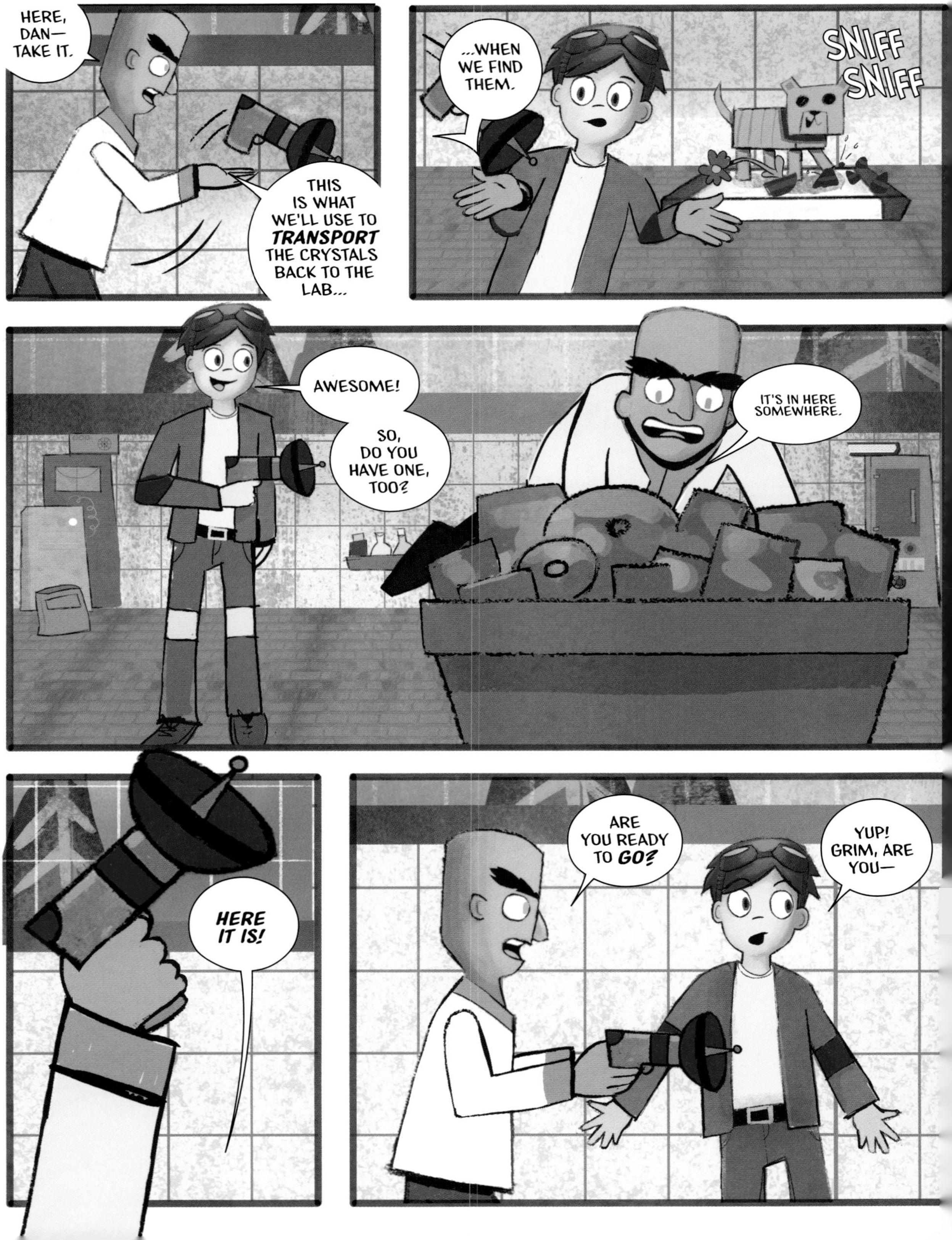
HERE, DAN— TAKE IT.
THIS IS WHAT WE'LL USE TO ***TRANSPORT*** THE CRYSTALS BACK TO THE LAB...
...WHEN WE FIND THEM.
SNIFF SNIFF
AWESOME!
SO, DO YOU HAVE ONE, TOO?
IT'S IN HERE SOMEWHERE.
HERE IT IS!
ARE YOU READY TO ***GO?***
YUP! GRIM, ARE YOU—

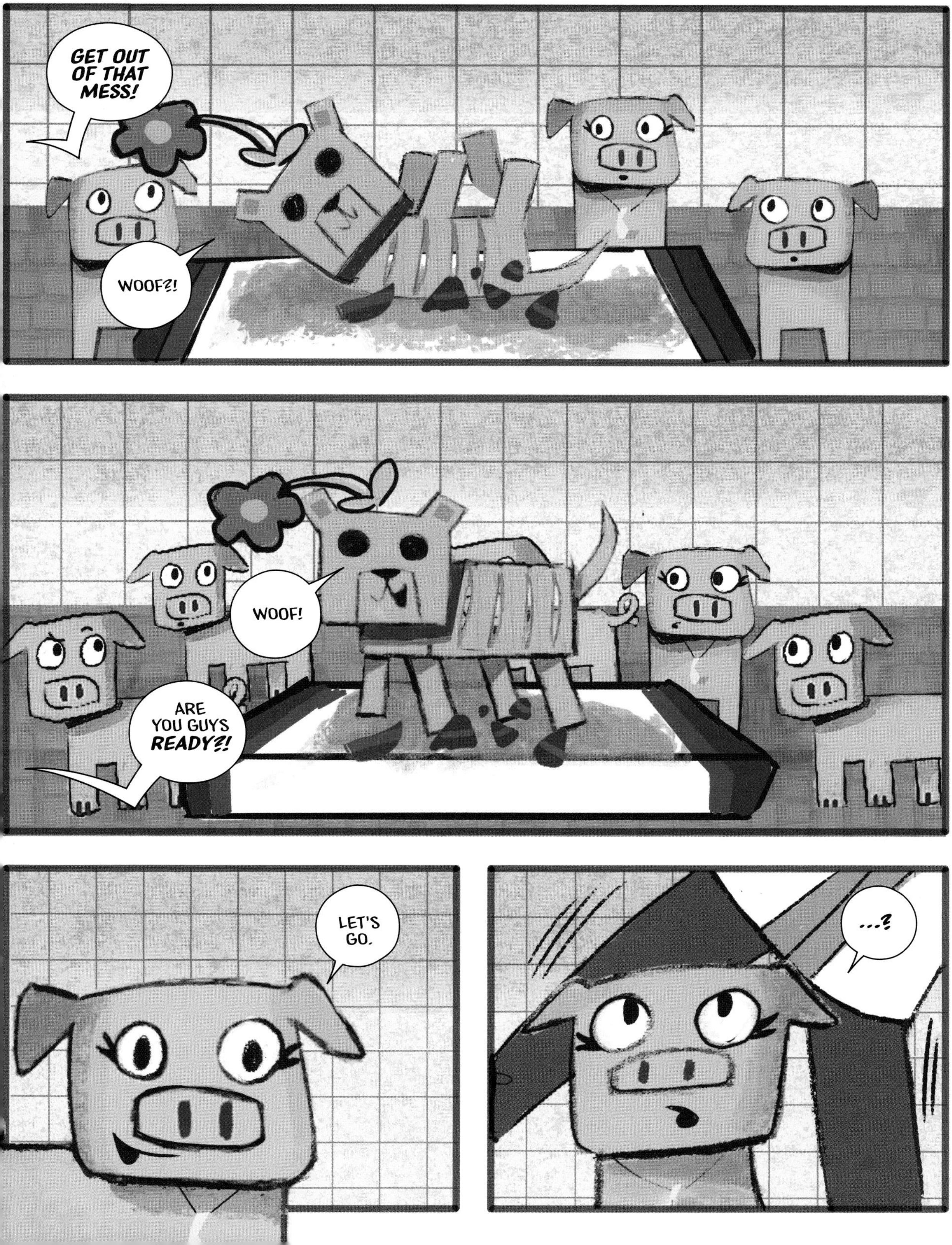
GET OUT OF THAT MESS!
WOOF?!
WOOF!
ARE YOU GUYS READY?!
LET'S GO.
...?

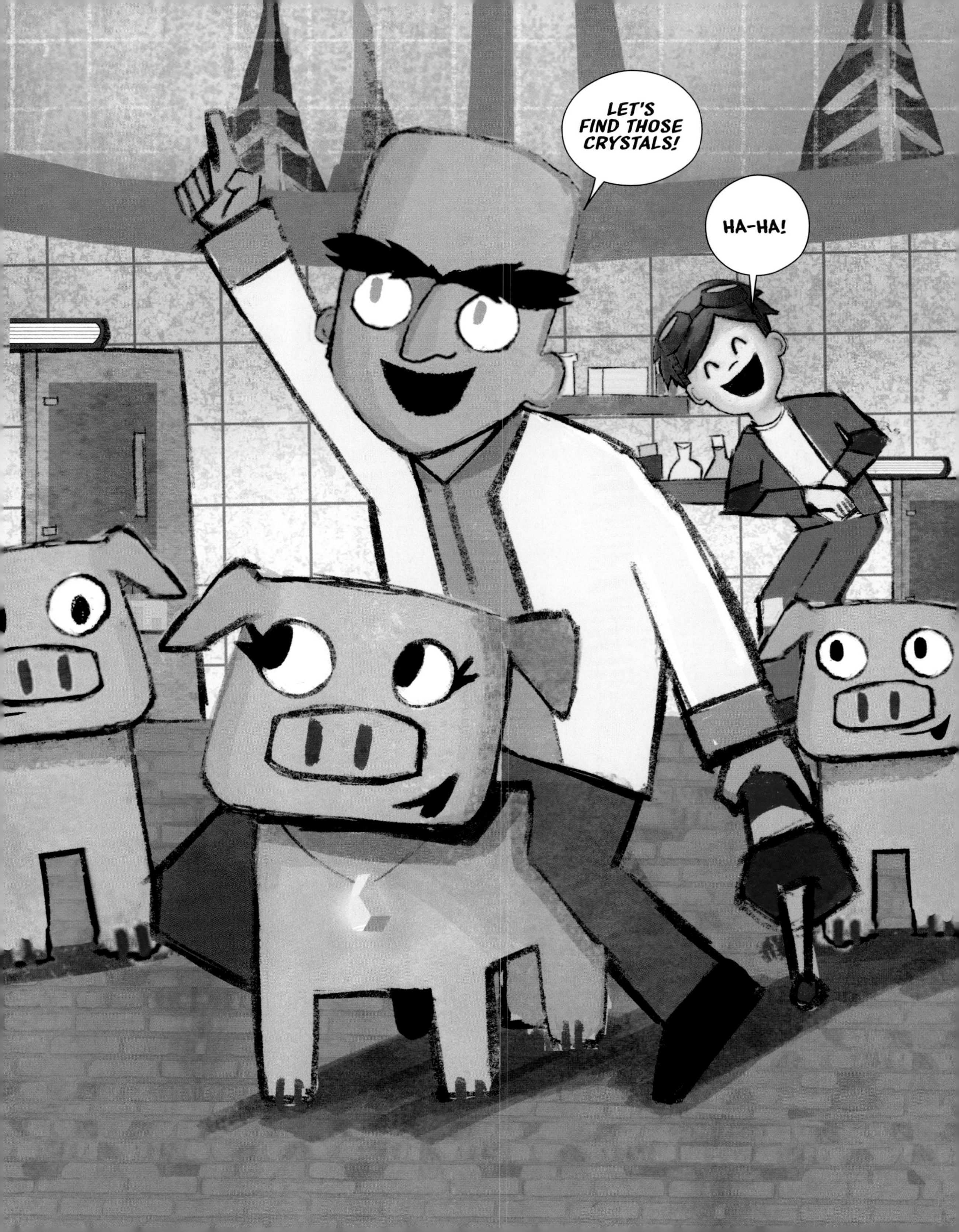
LET'S FIND THOSE CRYSTALS!
HA-HA!

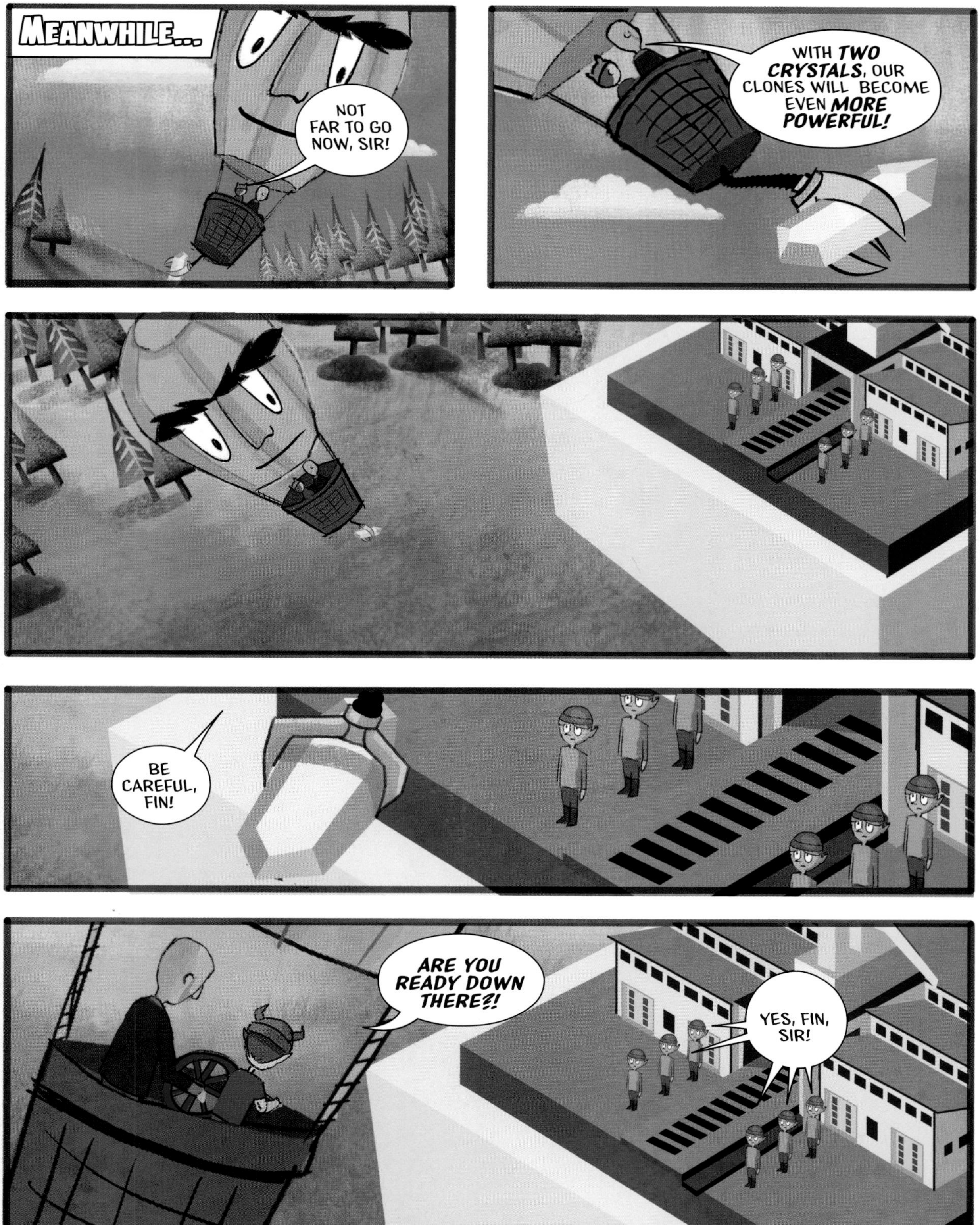
MEANWHILE...
NOT FAR TO GO NOW, SIR!
WITH **TWO CRYSTALS**, OUR CLONES WILL BECOME EVEN **MORE POWERFUL!**
BE CAREFUL, FIN!
ARE YOU READY DOWN THERE?!
YES, FIN, SIR!

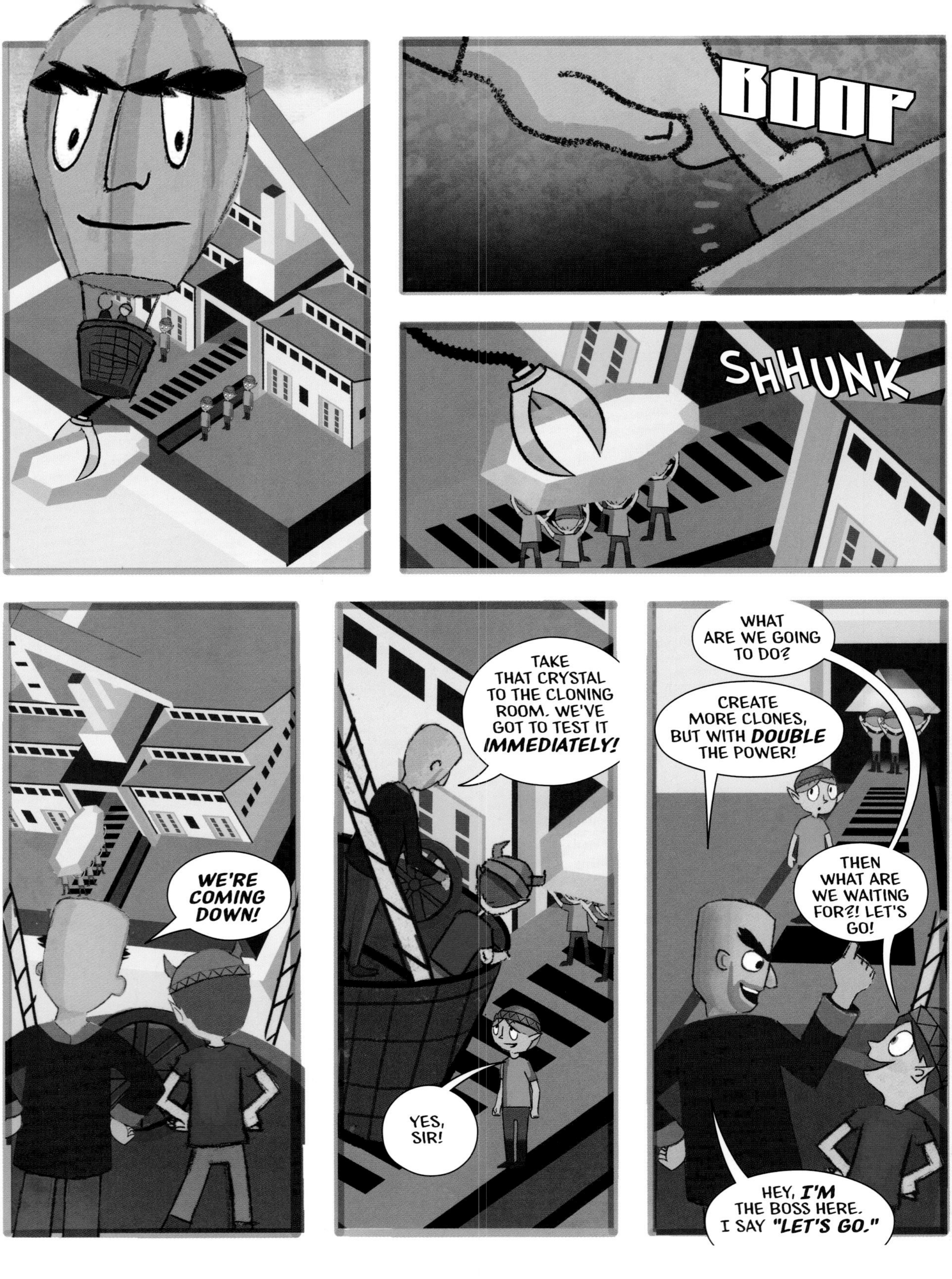
BOOP
SHHUNK
WE'RE COMING DOWN!
TAKE THAT CRYSTAL TO THE CLONING ROOM. WE'VE GOT TO TEST IT IMMEDIATELY!
YES, SIR!
WHAT ARE WE GOING TO DO?
CREATE MORE CLONES, BUT WITH DOUBLE THE POWER!
THEN WHAT ARE WE WAITING FOR?! LET'S GO!
HEY, I'M THE BOSS HERE. I SAY "LET'S GO."

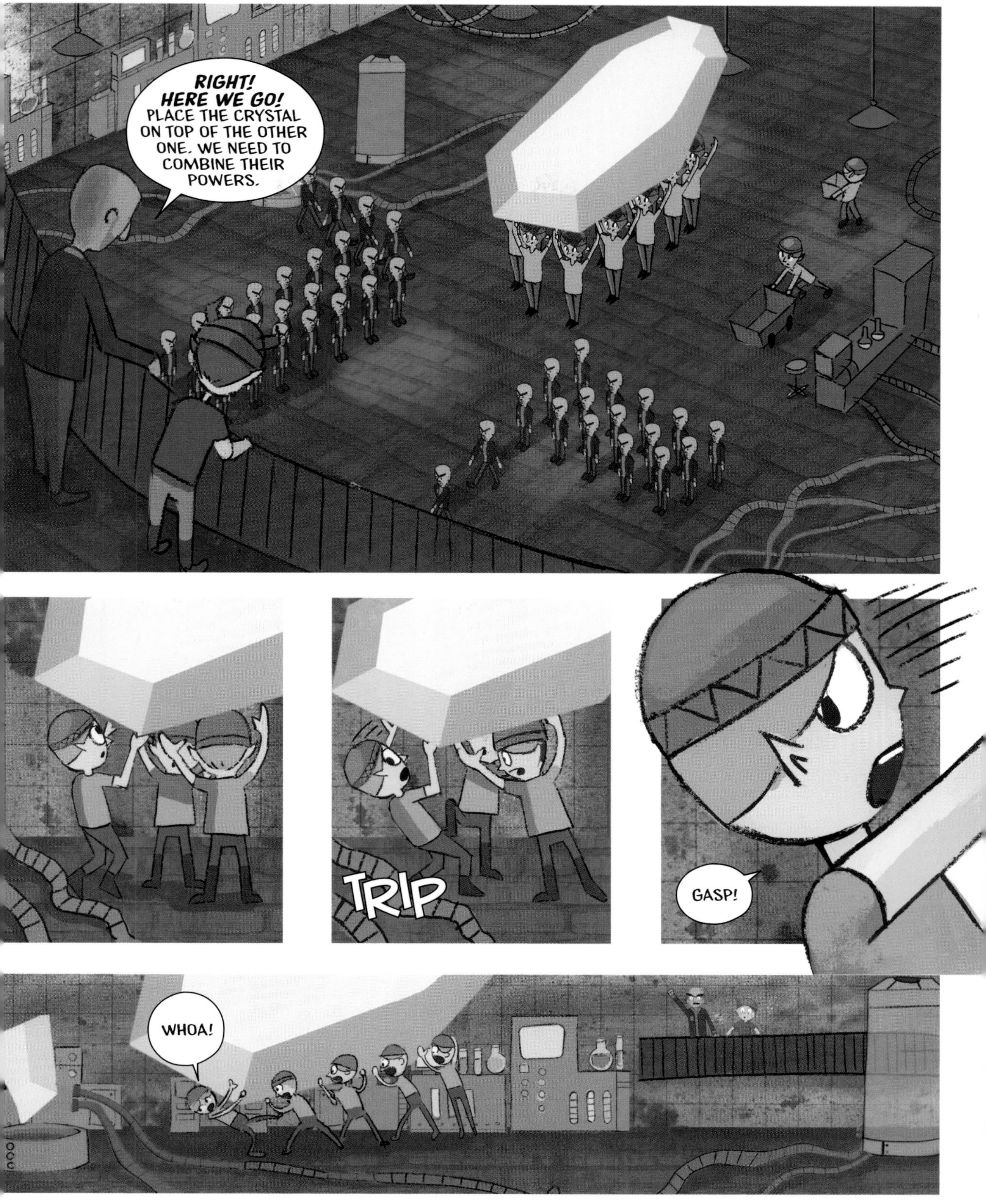
RIGHT! HERE WE GO! PLACE THE CRYSTAL ON TOP OF THE OTHER ONE. WE NEED TO COMBINE THEIR POWERS.
TRIP
GASP!
WHOA!

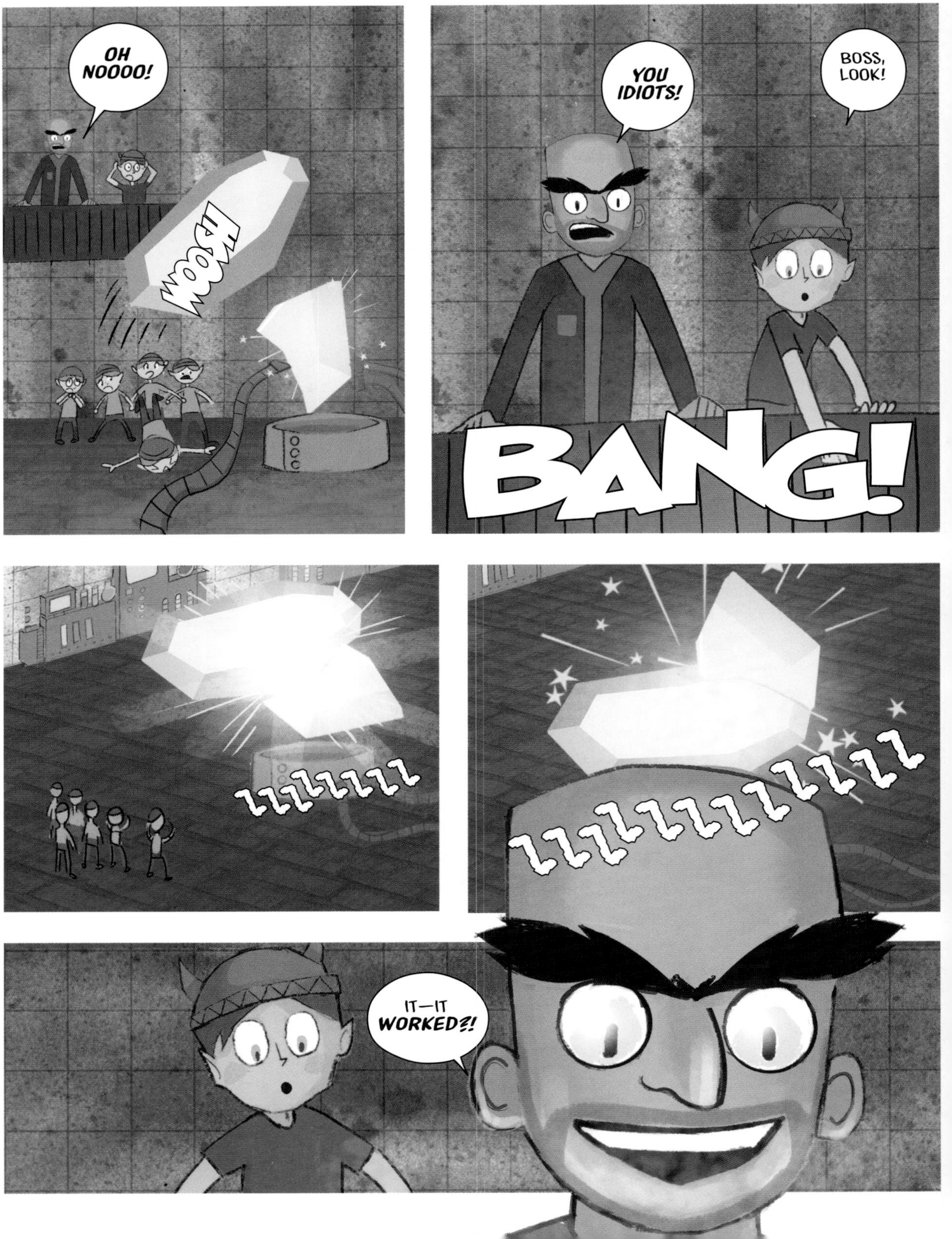
OH NOOOO!
FWOOM
YOU IDIOTS!
BOSS, LOOK!
BANG!
ZZZZZZZZ
ZZZZZZZZZZZZZ
IT—IT WORKED?!

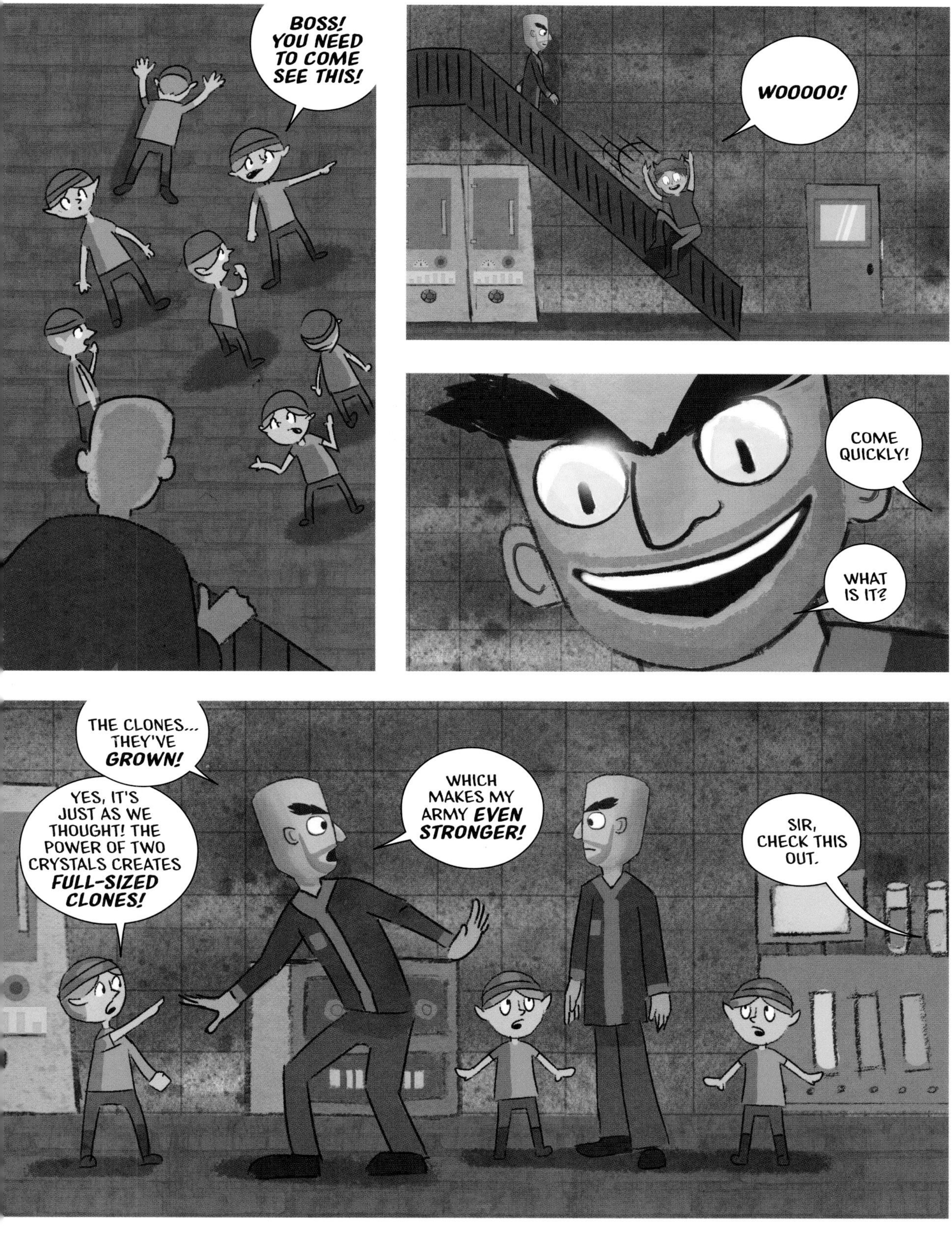
BOSS! YOU NEED TO COME SEE THIS!
WOOOOO!
COME QUICKLY!
WHAT IS IT?
THE CLONES... THEY'VE **GROWN!**
YES, IT'S JUST AS WE THOUGHT! THE POWER OF TWO CRYSTALS CREATES **FULL-SIZED CLONES!**
WHICH MAKES MY ARMY **EVEN STRONGER!**
SIR, CHECK THIS OUT.

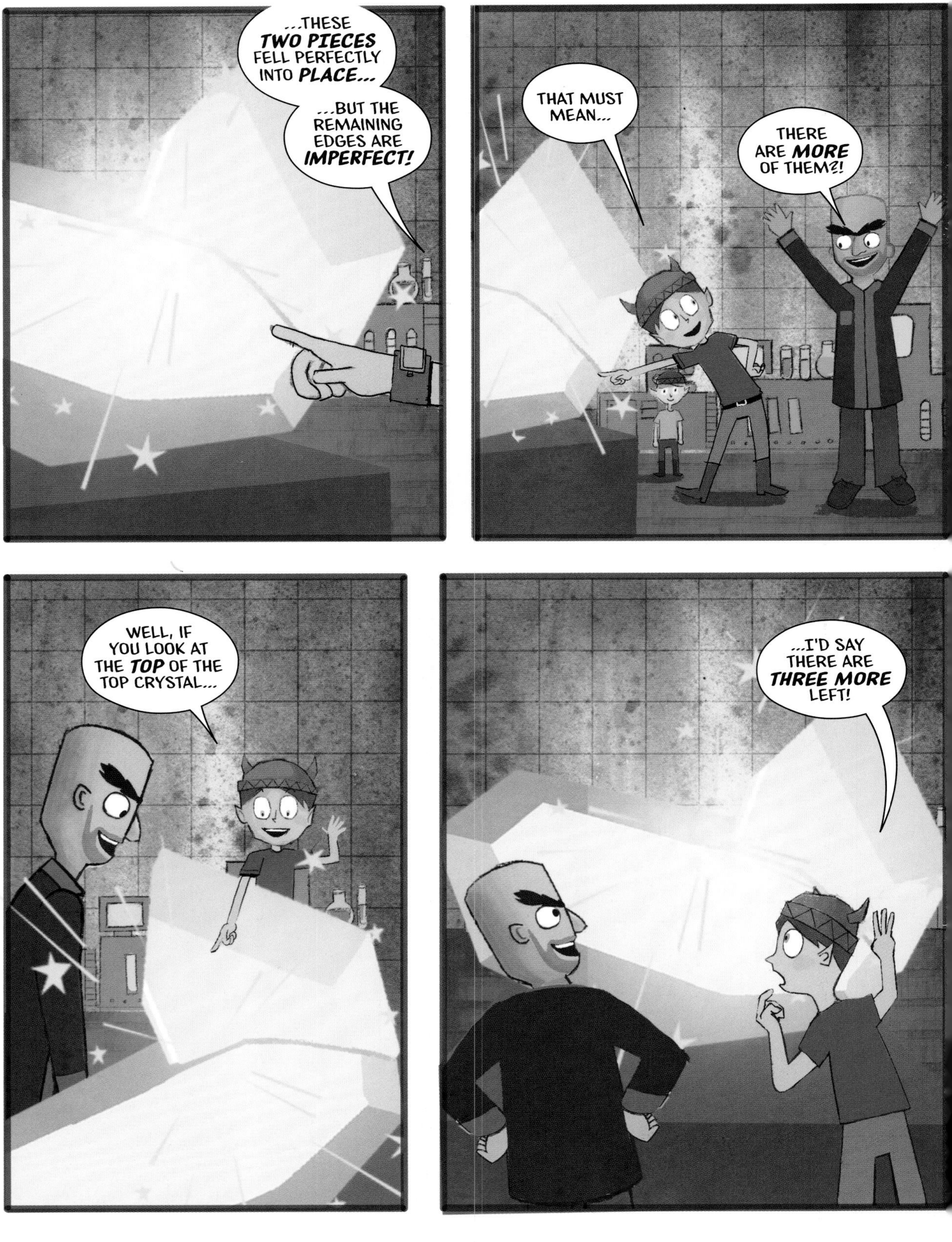

...THESE TWO PIECES FELL PERFECTLY INTO PLACE...
...BUT THE REMAINING EDGES ARE IMPERFECT!
THAT MUST MEAN...
THERE ARE MORE OF THEM?!
WELL, IF YOU LOOK AT THE TOP OF THE TOP CRYSTAL...
...I'D SAY THERE ARE THREE MORE LEFT!

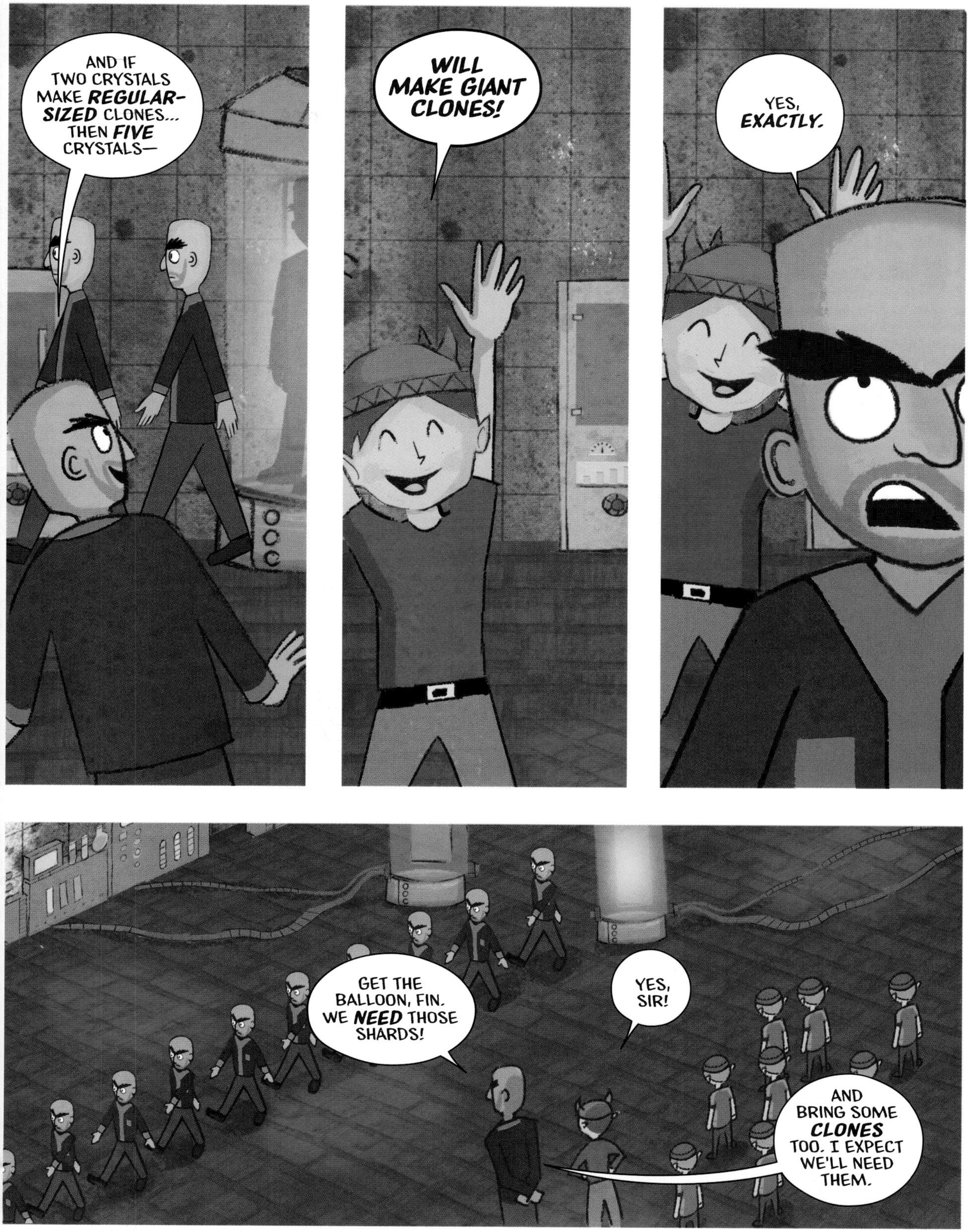
AND IF TWO CRYSTALS MAKE REGULAR-SIZED CLONES... THEN FIVE CRYSTALS—
WILL MAKE GIANT CLONES!
YES, EXACTLY.
GET THE BALLOON, FIN. WE NEED THOSE SHARDS!
YES, SIR!
AND BRING SOME CLONES TOO. I EXPECT WE'LL NEED THEM.

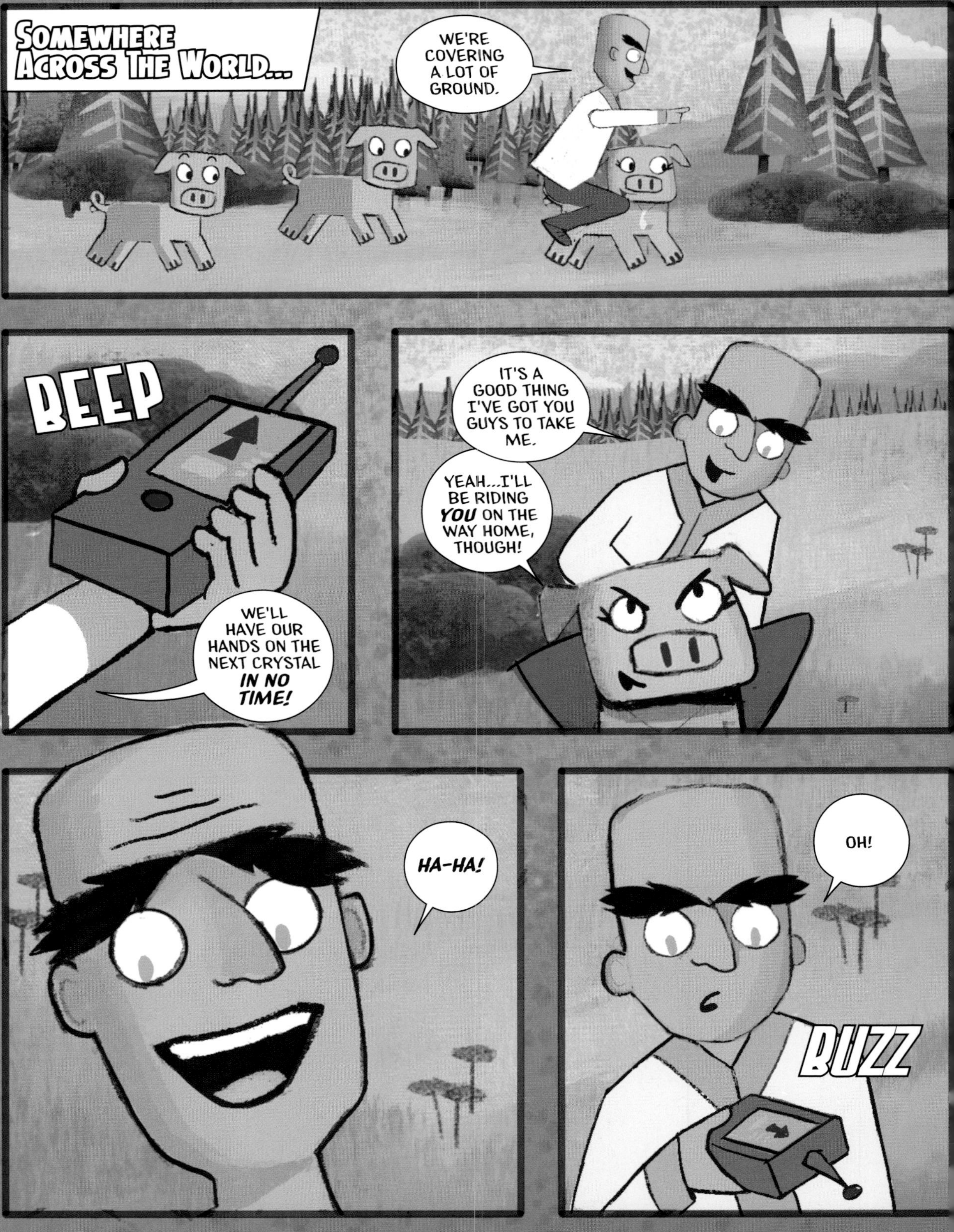
SOMEWHERE ACROSS THE WORLD...
WE'RE COVERING A LOT OF GROUND.
BEEP
WE'LL HAVE OUR HANDS ON THE NEXT CRYSTAL IN NO TIME!
IT'S A GOOD THING I'VE GOT YOU GUYS TO TAKE ME.
YEAH...I'LL BE RIDING YOU ON THE WAY HOME, THOUGH!
HA-HA!
OH!
BUZZ

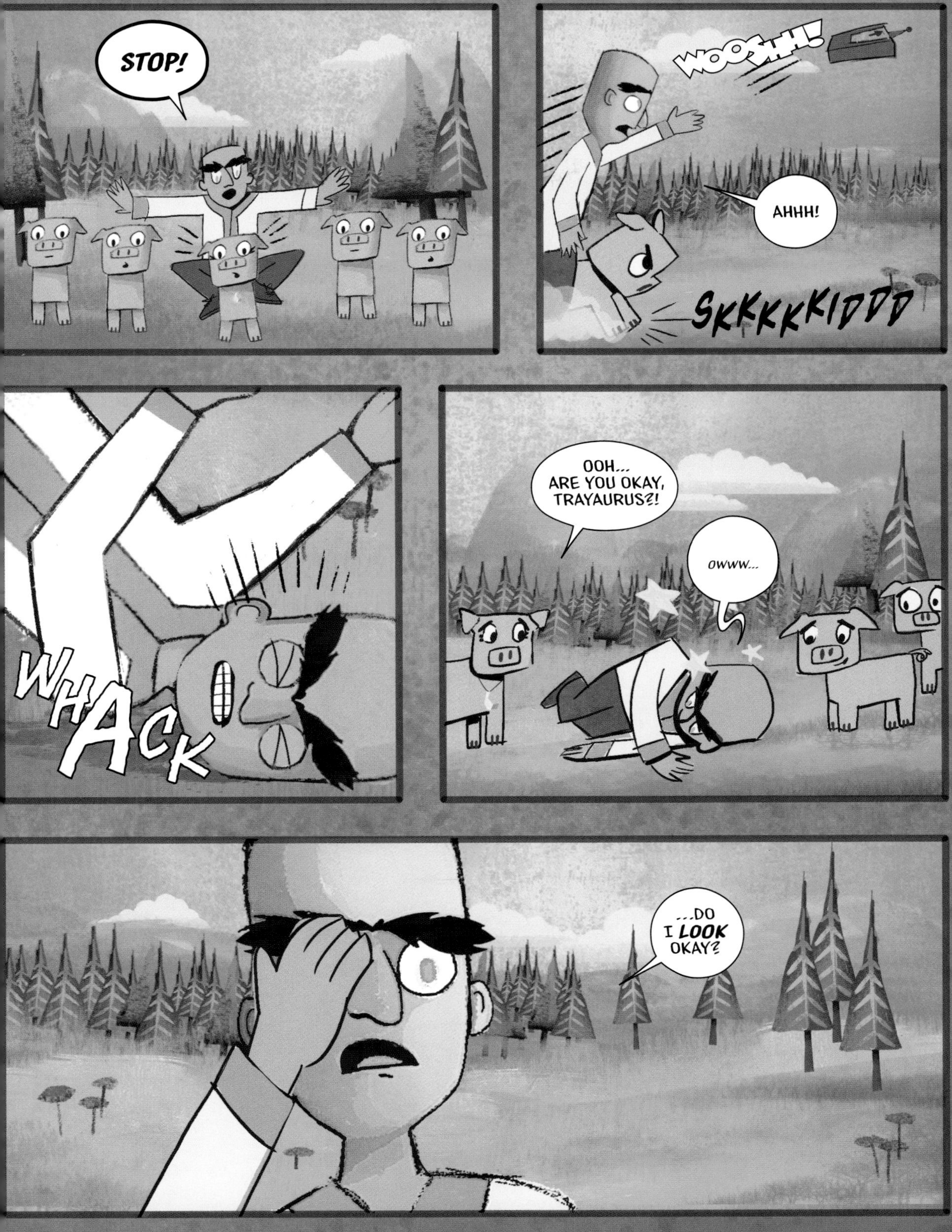
STOP!
WOOSHH!
AHHH!
SKKKKKIDDD
WHACK
OOH... ARE YOU OKAY, TRAYAURUS?!
OWWW...
...DO I LOOK OKAY?

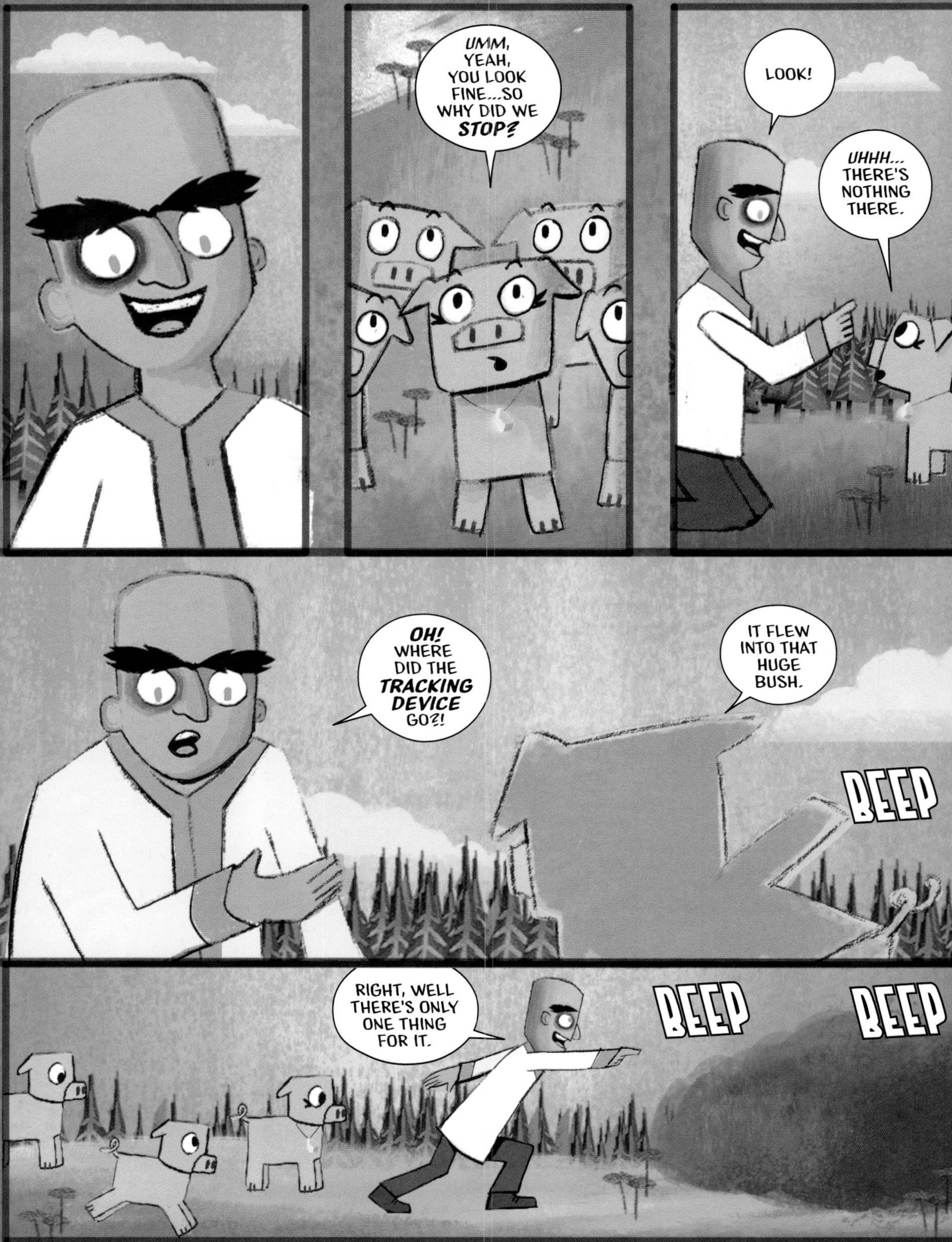
UMM, YEAH, YOU LOOK FINE...SO WHY DID WE STOP?
LOOK!
UHHH... THERE'S NOTHING THERE.
OH! WHERE DID THE TRACKING DEVICE GO?!
IT FLEW INTO THAT HUGE BUSH.
BEEP
RIGHT, WELL THERE'S ONLY ONE THING FOR IT.
BEEP
BEEP

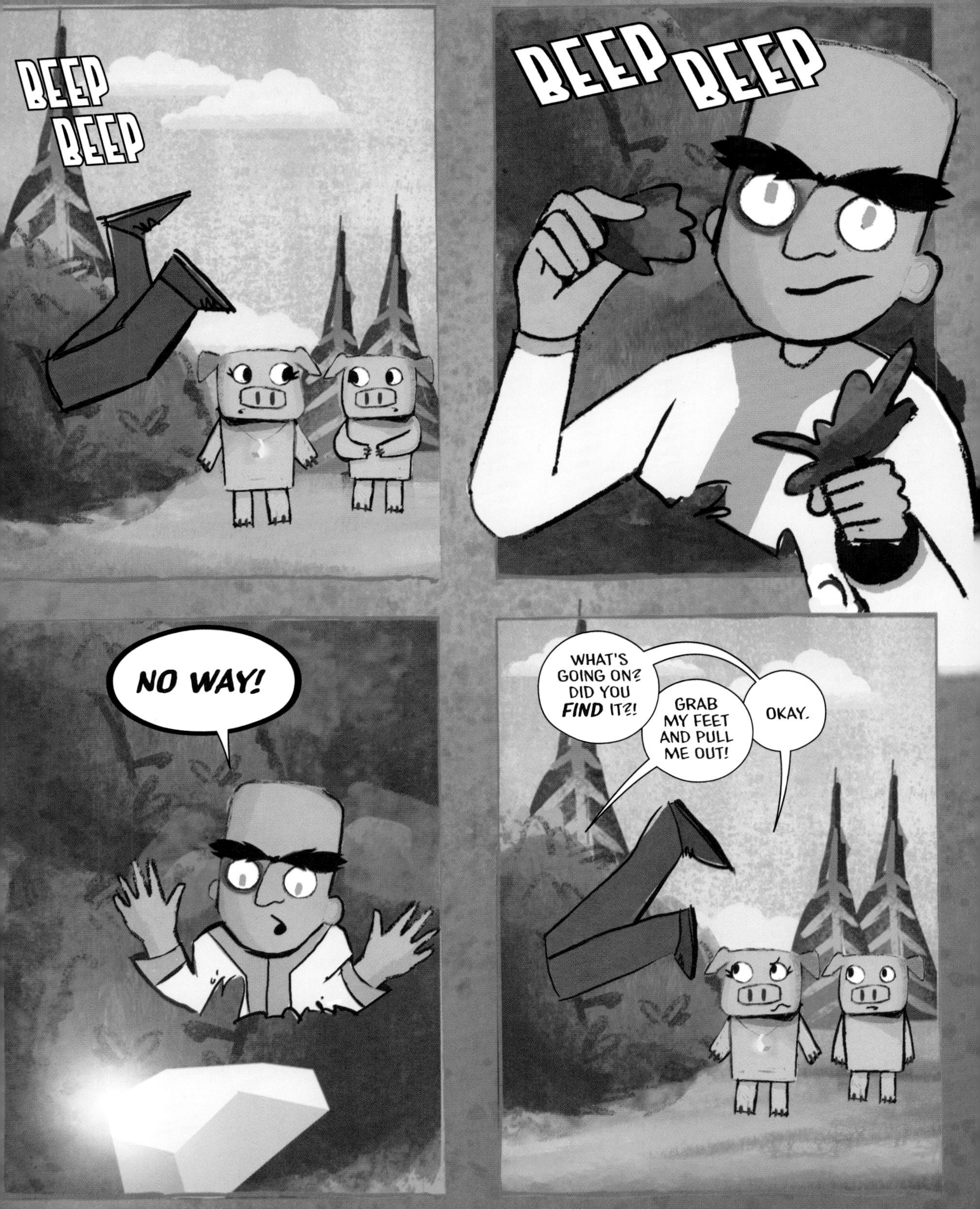
BEEP BEEP
BEEP BEEP
NO WAY!
WHAT'S GOING ON? DID YOU FIND IT?!
GRAB MY FEET AND PULL ME OUT!
OKAY.

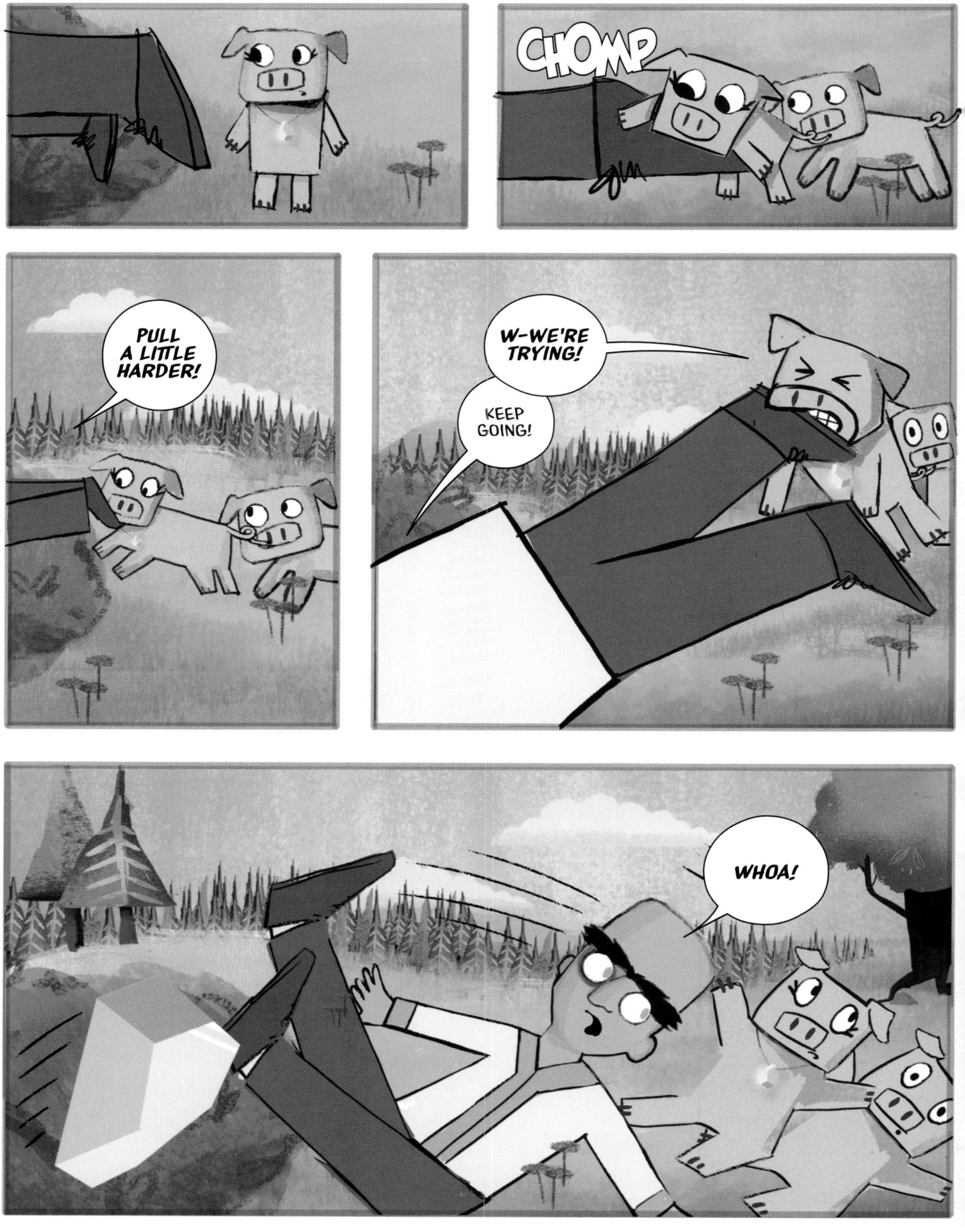
CHOMP
PULL A LITTLE HARDER!
W-WE'RE TRYING!
KEEP GOING!
WHOA!

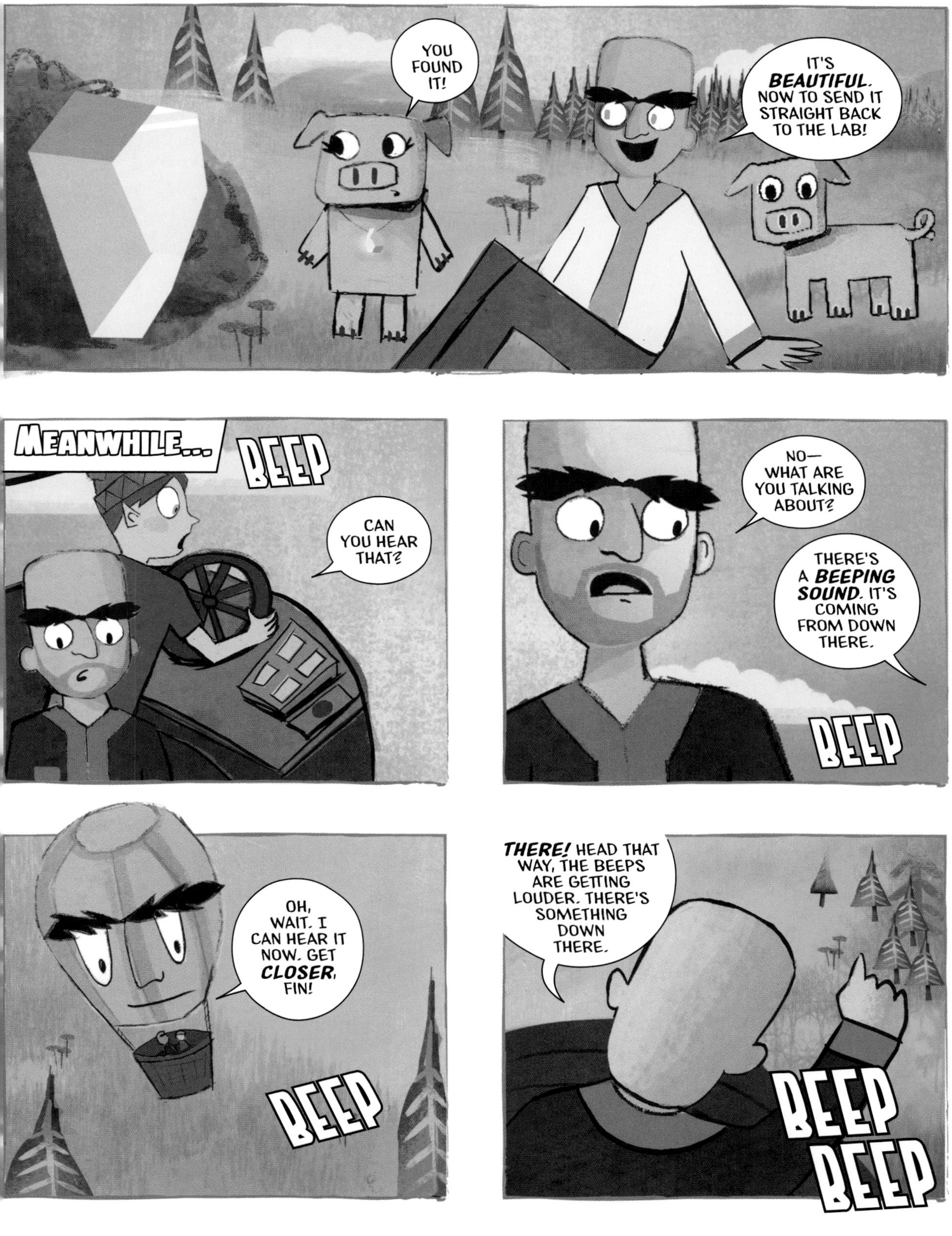
YOU FOUND IT!
IT'S BEAUTIFUL. NOW TO SEND IT STRAIGHT BACK TO THE LAB!
MEANWHILE...
BEEP
CAN YOU HEAR THAT?
NO— WHAT ARE YOU TALKING ABOUT?
THERE'S A BEEPING SOUND. IT'S COMING FROM DOWN THERE.
BEEP
OH, WAIT. I CAN HEAR IT NOW. GET CLOSER, FIN!
BEEP
THERE! HEAD THAT WAY, THE BEEPS ARE GETTING LOUDER. THERE'S SOMETHING DOWN THERE.
BEEP
BEEP

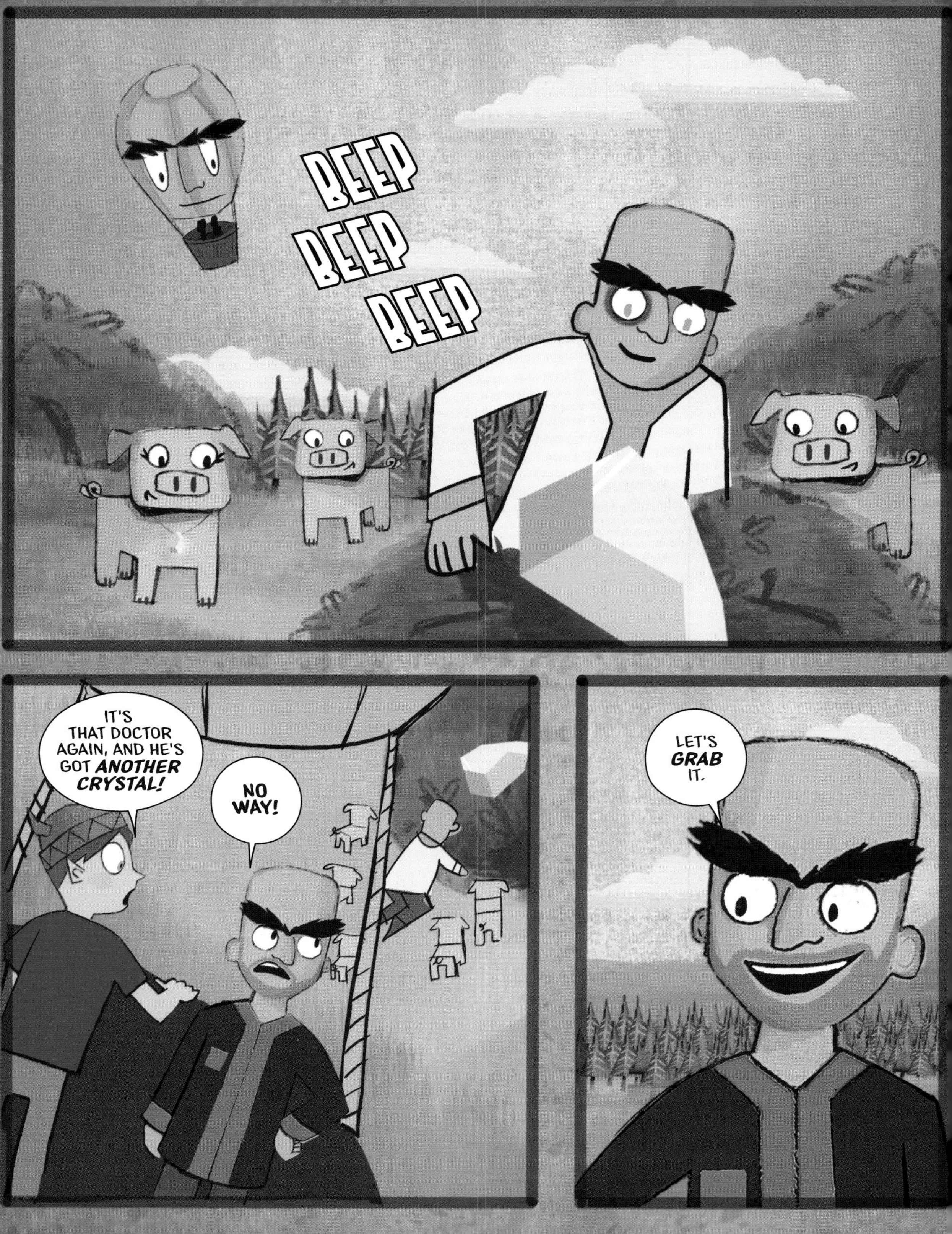
BEEP
BEEP
BEEP
IT'S THAT DOCTOR AGAIN, AND HE'S GOT ANOTHER CRYSTAL!
NO WAY!
LET'S GRAB IT.

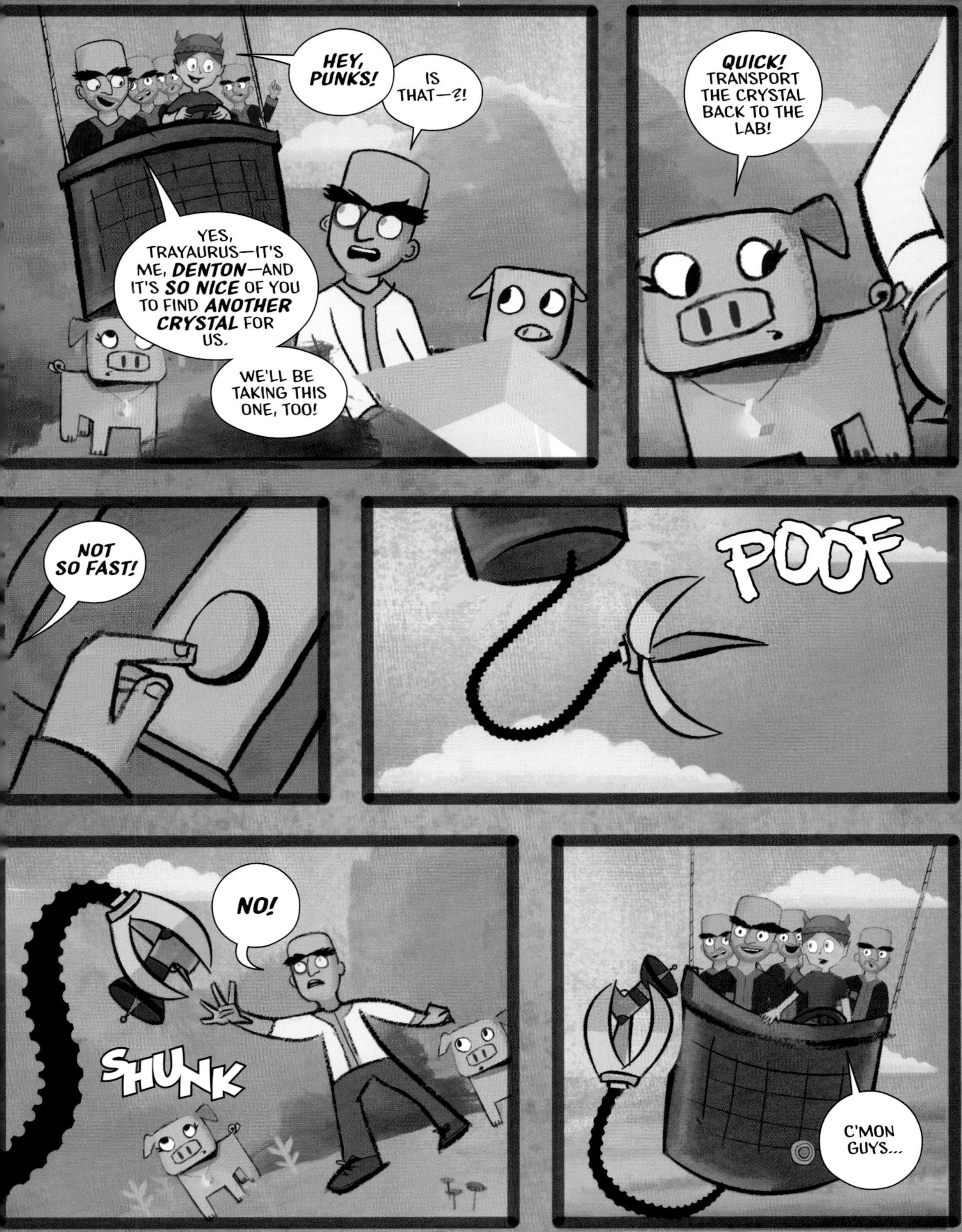
HEY, PUNKS!
IS THAT—?!
YES, TRAYAURUS—IT'S ME, DENTON—AND IT'S SO NICE OF YOU TO FIND ANOTHER CRYSTAL FOR US.
WE'LL BE TAKING THIS ONE, TOO!
QUICK! TRANSPORT THE CRYSTAL BACK TO THE LAB!
NOT SO FAST!
POOF
NO!
SHUNK
C'MON GUYS...

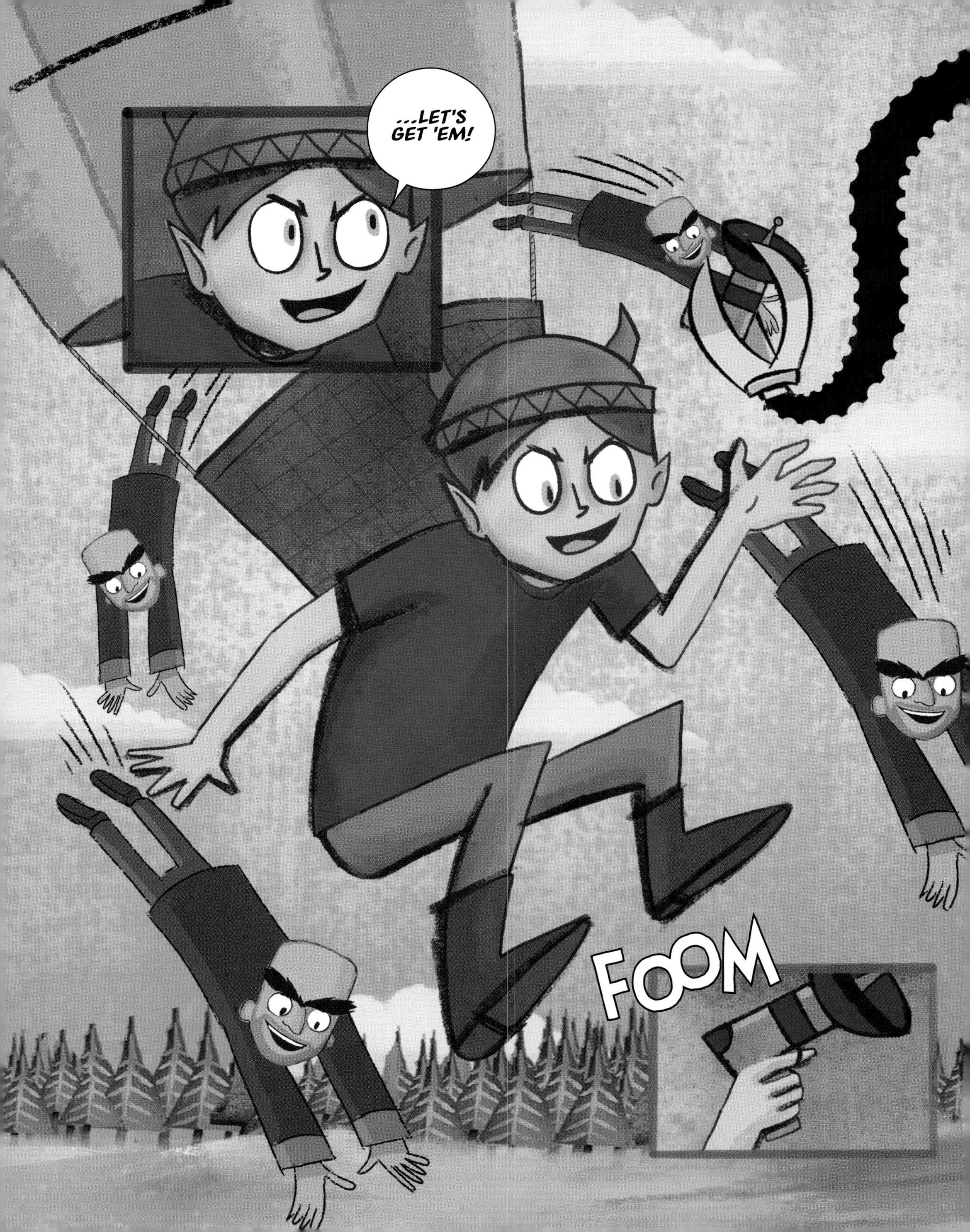
...LET'S GET 'EM!
FOOM

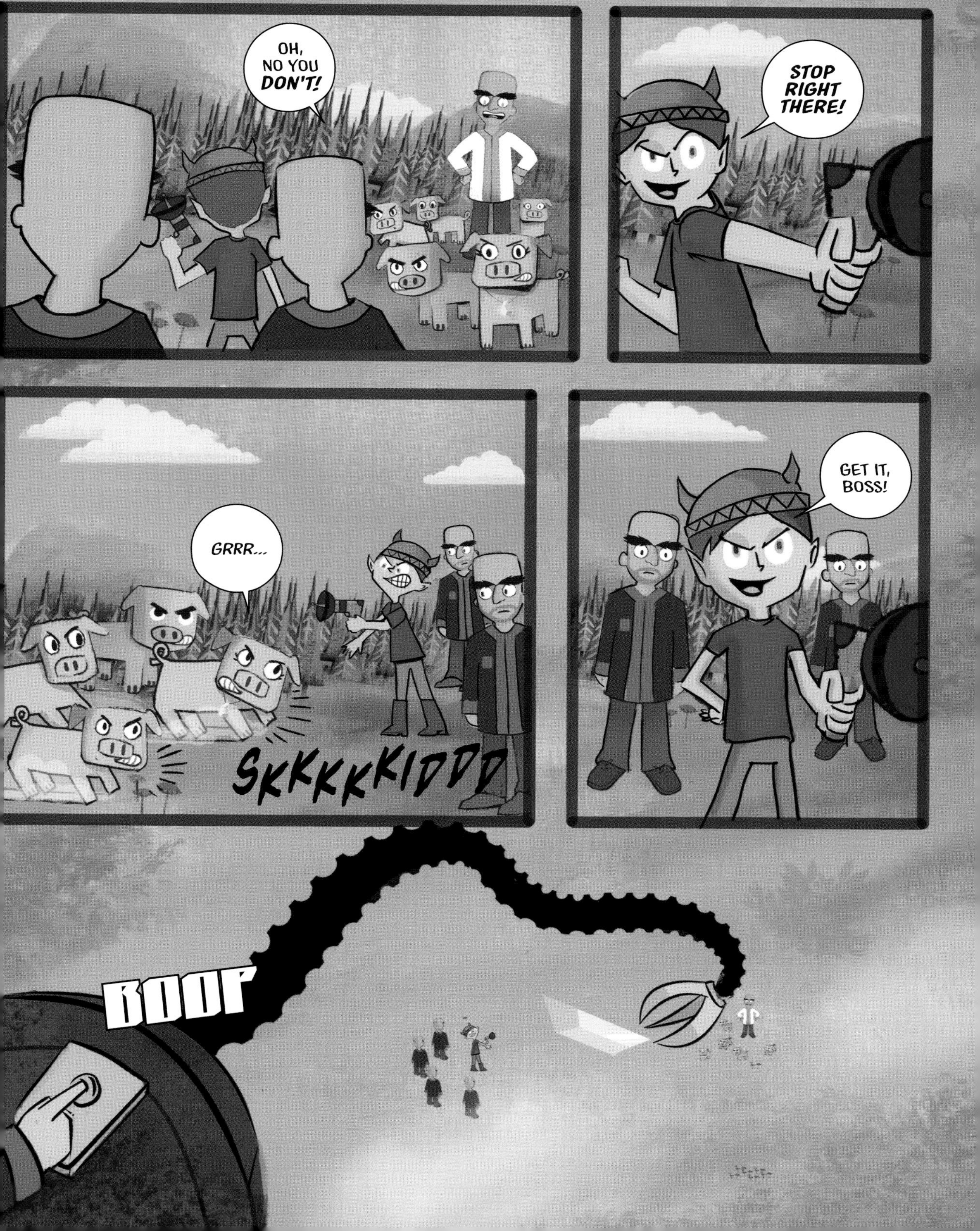
OH, NO YOU DON'T!
STOP RIGHT THERE!
GRRR...
SKKKKKIDDD
GET IT, BOSS!
BOOP

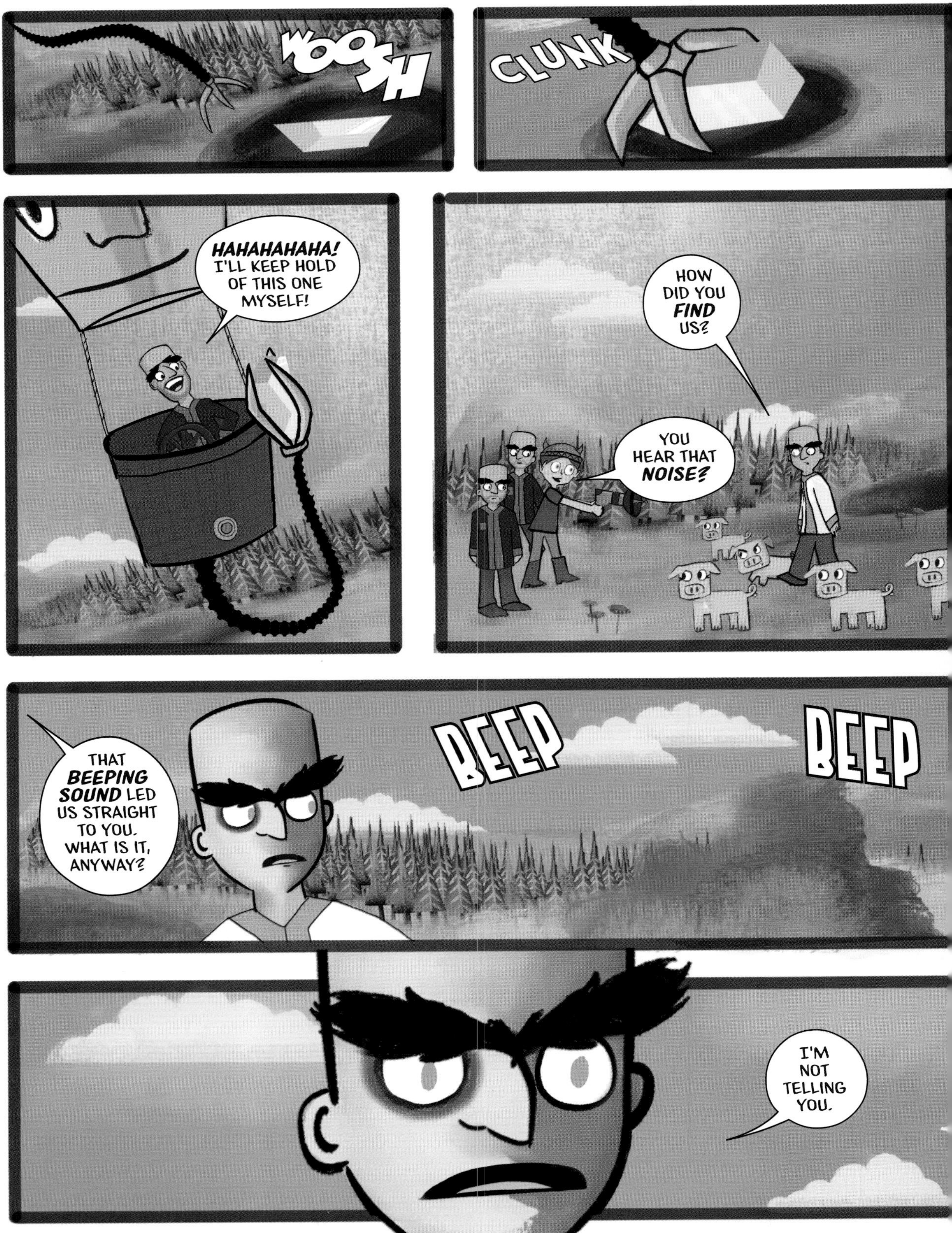
WOOSH
CLUNK
HAHAHAHAHA! I'LL KEEP HOLD OF THIS ONE MYSELF!
HOW DID YOU FIND US?
YOU HEAR THAT NOISE?
THAT BEEPING SOUND LED US STRAIGHT TO YOU. WHAT IS IT, ANYWAY?
BEEP
BEEP
I'M NOT TELLING YOU.

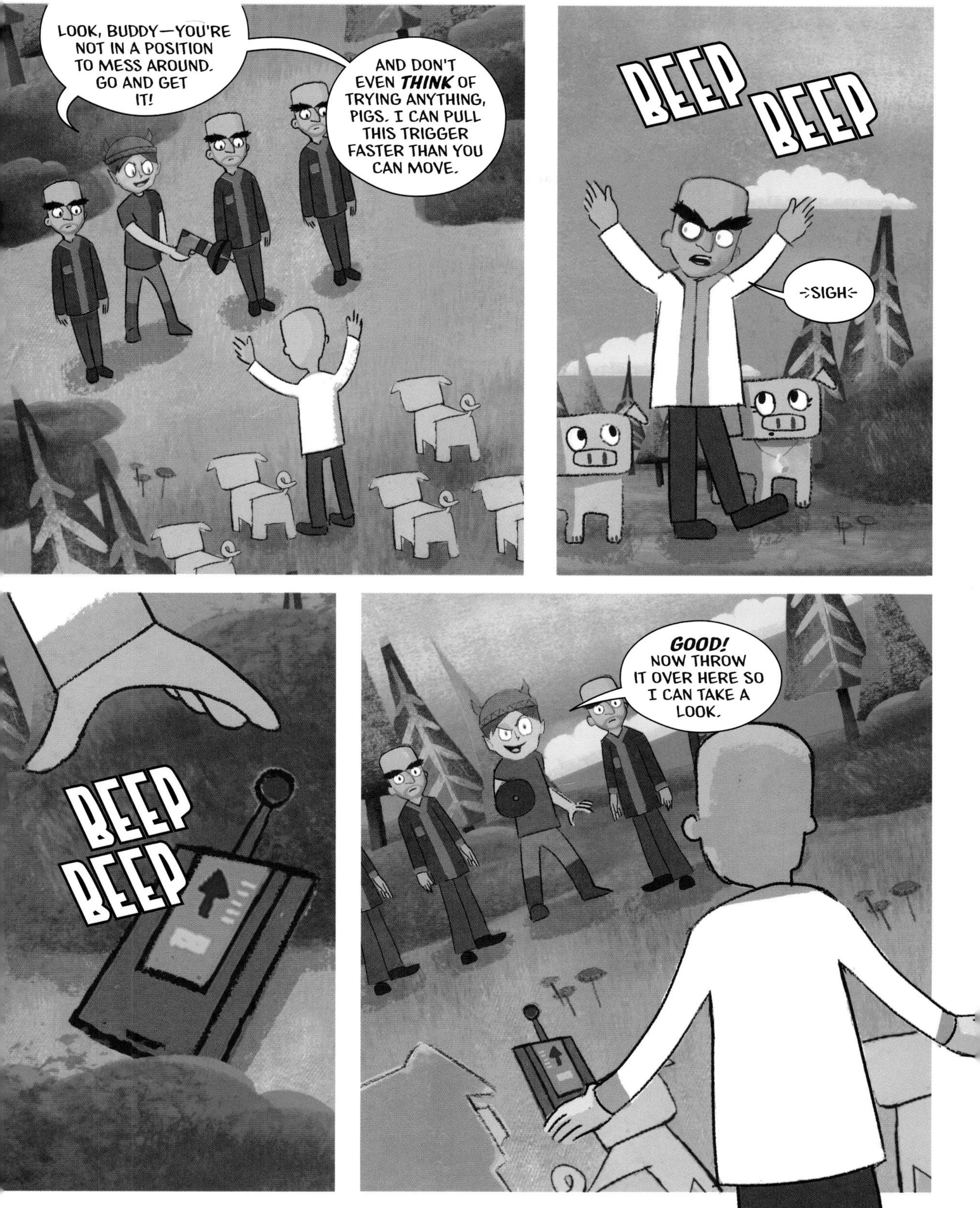
LOOK, BUDDY—YOU'RE NOT IN A POSITION TO MESS AROUND. GO AND GET IT!
AND DON'T EVEN *THINK* OF TRYING ANYTHING, PIGS. I CAN PULL THIS TRIGGER FASTER THAN YOU CAN MOVE.
BEEP BEEP
SIGH
BEEP BEEP
GOOD! NOW THROW IT OVER HERE SO I CAN TAKE A LOOK.

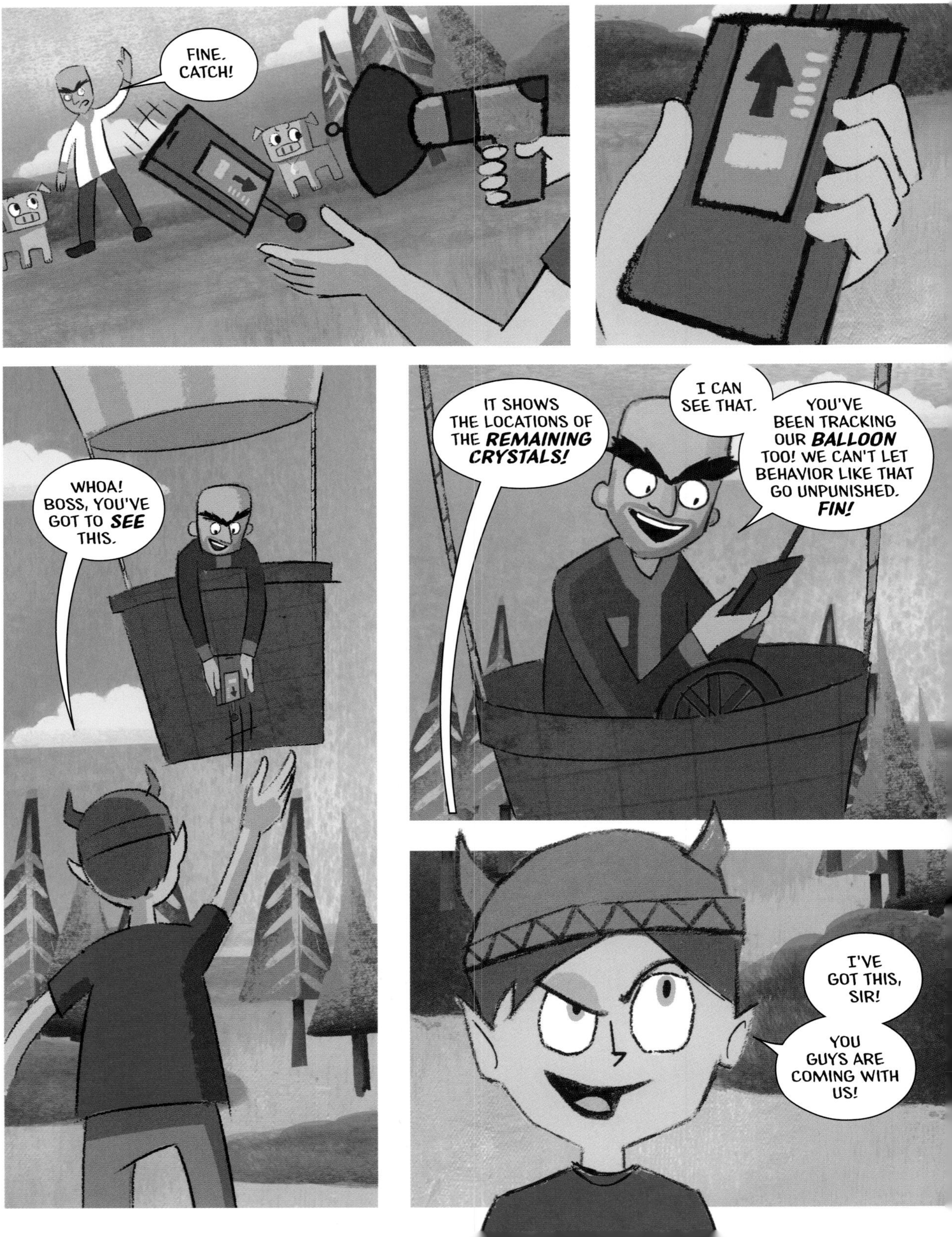
FINE. CATCH!
WHOA! BOSS, YOU'VE GOT TO SEE THIS.
IT SHOWS THE LOCATIONS OF THE REMAINING CRYSTALS!
I CAN SEE THAT.
YOU'VE BEEN TRACKING OUR BALLOON TOO! WE CAN'T LET BEHAVIOR LIKE THAT GO UNPUNISHED. FIN!
I'VE GOT THIS, SIR!
YOU GUYS ARE COMING WITH US!

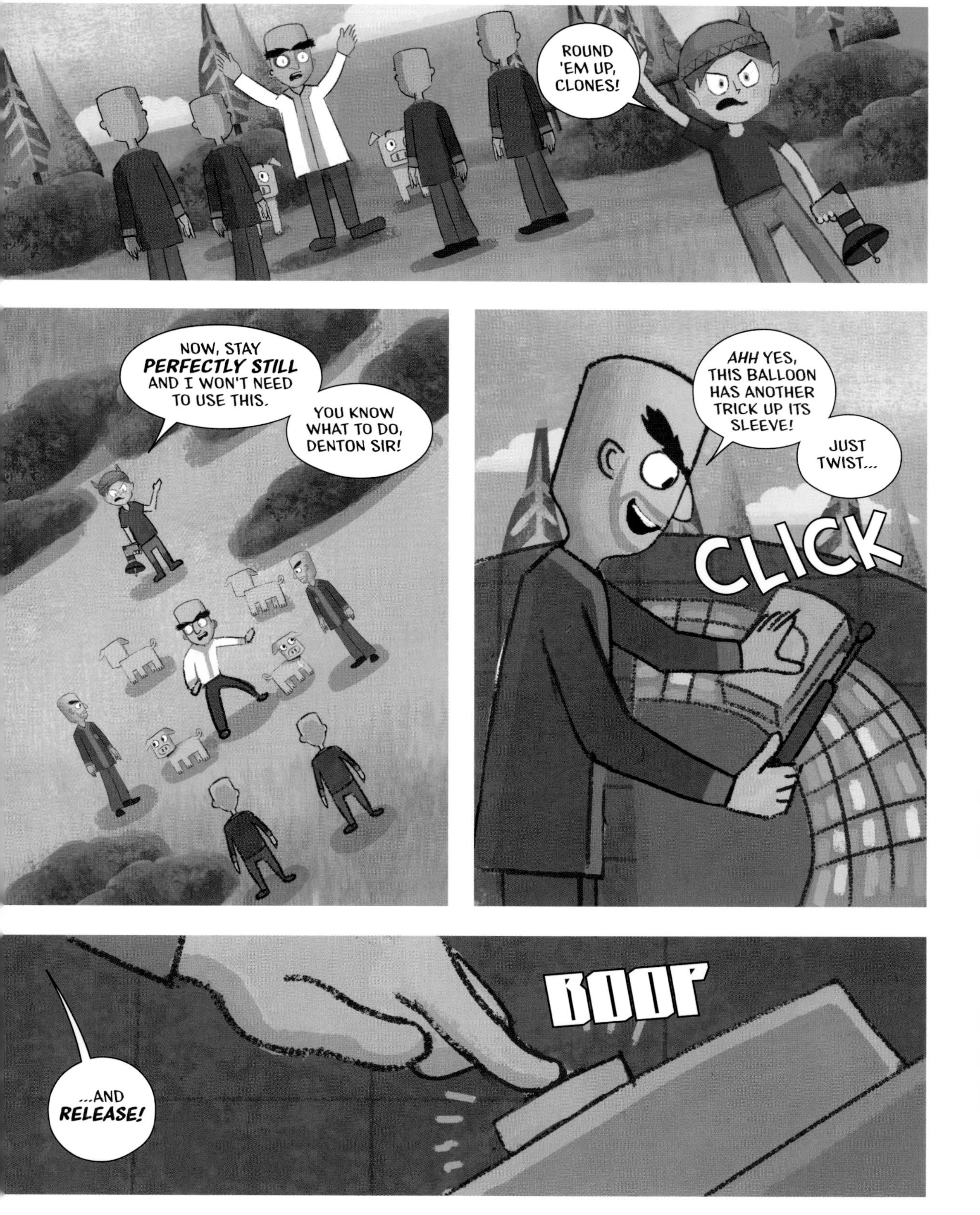
ROUND 'EM UP, CLONES!
NOW, STAY **PERFECTLY STILL** AND I WON'T NEED TO USE THIS.
YOU KNOW WHAT TO DO, DENTON SIR!
AHH YES, THIS BALLOON HAS ANOTHER TRICK UP ITS SLEEVE!
JUST TWIST...
CLICK
...AND ***RELEASE!***
BOOP

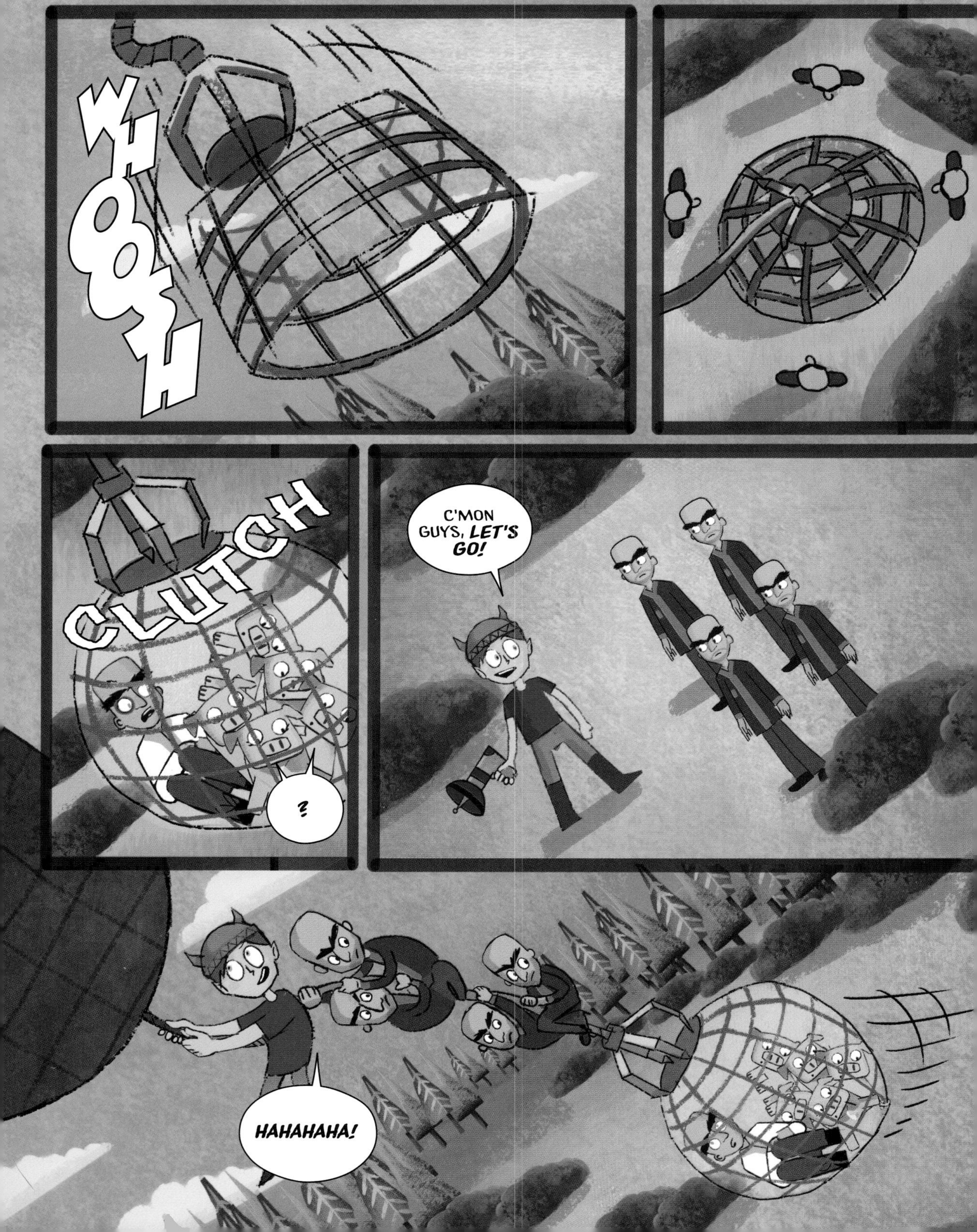
WHOOSH
CLUTCH
?
C'MON GUYS, LET'S GO!
HAHAHAHA!

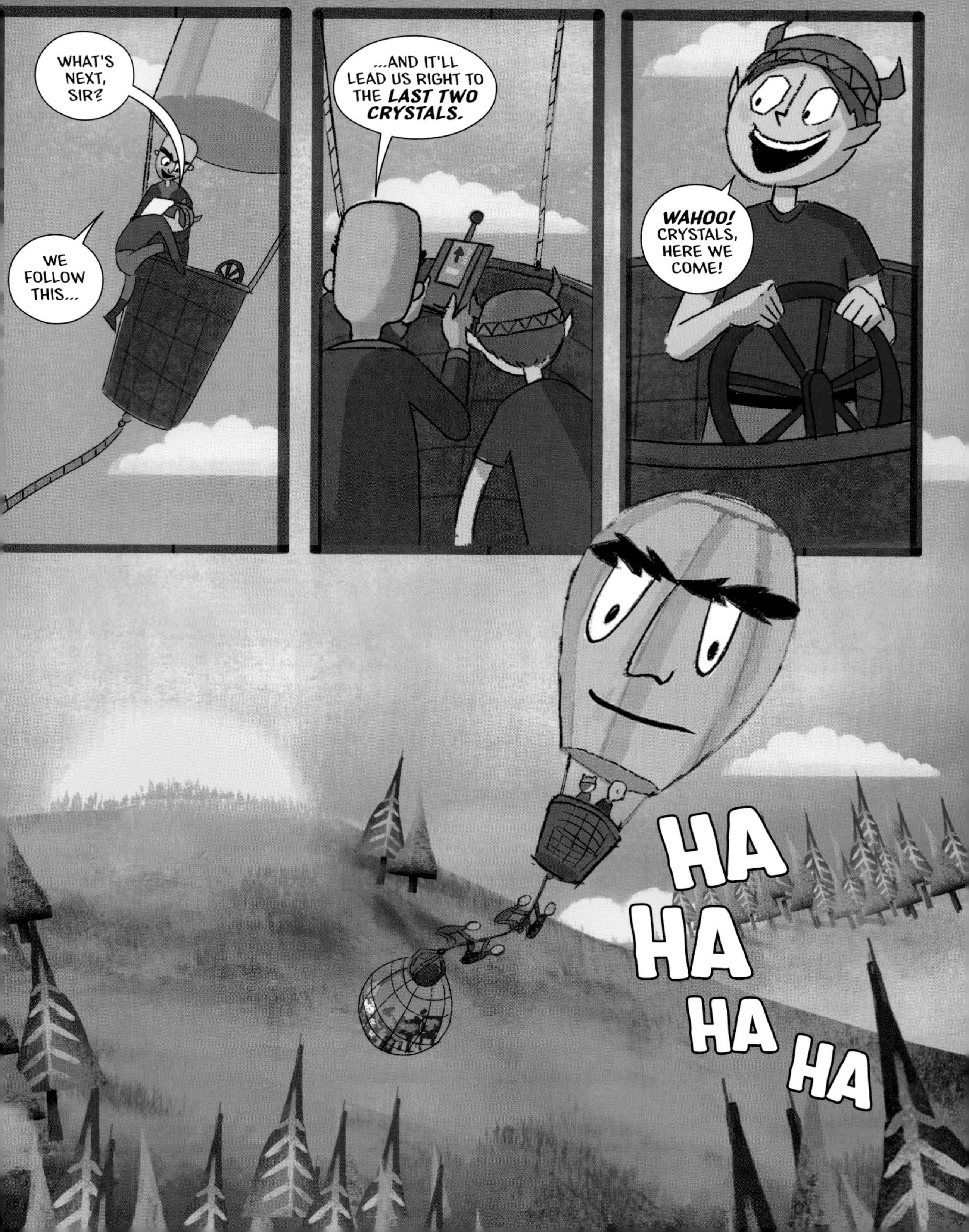
WHAT'S NEXT, SIR?
WE FOLLOW THIS...
...AND IT'LL LEAD US RIGHT TO THE **LAST TWO CRYSTALS.**
WAHOO! CRYSTALS, HERE WE COME!
HA
HA
HA
HA

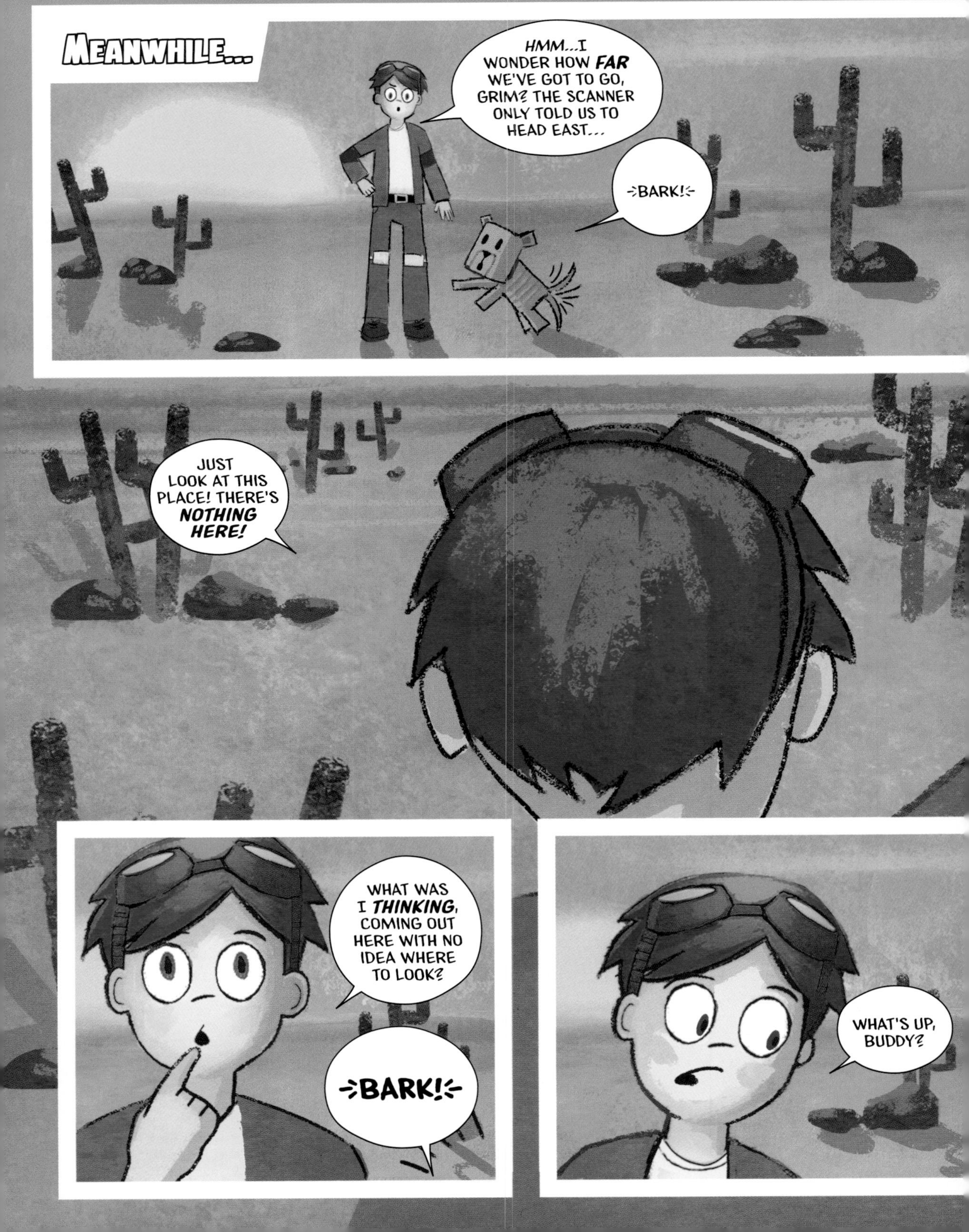
MEANWHILE...
HMM...I WONDER HOW FAR WE'VE GOT TO GO, GRIM? THE SCANNER ONLY TOLD US TO HEAD EAST...
BARK!
JUST LOOK AT THIS PLACE! THERE'S NOTHING HERE!
WHAT WAS I THINKING, COMING OUT HERE WITH NO IDEA WHERE TO LOOK?
BARK!
WHAT'S UP, BUDDY?

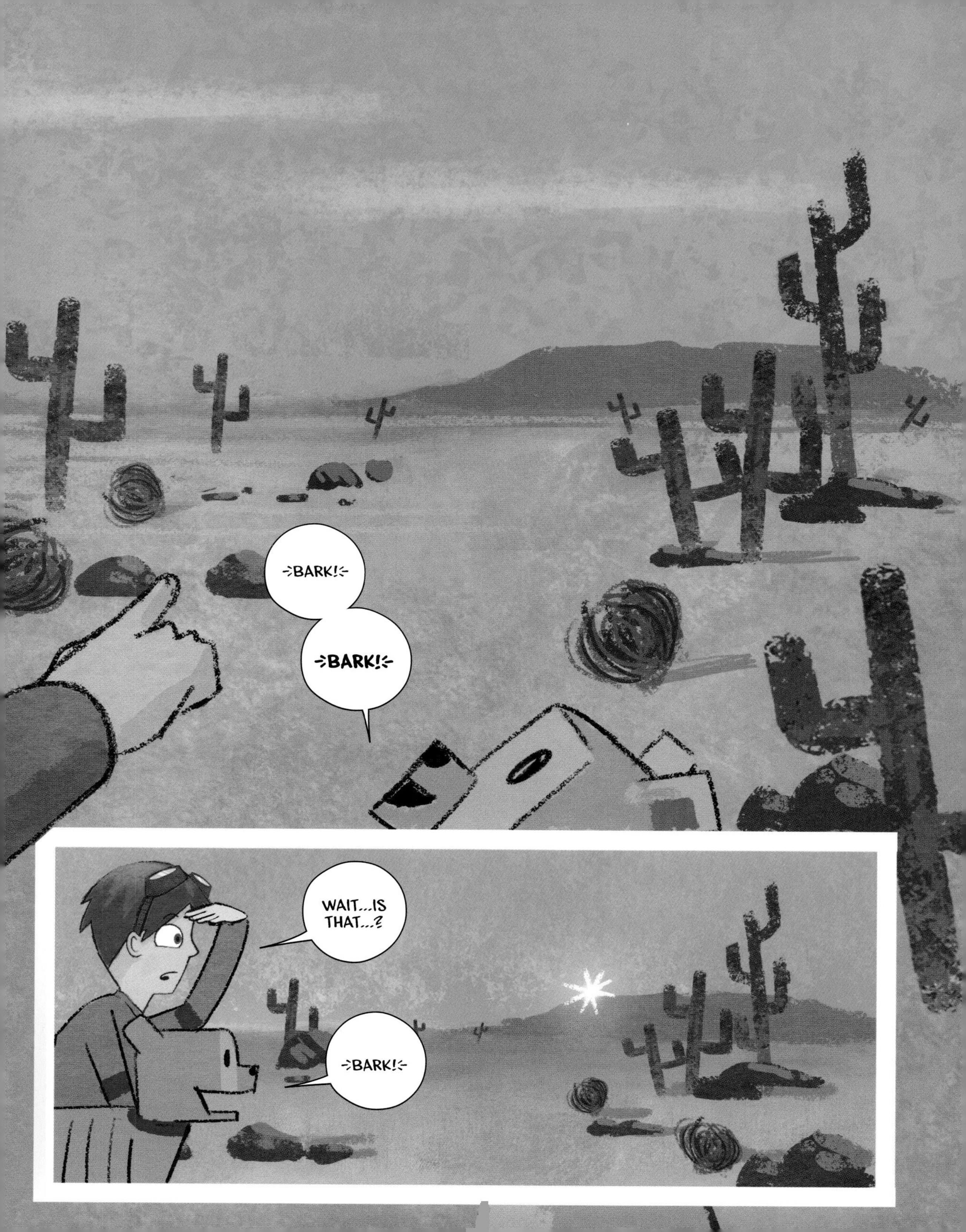
BARK!
BARK!
WAIT...IS THAT...?
BARK!

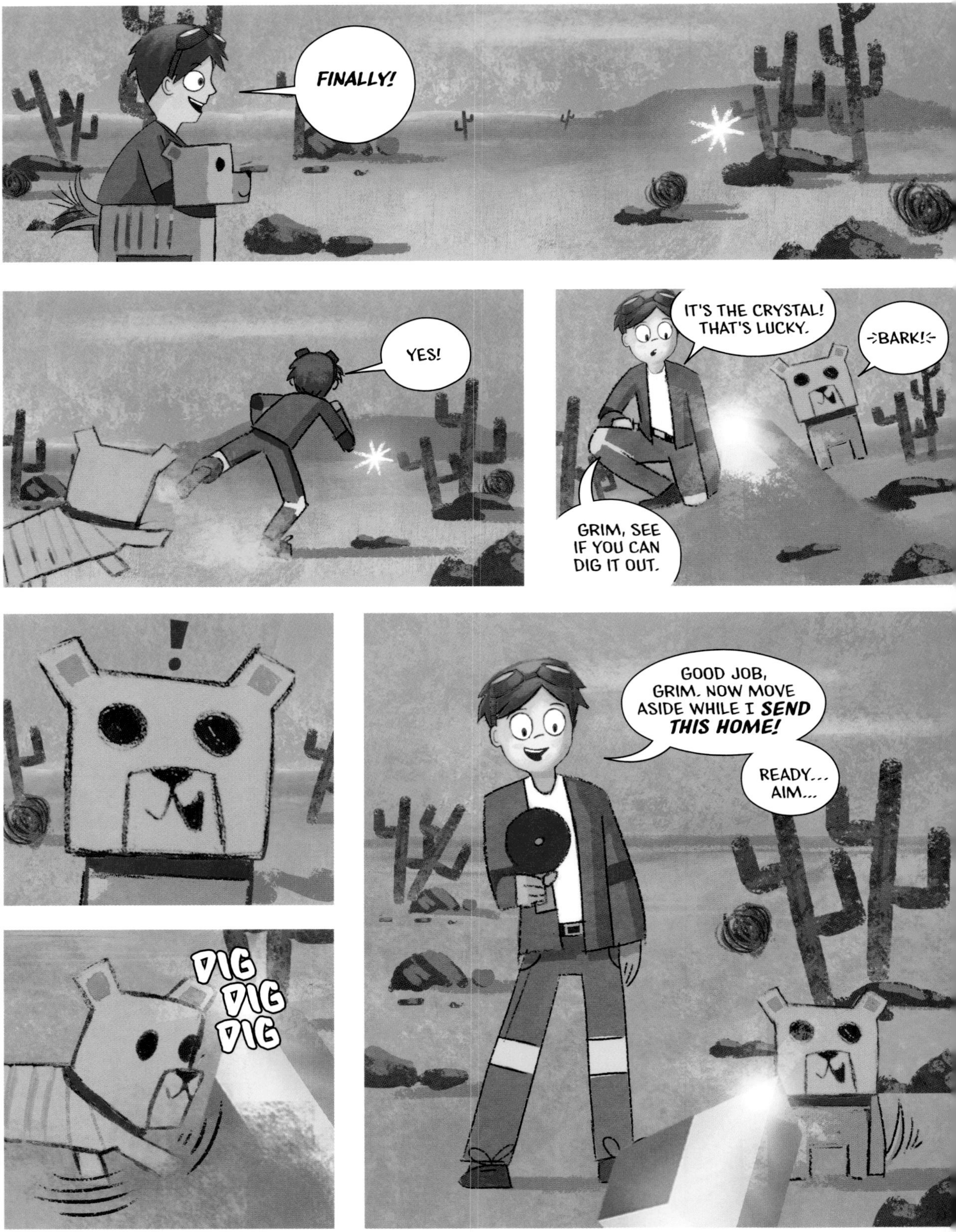
FINALLY!
YES!
IT'S THE CRYSTAL! THAT'S LUCKY.
BARK!
GRIM, SEE IF YOU CAN DIG IT OUT.
!
DIG DIG DIG
GOOD JOB, GRIM. NOW MOVE ASIDE WHILE I SEND THIS HOME!
READY... AIM...

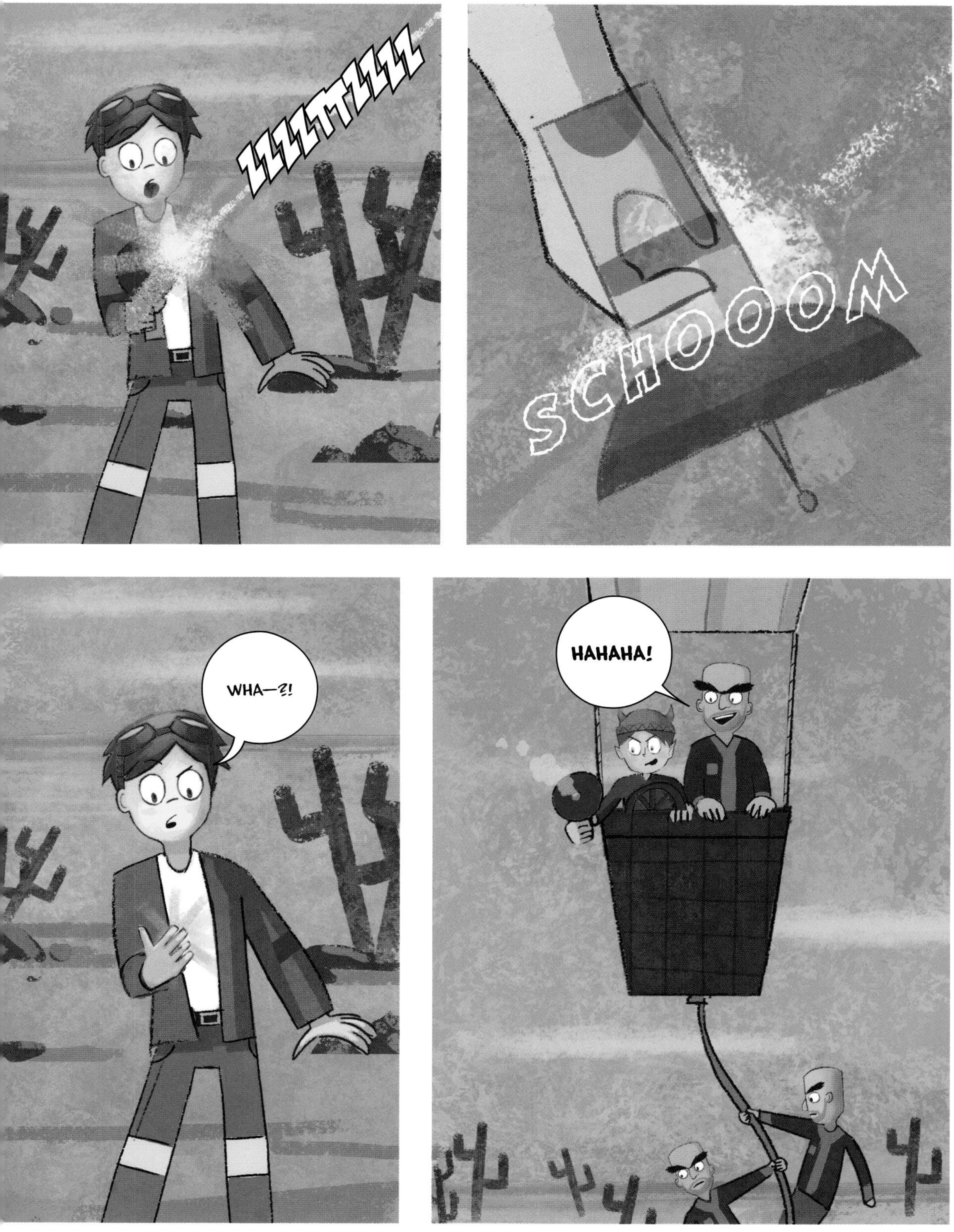
ZZZZZTTZZZZZ
SCHOOOM
WHA—?!
HAHAHA!

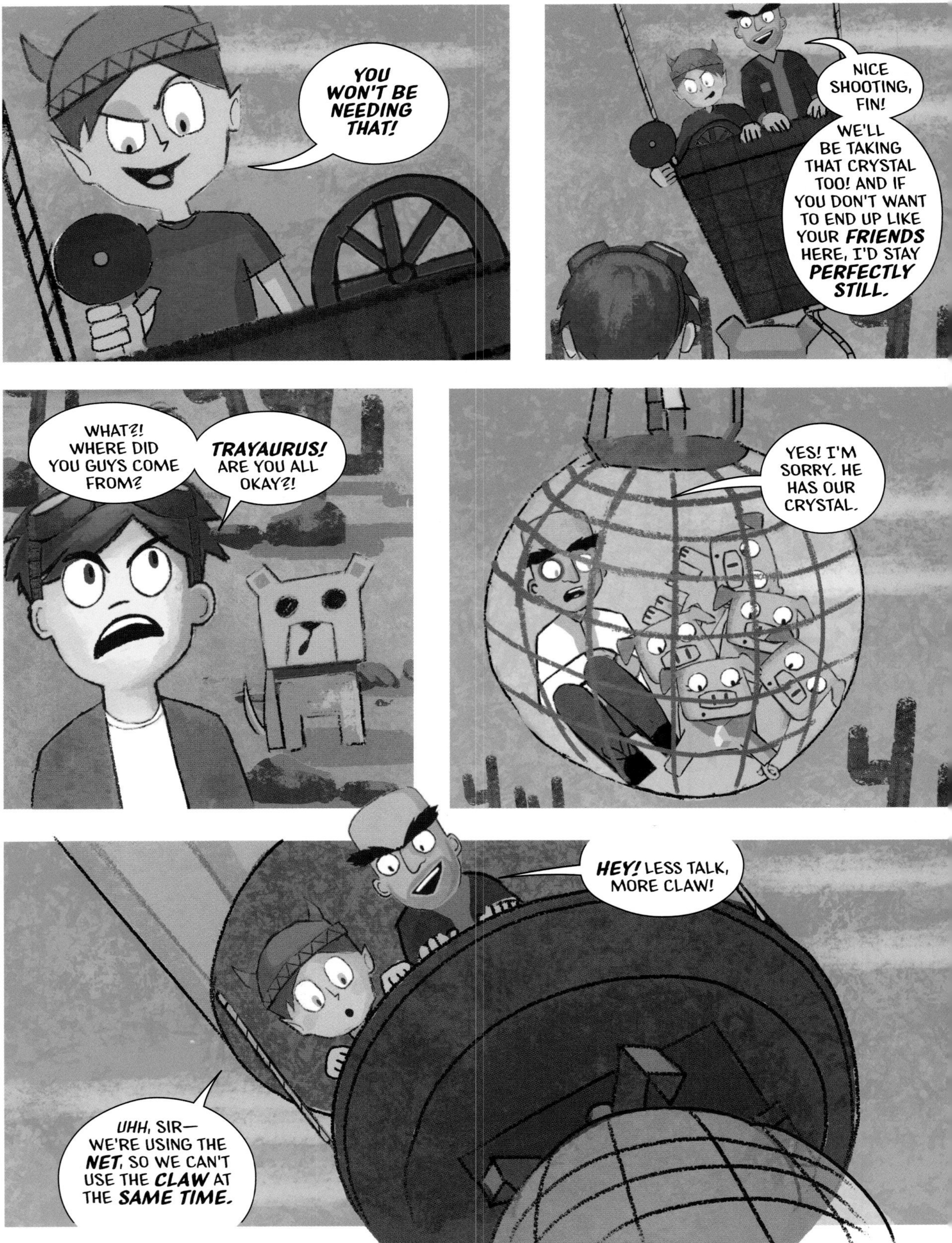
YOU WON'T BE NEEDING THAT!
NICE SHOOTING, FIN!
WE'LL BE TAKING THAT CRYSTAL TOO! AND IF YOU DON'T WANT TO END UP LIKE YOUR FRIENDS HERE, I'D STAY PERFECTLY STILL.
WHAT?! WHERE DID YOU GUYS COME FROM?
TRAYAURUS! ARE YOU ALL OKAY?!
YES! I'M SORRY. HE HAS OUR CRYSTAL.
HEY! LESS TALK, MORE CLAW!
UHH, SIR— WE'RE USING THE NET, SO WE CAN'T USE THE CLAW AT THE SAME TIME.

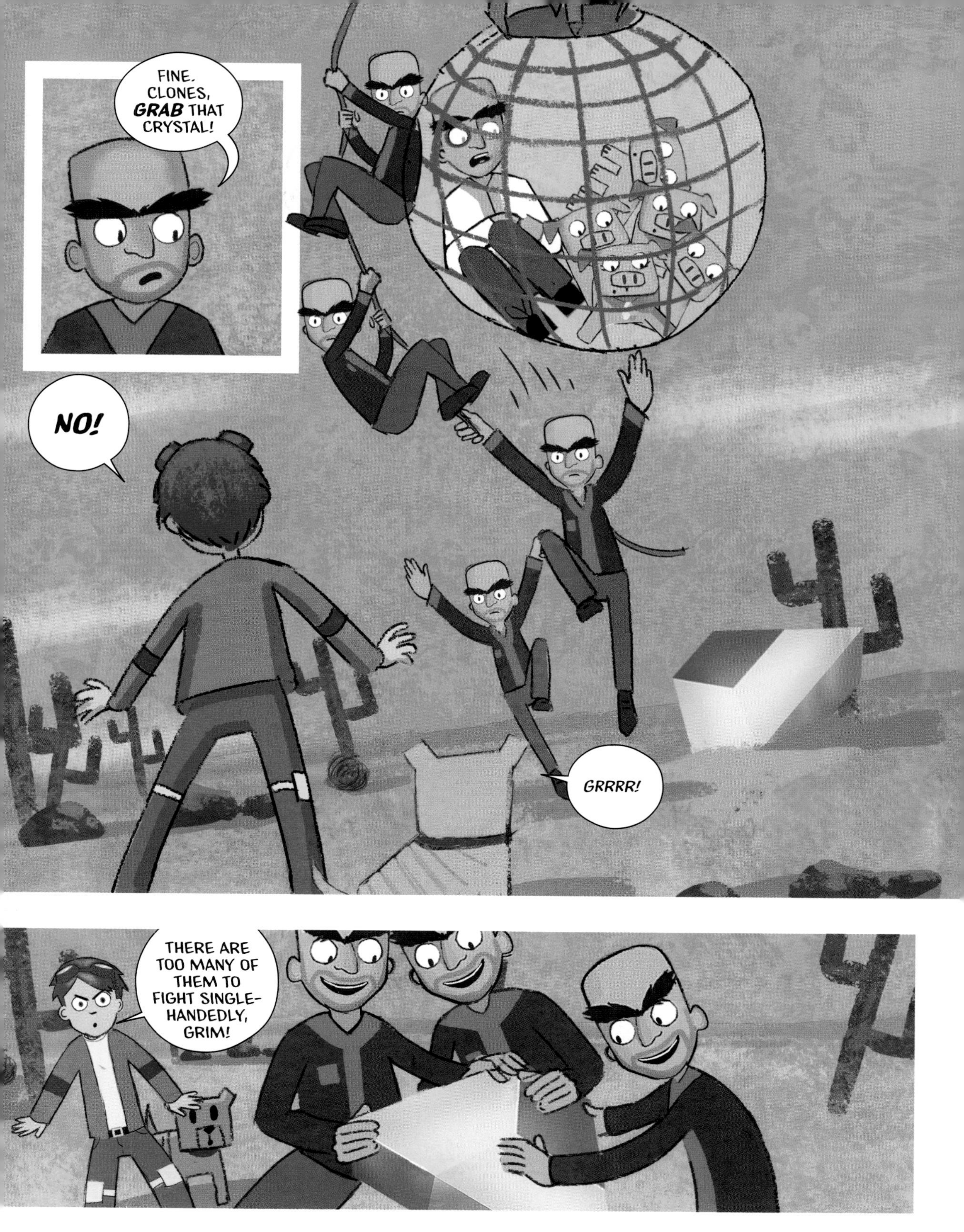
FINE. CLONES, **GRAB** THAT CRYSTAL!
NO!
GRRRR!
THERE ARE TOO MANY OF THEM TO FIGHT SINGLE-HANDEDLY, GRIM!

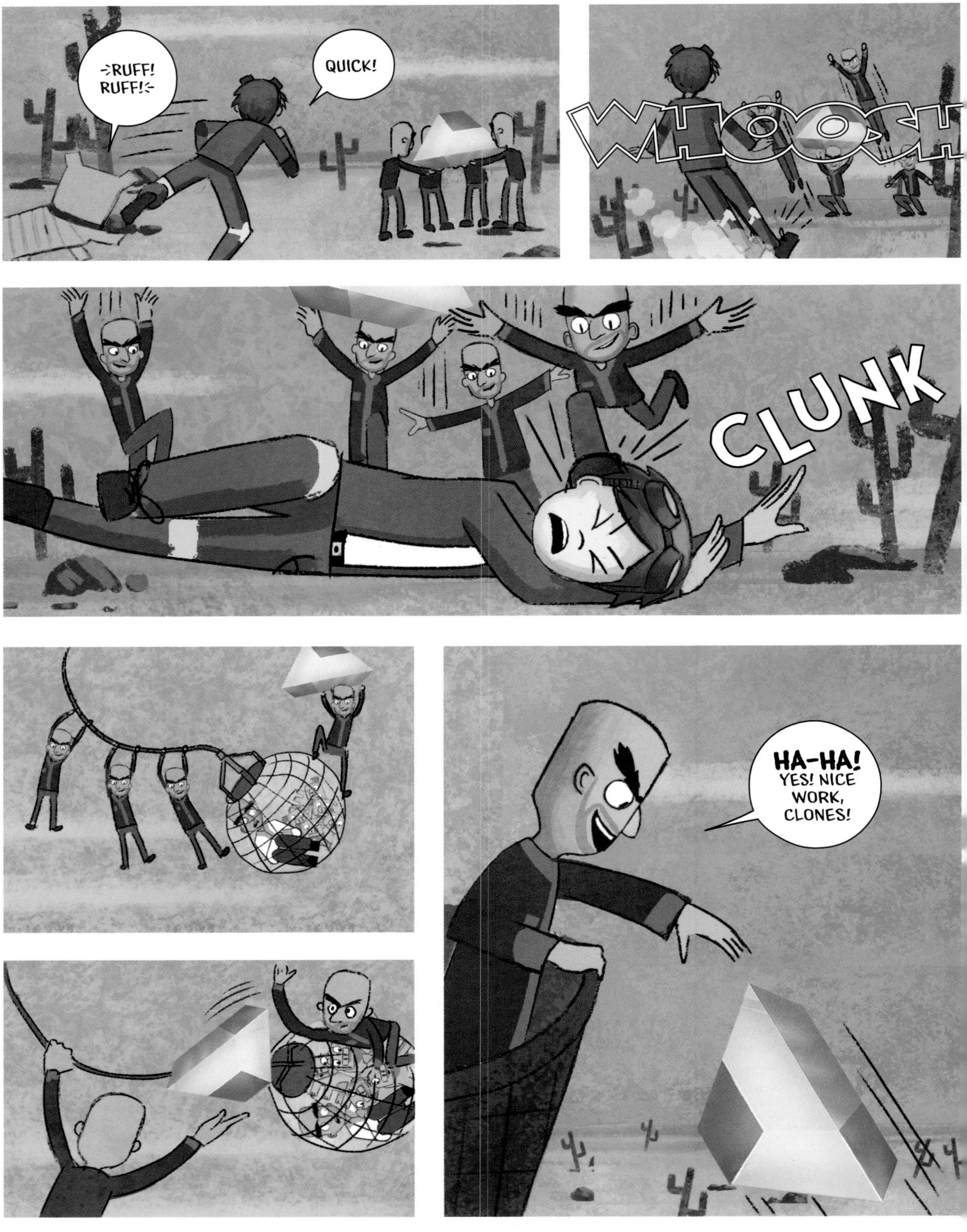

⇀RUFF! RUFF!↼
QUICK!
WHOOSH
CLUNK
HA-HA! YES! NICE WORK, CLONES!

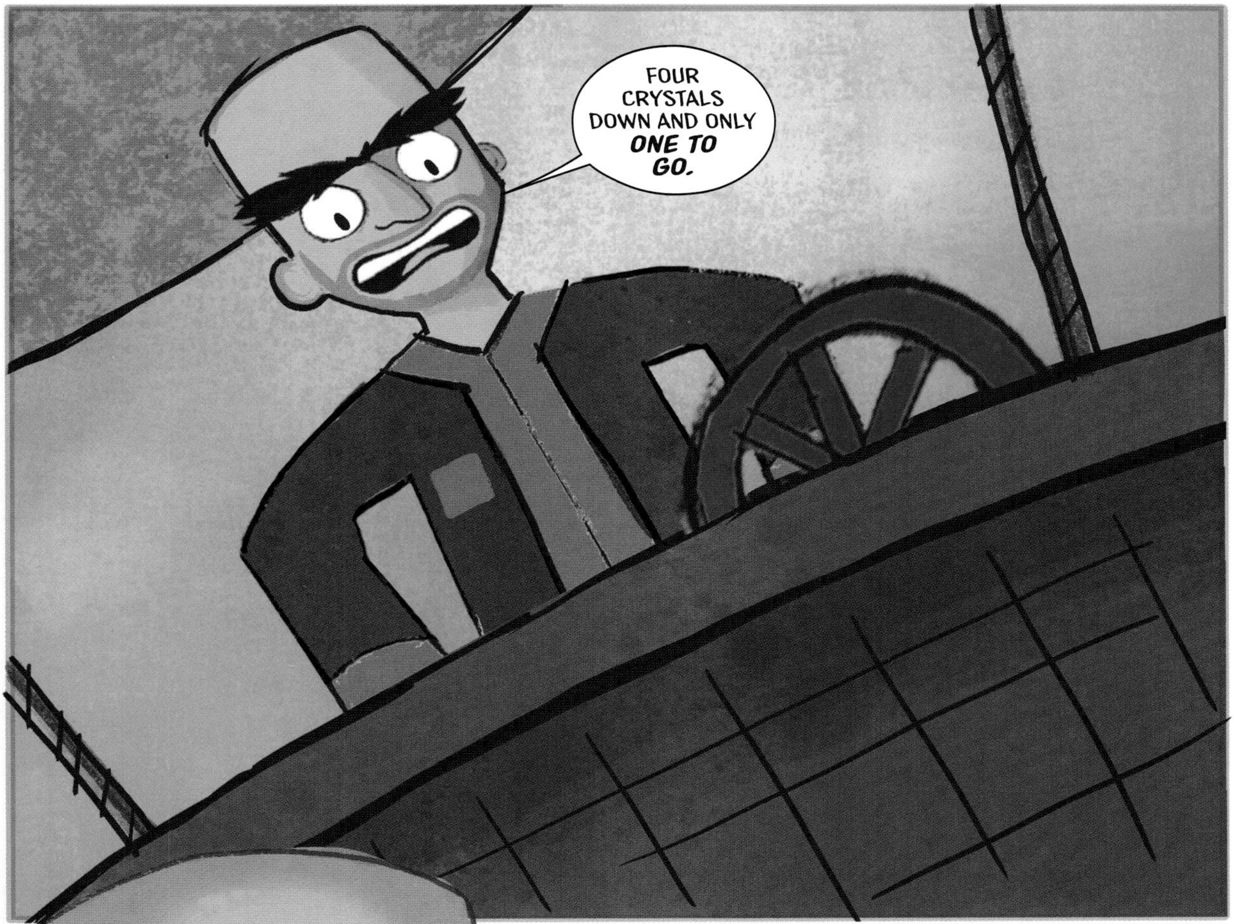
FOUR CRYSTALS DOWN AND ONLY ONE TO GO.

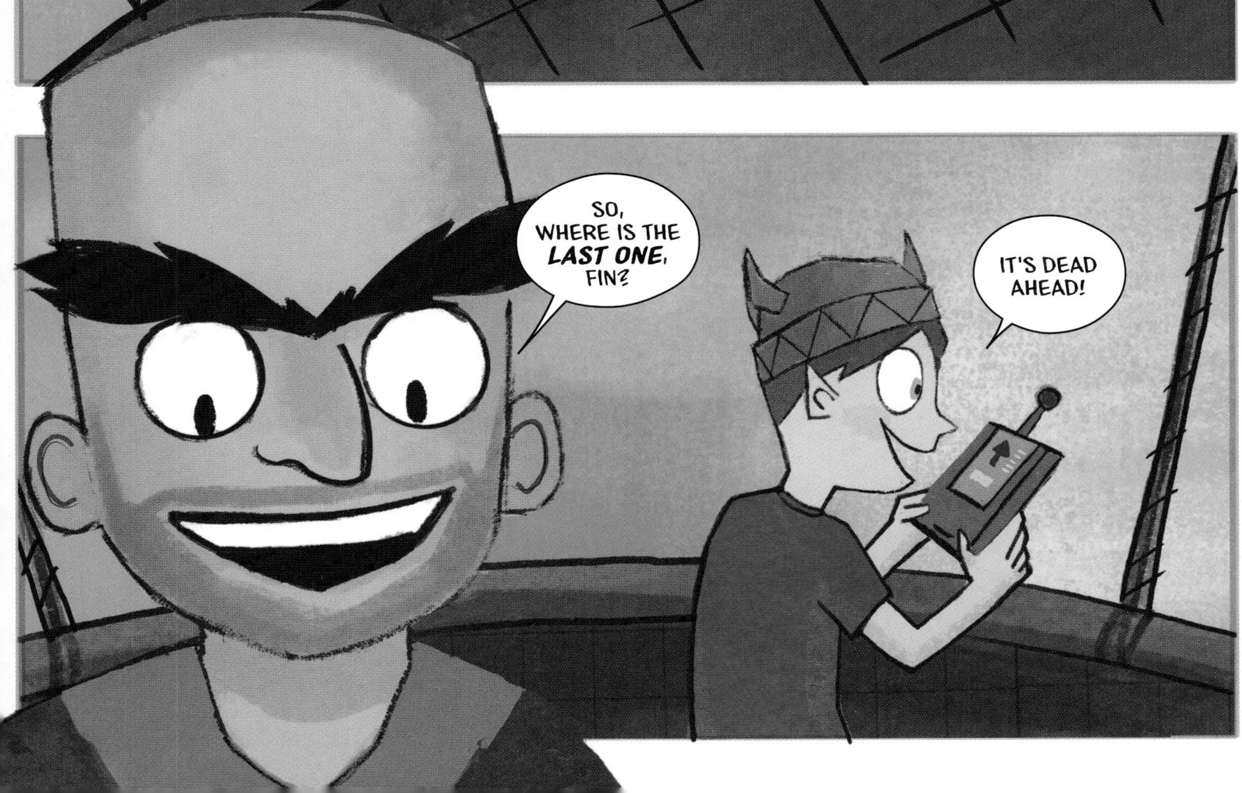
SO, WHERE IS THE LAST ONE, FIN?
IT'S DEAD AHEAD!

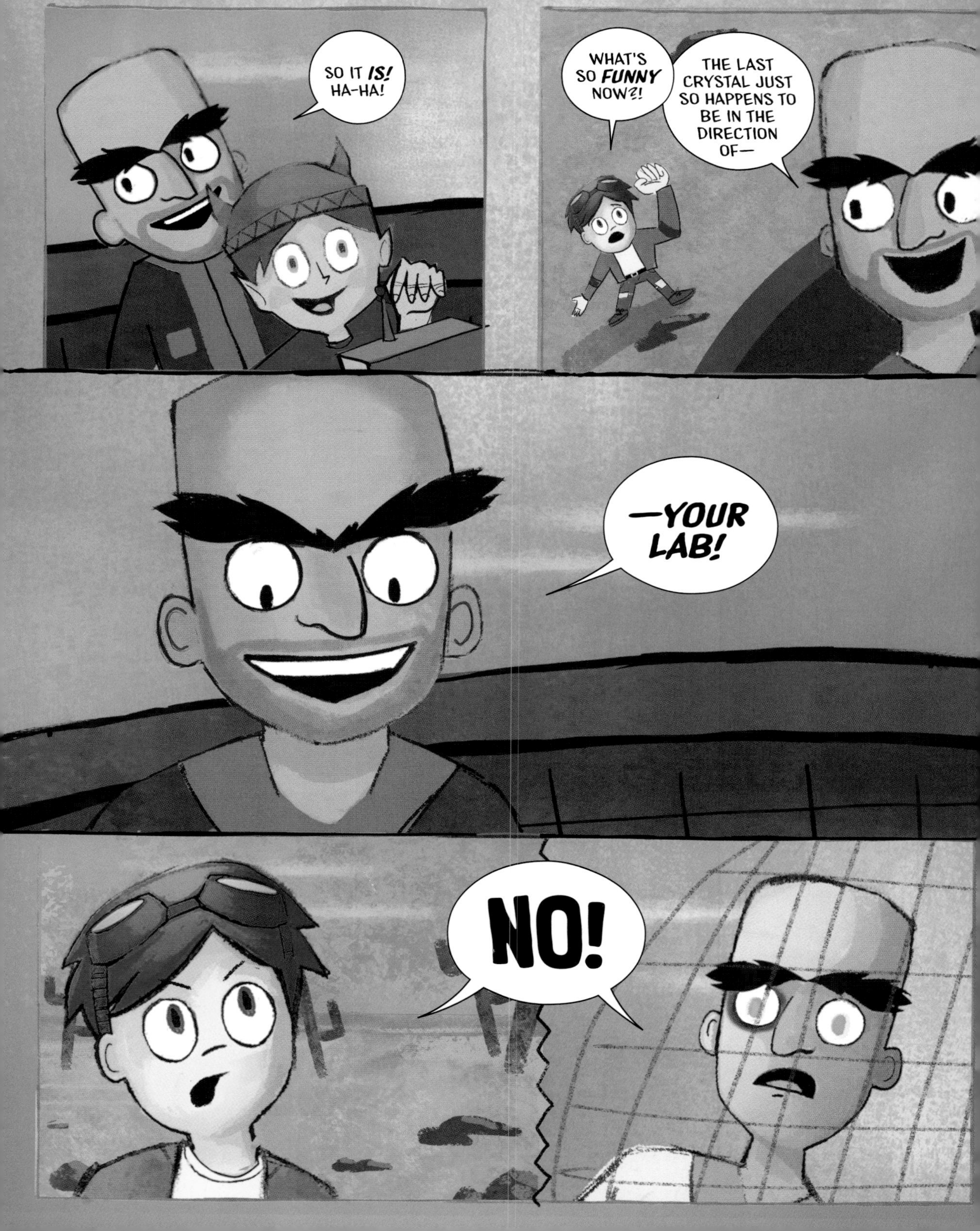
SO IT *IS!* HA-HA!
WHAT'S SO *FUNNY* NOW?!
THE LAST CRYSTAL JUST SO HAPPENS TO BE IN THE DIRECTION OF—
—*YOUR LAB!*
NO!

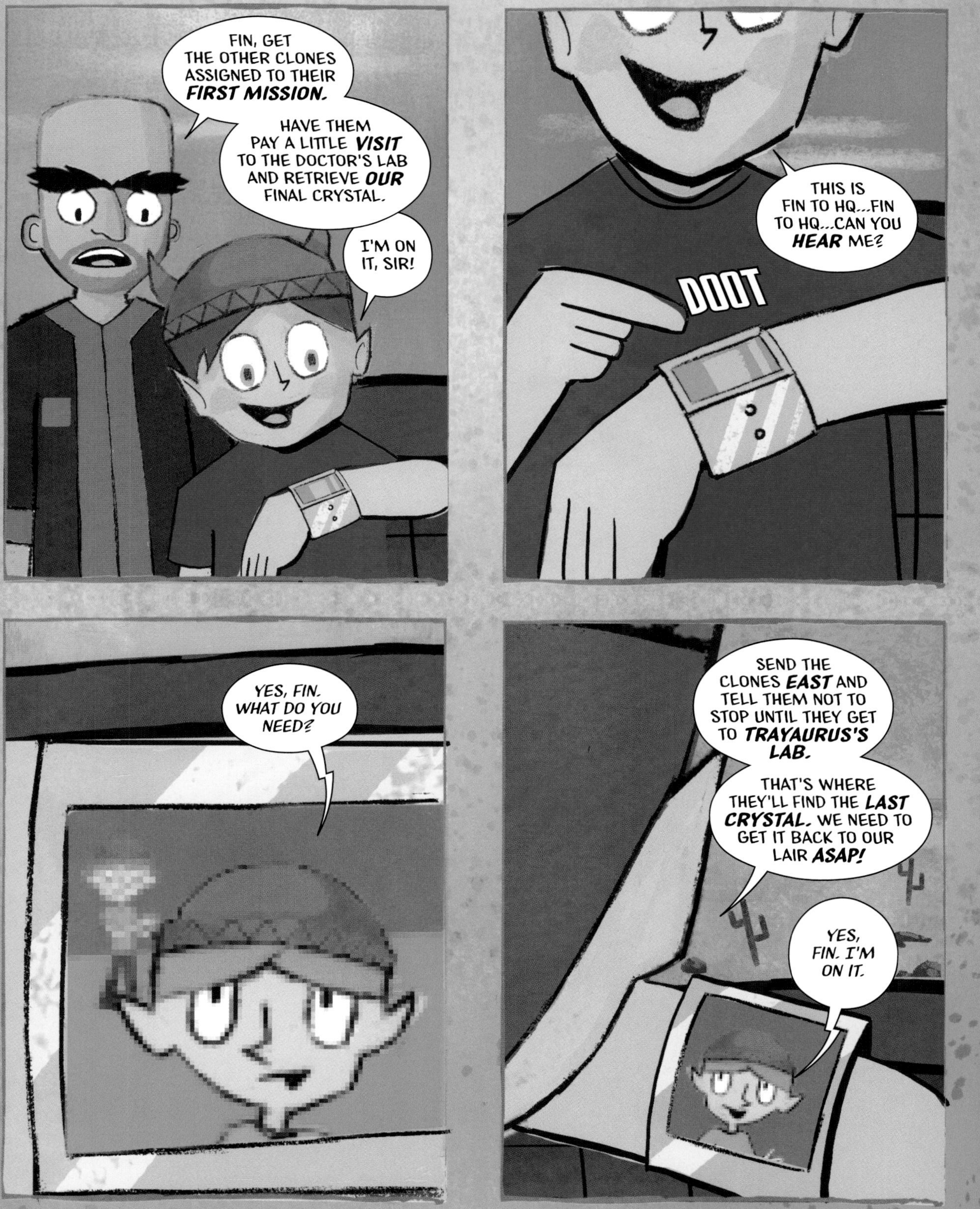
FIN, GET THE OTHER CLONES ASSIGNED TO THEIR FIRST MISSION.
HAVE THEM PAY A LITTLE VISIT TO THE DOCTOR'S LAB AND RETRIEVE OUR FINAL CRYSTAL.
I'M ON IT, SIR!
THIS IS FIN TO HQ...FIN TO HQ...CAN YOU HEAR ME?
DOOT
YES, FIN. WHAT DO YOU NEED?
SEND THE CLONES EAST AND TELL THEM NOT TO STOP UNTIL THEY GET TO TRAYAURUS'S LAB.
THAT'S WHERE THEY'LL FIND THE LAST CRYSTAL. WE NEED TO GET IT BACK TO OUR LAIR ASAP!
YES, FIN. I'M ON IT.

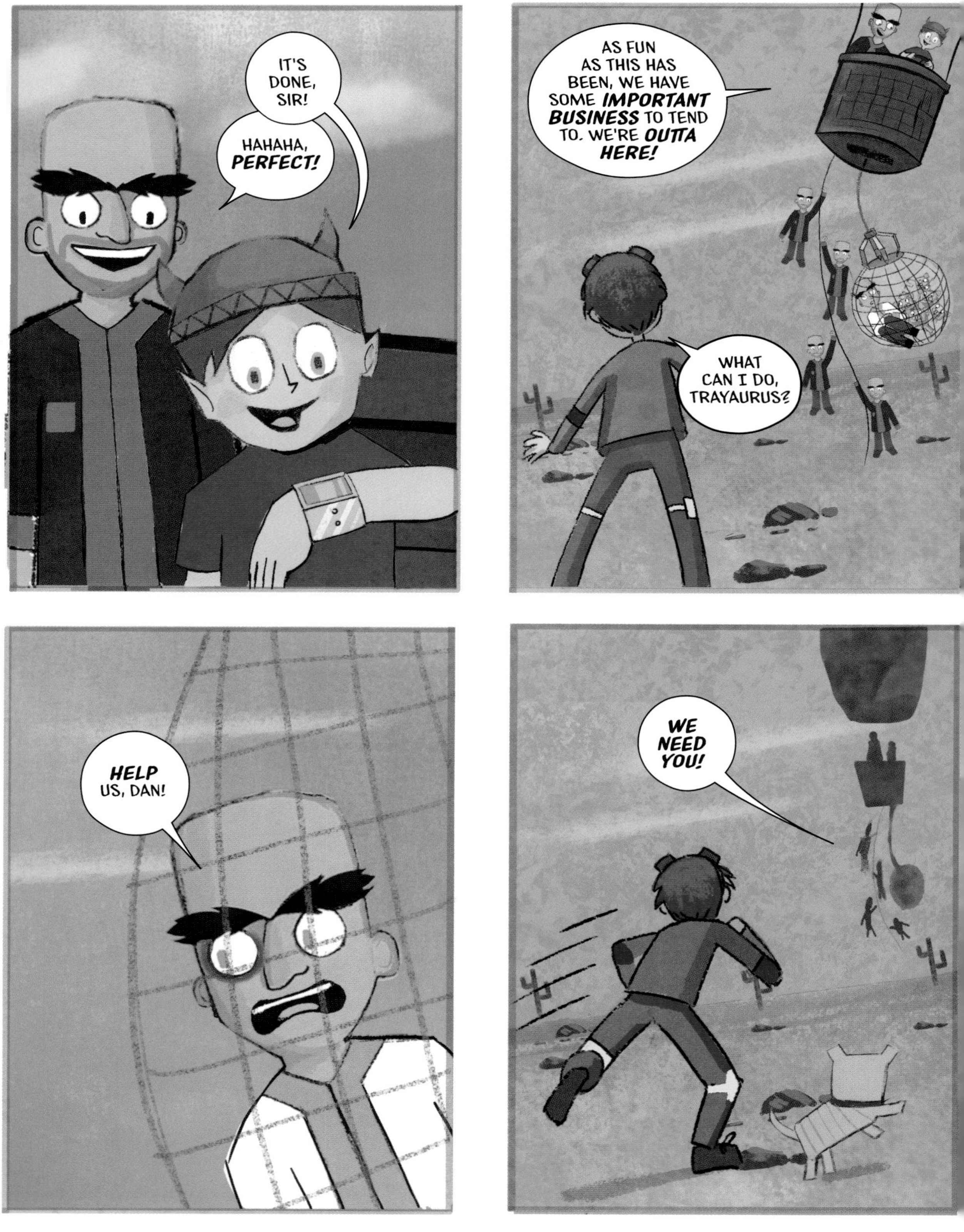
IT'S DONE, SIR!
HAHAHA, PERFECT!
AS FUN AS THIS HAS BEEN, WE HAVE SOME IMPORTANT BUSINESS TO TEND TO. WE'RE OUTTA HERE!
WHAT CAN I DO, TRAYAURUS?
HELP US, DAN!
WE NEED YOU!

LISTEN UP, CHUMPS!

RELEASE THE CLONES!

CLICK

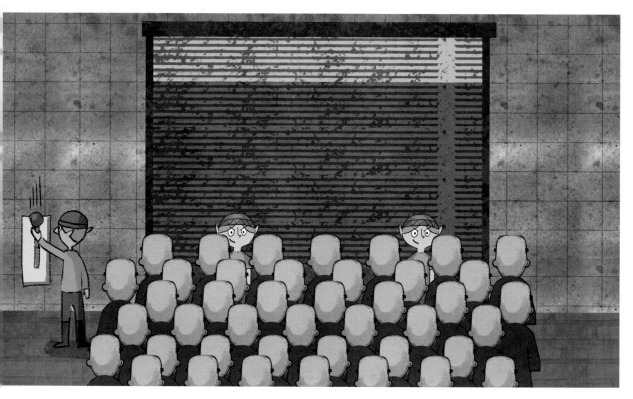

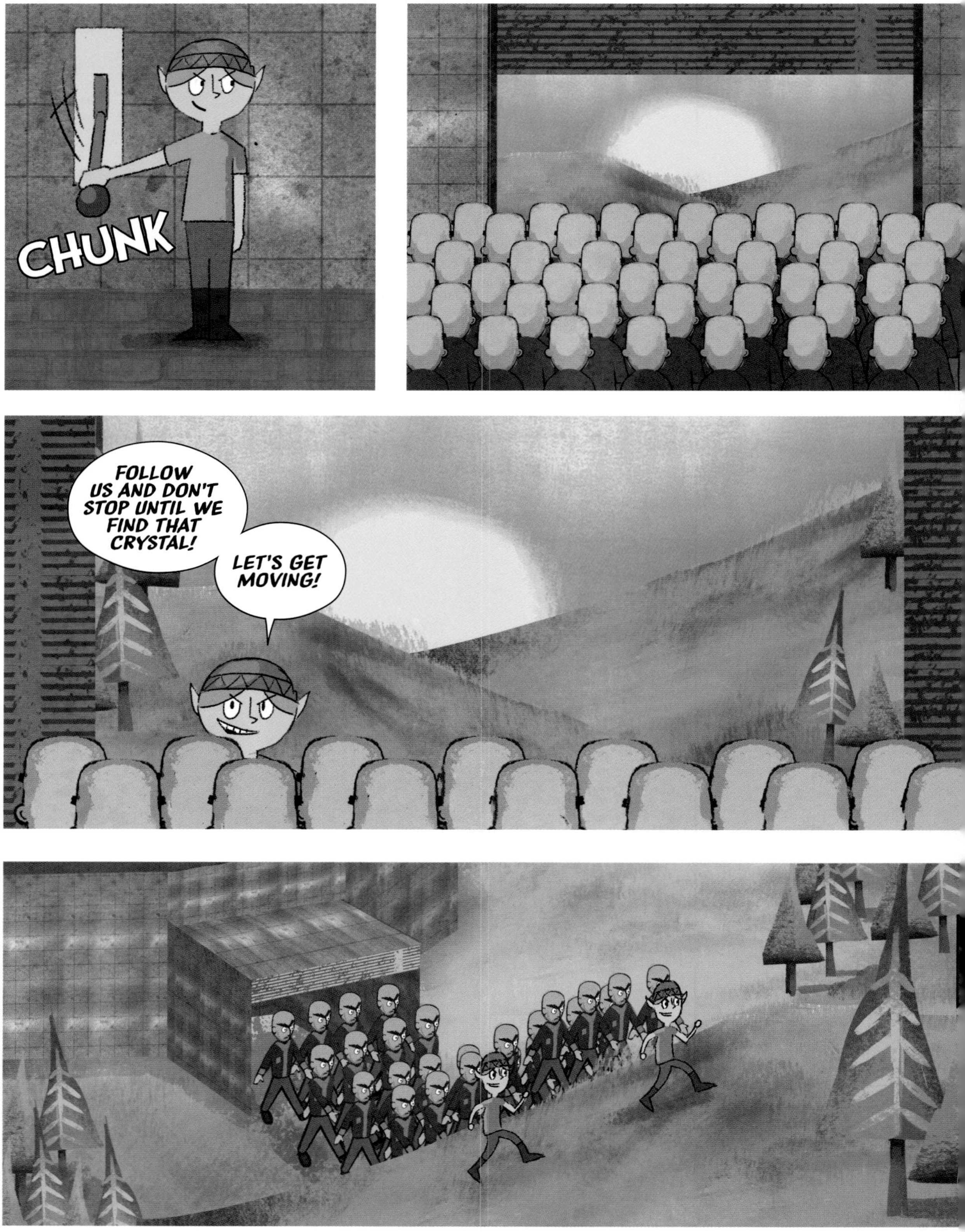
CHUNK
FOLLOW US AND DON'T STOP UNTIL WE FIND THAT CRYSTAL!
LET'S GET MOVING!

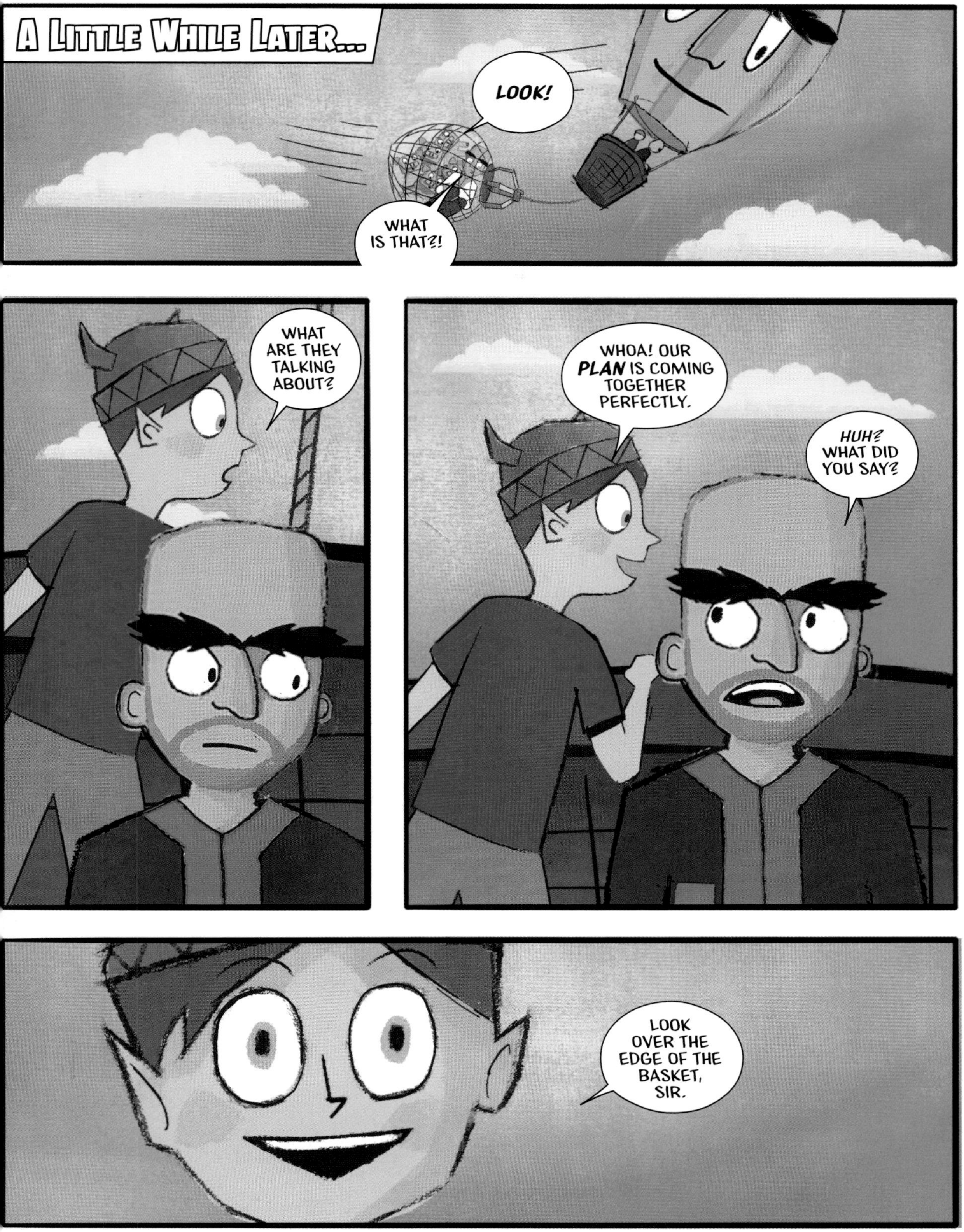
A LITTLE WHILE LATER...
LOOK!
WHAT IS THAT?!
WHAT ARE THEY TALKING ABOUT?
WHOA! OUR PLAN IS COMING TOGETHER PERFECTLY.
HUH? WHAT DID YOU SAY?
LOOK OVER THE EDGE OF THE BASKET, SIR.

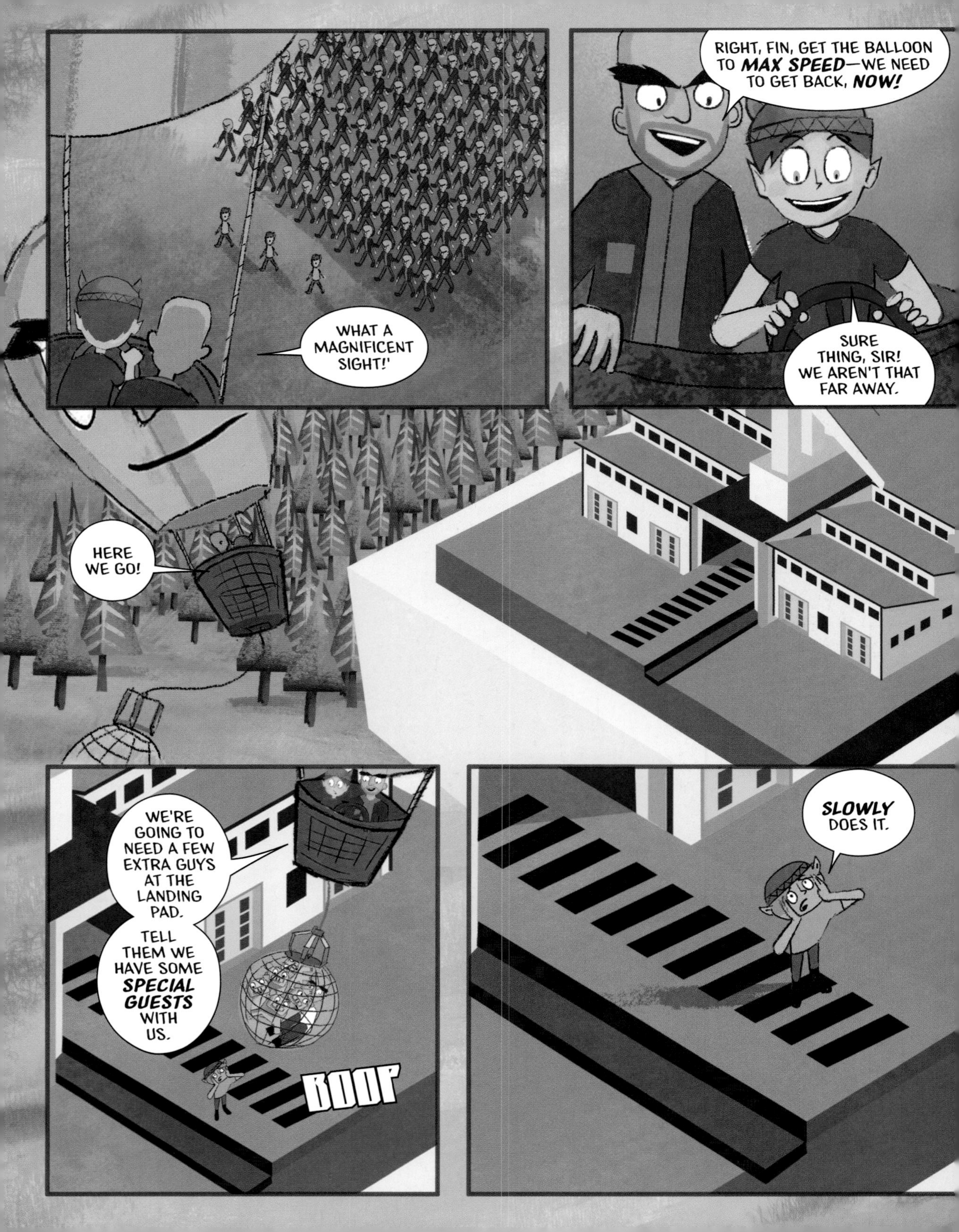
WHAT A MAGNIFICENT SIGHT!'
RIGHT, FIN, GET THE BALLOON TO MAX SPEED—WE NEED TO GET BACK, NOW!
SURE THING, SIR! WE AREN'T THAT FAR AWAY.
HERE WE GO!
WE'RE GOING TO NEED A FEW EXTRA GUYS AT THE LANDING PAD.
TELL THEM WE HAVE SOME SPECIAL GUESTS WITH US.
BOOP
SLOWLY DOES IT.

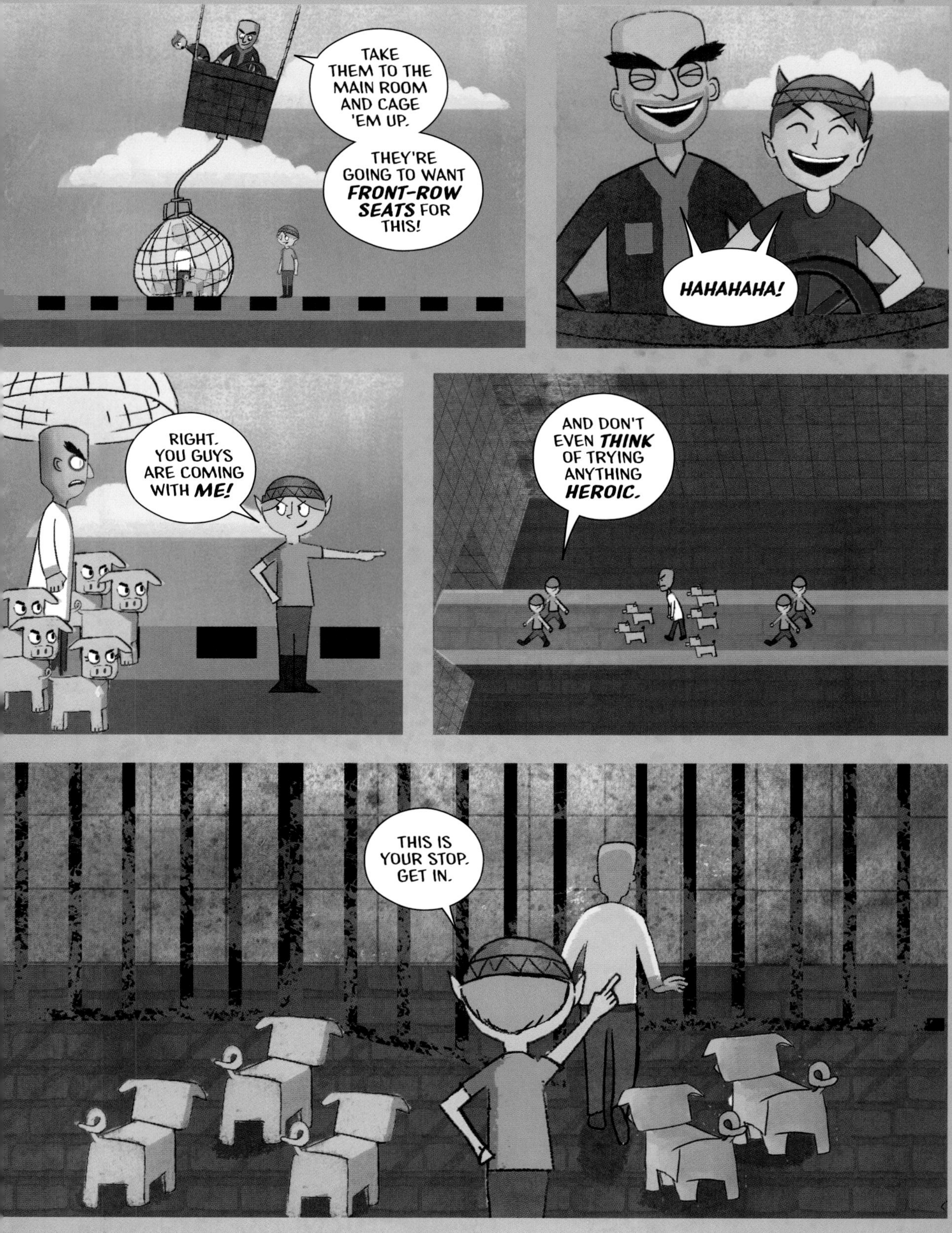
TAKE THEM TO THE MAIN ROOM AND CAGE 'EM UP.
THEY'RE GOING TO WANT FRONT-ROW SEATS FOR THIS!
HAHAHAHA!
RIGHT. YOU GUYS ARE COMING WITH ME!
AND DON'T EVEN THINK OF TRYING ANYTHING HEROIC.
THIS IS YOUR STOP. GET IN.

CLANG!

I WONDER IF WE'LL GET A PROMOTION FOR THIS?

I DON'T LIKE THESE GUYS *ONE BIT.* BUT YOU HAVE TO ADMIT, THEY'VE GOT A *PRETTY* IMPRESSIVE PLACE HERE.

LOOKS LIKE YOU WERE RIGHT, TRAYAURUS.

ABOUT *WHAT?*

THEY'RE USING THE POWER OF THE CRYSTALS TO MAKE A *CLONE ARMY.*

I KNEW IT!

AND WITH *TWO* CRYSTALS THE CLONES ARE *MUCH BIGGER.*

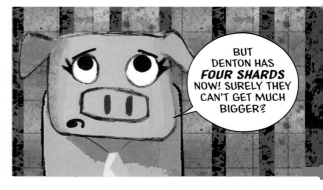

BUT DENTON HAS *FOUR SHARDS* NOW! SURELY THEY CAN'T GET MUCH BIGGER?

I HOPE NOT! BUT I THINK WE'LL SOON FIND OUT.

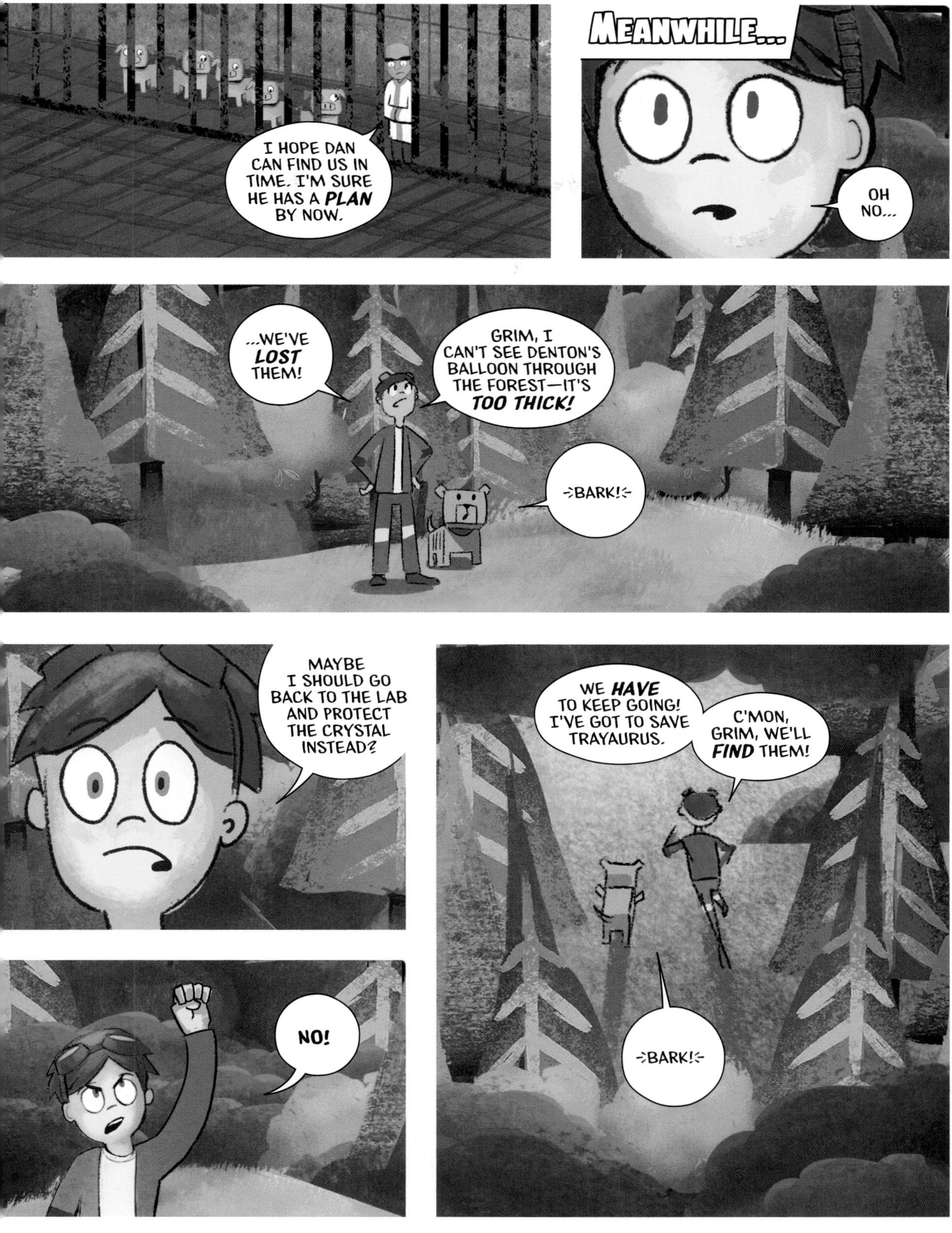
I HOPE DAN CAN FIND US IN TIME. I'M SURE HE HAS A *PLAN* BY NOW.
MEANWHILE...
OH NO...
...WE'VE *LOST* THEM!
GRIM, I CAN'T SEE DENTON'S BALLOON THROUGH THE FOREST—IT'S *TOO THICK!*
BARK!
MAYBE I SHOULD GO BACK TO THE LAB AND PROTECT THE CRYSTAL INSTEAD?
NO!
WE *HAVE* TO KEEP GOING! I'VE GOT TO SAVE TRAYAURUS.
C'MON, GRIM, WE'LL *FIND* THEM!
BARK!

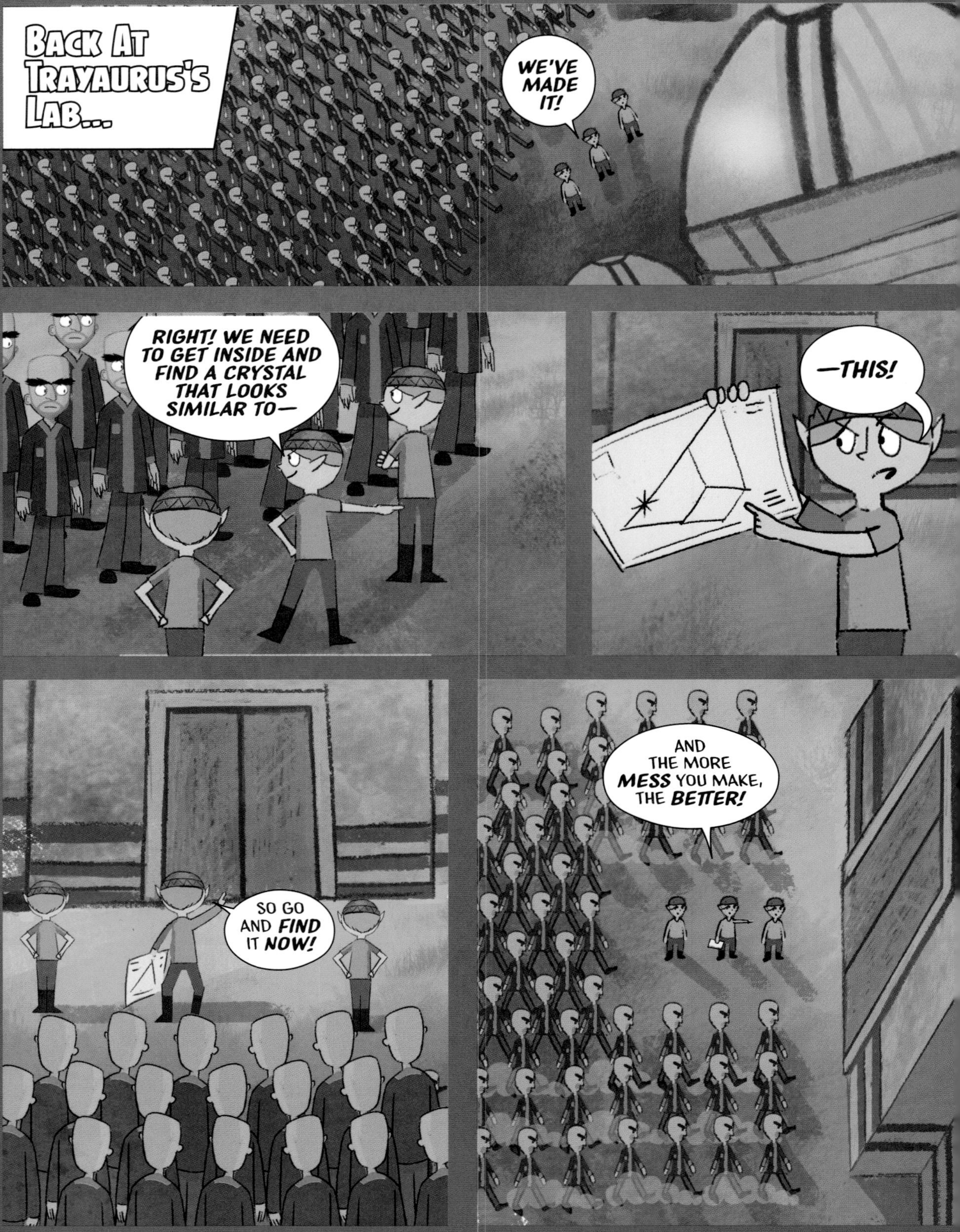
BACK AT TRAYAURUS'S LAB...
WE'VE MADE IT!
RIGHT! WE NEED TO GET INSIDE AND FIND A CRYSTAL THAT LOOKS SIMILAR TO—
—THIS!
SO GO AND FIND IT NOW!
AND THE MORE MESS YOU MAKE, THE BETTER!

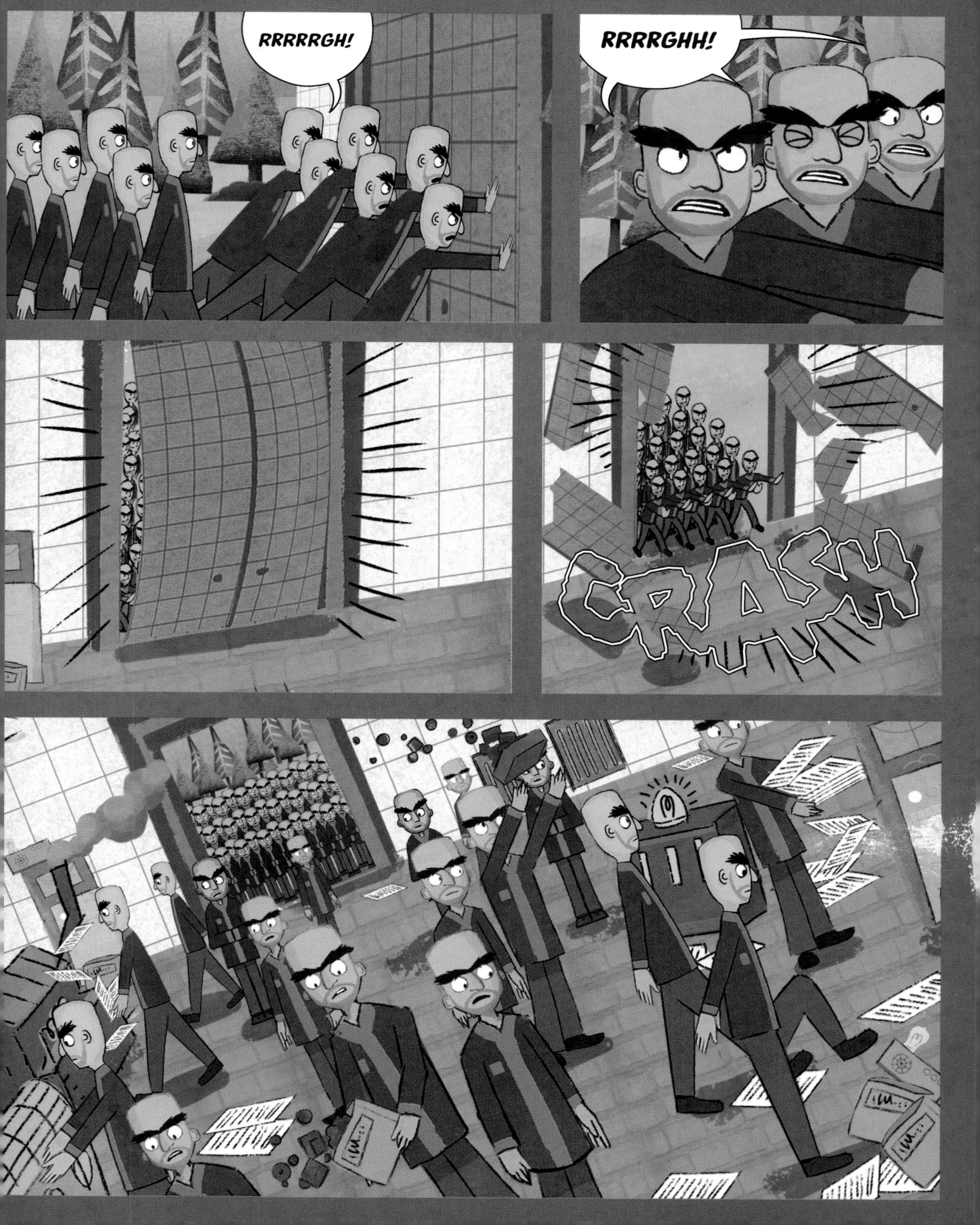
RRRRRGH!
RRRRGHH!
CRASH

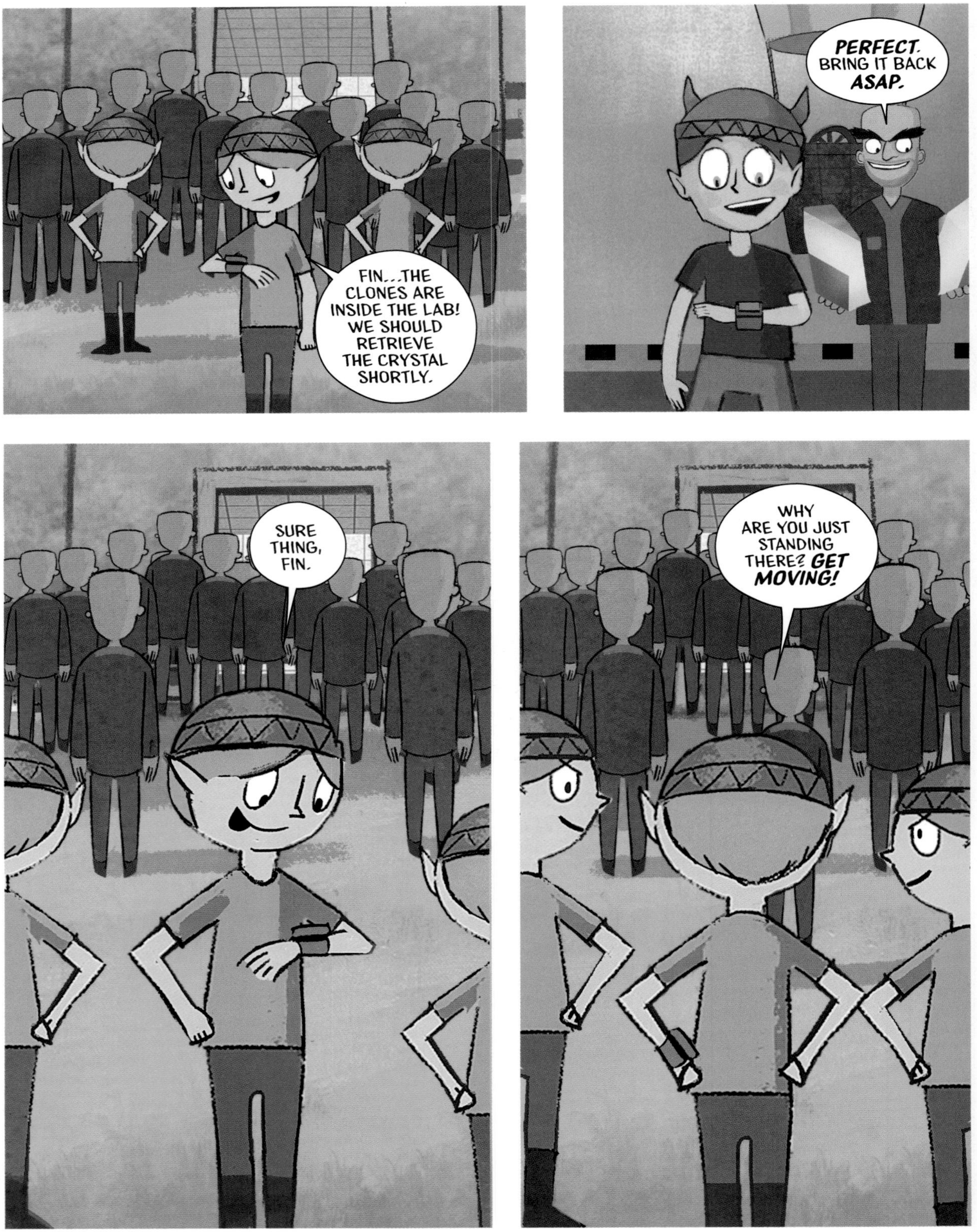
FIN...THE CLONES ARE INSIDE THE LAB! WE SHOULD RETRIEVE THE CRYSTAL SHORTLY.
PERFECT. BRING IT BACK ASAP.
SURE THING, FIN.
WHY ARE YOU JUST STANDING THERE? GET MOVING!

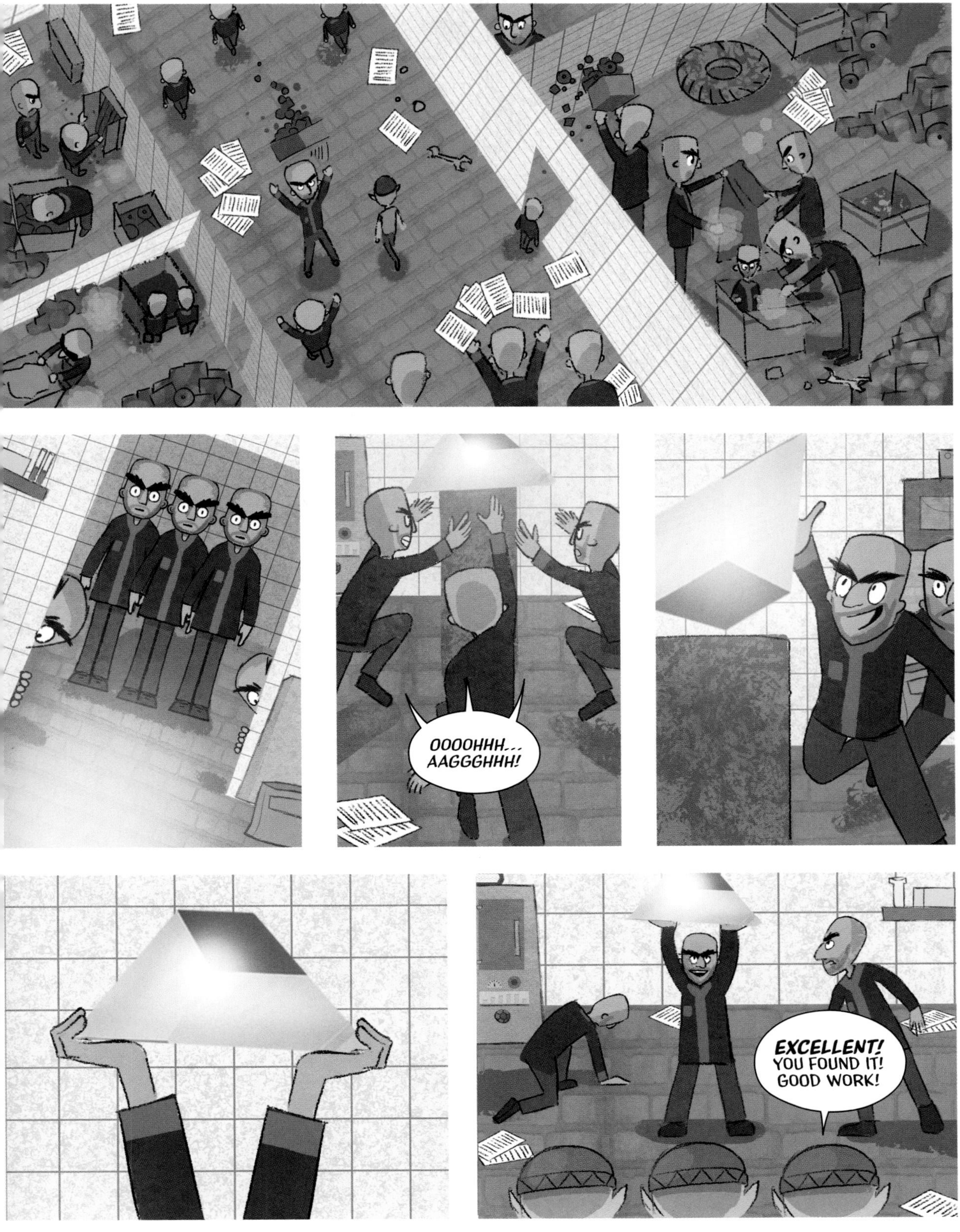
OOOOHHH...
AAGGGHHH!
EXCELLENT!
YOU FOUND IT!
GOOD WORK!

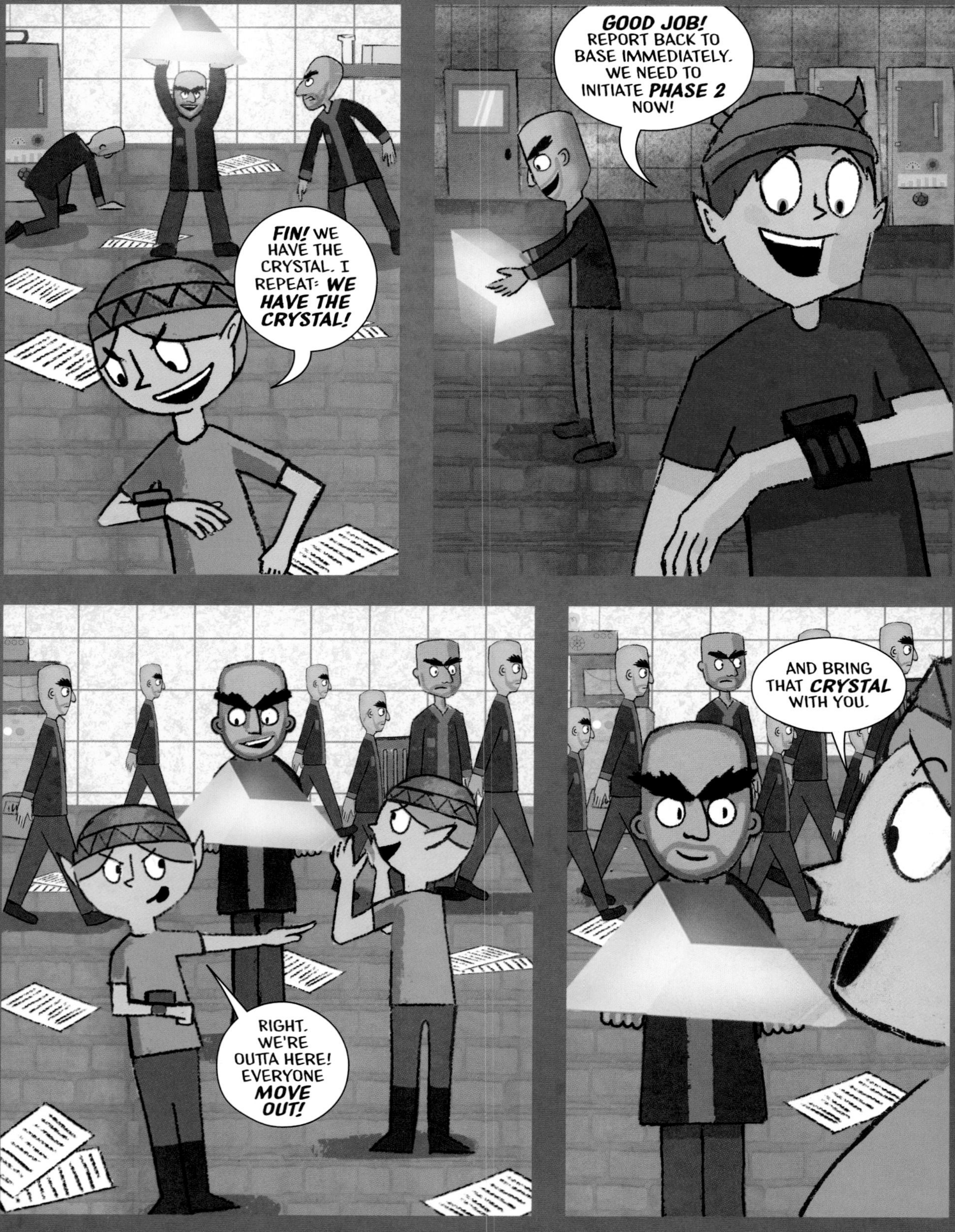
FIN! WE HAVE THE CRYSTAL. I REPEAT: WE HAVE THE CRYSTAL!
GOOD JOB! REPORT BACK TO BASE IMMEDIATELY. WE NEED TO INITIATE PHASE 2 NOW!
RIGHT. WE'RE OUTTA HERE! EVERYONE MOVE OUT!
AND BRING THAT CRYSTAL WITH YOU.

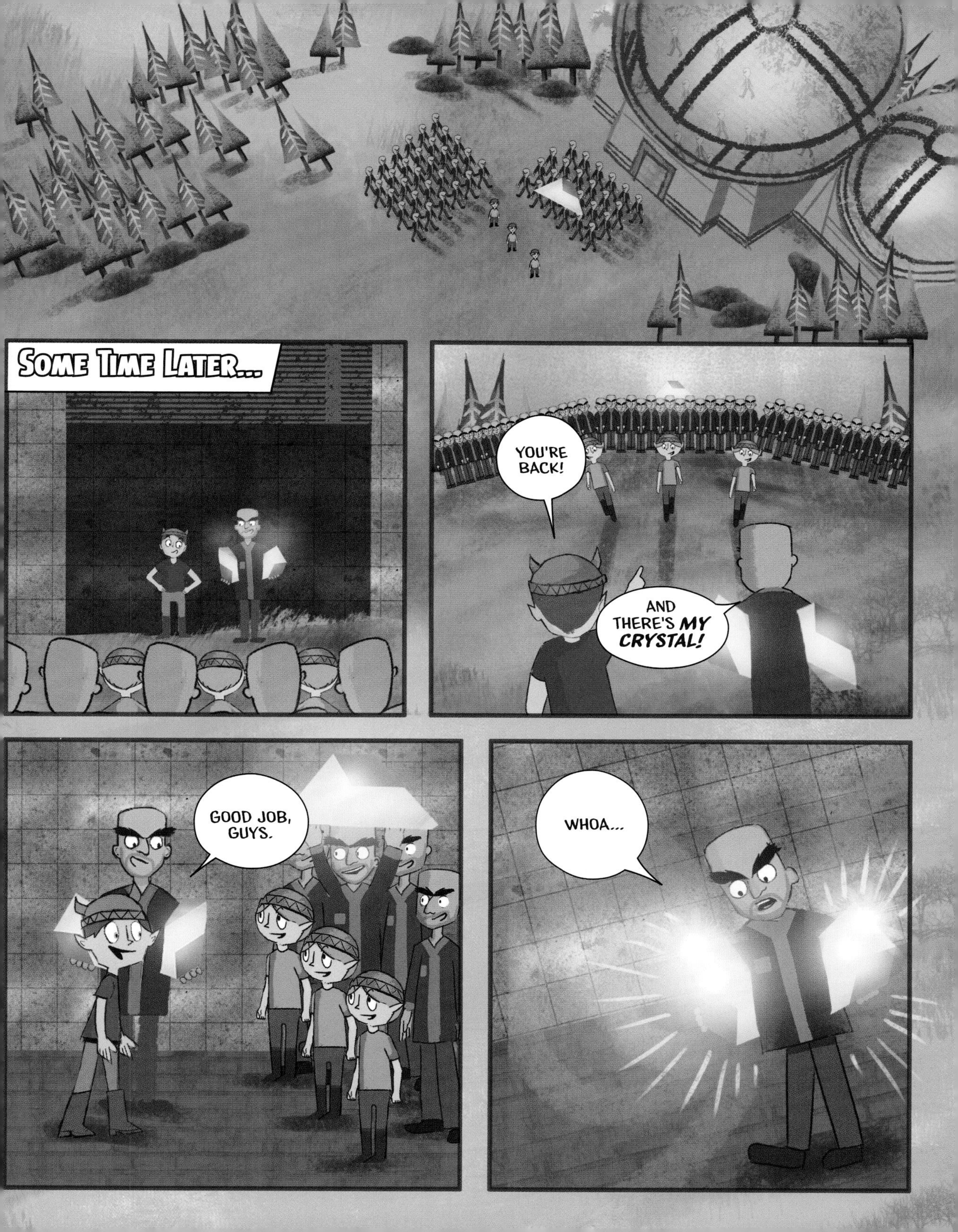
SOME TIME LATER...
YOU'RE BACK!
AND THERE'S MY CRYSTAL!
GOOD JOB, GUYS.
WHOA...

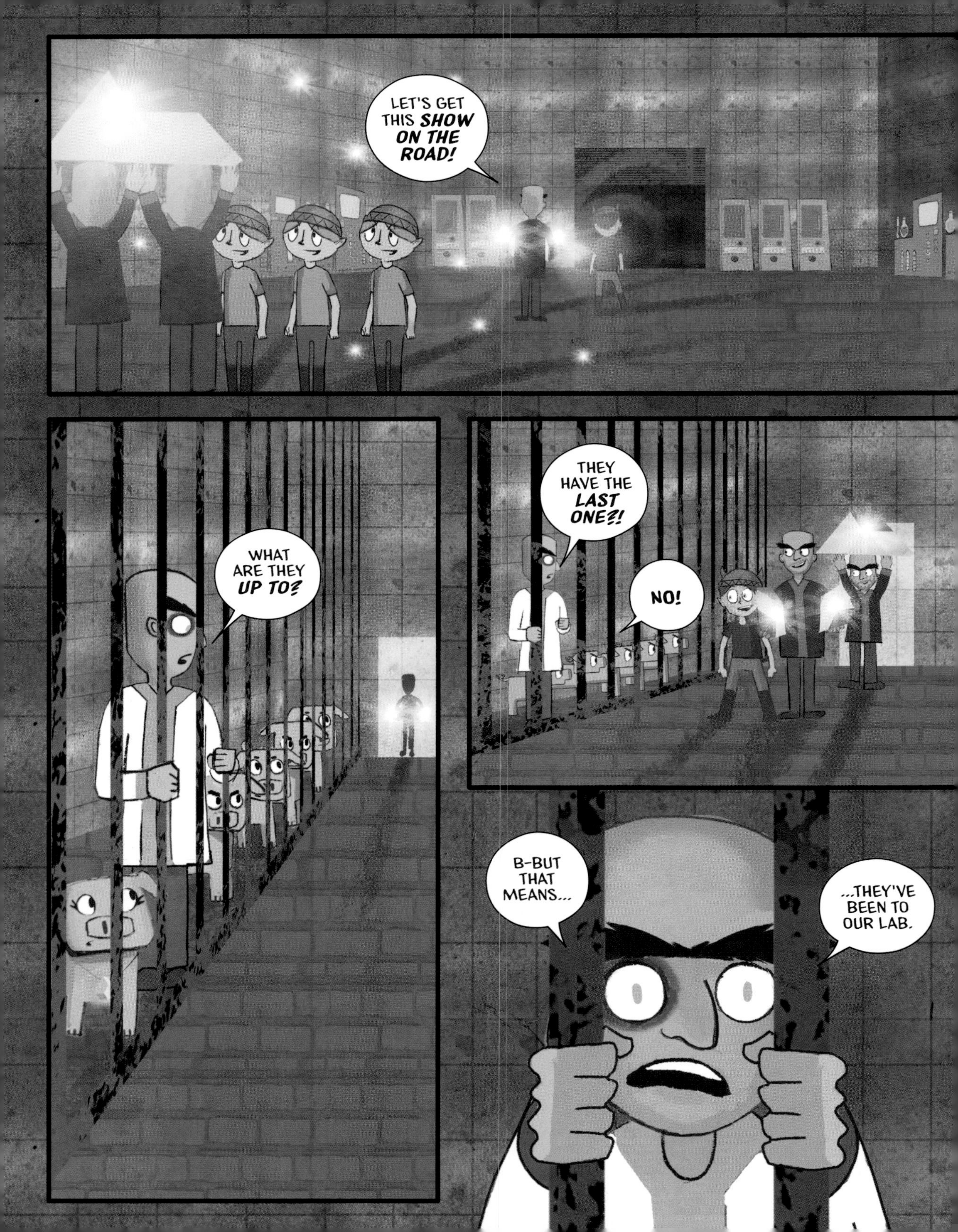
LET'S GET THIS SHOW ON THE ROAD!
WHAT ARE THEY UP TO?
THEY HAVE THE LAST ONE?!
NO!
B-BUT THAT MEANS...
...THEY'VE BEEN TO OUR LAB.

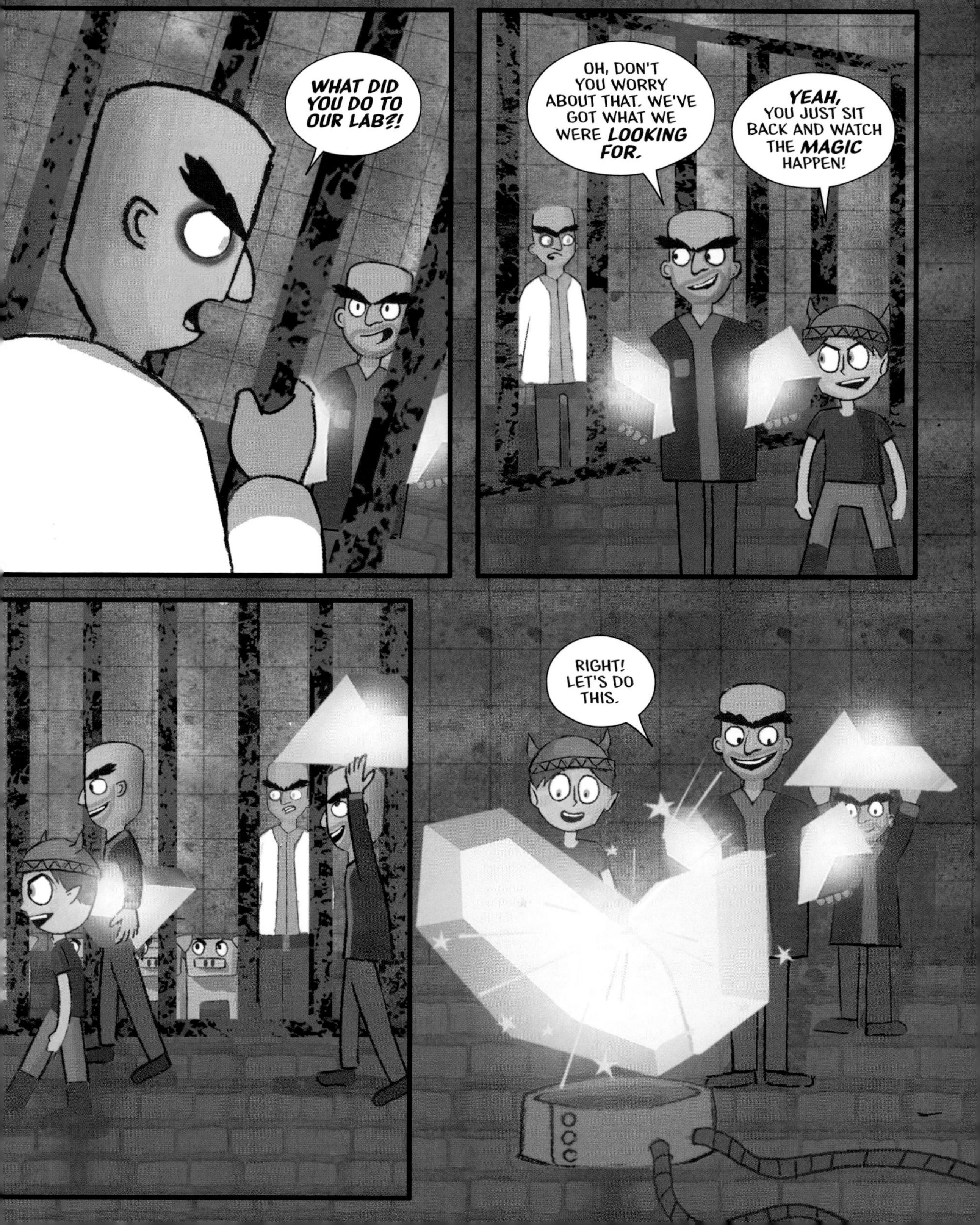
WHAT DID YOU DO TO OUR LAB?!
OH, DON'T YOU WORRY ABOUT THAT. WE'VE GOT WHAT WE WERE LOOKING FOR.
YEAH, YOU JUST SIT BACK AND WATCH THE MAGIC HAPPEN!
RIGHT! LET'S DO THIS.

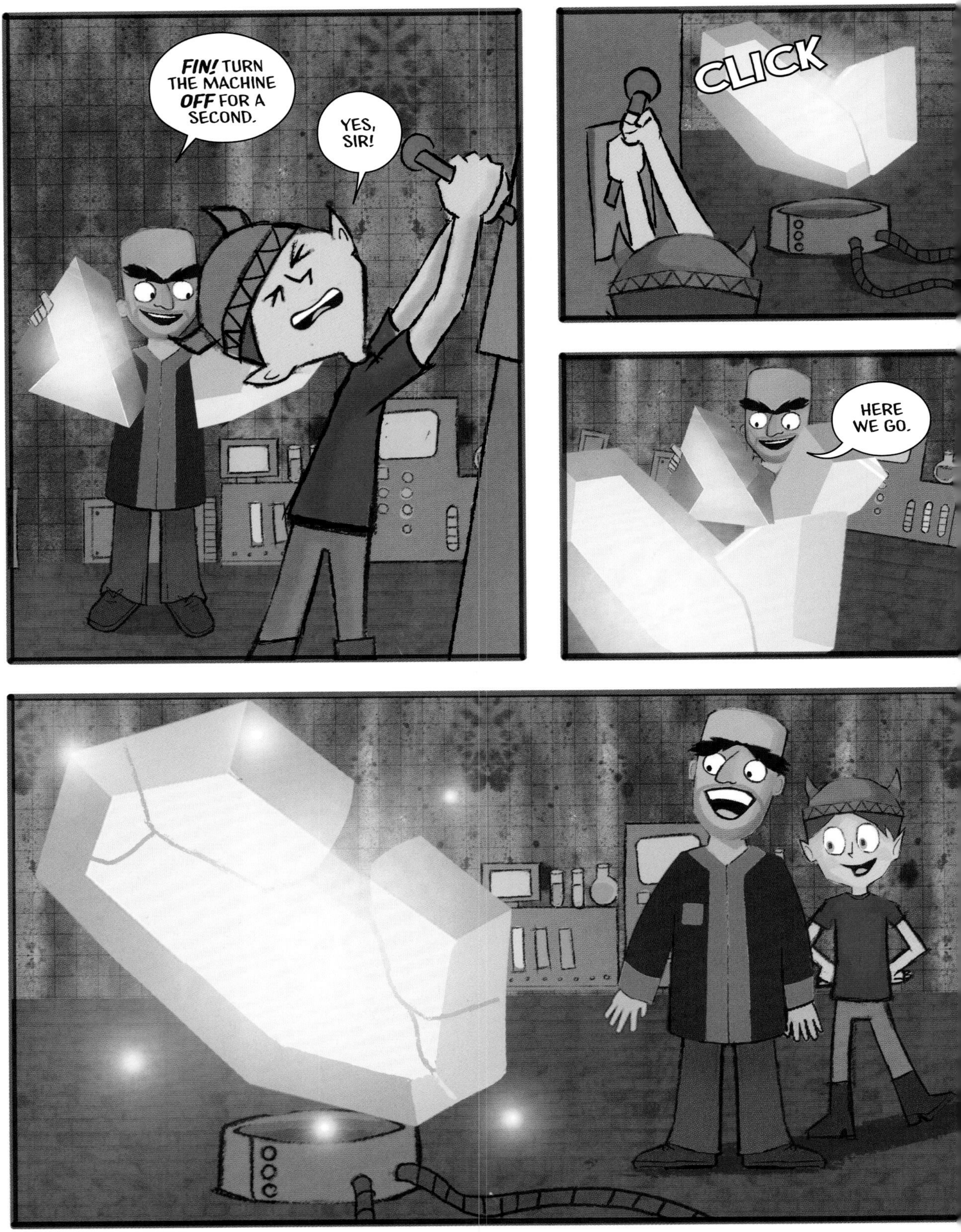
FIN! TURN THE MACHINE OFF FOR A SECOND.
YES, SIR!
CLICK
HERE WE GO.

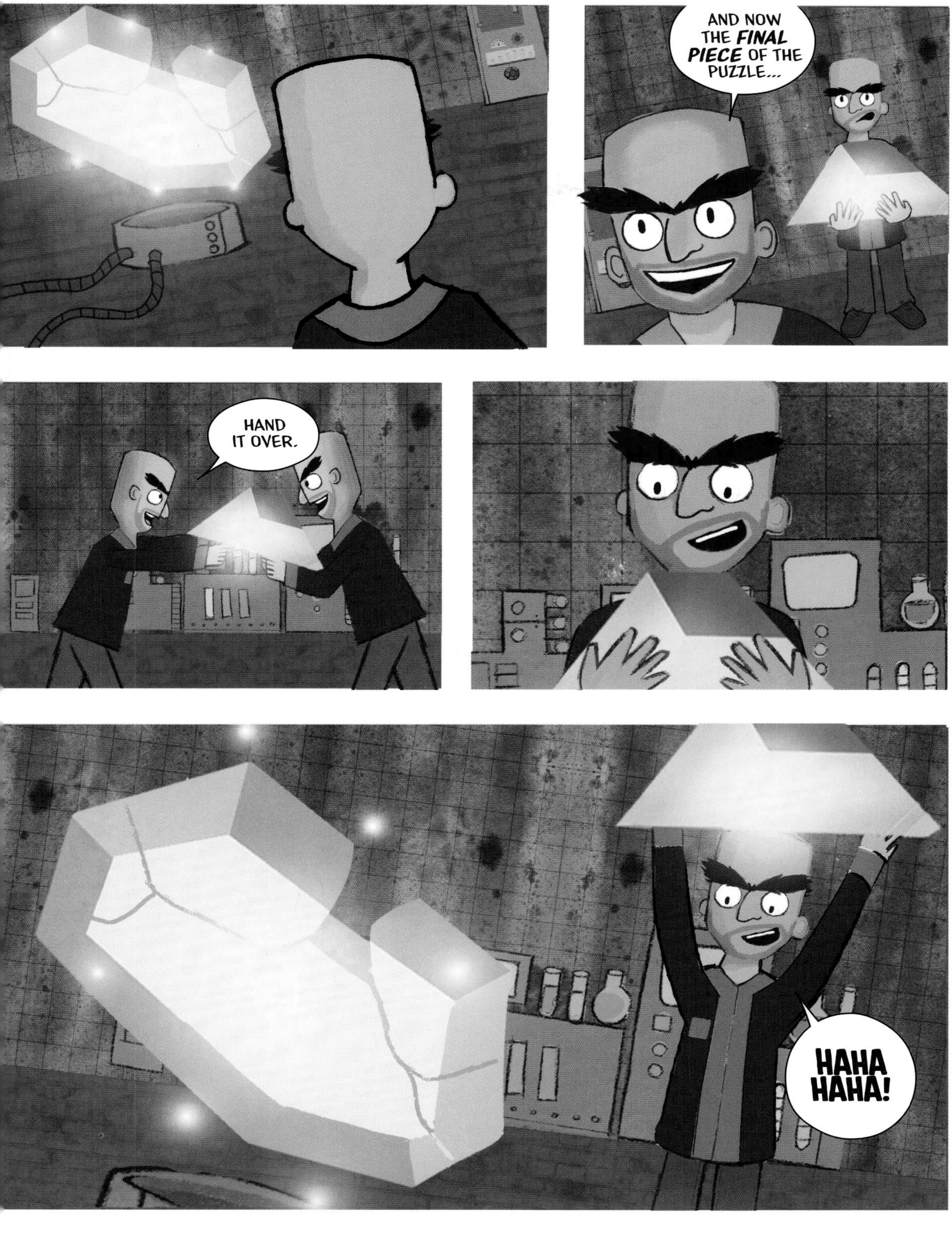
AND NOW THE FINAL PIECE OF THE PUZZLE...
HAND IT OVER.
HAHA HAHA!

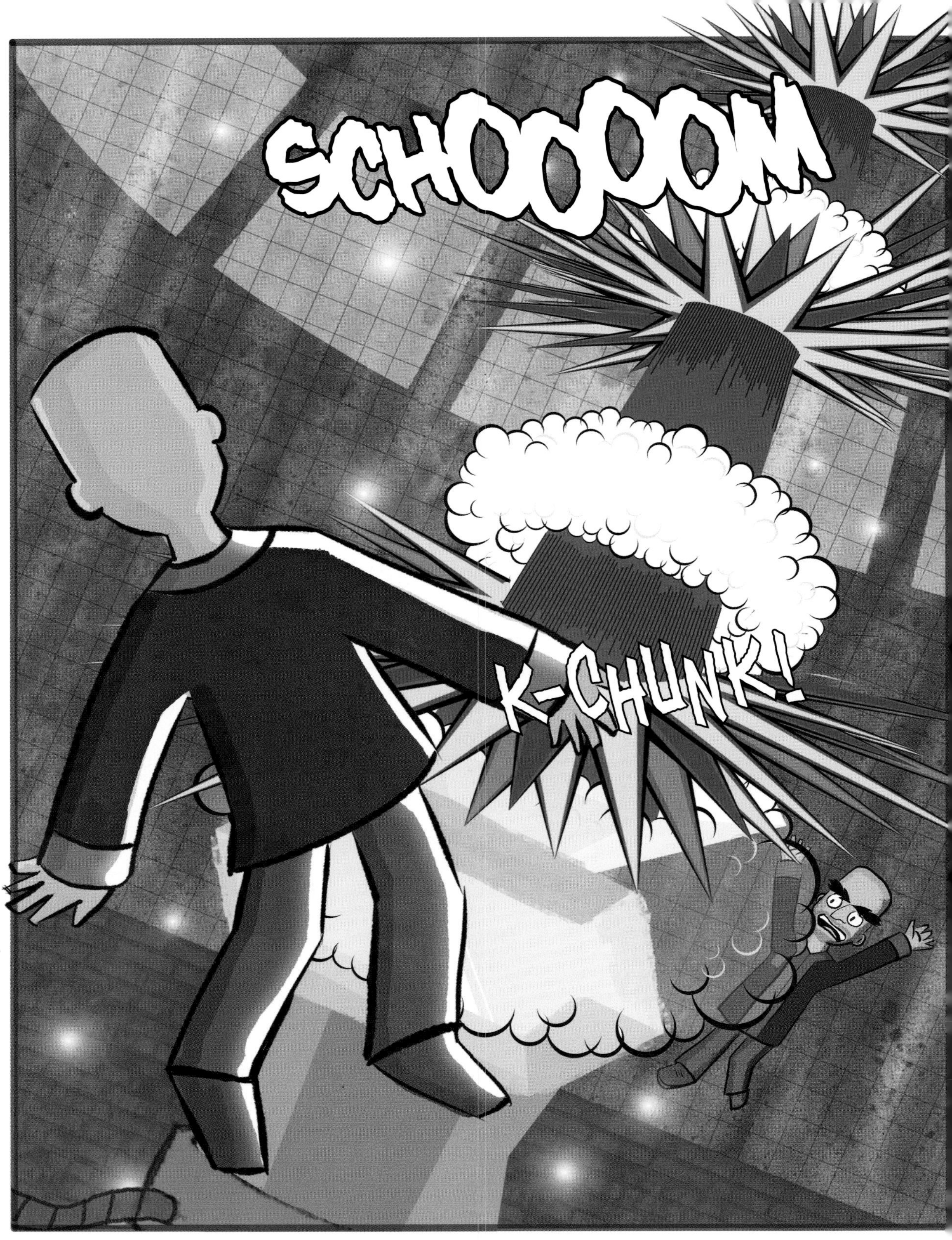
SCHOOOOOM
K-CHUNK!

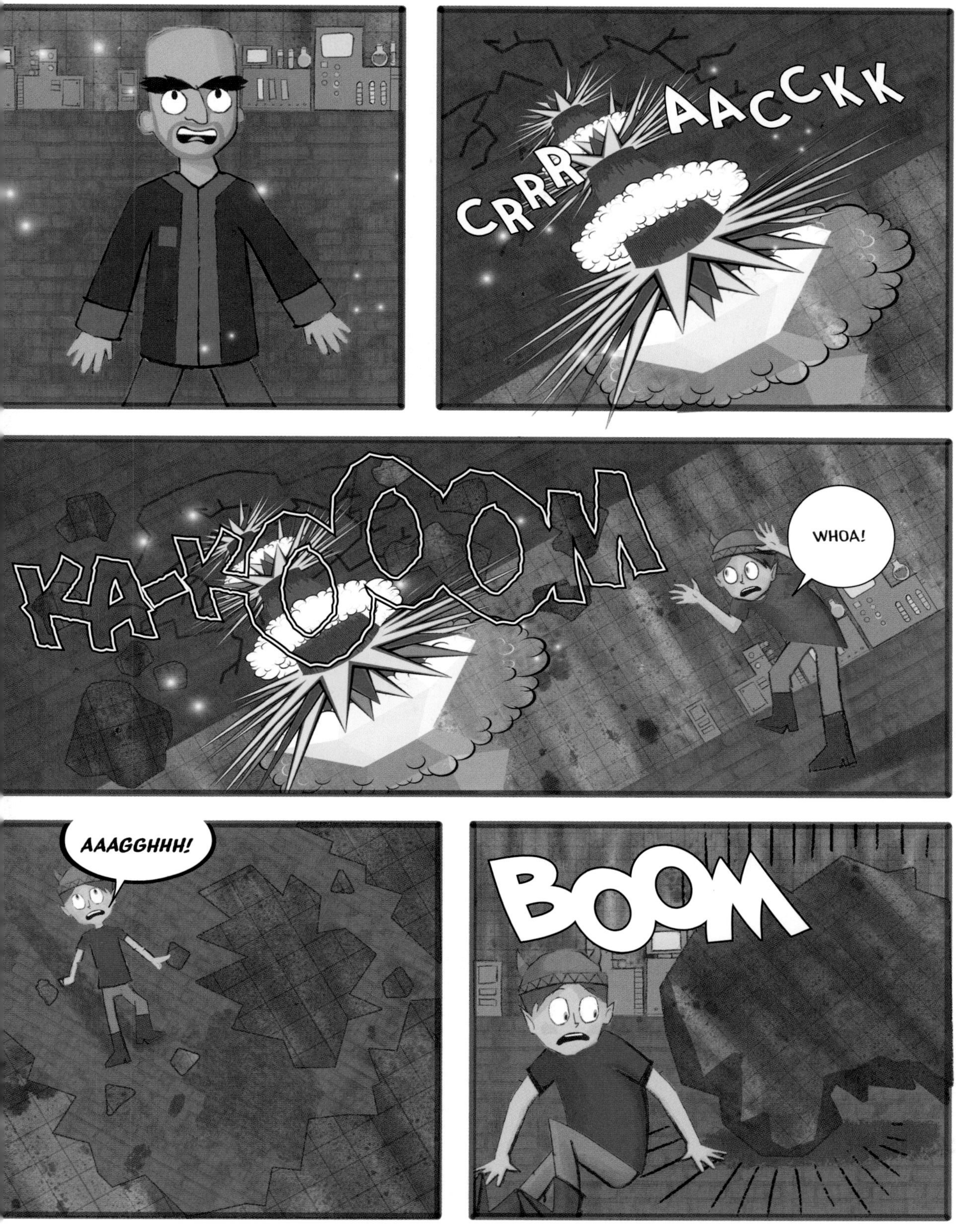
CRRRAACCKK
KA-KOOOOM
WHOA!
AAAGGHHH!
BOOM

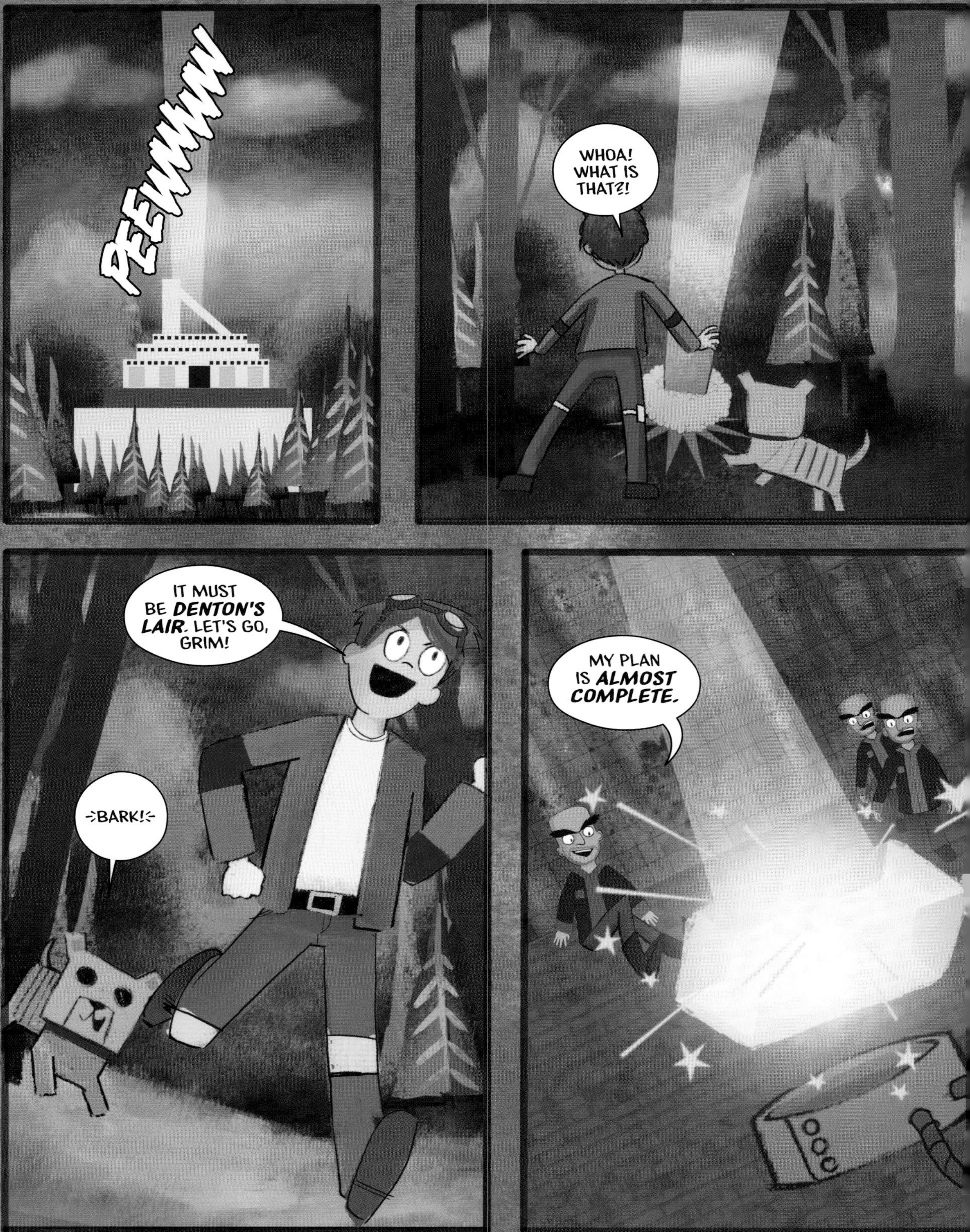
PEEWWWW
WHOA! WHAT IS THAT?!
IT MUST BE **DENTON'S LAIR**. LET'S GO, GRIM!
BARK!
MY PLAN IS **ALMOST COMPLETE.**

NOW WE JUST TURN THE MACHINE BACK **ON** AND—

—*ACTIVATE!*

CLUNK

WUUUMM

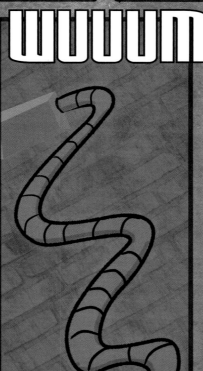

HERE.... WE.... **GO!**

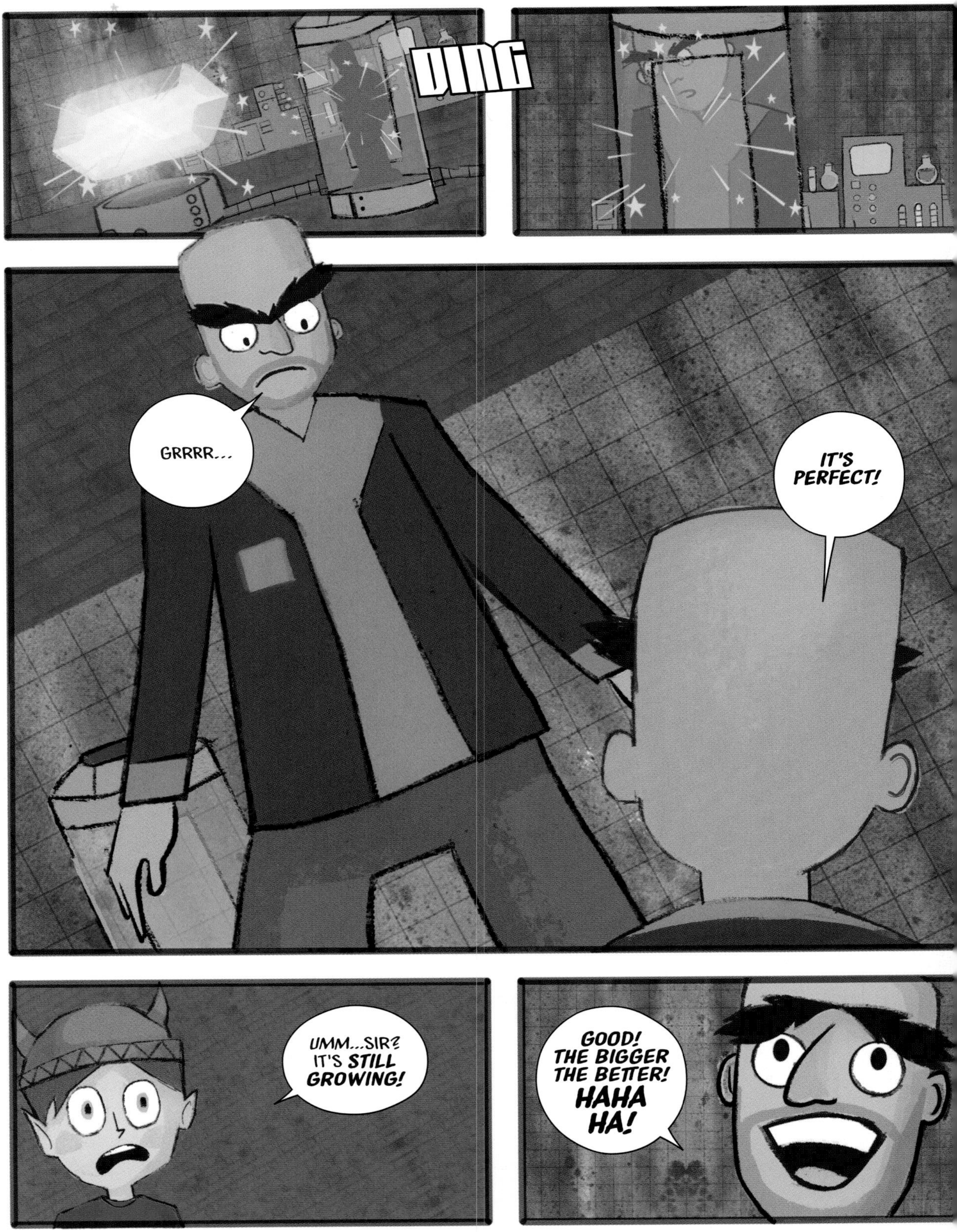
DING
GRRRR...
IT'S PERFECT!
UMM...SIR? IT'S STILL GROWING!
GOOD! THE BIGGER THE BETTER! HAHA HA!

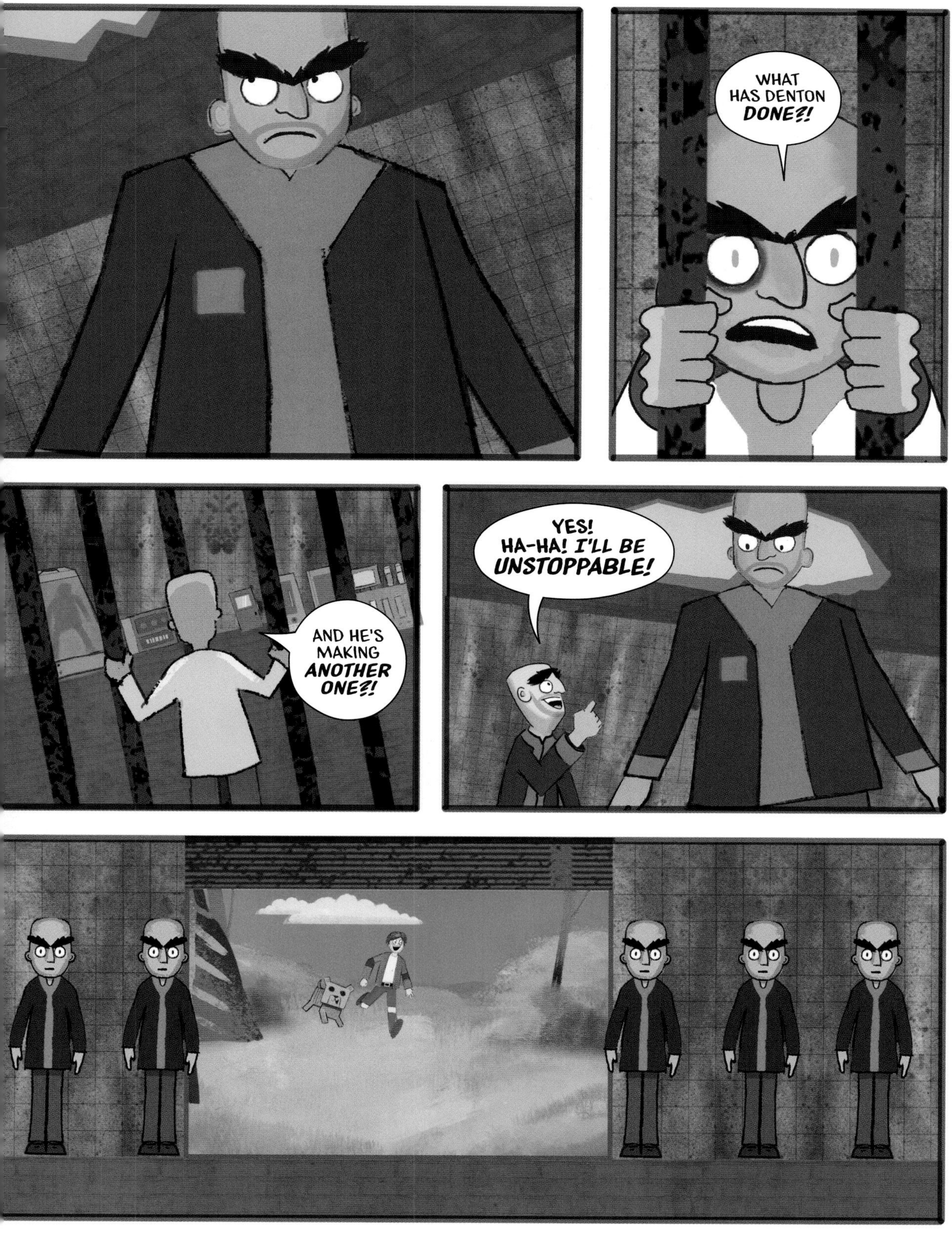
WHAT HAS DENTON DONE?!
AND HE'S MAKING ANOTHER ONE?!
YES! HA-HA! I'LL BE UNSTOPPABLE!

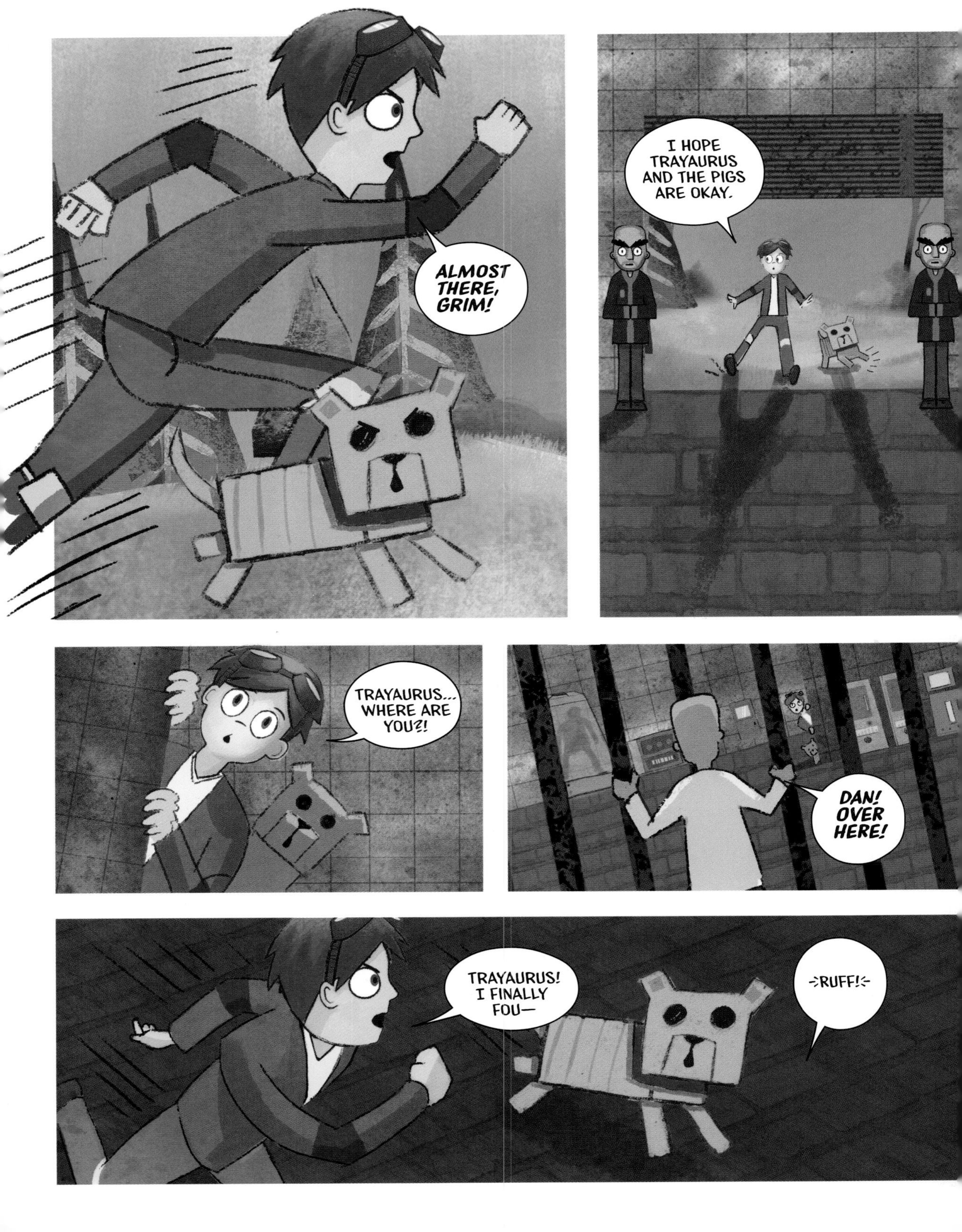
ALMOST THERE, GRIM!
I HOPE TRAYAURUS AND THE PIGS ARE OKAY.
TRAYAURUS... WHERE ARE YOU?!
DAN! OVER HERE!
TRAYAURUS! I FINALLY FOU—
RUFF!

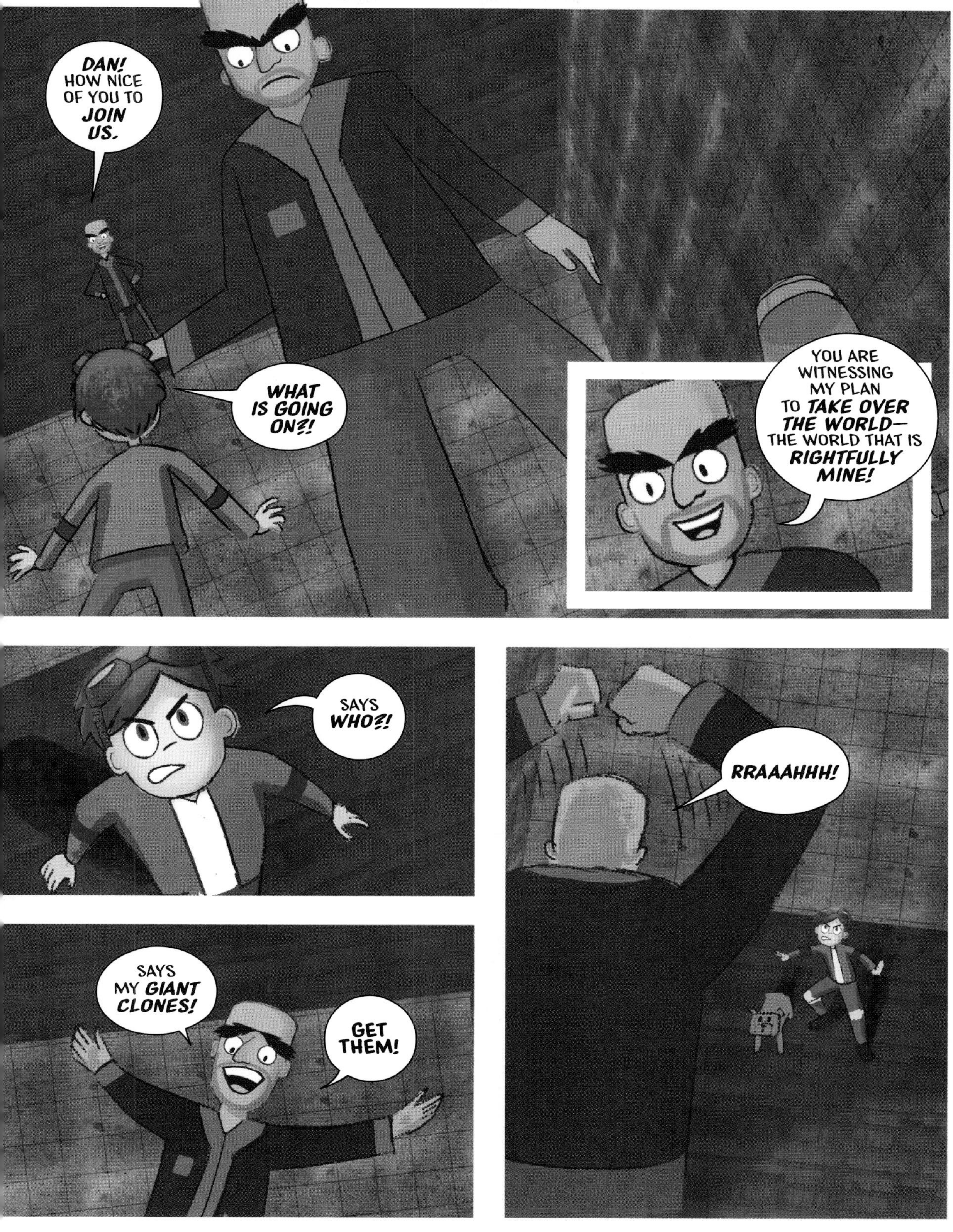
DAN! HOW NICE OF YOU TO JOIN US.
WHAT IS GOING ON?!
YOU ARE WITNESSING MY PLAN TO TAKE OVER THE WORLD— THE WORLD THAT IS RIGHTFULLY MINE!
SAYS WHO?!
SAYS MY GIANT CLONES!
GET THEM!
RRAAAHHH!

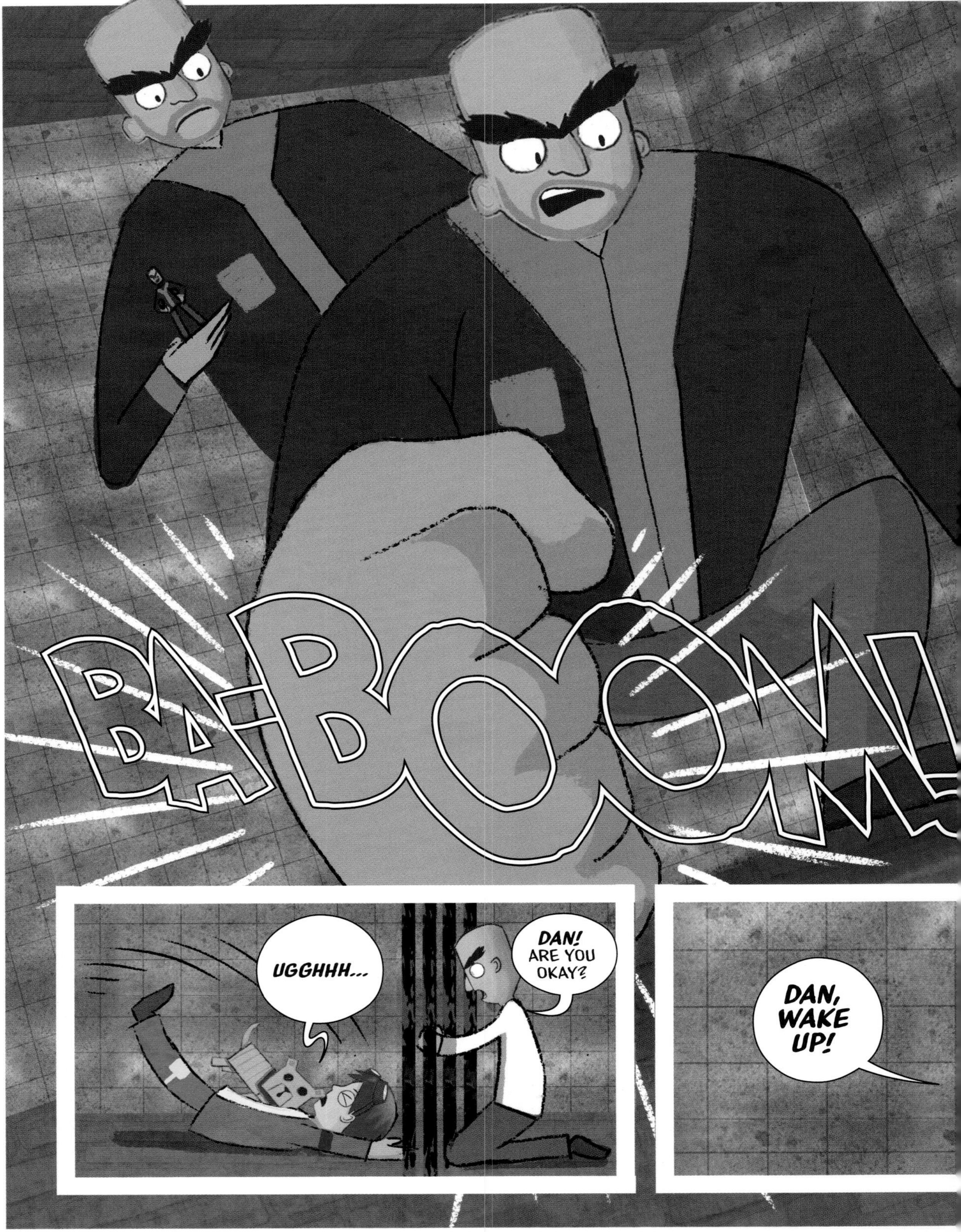
BA-BOOM!
UGGHHH...
DAN! ARE YOU OKAY?
DAN, WAKE UP!

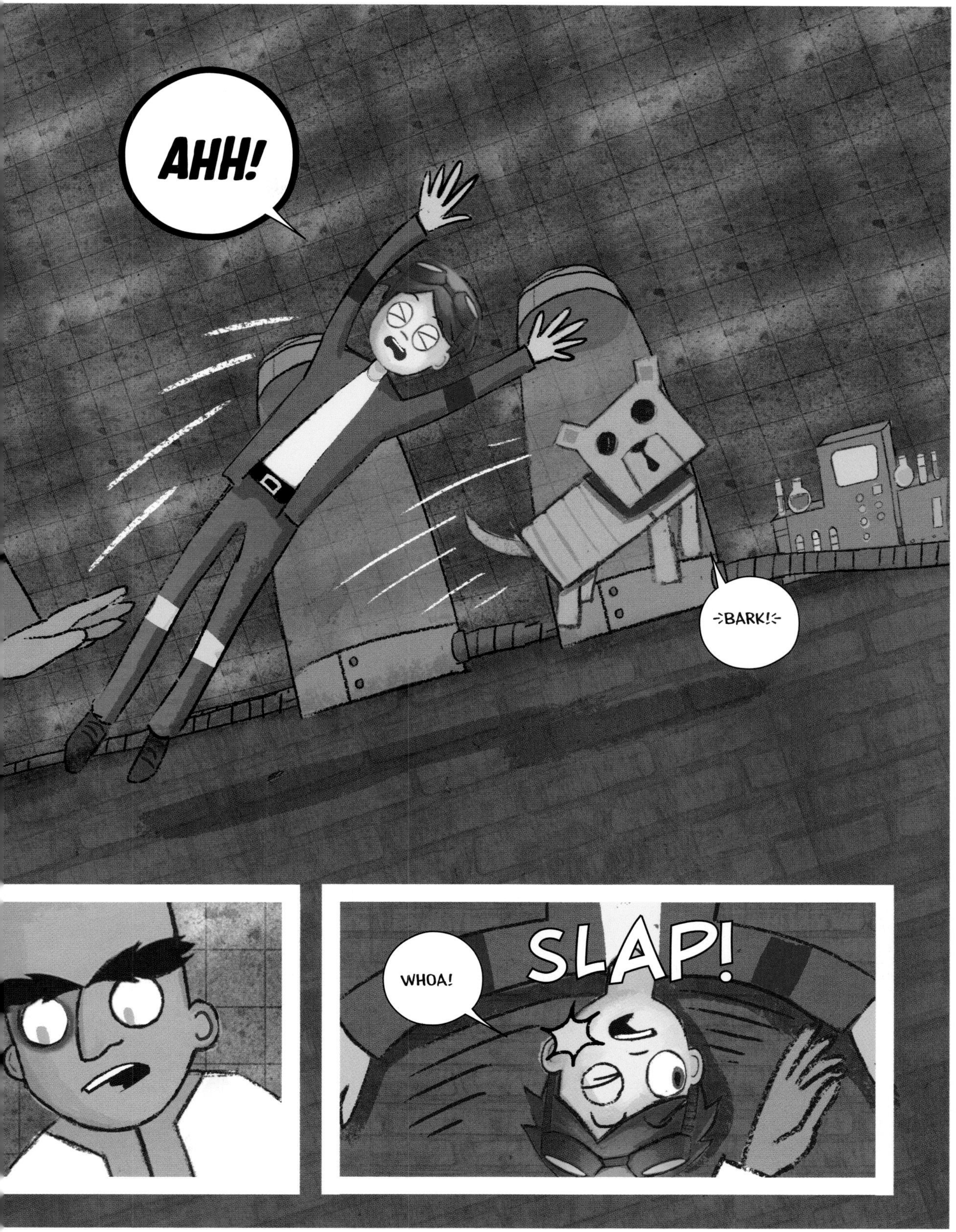
AHH!
BARK!
WHOA!
SLAP!

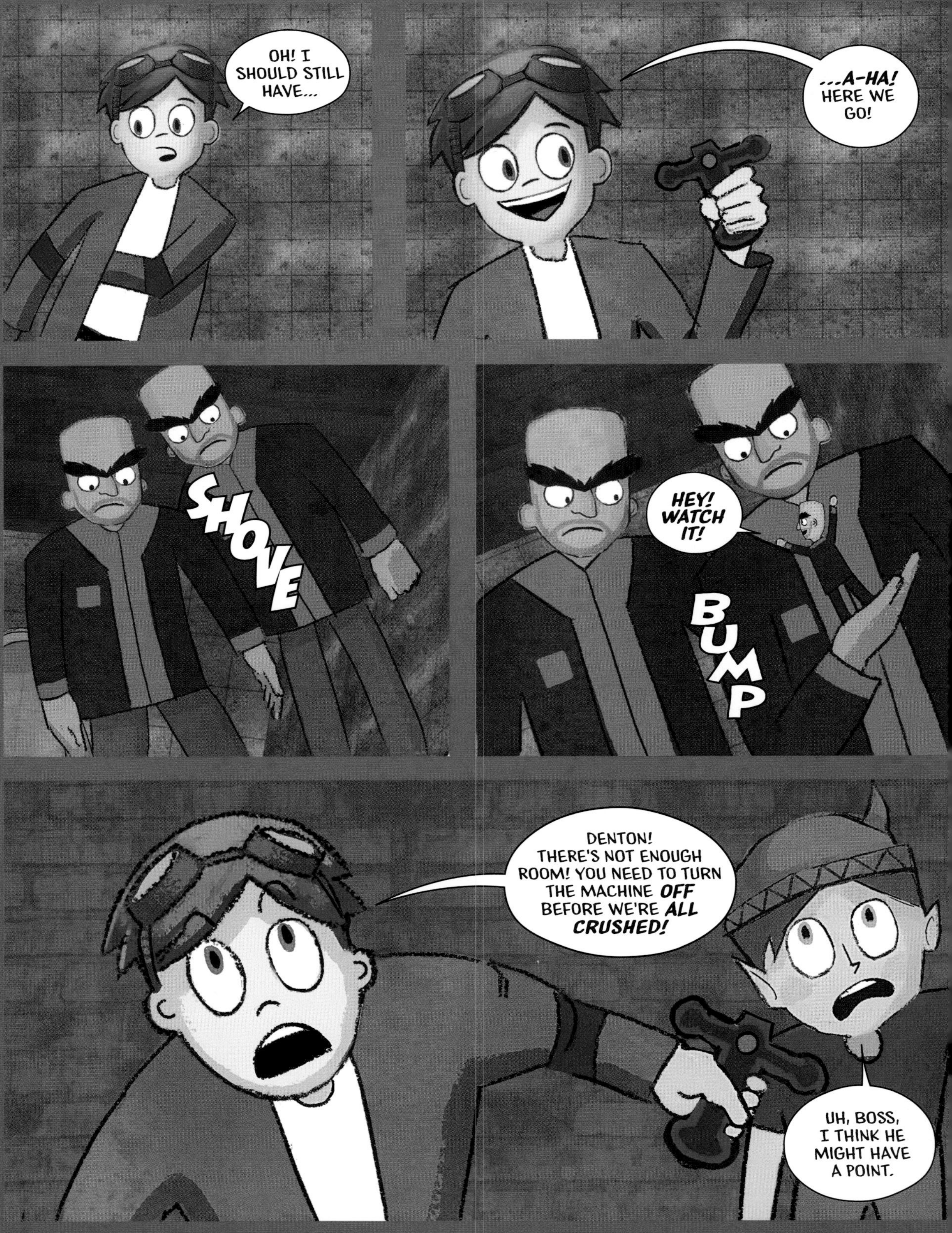
OH! I SHOULD STILL HAVE...
...A-HA! HERE WE GO!
SHOVE
HEY! WATCH IT!
BUMP
DENTON! THERE'S NOT ENOUGH ROOM! YOU NEED TO TURN THE MACHINE *OFF* BEFORE WE'RE ***ALL CRUSHED!***
UH, BOSS, I THINK HE MIGHT HAVE A POINT.

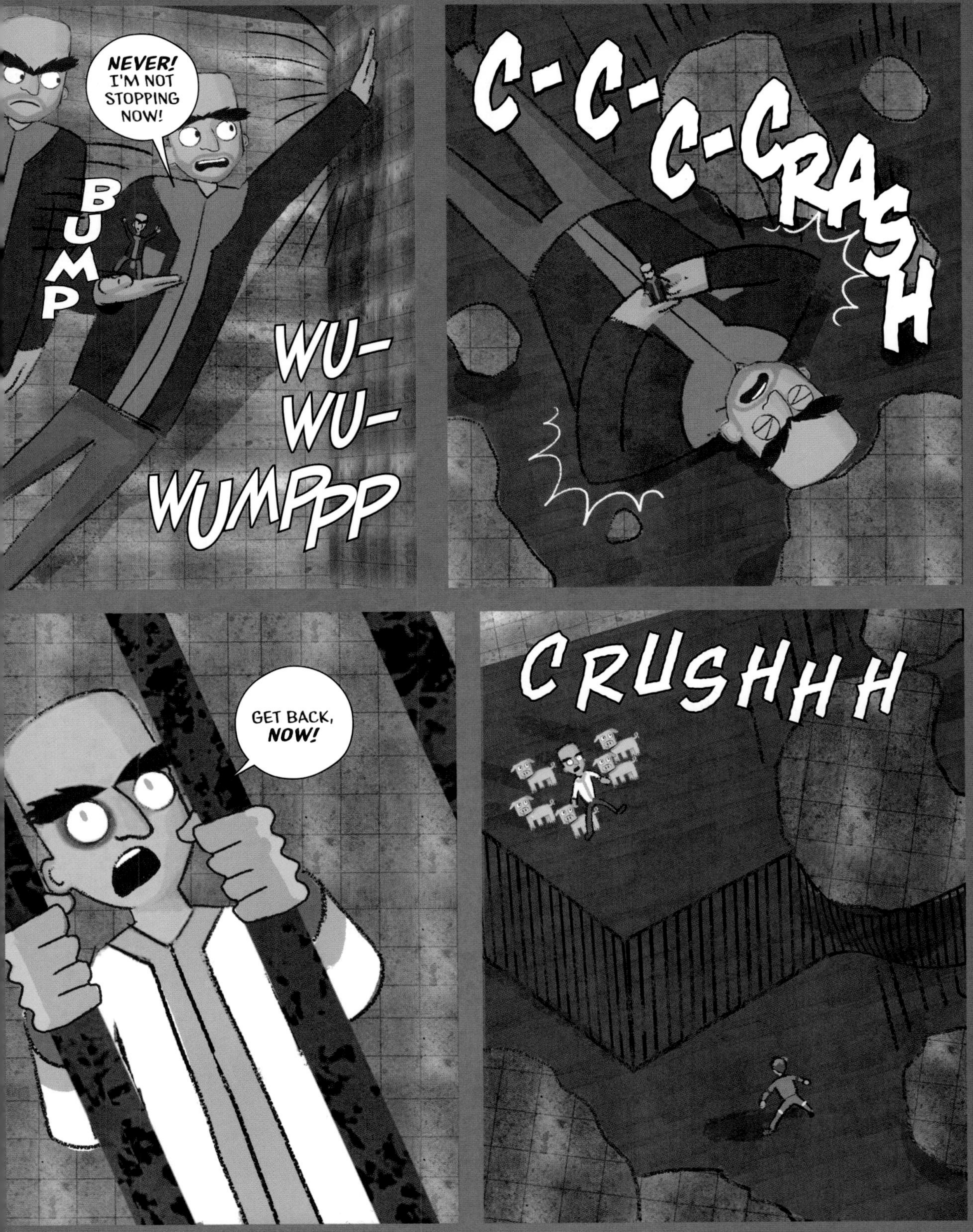
NEVER! I'M NOT STOPPING NOW!
BUMP
WU- WU- WUMPPP
C-C-C-CRASH
GET BACK, NOW!
CRUSHHH

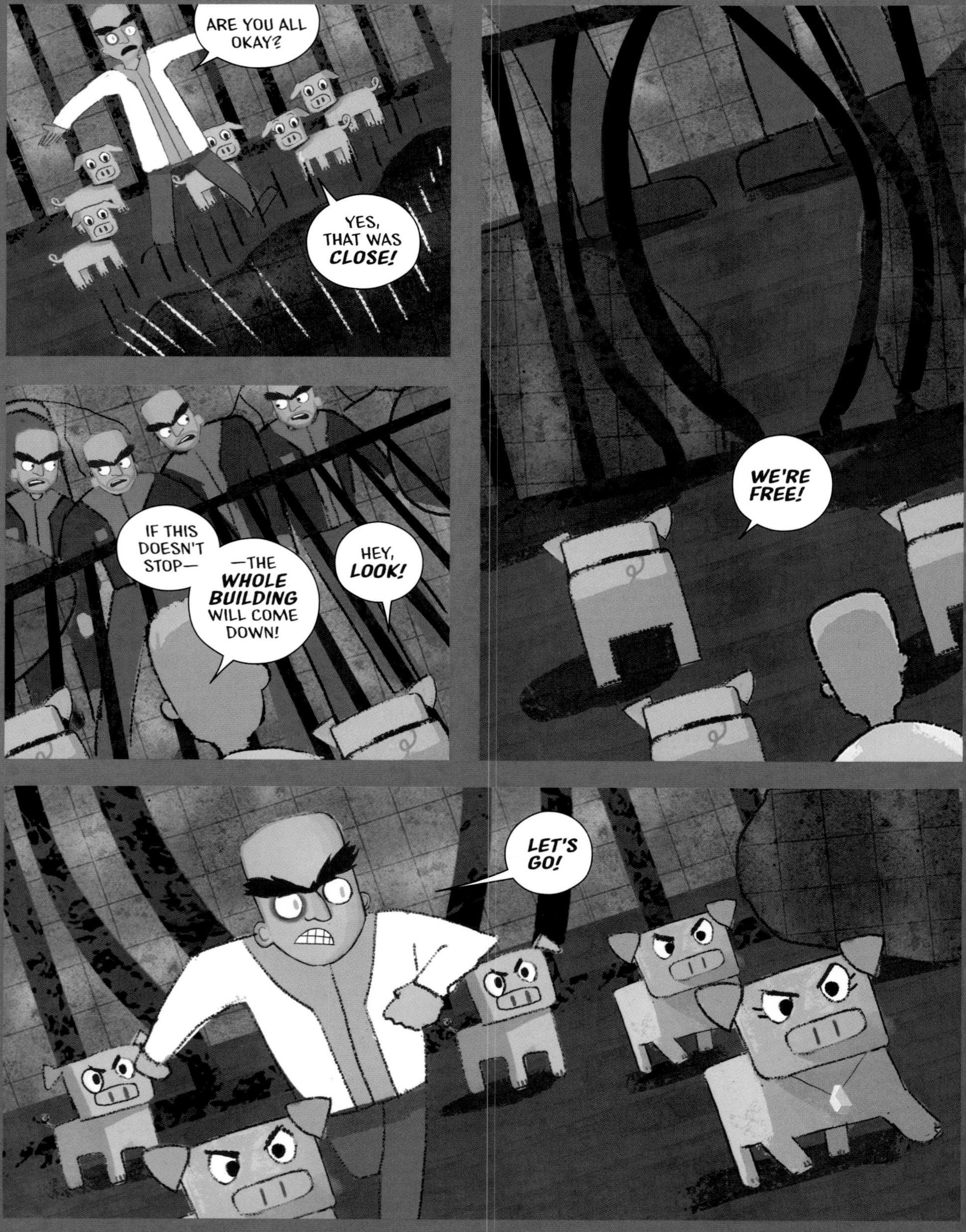
ARE YOU ALL OKAY?
YES, THAT WAS CLOSE!
IF THIS DOESN'T STOP—
—THE WHOLE BUILDING WILL COME DOWN!
HEY, LOOK!
WE'RE FREE!
LET'S GO!

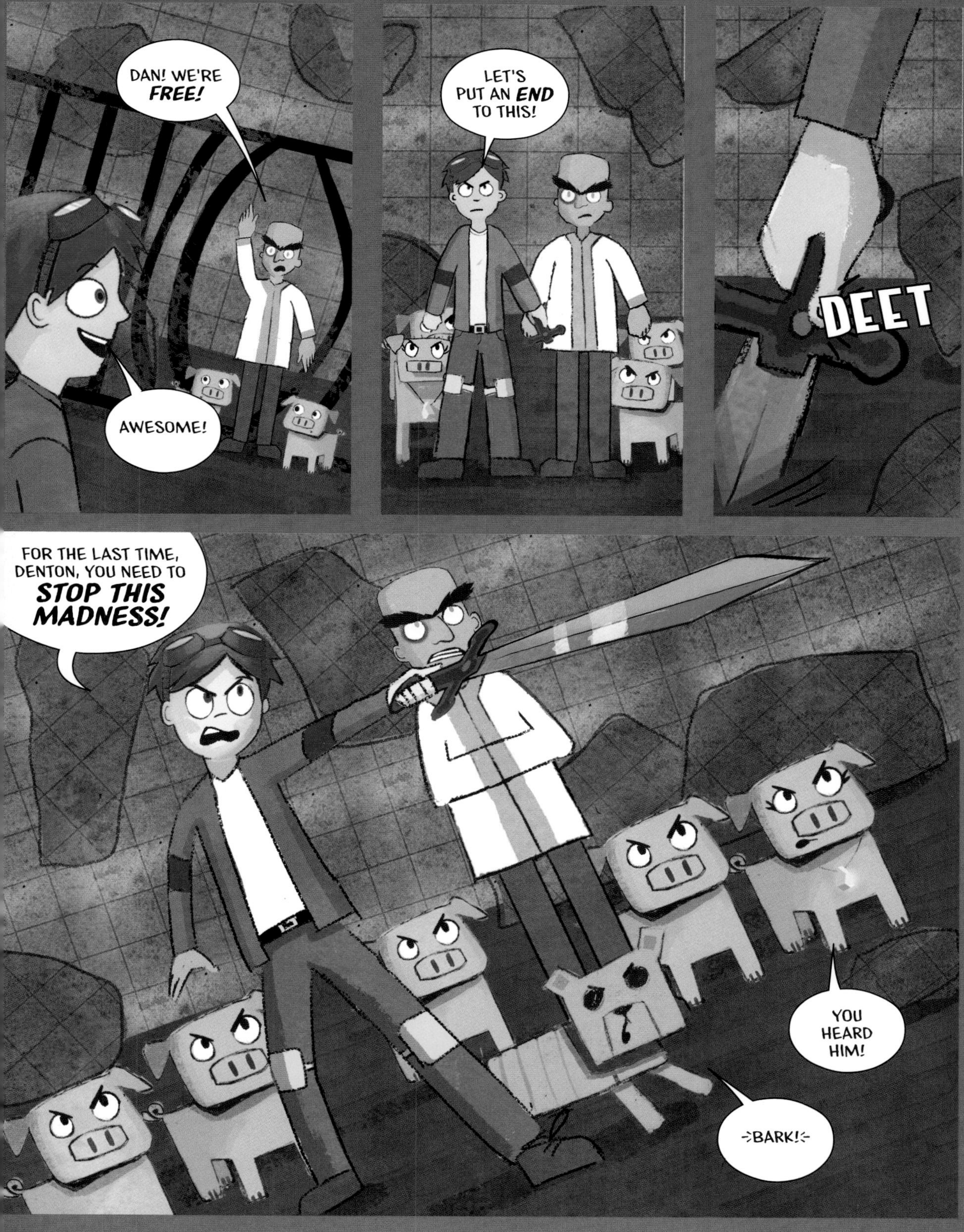
DAN! WE'RE FREE!
AWESOME!
LET'S PUT AN END TO THIS!
DEET
FOR THE LAST TIME, DENTON, YOU NEED TO STOP THIS MADNESS!
YOU HEARD HIM!
BARK!

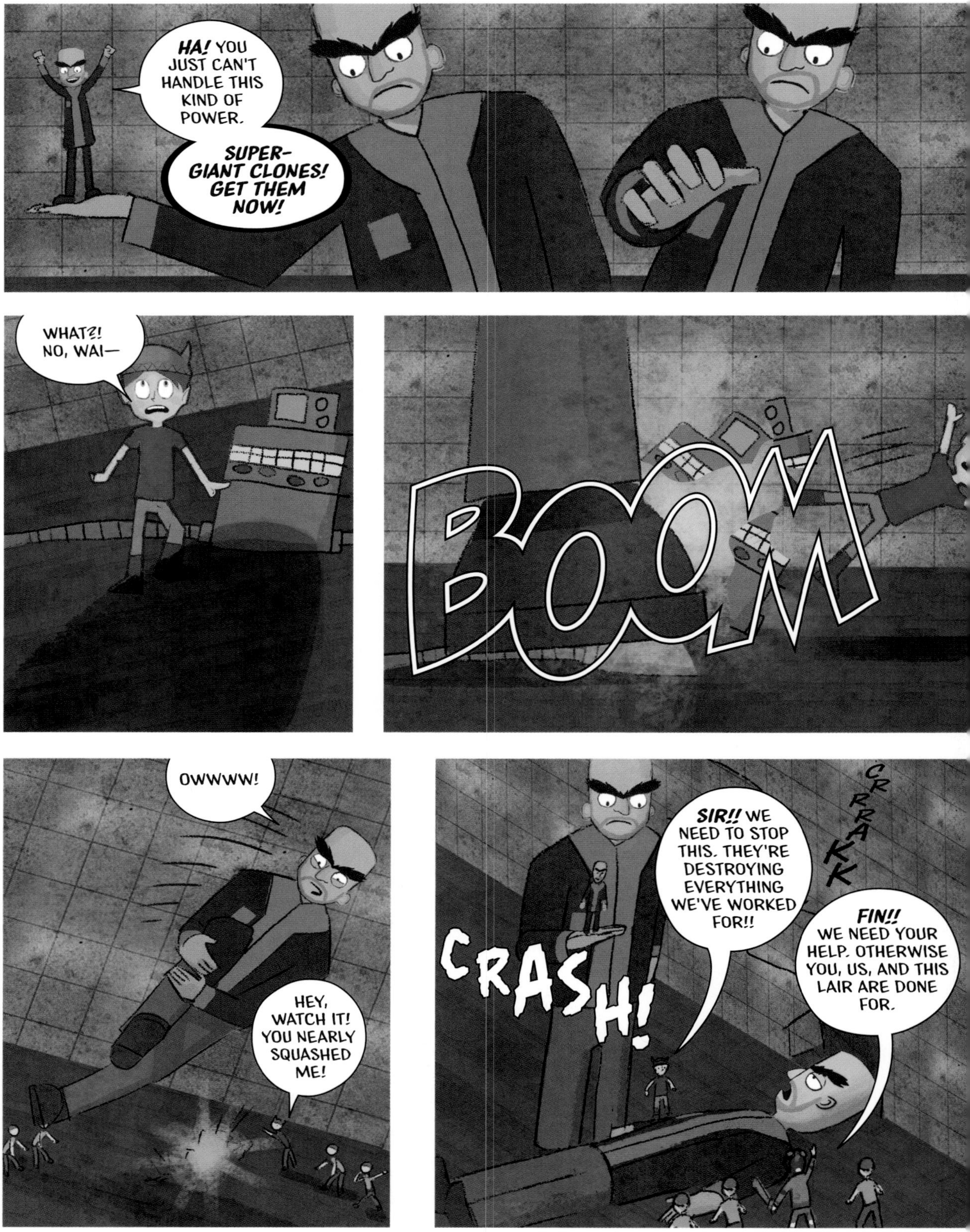
HA! YOU JUST CAN'T HANDLE THIS KIND OF POWER.
SUPER-GIANT CLONES! GET THEM NOW!
WHAT?! NO, WAI—
BOOM
OWWWW!
HEY, WATCH IT! YOU NEARLY SQUASHED ME!
CRASH!
SIR!! WE NEED TO STOP THIS. THEY'RE DESTROYING EVERYTHING WE'VE WORKED FOR!!
CRRRAKK
FIN!! WE NEED YOUR HELP. OTHERWISE YOU, US, AND THIS LAIR ARE DONE FOR.

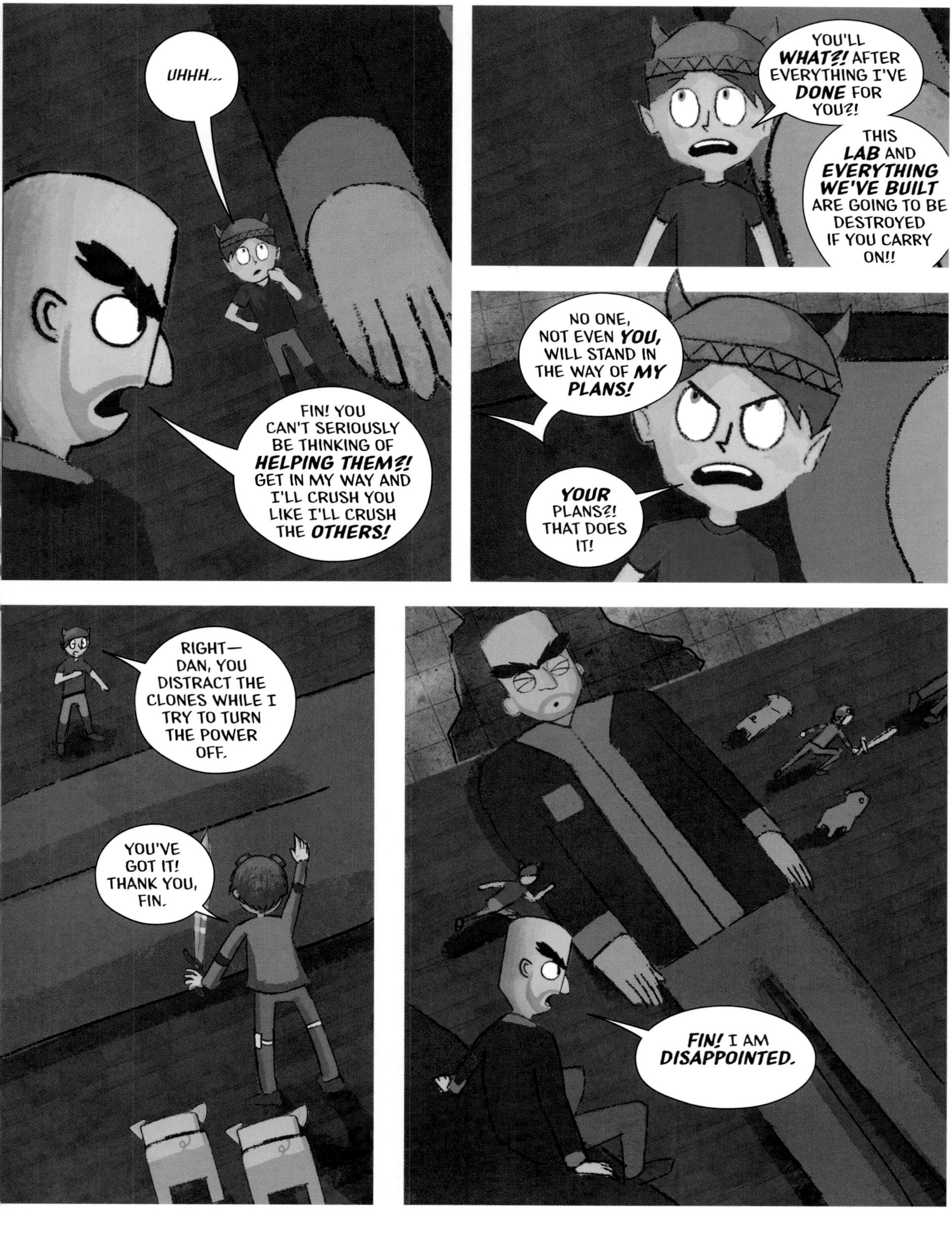
UHHH...
FIN! YOU CAN'T SERIOUSLY BE THINKING OF HELPING THEM?! GET IN MY WAY AND I'LL CRUSH YOU LIKE I'LL CRUSH THE OTHERS!
YOU'LL WHAT?! AFTER EVERYTHING I'VE DONE FOR YOU?!
THIS LAB AND EVERYTHING WE'VE BUILT ARE GOING TO BE DESTROYED IF YOU CARRY ON!!
NO ONE, NOT EVEN YOU, WILL STAND IN THE WAY OF MY PLANS!
YOUR PLANS?! THAT DOES IT!
RIGHT— DAN, YOU DISTRACT THE CLONES WHILE I TRY TO TURN THE POWER OFF.
YOU'VE GOT IT! THANK YOU, FIN.
FIN! I AM DISAPPOINTED.

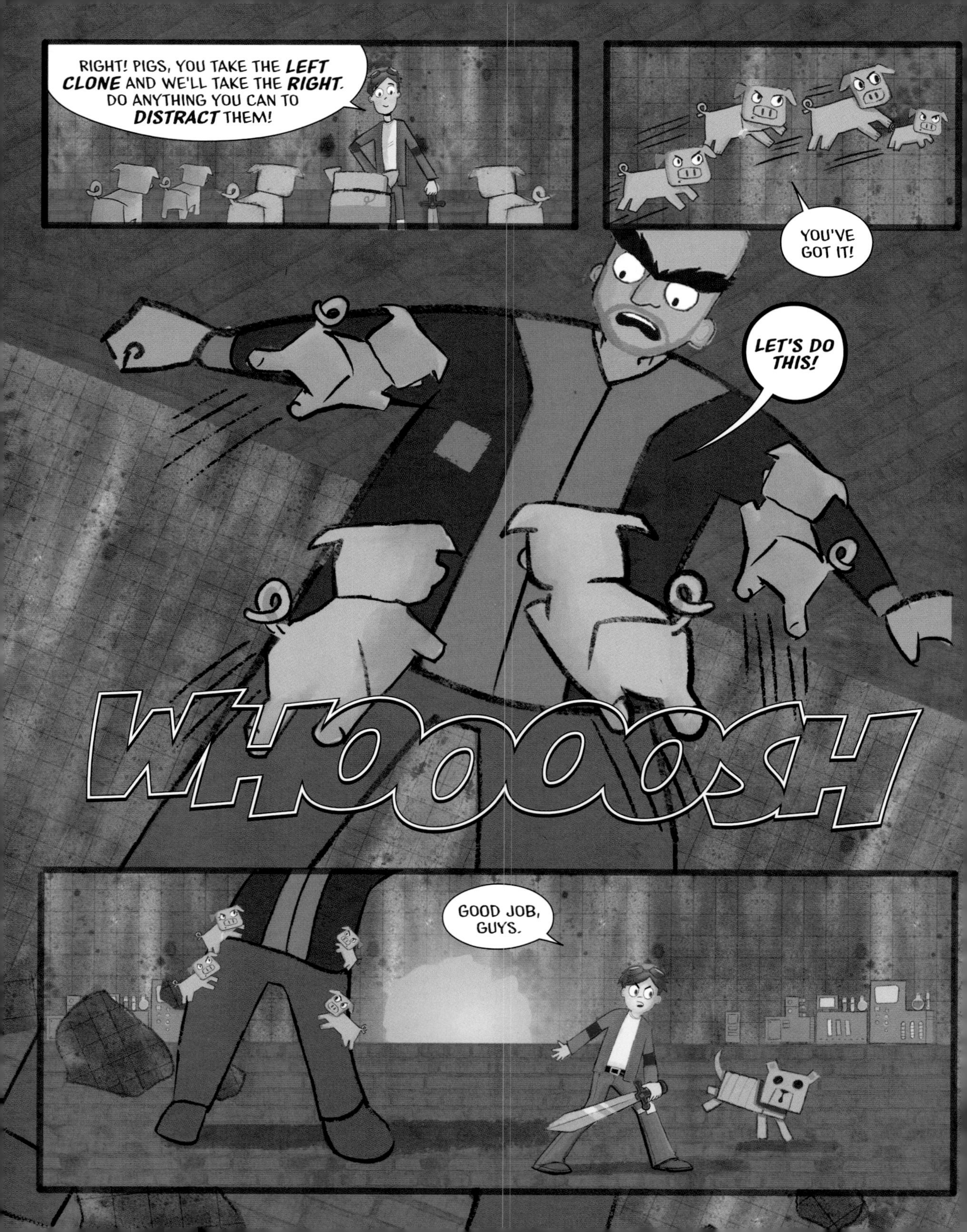
RIGHT! PIGS, YOU TAKE THE LEFT CLONE AND WE'LL TAKE THE RIGHT. DO ANYTHING YOU CAN TO DISTRACT THEM!
YOU'VE GOT IT!
LET'S DO THIS!
WHOOOOSH
GOOD JOB, GUYS.

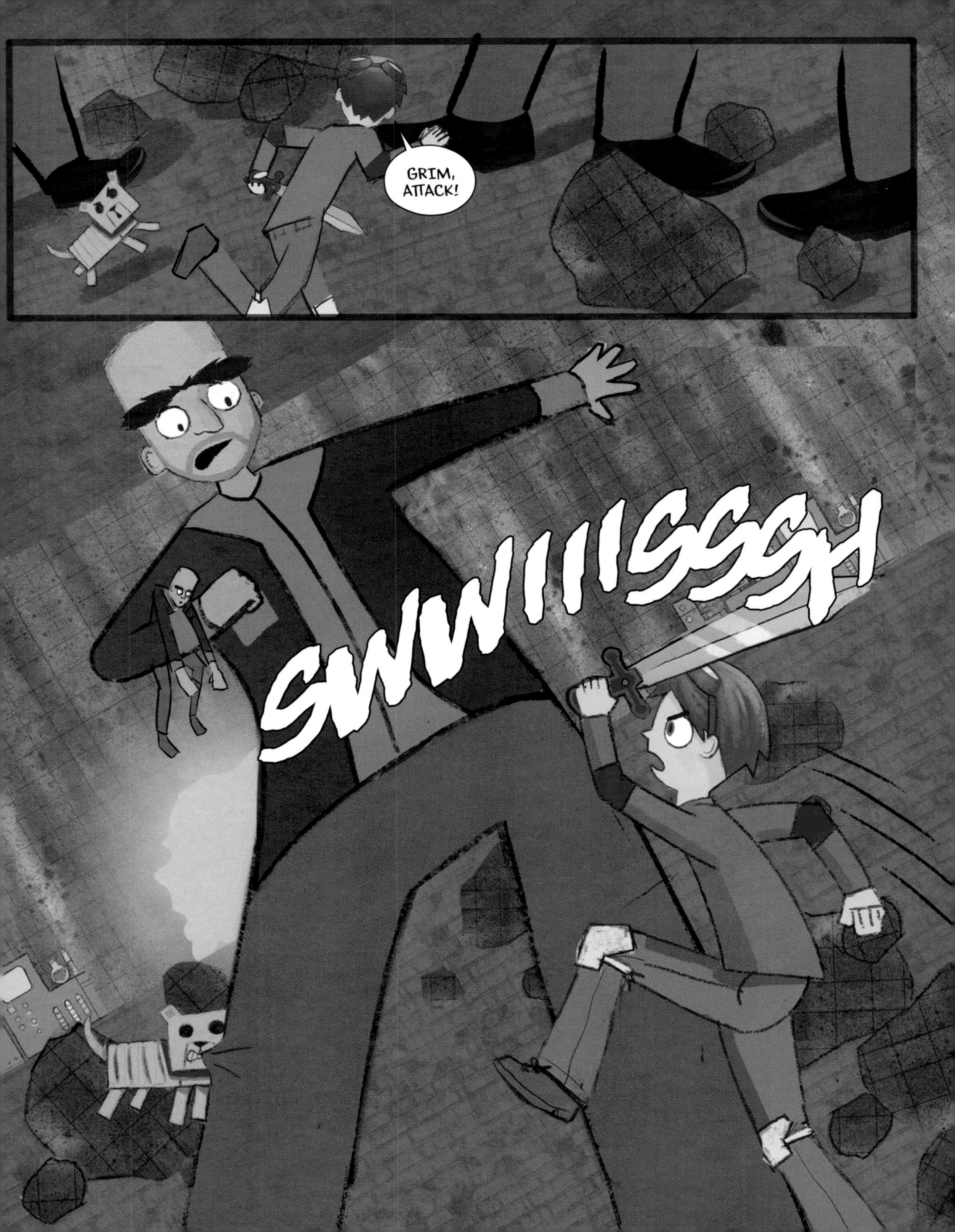
GRIM, ATTACK!
SWIIISSSH

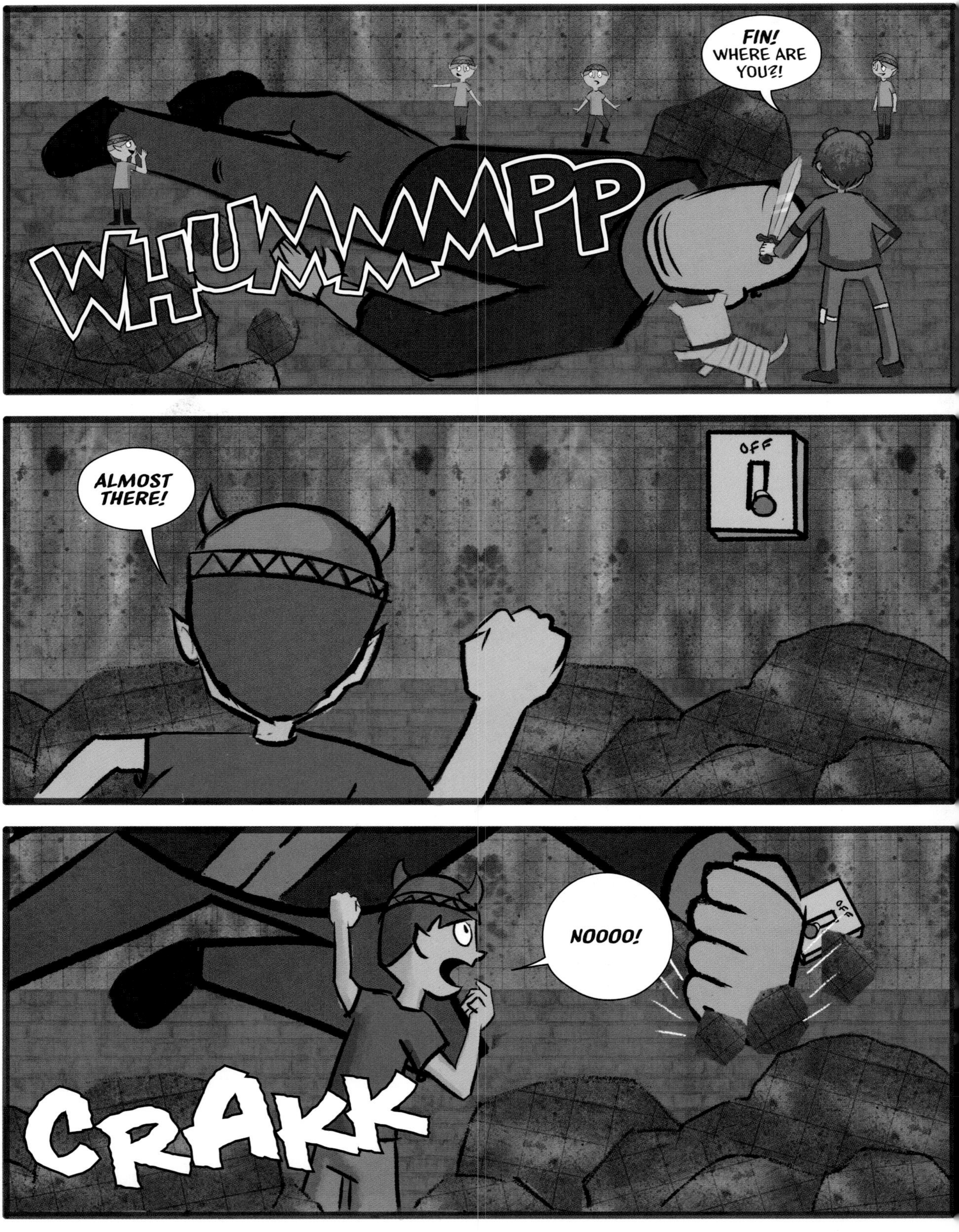
FIN! WHERE ARE YOU?!
WHUMMMPP
ALMOST THERE!
OFF
OFF
NOOOO!
CRAKK

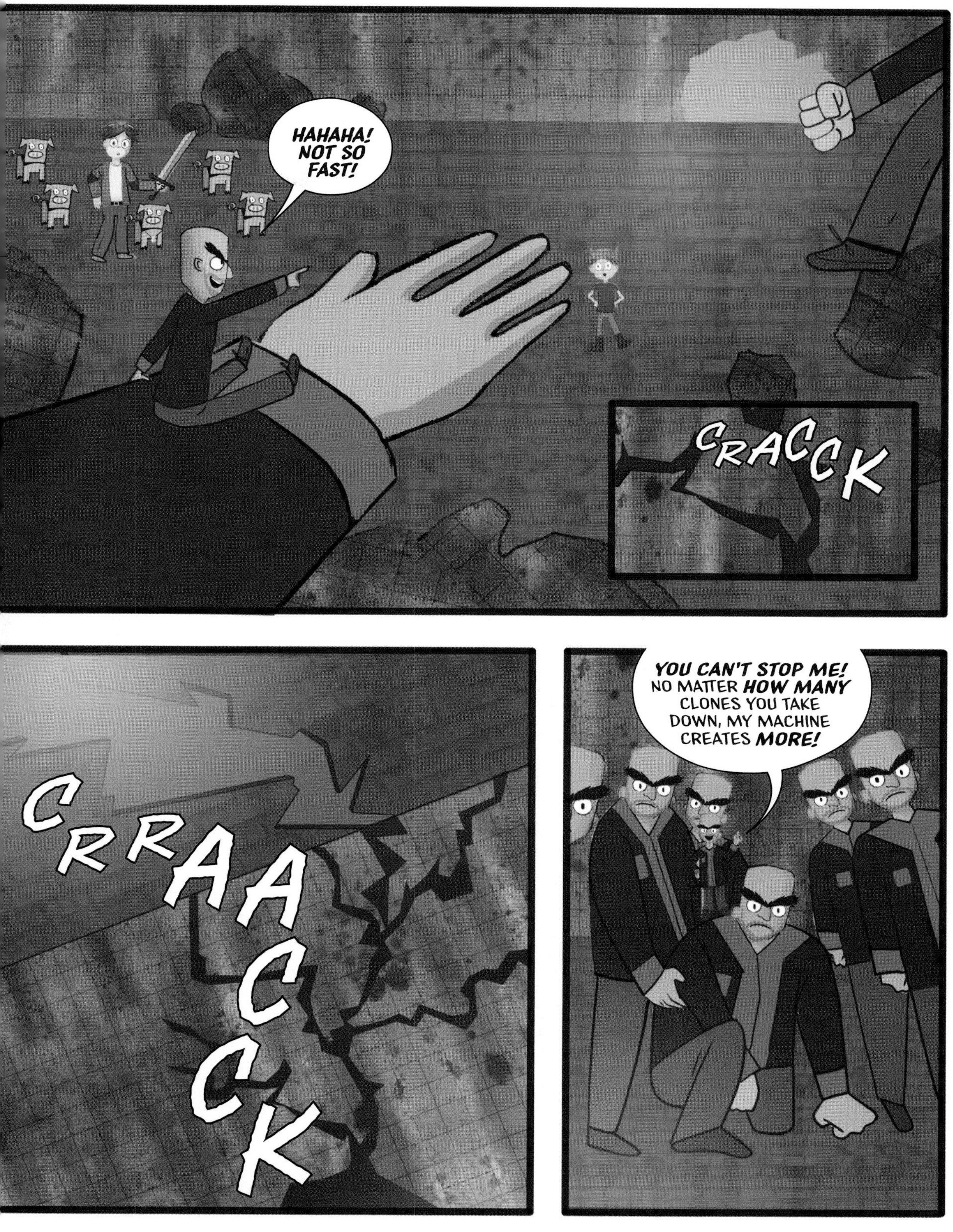
HAHAHA! NOT SO FAST!
CRACCK
CRRAACCK
YOU CAN'T STOP ME! NO MATTER HOW MANY CLONES YOU TAKE DOWN, MY MACHINE CREATES MORE!

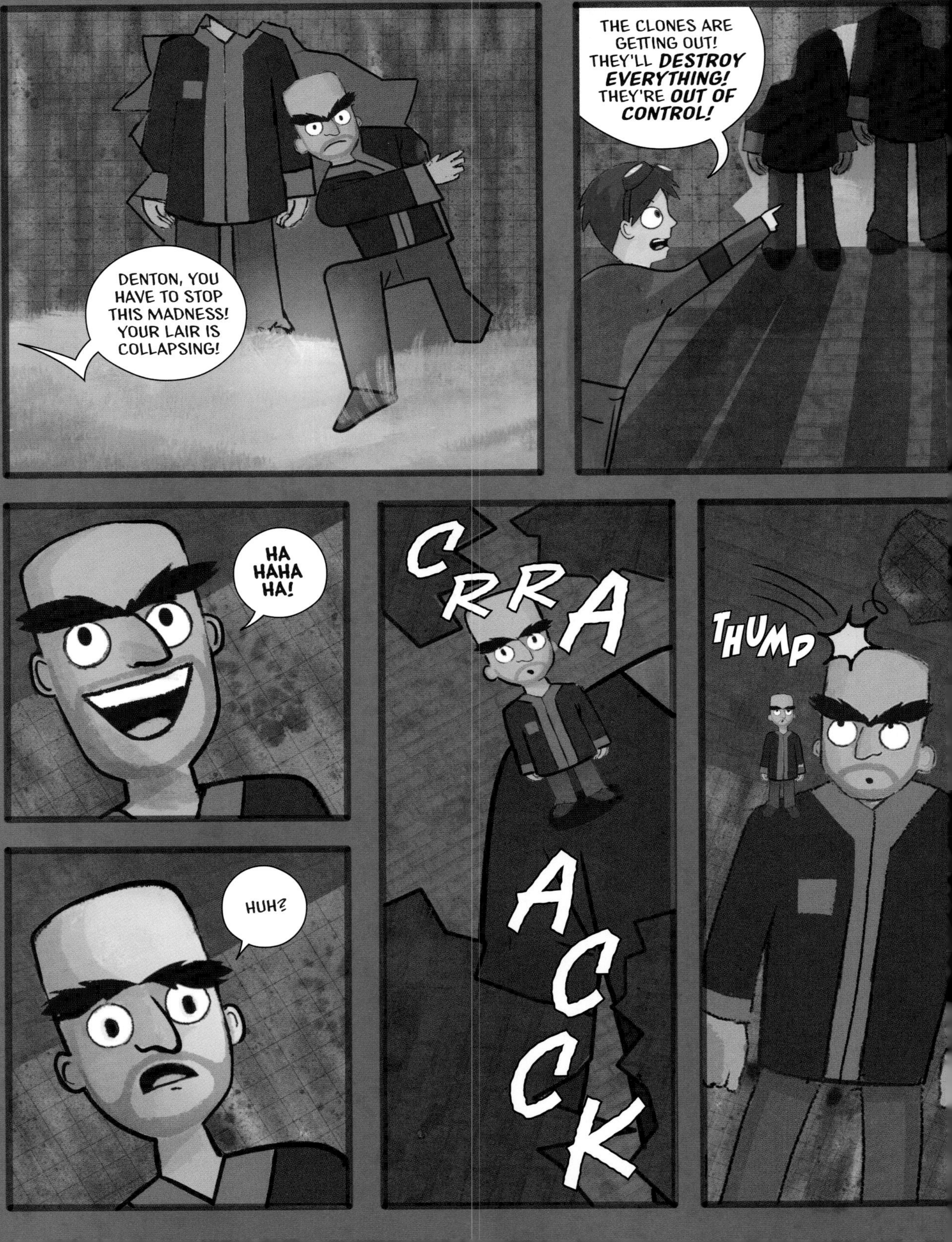
DENTON, YOU HAVE TO STOP THIS MADNESS! YOUR LAIR IS COLLAPSING!
THE CLONES ARE GETTING OUT! THEY'LL DESTROY EVERYTHING! THEY'RE OUT OF CONTROL!
HA HAHA HA!
HUH?
CRRA ACCK
THUMP

AHHH!
WHUMP!
DENTON!
THIS IS OUT OF CONTROL! TELL ME HOW TO STOP THE MACHINE, NOW!
DON'T FORCE ME TO USE THIS.

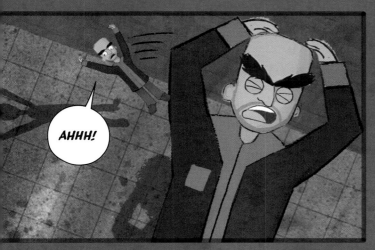

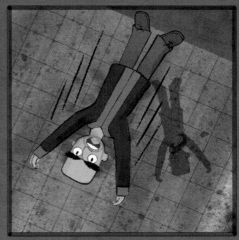

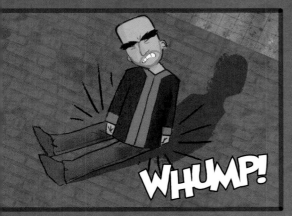

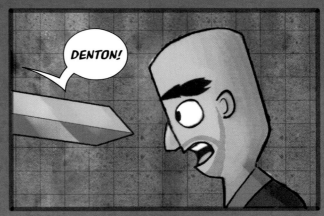

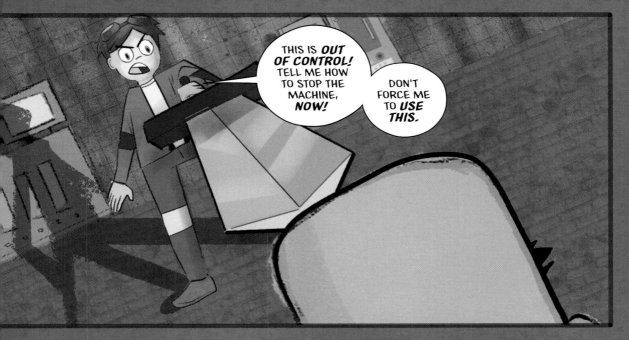

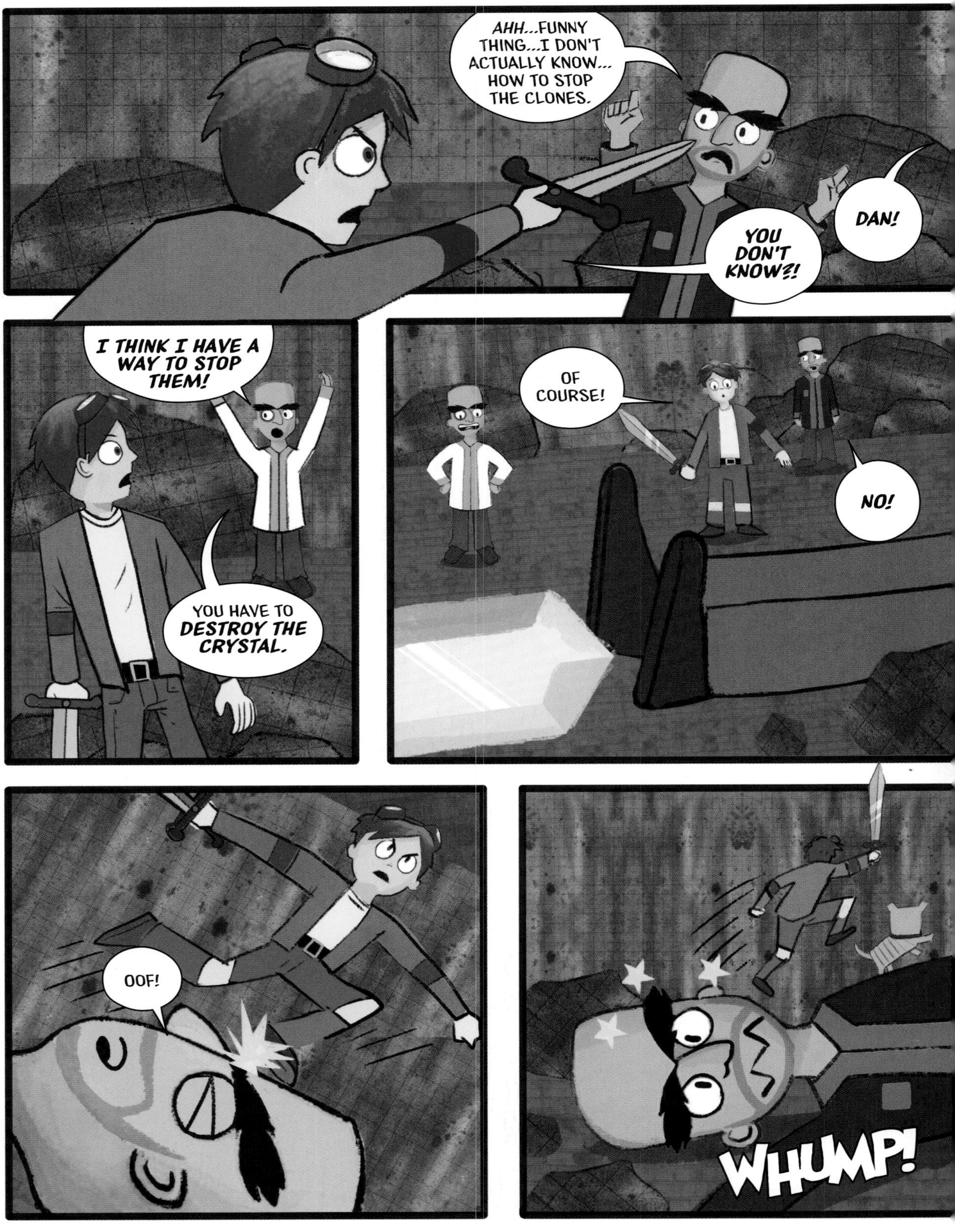
AHH...FUNNY THING...I DON'T ACTUALLY KNOW... HOW TO STOP THE CLONES.
YOU DON'T KNOW?!
DAN!
I THINK I HAVE A WAY TO STOP THEM!
YOU HAVE TO DESTROY THE CRYSTAL.
OF COURSE!
NO!
OOF!
WHUMP!

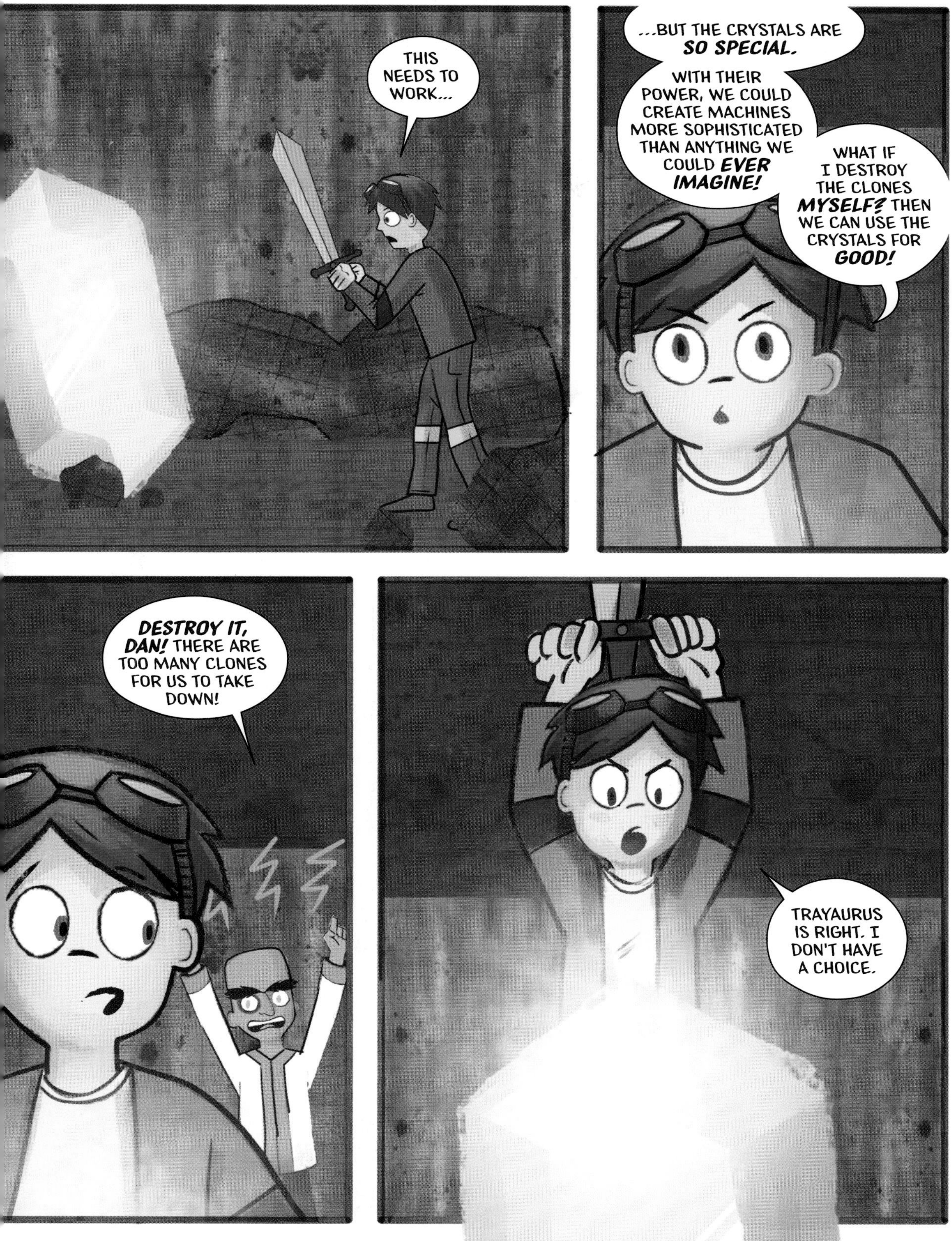
THIS NEEDS TO WORK...
...BUT THE CRYSTALS ARE SO SPECIAL.
WITH THEIR POWER, WE COULD CREATE MACHINES MORE SOPHISTICATED THAN ANYTHING WE COULD EVER IMAGINE!
WHAT IF I DESTROY THE CLONES MYSELF? THEN WE CAN USE THE CRYSTALS FOR GOOD!
DESTROY IT, DAN! THERE ARE TOO MANY CLONES FOR US TO TAKE DOWN!
TRAYAURUS IS RIGHT. I DON'T HAVE A CHOICE.

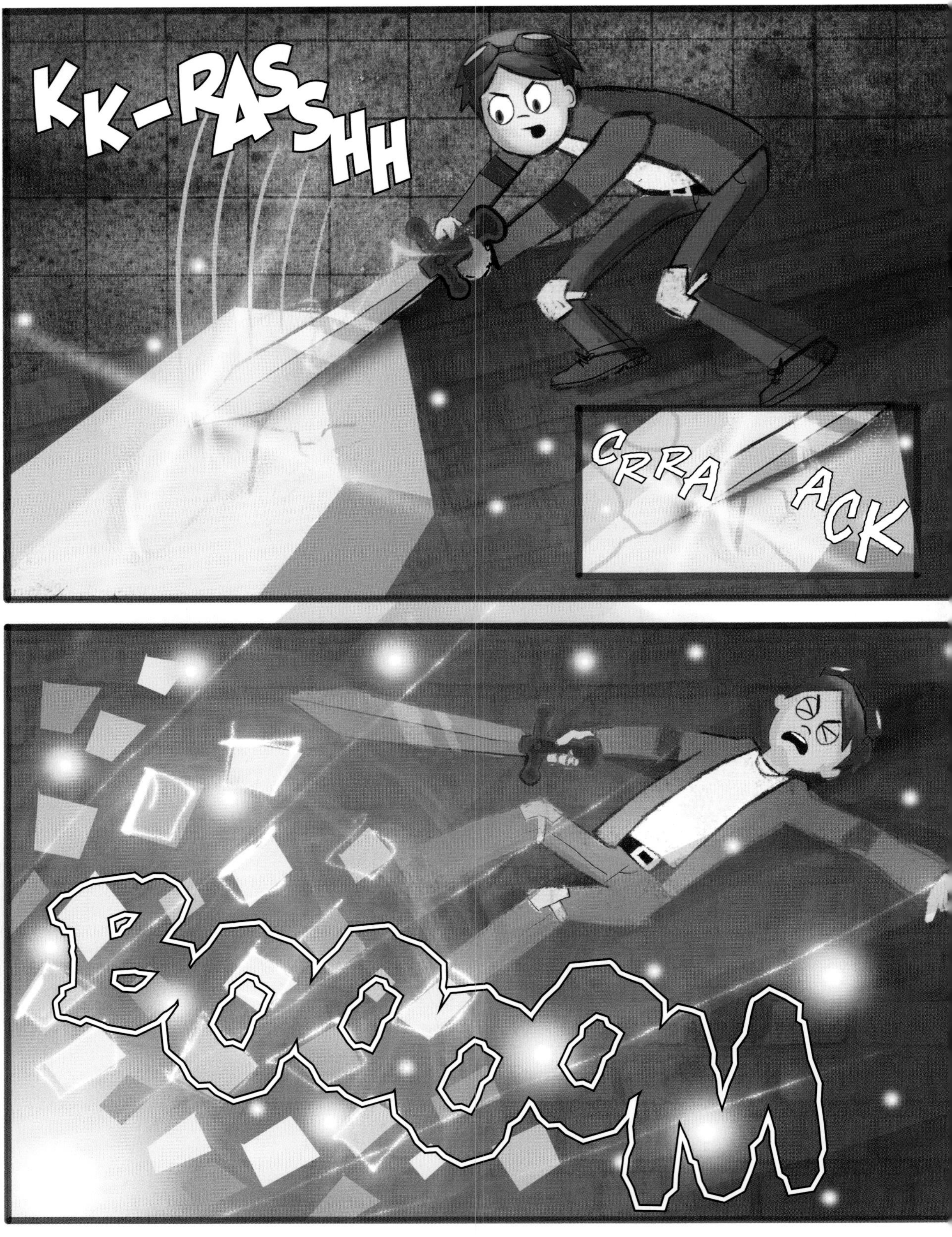
KK-RASSHH
CRRAACK
BOOOOM

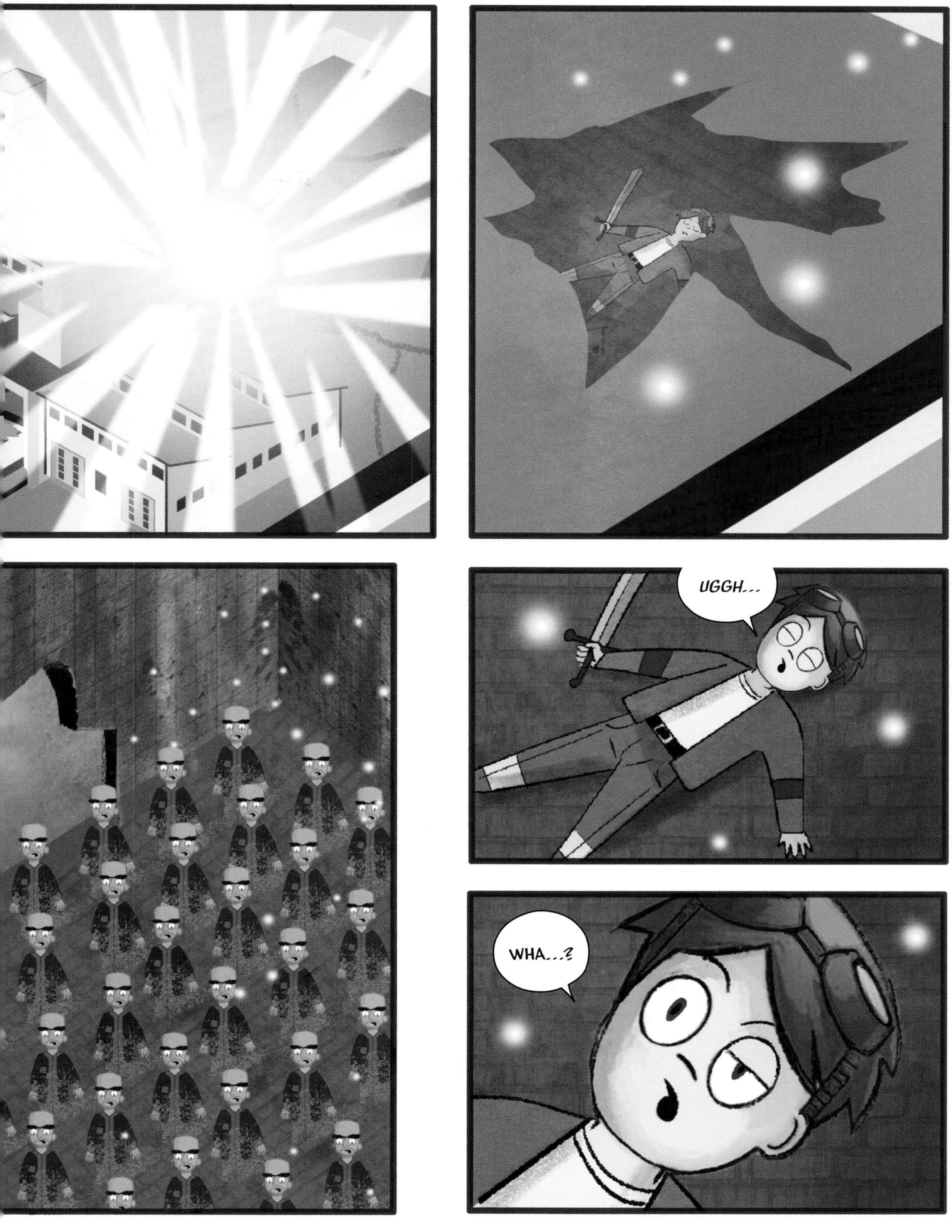
UGGH...
WHA...?

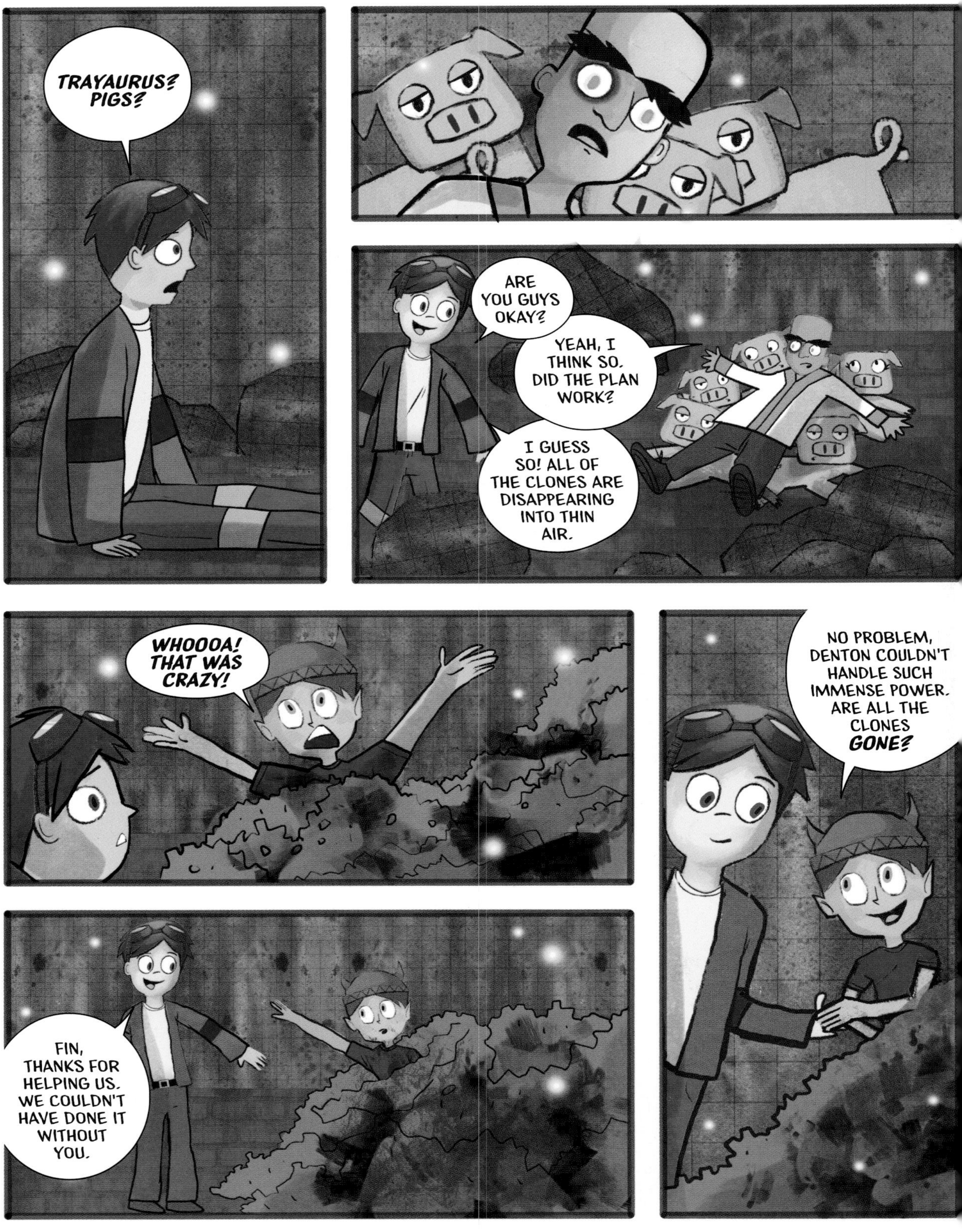
TRAYAURUS? PIGS?
ARE YOU GUYS OKAY?
YEAH, I THINK SO. DID THE PLAN WORK?
I GUESS SO! ALL OF THE CLONES ARE DISAPPEARING INTO THIN AIR.
WHOOOA! THAT WAS CRAZY!
FIN, THANKS FOR HELPING US. WE COULDN'T HAVE DONE IT WITHOUT YOU.
NO PROBLEM, DENTON COULDN'T HANDLE SUCH IMMENSE POWER. ARE ALL THE CLONES GONE?

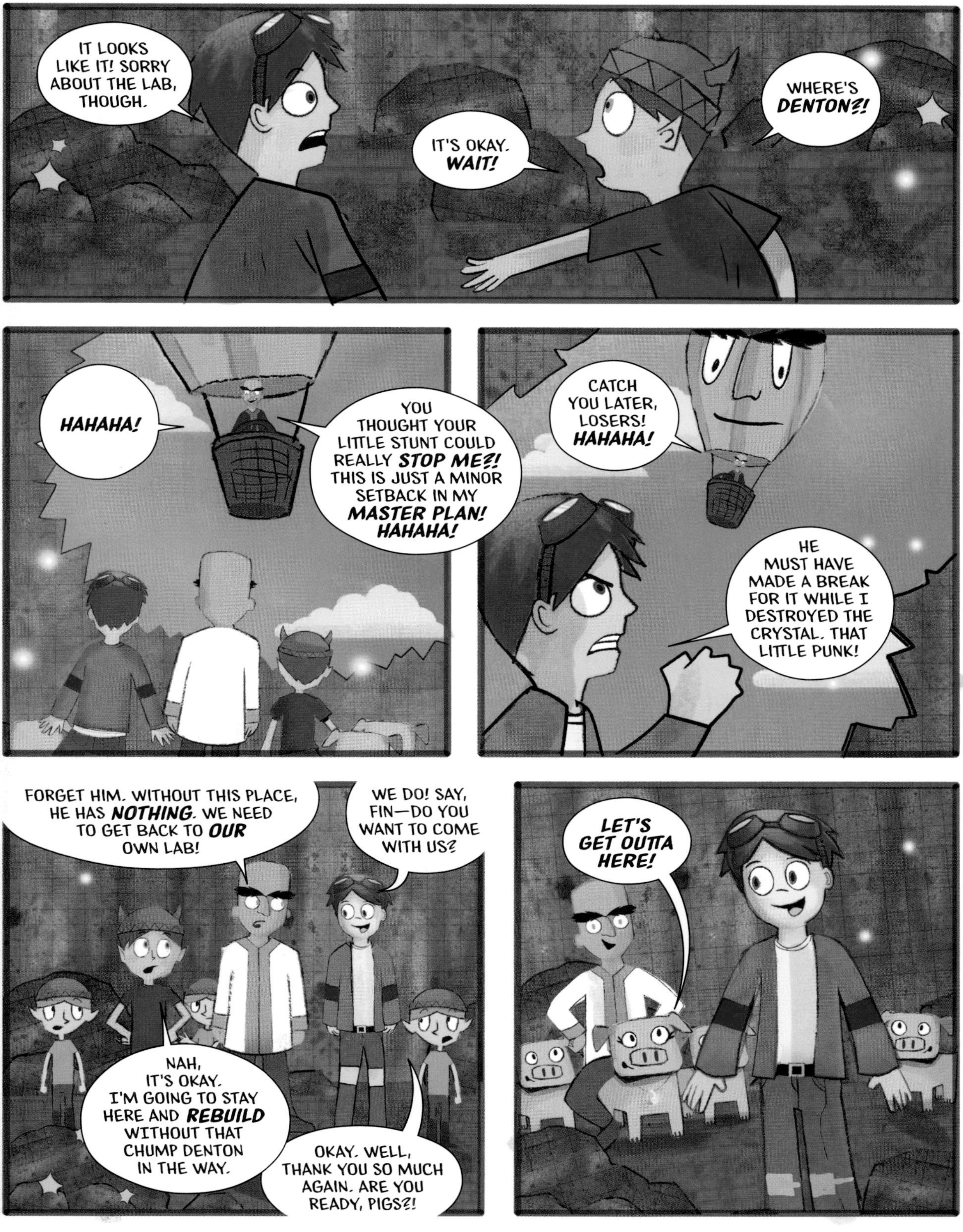
IT LOOKS LIKE IT! SORRY ABOUT THE LAB, THOUGH.
IT'S OKAY. WAIT!
WHERE'S DENTON?!
HAHAHA!
YOU THOUGHT YOUR LITTLE STUNT COULD REALLY STOP ME?! THIS IS JUST A MINOR SETBACK IN MY MASTER PLAN! HAHAHA!
CATCH YOU LATER, LOSERS! HAHAHA!
HE MUST HAVE MADE A BREAK FOR IT WHILE I DESTROYED THE CRYSTAL. THAT LITTLE PUNK!
FORGET HIM. WITHOUT THIS PLACE, HE HAS NOTHING. WE NEED TO GET BACK TO OUR OWN LAB!
WE DO! SAY, FIN—DO YOU WANT TO COME WITH US?
NAH, IT'S OKAY. I'M GOING TO STAY HERE AND REBUILD WITHOUT THAT CHUMP DENTON IN THE WAY.
OKAY. WELL, THANK YOU SO MUCH AGAIN. ARE YOU READY, PIGS?!
LET'S GET OUTTA HERE!

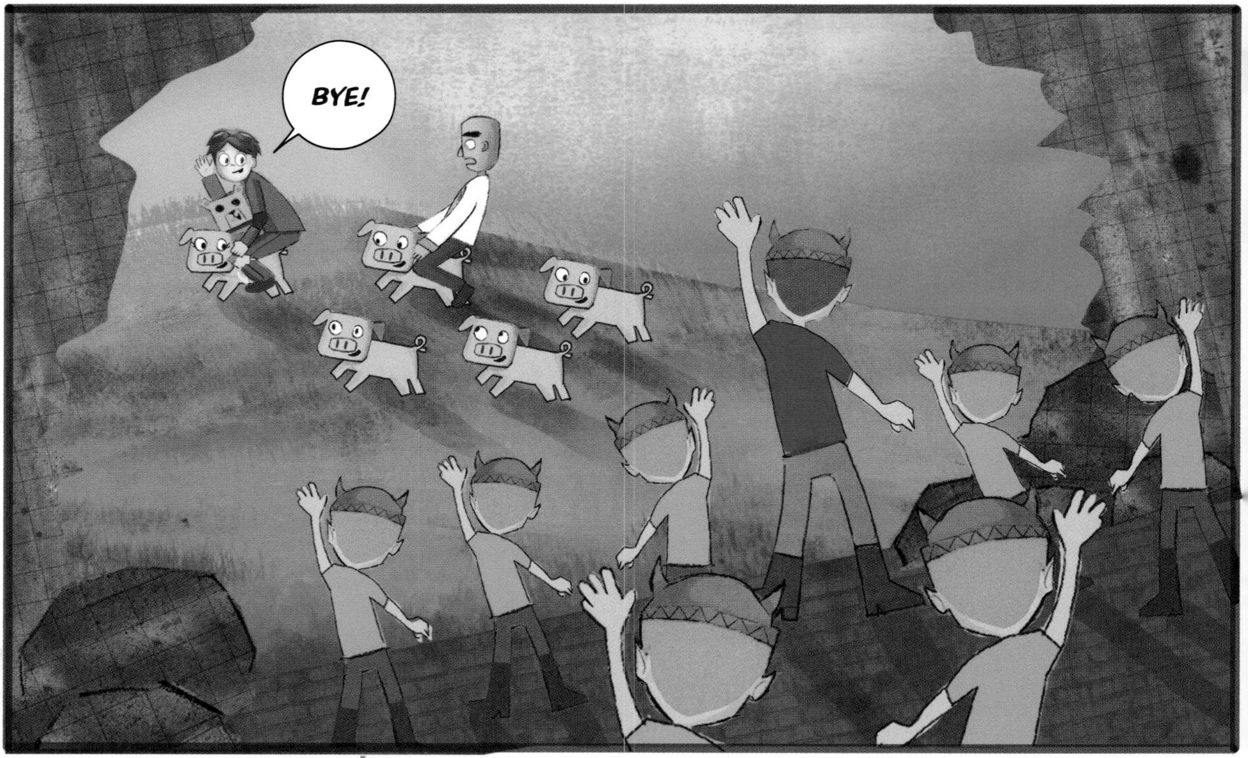
BYE!

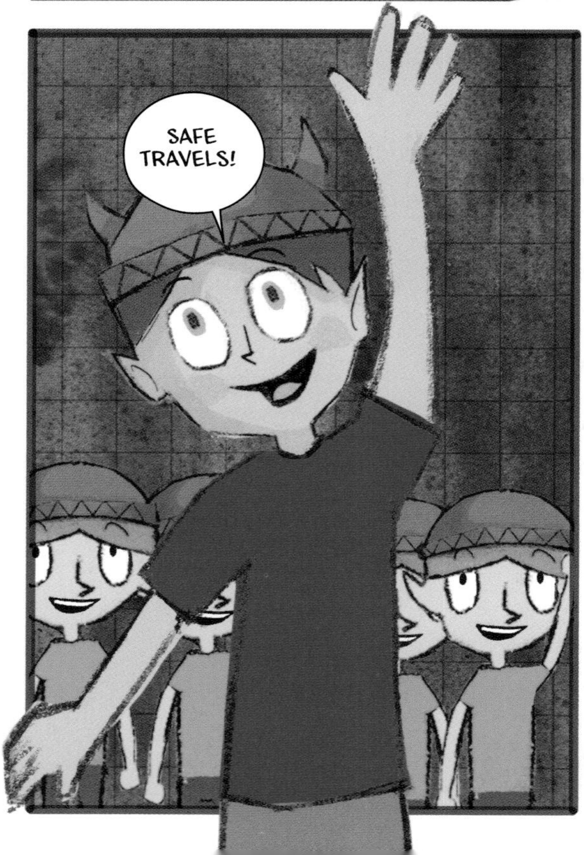
SAFE TRAVELS!

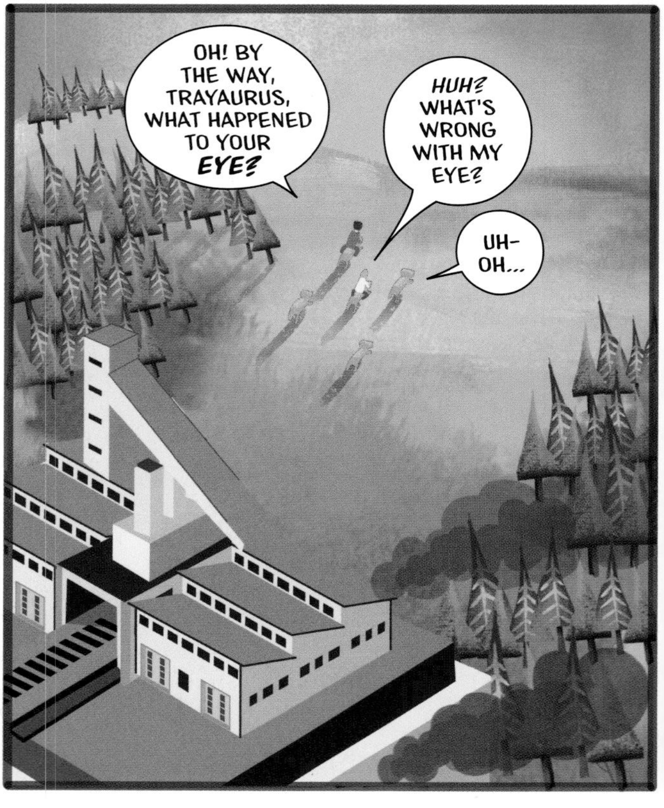
OH! BY THE WAY, TRAYAURUS, WHAT HAPPENED TO YOUR *EYE?*
HUH? WHAT'S WRONG WITH MY EYE?
UH-OH...

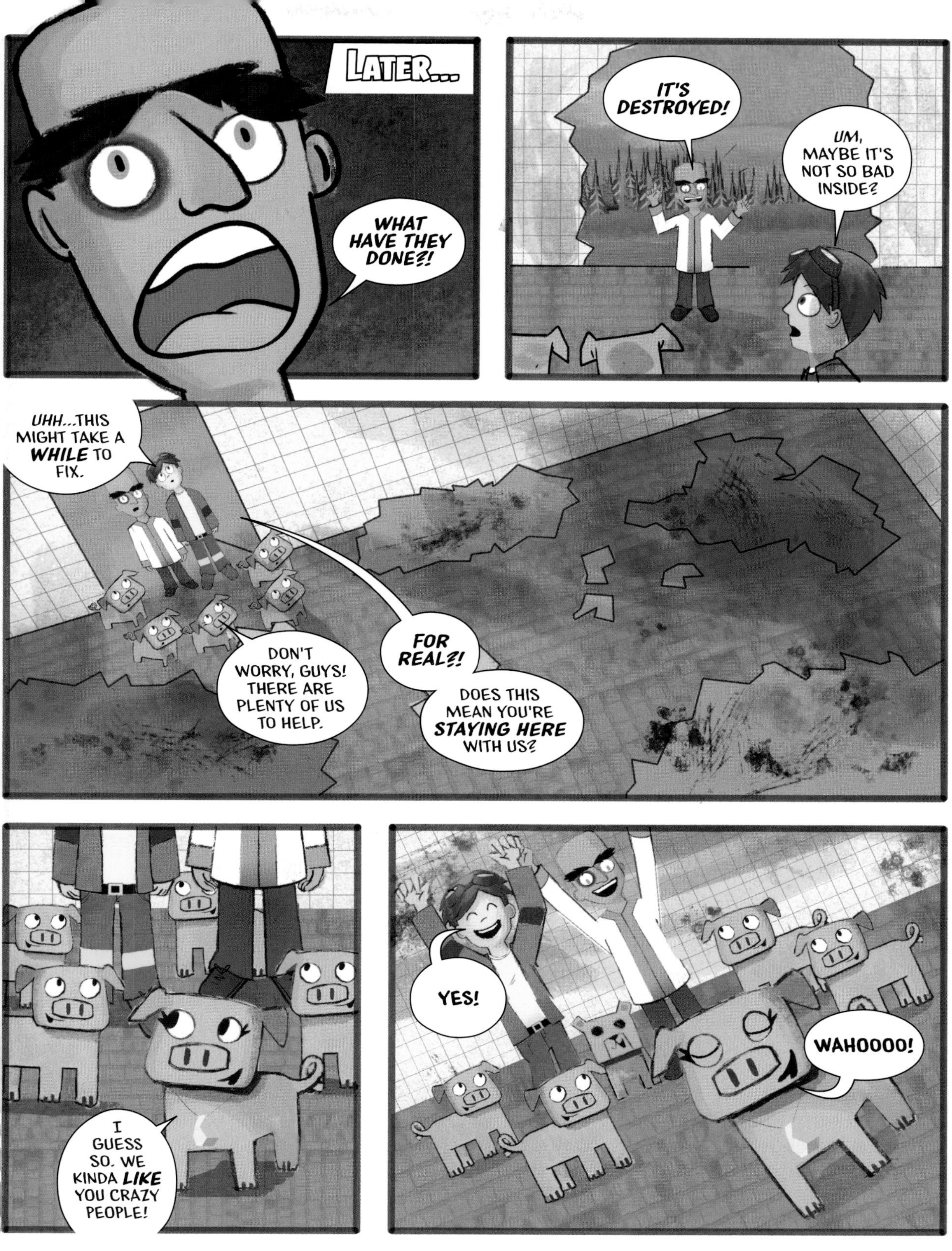
LATER...
WHAT HAVE THEY DONE?!
IT'S DESTROYED!
UM, MAYBE IT'S NOT SO BAD INSIDE?
UHH...THIS MIGHT TAKE A WHILE TO FIX.
FOR REAL?!
DOES THIS MEAN YOU'RE STAYING HERE WITH US?
DON'T WORRY, GUYS! THERE ARE PLENTY OF US TO HELP.
I GUESS SO. WE KINDA LIKE YOU CRAZY PEOPLE!
YES!
WAHOOOO!

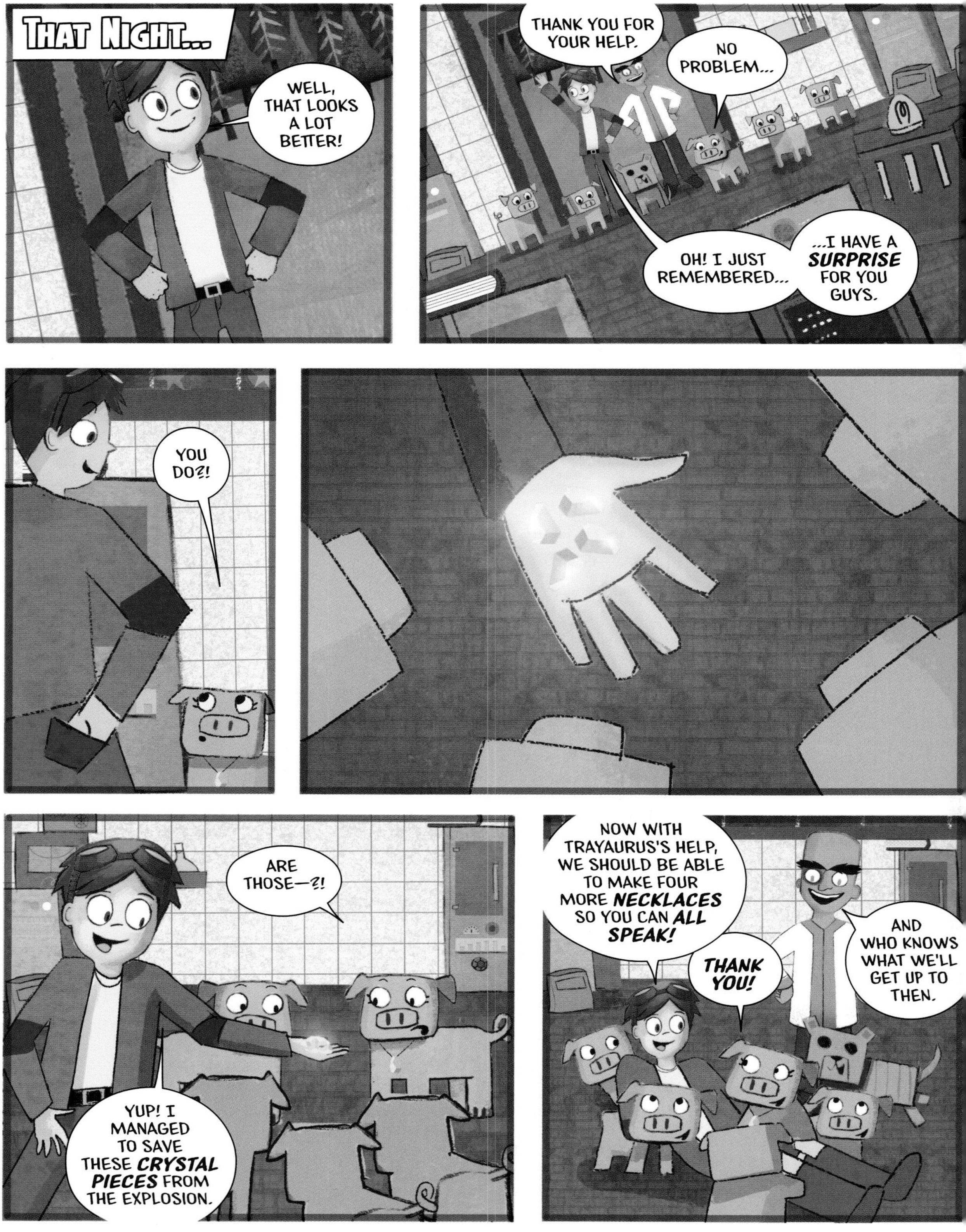
THAT NIGHT...
WELL, THAT LOOKS A LOT BETTER!
THANK YOU FOR YOUR HELP.
NO PROBLEM...
OH! I JUST REMEMBERED...
...I HAVE A SURPRISE FOR YOU GUYS.
YOU DO?!
ARE THOSE—?!
YUP! I MANAGED TO SAVE THESE CRYSTAL PIECES FROM THE EXPLOSION.
NOW WITH TRAYAURUS'S HELP, WE SHOULD BE ABLE TO MAKE FOUR MORE NECKLACES SO YOU CAN ALL SPEAK!
THANK YOU!
AND WHO KNOWS WHAT WE'LL GET UP TO THEN.

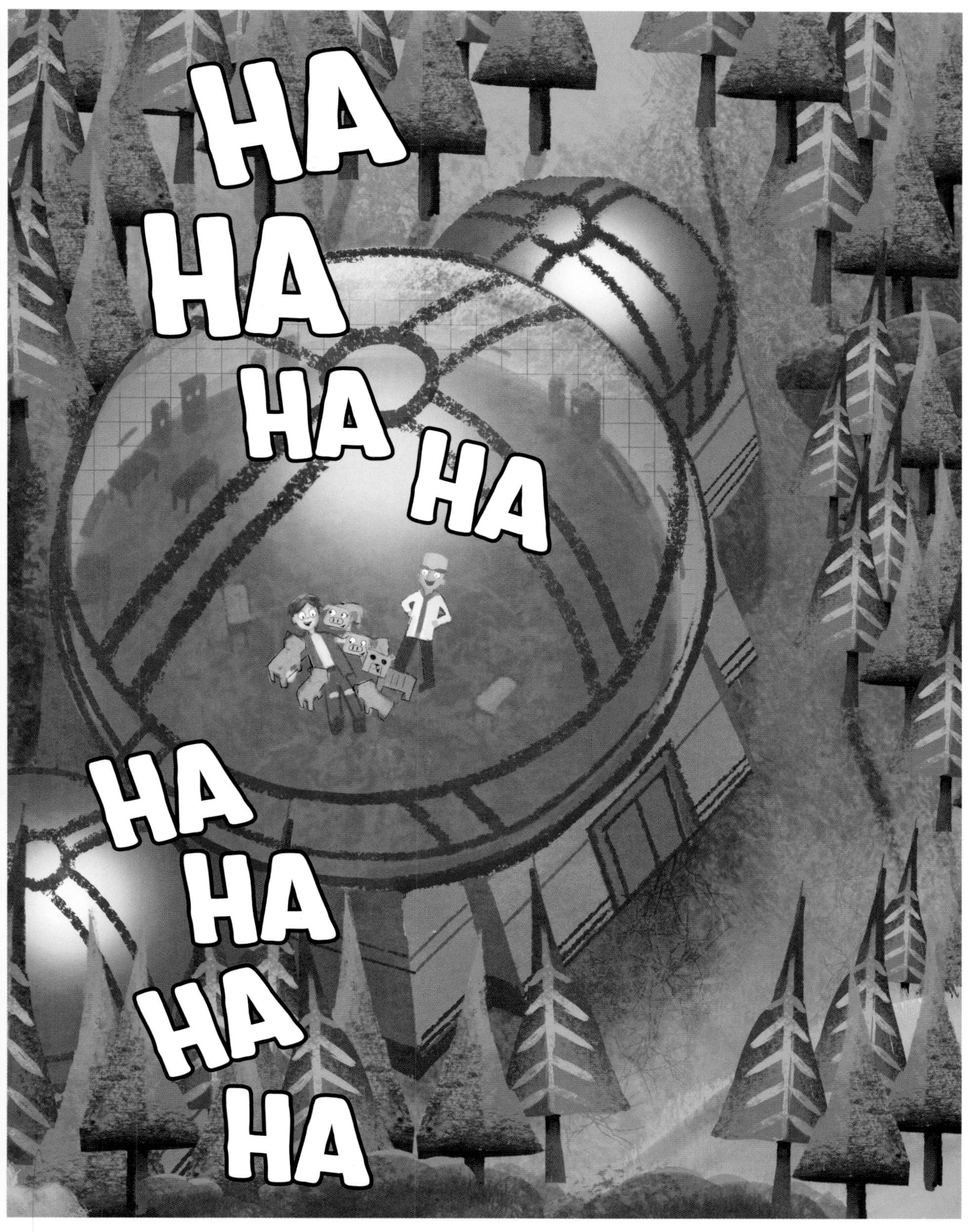
HA
HA
HA
HA
HA
HA
HA
HA

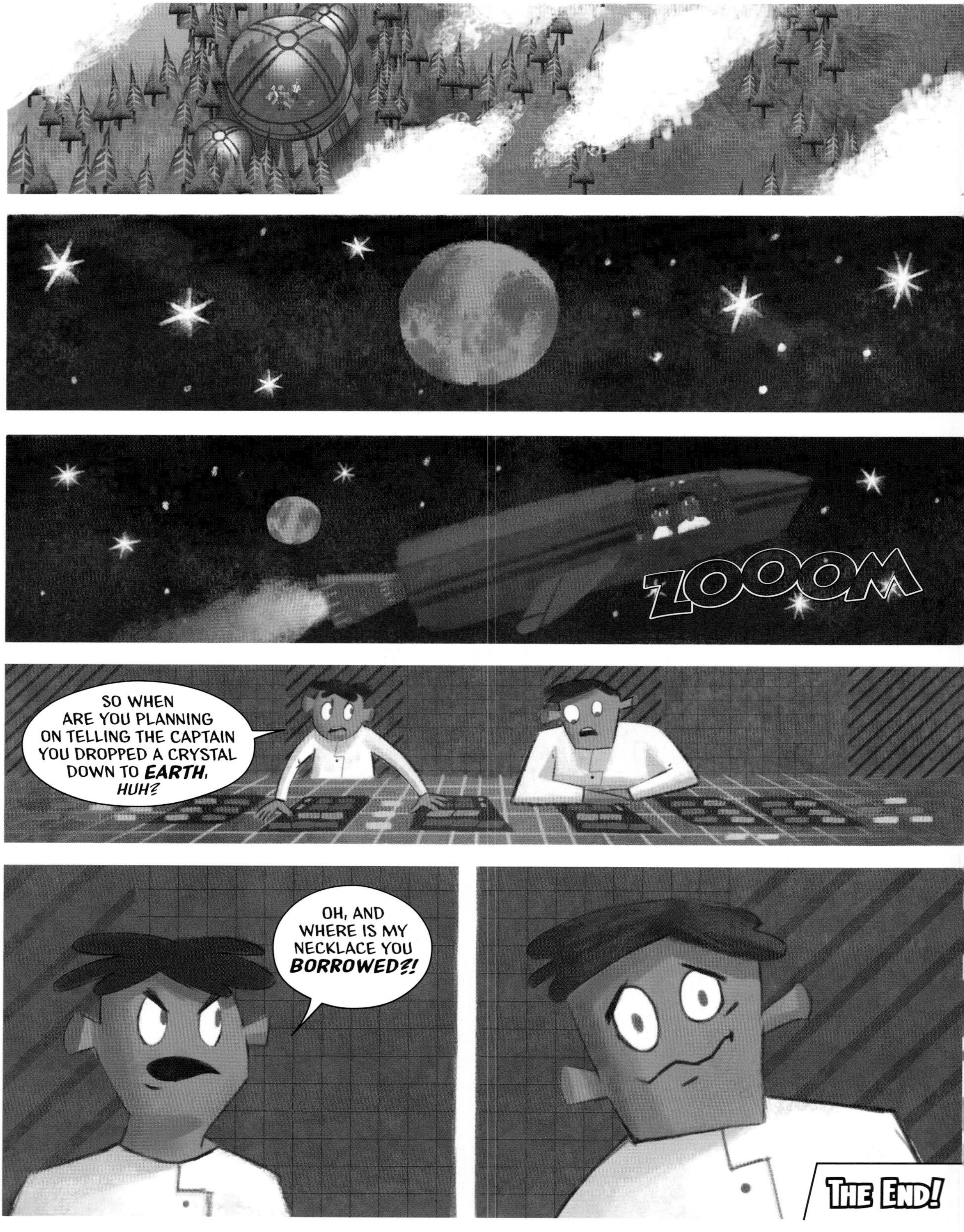
ZOOOM
SO WHEN ARE YOU PLANNING ON TELLING THE CAPTAIN YOU DROPPED A CRYSTAL DOWN TO EARTH, HUH?
OH, AND WHERE IS MY NECKLACE YOU BORROWED?!
THE END!

MEET TEAM DANTDM...

DANTDM

WROTE THE STORY LINE, CREATED THE
CHARACTERS, AND OVERSAW THE WHOLE
BOOK THAT YOU'RE READING TODAY!

MIKE MARTS

IS THE PERSON WHO BROKE DOWN DAN'S
SCRIPT AND CREATED THE COOL, FAST-PACED
NARRATIVE TO ACCOMPANY THE PICTURES.

CORY PETIT

IS THE MASTERMIND BEHIND THE
AWESOME VISUAL SOUND EFFECTS,
LETTERING, AND SPEECH BUBBLES.

DOREEN MULRYAN

IS THE WONDERFULLY CREATIVE ARTIST
WHO SET THE STYLE FOR THE STORY AND
TRANSFORMED DAN'S WORDS INTO PICTURES.

MIKE LOVE

IS THE EXTREMELY TALENTED
SUPPORT ARTIST WHO HELPED BRING
THE WORLD OF DANTDM TO LIFE.

JULYAN BAYES

IS THE DESIGNER WHO HELPED TO
ADD THAT ALL-IMPORTANT SPARKLE
TO THE REST OF THE BOOK.

A SPECIAL THANK-YOU TO
EMMA KUBERT, LISA FOWLER LUBERA, MARKI WOLFSON, JARED OSBORN,
AND DAVID FORREST AND HIS TEAM AT KINETIC UNDERGROUND.